ENCHANTRESS MINE

BERTRICE SMALL

ENCHANTRESS MINE

NEW AMERICAN LIBRARY

New American Library
Published by New American Library, a division of
Penguin Group (USA) Inc., 375 Hudson Street,
New York, New York 10014, U.S.A.
Penguin Books Ltd, 80 Strand,
London WC2R 0RL, England
Penguin Books Australia Ltd, 250 Camberwell Road,
Camberwell, Victoria 3124, Australia
Penguin Books Canada Ltd, 10 Alcorn Avenue,
Toronto, Ontario, Canada M4V 3B2
Penguin Books (N.Z.) Ltd, Cnr Rosedale and Airborne Roads,
Albany, Auckland 1310, New Zealand

Penguin Books Ltd, Registered Offices:
80 Strand, London WC2R 0RL, England

Published by New American Library, a division of Penguin Group (USA) Inc.
Previously published in an Onyx edition.

First New American Library Trade Paperback Printing, January 2004
10 9 8 7 6 5 4 3

 REGISTERED TRADEMARK—MARCA REGISTRADA

Set in Goudy
Designed by Leonard Telesca

Printed in the United States of America

To Morgan Llywelyn, with love,

from her sibling through time

Prologue

Brittany, 1056

"The child is a bastard, uncle, and must be declared so!" Blanche St. Ronan compressed her thin lips into a narrow line, and her hard blue eyes stared unflinchingly into those of her uncle. "I did not marry Ciaran St. Ronan and agree to live in the Argoat so that my child might be passed over in favor of that brat!" Her slender fingers worried at her full indigo blue silk skirt. He noted that each one of those fingers wore a gold ring encrusted with a colored gemstone. "You must help me, uncle! *You must!*"

The bishop of St. Brieuc looked directly at his niece, and felt the same sensuous pleasure he always felt when he looked at her. She was an absolutely beautiful girl, her pale golden hair braided with colorful ribbons, her white-rose skin, and those perfect sky-blue eyes. He felt a sting of regret. She was fit for a king, but because she was the last of his sister's children she had only had a small dowry. Her parents had thought to send her to a convent, but Blanche had rebelled and he had supported her in her rebellion for she was far too lovely to be shut away. It had been he who had arranged her marriage to the Sieur St. Ronan, a man of impeccable Breton lineage and a pleasant estate, but little other wealth.

Ciaran St. Ronan was a widower who had a small daughter from his first marriage. Blanche had detested the child on sight, but she had hidden her dislike long enough to marry the Sieur St. Ronan. Now she was with child, and although the bishop understood his niece's concern, he was a cautious man. Blanche could simply not dispose of her stepdaughter as if she were an unwanted puppy. He made another attempt at reasoning with her.

"If the infant you carry is a son, Blanche, there is no question at all of his position. All the daughter will have is a small dowry. In another year

3

or two she will be old enough to go to her future husband's family, and they will raise her; or we may place her in a convent, and that will be the end of it. There is no need for you to upset yourself, my precious girl." A fat, dimpled hand reached out, and he stroked her silken head. "You are young. At fourteen you have many years ahead of you, and you will undoubtedly bear many sons for your lord husband."

"Ciaran is dying, uncle! There is only this child! If it is another daughter then it is the girl, Mairin, who will inherit, and my child will be left with nothing! You cannot let that happen to me, uncle! You cannot!" Her voice was tinged with growing hysteria. "It is a female that I carry, uncle. *She* has said it! Help me!"

"No one can know if the babe that you carry is a son or a daughter until the child is born, Blanche. Who has told you that you will bear a daughter? Surely you have not listened to the old women in the village with their stories, and their signs that usually mean nothing?"

"*Mairin* has said it, uncle. You know that the child has second sight! We do not discount these things here in Brittany, for we are a Celtic race. Several weeks ago the brat greeted me in the morning with the words, 'How fare you this morning, my lady Blanche? And how fares my little sister?' Ciaran was with me, for it was before his accident, and he lifted the little brat into his arms saying, 'So it is a sister you see, Mairin?', and she answered, 'Aye, my father. A sister, and she will be as pretty as the lady Blanche.'"

The bishop sat back in his chair and contemplated his niece's words. The church did not approve of second sight, but as Blanche had pointed out to him, they were Bretons. Theirs was a Celtic race, and whatever the church might say on the subject, Bretons believed in second sight. His niece's stepchild was known to possess it, although being but five and a half years of age she could but innocently speak of what she saw, but had not real power over her gift. If Ciaran St. Ronan died of his injuries, and Blanche's child was a female, their family would certainly lose the St. Ronan lands for the elder daughter would indeed be the heiress. Mairin was a healthy child, however, and although he would never countenance violence against a child, his niece did have a valid point.

"What do the physicians say about your husband's condition, my precious girl?" the bishop gently queried. "Are they truly convinced that he is dying?"

"Aye," she answered him irritably. "His condition is disgusting, uncle, for his bowels run constantly. He grows weaker every day, and the doctor holds little hope for him. I will be widowed long before my baby is born, and all because he and the Comte de Combourg must play their stupid game! Will the comte look after my child and me when Ciaran is dead and buried? He will not! This is all his fault, but it is I who must suffer!"

"Blanche, Blanche," soothed the bishop, and he squeezed her delicate shoulder in his pudgy hand, "Ciaran and the comte have been friends since boyhood, and they played the game they enjoyed each time the comte visited Landerneau. Leaping the castle moat from the narrow ribbon of land below the walls to the other side takes great skill, and both men had fallen into the moat in the past. It is unfortunate that this time Ciaran's horse fell on him, and that he swallowed so much water."

"Yes," Blanche St. Ronan said bitterly, "it is indeed unfortunate, uncle, but now I must protect my baby alone. Mairin must be declared a bastard lest my own child suffer. Why should I care what happens to Mairin? She is not mine! Why should I be left to care for the bastard spawn of some Irish savage? If I wait until Ciaran is dead, people will say I make the claim out of malice, but if you will help me now, dearest uncle, who will dispute the church's decision? If it is done before my husband dies, and he protests not, who will dare to criticize me?"

"Ciaran St. Ronan loves his daughter, Blanche. I do not believe he will allow you to do this thing."

"Ciaran St. Ronan will never know, uncle. Once the deed is done I will permit no one to come near him but me, and my chosen servants. To the world his lack of protest will appear acquiescence!" She smiled at the bishop triumphantly, her small and perfect teeth glistening whitely against the rose-pink of her mouth.

"What is it exactly that you want me to do, Blanche?" His niece had certainly considered it all very carefully, he thought, impressed by her determination.

"The church must declare that the child known as Mairin St. Ronan is bastard-born, and therefore, not entitled to inherit her father's estates as his heiress," came the cold reply. "The church must declare that the true heir to Ciaran St. Ronan is the child I now carry in my belly."

"And on what grounds shall the church do this, Blanche? We must have legitimate evidence if we are to succeed in disinheriting little Mairin, else I be accused of favoring my own."

"Uncle! There is no proof whatsoever of my lord husband's marriage to the brat's mother. No one here in Brittany ever laid eyes upon the woman for she was Irish, and is said to have died in Ireland before Ciaran could bring her here. There is nothing, however, to prove such facts. It is only upon the word of my lord husband that the child has been accepted at all."

"What was the woman's name?" the bishop asked. "Do you know anything about her?"

"Her name was Maire Tir Connell. Ciaran has said that she was of royal blood, but I do not believe it for a moment! She was probably some savage peasant whore with whom my lord amused himself during his time in Ireland. It is said that my husband was wild in his youth. The whore's child might not even be his, uncle! Perhaps this Maire Tir Connell did die, and Ciaran took the child to raise himself. You know how softhearted he is. How can we allow Landerneau to fall into the hands of a bastard whose father is unknown when I carry the true heir to the estate?"

"Why was Baron St. Ronan in Ireland?" The bishop was curious.

"Ciaran's mother was Irish. After his father died she remarried an old friend with whom she had grown up in Ireland. Several years ago she grew ill, and my lord's stepfather sent for him that he might be with his mother in her final days. While he was there he claims to have met and wed with this Maire Tir Connell, but he has never showed me any proof of that marriage, uncle, nor can I find any. Believe me when I tell you I have looked everywhere for such evidence."

The bishop smiled tightly. He had absolutely no doubt that his darling Blanche had sought thoroughly for proof of her husband's first marriage with an eye to destroying it.

"When this Irish woman gave birth to my lord's daughter, he says she was weakened, and made ill by her months of confinement," continued Blanche. "Ciaran returned home to Brittany leaving her to regain her strength before making the long journey here. He had been gone over a year, and felt it necessary to show himself on his estates. His mother had died shortly after the child's birth. When he went back to Ireland to fetch the woman and her baby she was dead. He brought Mairin back with him. This is what he says, uncle, but I think he says it to protect the bastard. There are neither documents nor witnesses to this marriage. *Nothing!*"

"You are certain, ma petite Blanche?" If she were, he thought, then his clever girl had indeed found a way to disinherit her stepchild.

"Absolutely certain, uncle," came the firm reply.

"What of the Irish giant who guards the child, my precious? Was he not a servant of Mairin's mother? Perhaps he knows something of the truth. Have you spoken with him?"

"Dagda? He could not possibly know anything of value to us, uncle. The creature is stupid beyond belief. With your help nothing can stand in my way!"

The bishop of St. Brieuc smiled benevolently at his favorite niece, thinking again of how lovely she was. Blanche had always had a marvelous instinct for style. The blues she wore today complimented her fair hair and her beautiful eyes. The full, flowing skirt was just a shade darker than the tunic top which was embroidered at the neck and about the sleeves in gold thread and tiny freshwater pearls. Her pale gold braids with their rose-colored silk ribbons were looped fashionably about her ears, and her head was crowned with a chaplet of delicate filigreed gold that had been set with tiny, sparkling gemstones. She was a marvelous girl, he thought fondly, and she deserved only the best that life had to offer.

"If you are certain of what you say, Blanche," he said with a beneficent smile, "then I shall arrange to solve this little problem for you. Unlike your careless husband, ma petite, you shall have a document, both stamped and sealed, that will attest to the validity of your word. Mairin St. Ronan will be declared bastard-born, and she will therefore be unable to inherit her father's possessions. Ciaran St. Ronan's lands will belong to your child alone, and you will hold them until that child either marries, should it indeed be female, or comes of age if you bear a son. Is that satisfactory?"

She arose from her chair, and slipped her arms about his neck as she had done so often as a child. With a little smile she settled herself into his ample lap, wriggling her bottom suggestively as she did. "Oh, uncle," she said softly as she looked up into his fat face, "you are always so good to me!"

He beamed back at her, feeling a trifle breathless, and finally drawing a breath in he was almost overwhelmed by the wonderful perfume that she wore. It smelt of lilies of the valley. "Dearest Blanche," he said, and he patted her dainty little hand, "how can I not be good to you? I adore you, and you are more than well aware of it, petite méchante."

Blanche St. Ronan leaned heavily against her uncle, and the tip of her little pointed tongue flicked out from between her pink lips to run along his fleshy mouth in a teasing manner. Then she kissed him, her full breasts pressing against him as she did so. "Let it be as it was between us, uncle, before I came to Landerneau," she murmured huskily against his lips. "Make love to me!"

The cleric's breath came in hard, little pants, and unable to restrain himself he fondled his niece's breasts with a groan of unconcealed desire. "You are with child, and I would harm neither you nor the baby you carry, ma petite Blanche," he protested, but faintly.

"*Uncle dearest*," she breathed with scented breath into his ear, "I have not even begun to show. You will not hurt us, and I burn for your touch! I am wed to a sick and disgusting man who has never been as virile with me as you always were. I wonder that he bothered to take a wife." She licked the inside of his ear teasingly.

"You are fortunate indeed that he did, ma petite, else you'd be in a convent now instead of the lap of luxury," the bishop reminded her, and felt his manhood begin to stir.

"But he never had your charm, uncle." She pouted, and added, "I will come to your apartments as soon as I have seen the castle settled for the night." She smiled at him, showing her perfect little teeth. "Surely, dearest uncle, you will offer me comfort in my distress?"

The bishop's heart pounded with excitement, and beneath the holy robes of his office he felt himself growing more lustful for his niece as each moment passed. He had taken her maidenhead in the confessional when she was twelve, and now as she rubbed herself against him he remembered other times, and other places. She was deliciously insatiable. He realized now how very much he had missed her since she had married Ciaran St. Ronan. Though he never lacked for companions, no woman had ever aroused him as did Blanche. Reaching up he stroked her soft cheek, and said in a pious tone, "My doors will be open to you, dearest niece, should you desire to make your confession to me later on this evening."

"I shall welcome any penance you impose upon me, *uncle*," she returned demurely. Then she was gone from the tiny private room. As she exited there was a triumphant smile upon her face, and she was certain of her total success. She had learned quickly, and early that a woman's body was a potent weapon in the war between the sexes! The brat, Mairin, would be disposed of and dispossessed. Blanche's child would inherit the St. Ronan lands! She thanked God and the Blessed Mother for her lustful uncle, else she and her baby might have been forced to accept their very bread from that little bastard. Of course, Blanche decided, she would have to get rid of the wench as quickly as possible. Once it became known what had been arranged, the tongues would wag, but they would wag less if Mairin were not around to remind everyone of what Blanche had done. Besides, who would take the brat's part against her father's legal widow? The lady of St. Ronan cared little what people might think as long as she and her child were victorious. Blanche St. Ronan smiled broadly, but the smile never reached her cold blue eyes.

Part One

The Saxon's Daughter

England, 1056–1063

Chapter 1

 ithin the Forest of the Argoat all was silent, but for the occasional trill of a bird, or a soft whisper of a breeze. The beeches and the oaks soared skyward, reaching with strong green fingers toward the life-giving warmth of the sun above them. Great mossy boulders that had been contoured by the passage of time and worn into strange, almost mysterious shapes by centuries of wind and rain littered the forest floor. Following the almost invisible path that wound its way through those huge rocks, one came upon a stream that tumbled breathlessly over the large stones in its wake, only to disappear around a sharp curve and slip silently off into the deep woods.

Somehow the warm late-summer sun managed to break through the thick stands of trees casting a pale green light over everything it touched; skimming across the dark pool within the sudden clearing where a great antlered stag had stopped to drink. A shaft of light touched the dark chestnut velvet of his flank, but so secure was the beast within this magical realm that he barely raised his head to gaze with liquid eyes as with the faintest rustle the underbrush gave way for but a moment to allow a small figure to enter within the charmed circle. It was a child. A little girl of such delicate structure and beauty that it seemed as if the faintest puff of wind would blow her away.

Seeing the stag, Mairin St. Ronan stopped to greet the beast. "Hail, Hearn!" came her soft childish voice, and the stag lowered his head to once again drink, knowing instinctively that this was no enemy.

The child's skin was snow-white and of such translucent quality that it contrasted sharply with the soft light within the clearing. The sunlight touching the crown of her head lit a flame of red-gold so intense that many seeing the little girl's mass of fiery hair for the first time were amazed by the beautiful color. Some fingered the great cloud of softness as if unable to believe the evidence of their own sight. It was unusual for a child so young to be so beautiful, and there was speculation as to what she would look like when she was grown. She was strangely adult for one so young, and this coupled with her rare beauty made many uncomfortable. There were even rumors that she visited old Catell, the witch woman, and because the child's knowledge of healing was beyond her years, many believed her to be a young enchantress. After all, had not Brittany been the home of the Great Sorcerer, Merlin, and the famed enchantress Vivian?

The child ran to the edge of the pool, and kneeling, dipped her tiny hand into the black water, letting its coolness drizzle back into the pond. The smooth, dark mirror reflected back at Mairin her own face, and looking at it the little girl saw a small square chin, a short, straight nose that her father assured her would eventually grow, and a mouth that her stepmother declared was much too large, and even a trifle vulgar for a female of good breeding. Mairin made a little moue with her mouth as she stared into the water. She knew certain charms and spells for whitening one's skin and lightening one's hair, but there was no way that she knew of for changing the shape of one's mouth.

As for the lady Blanche with her cold blue eyes and her rosebud lips that always seemed pursed with discontentment, Mairin knew full well that her father's new wife did not like her, although she did not know why that should be so. She was happy her father had finally remarried, for she understood his need for a son. He would not have one for Mairin knew the baby her stepmother carried was a daughter, and alas, her father now lay dying. She could see it in his sad eyes. A tear rolled down her cheek, but she impatiently brushed it away. Death was but a doorway into another life. There was nothing she could do to prevent her father's fate.

Shrugging she arose, thanking the pond as she did for its smooth surface which had allowed her to glimpse herself. Then, walking about the little body of water, she looked carefully for any plants that might be of use to her, or to old Catell, the witch woman of these woods, who had taught her so much about healing.

There were a few green acorns that had fallen, but acorns were best when ripe, and so she ignored them. Here and there upon the ground there were pine cones, but the best cones were those with their seeds, and she had gathered them in the late spring when they were newly fallen before the squirrels and birds got at them. On a patch of dry and rocky ground, however, she found some capers growing, and these she plucked carefully, putting them into the little linen pouch that hung from her girdle. As a decoction capers were very good for easing toothache, but one had to be careful when using them for capers were also known to draw blood and sperm into the urine, and the only antidote for that was apple vinegar.

"*Mairin.*"

She whirled and her generous mouth turned up into a welcoming smile. "How is it, Dagda, that such a big man can tread so lightly?" she demanded of him. "My ears are as sharp as the fox's, and yet it is rarely that I hear you come."

Dagda, who stood seven feet in height, and had a mop of unruly silver-colored hair, smiled down at the litte girl. It was a smile that crinkled the corners of his deep blue eyes and was filled with his deep love for Mairin St. Ronan. He had raised her even as he had raised her mother long ago in Ireland. He thought of Mairin as his child even as her mother had been his child. Just before she had died Maire Tir Connell had begged him to care for Mairin as he had once cared for her. Of course he had agreed, and she had given him his freedom, unfastening the slave collar from his thick neck with trembling fingers, touching gently with a sad sigh the scar tissue that had built up from the chafing of the collar in the first years he had worn it. Dagda had caught at her hand and kissed those dainty fingers, the unashamed tears rushing down his face.

Maire Tir Connell had died then. She had died in the comforting cradle of his big arms, the breath fleeing her slender body in a soft whisper, but he had continued to hold her for the longest time because he could simply not believe that she who had always been so loving and so filled with life was truly dead. Finally the old women had come, and with sympathetic hands that had loosened his hold upon Maire Tir Connell, they had taken the body away to prepare it for its burial. That had been almost five years ago.

When Mairin was a year old her father returned to Ireland for his wife and child. Ciaran St. Ronan was first shown his wife's grave and then shown his beautiful daughter. He had wept bitter tears for Maire Tir Connell. Then he had gotten drunk, and stayed that way for a week. Finally pulling himself together he had gone to speak with the king, his late wife's father. It was decided that Mairin would go with her father to Brittany. When they departed Dagda had accompanied them. He had made a promise to Maire Tir Connell, and only death would make him break his word to her.

It had been a pleasant life these last few years in Brittany, for Ciaran St. Ronan, the Sieur de Landerneau, was a good man. He had never once questioned his late wife's dying wish with regard to their child. Dagda had raised Maire Tir Connell, and she had been perfect in Ciaran's eyes. He expected that his little daughter, Mairin, raised by the same gentle giant, would be no less perfect. So despite the wagging tongues of the good-wives, and the shaking of heads by the elderly remainder of Ciaran St. Ronan's family, Dagda had remained as nursemaid and guardian to the Sieur de Landerneau's only child.

Looking down now at his precious charge, Dagda shook his shaggy silver head, and thought that it was indeed fortunate that he was Mairin's watchdog, especially since the lady Blanche had entered their lives.

Ciaran St. Ronan's second wife was a spiteful and cruel young woman. She reminded him of a golden rose, full-blown and totally perfect until you bent to sniff its fragrance, and discovered that it was rotten.

Aye! Mairin needed him now. *Particularly now.* Bending, he lifted his little mistress into his arms. "Your father," he said quietly, and without any preamble, "has just died. Whatever happens now, I don't want you to be frightened for I will be with you, my little lady. Do you understand me?"

The child's face crumbled with her grief. She had known before he had even spoken what he had come to tell her. Her father had left her, and she was alone. A small sob escaped her, but then recovering herself she said, "Did he want to see me, Dagda? Did my father not ask for me at the end?"

"He did, but *she* pretended that you could not be found, and her uncle, the wily bishop, then began fussing with your father over his last confession, and the absolution."

A tear slid down the child's beautiful face. "Oh, Dagda," she said brokenly, "why does the lady Blanche hate me so? Why did she keep my father and me from our farewells?"

"She is jealous of you, child. How could she not be? Your father loved you above all people including the lady Blanche. Now she will seek to strike out at you in order to protect the child she will bear in a few months' time."

"But I would not harm my sister, Dagda," said Mairin in her innocence.

"Of course you wouldn't," he replied soothingly, "but that is not why she fears you. You are your father's heiress, Mairin. With Ciarin St. Ronan, the Sieur de Landerneau, dead, my child, you become the Demoiselle de Landerneau. The lady Blanche and her child will be obligated to you for their very living. This is what the bitch fears."

"But I would take nothing from them!" protested Mairin. "Has not Père Caolan taught me to honor my parents, and is not the lady Blanche my stepmother?"

Dagda sighed deeply. How could he possibly explain to a sweet and totally innocent child like Mairin the greed and venality of the world? Mairin's wisdom was of a different sort, and in a sense he was responsible for he had encouraged her to learn the ancient ways of their people. She had never been exposed to selfishness or avarice, but these were qualities that he knew the lady Blanche possessed, and he feared for the little girl in his charge. He would protect her with his life if need be, but right now he knew not from where the first blow would come.

"We must return to the castle," he said. "If we do not come soon they will wonder where we are and send others after us."

She snuggled into his arms. "Please stop at old Catell's cottage, Dagda. I found some capers, and would leave them with her for I know not when I will see her again." Abruptly Mairin shivered, and she cried out sharply. "Stop, Dagda!"

"What is it, my child?" He slowed his pace.

"Let me down," she begged him, and when he did she looked up at him, her little face dirty with the tears that ran down it now, and she said, "*I will never see this place again, Dagda!* Suddenly I know that. I shall not come to these woods again."

"Are you threatened?" he demanded, not for one moment doubting her words.

She thought for a long moment, and then replied slowly, "Not my life, Dagda. No, not my life." Then running a little ways back along the path to the dark pool she said to the trees and the water, and the rocks, "Farewell, my friends. I shall not forget your kindness to me. I will remember you always!"

To Dagda, who stood watching, it seemed as if the trees bowed their branches to her, and the waters in the normally still pond wavered distinctly. She is magic, he thought. She has the touch. If we remain here perhaps old Catell could teach her some of the old ways, for my little enchantress needs more than I can give her. Feeling Mairin slip her little hand into his large one he set his steps toward the castle once again. Old Catell was now forgotten for the day was beginning to wane and there was no time left.

They met Mairin's old wet-nurse, Melaine, hurrying along to find them. "Quickly, quickly, my precious. *She* is already in a rage that you are not found. We must go to her swiftly!"

"Not until demoiselle is washed, and properly dressed," said Dagda firmly.

"Sweet Mother Marie! How am I to hold her off then? She insists that the petite mistress be found!"

"She was not so insistent when the good Sieur Ciaran lay dying. She would allow no one to seek out the demoiselle then that the child and her father might make their farewells. She is evil, that one! Whatever it is that she wants, at least let the demoiselle Mairin face that woman at her best."

Melaine nodded her agreement, and crossed herself for luck. She had heard terrible gossip from her sister whose daughter worked as a dairymaid for the bishop of St. Brieuc. She knew that Dagda had not heard the rumors for during the last few weeks he had spent his time being particularly vigilant over the little mistress. Melaine wondered if the Sieur St. Ronan had heard the gossip. If so he had not refuted it, so perhaps then it was true. Whatever the truth, her former nursling was in for a great deal of difficulty from the lady Blanche.

"I will distract the guards at the portcullis while you and the child pass by them," said Melaine, and then she chuckled at the idea of Dagda sneaking by anyone.

Yet with her help they were able to gain entry to the castle quickly, and without being noticed. Carrying Mairin, Dagda made his way up the stairs to the tiny room that belonged to the little girl. Lowering her he pushed her into the cubicle, hissing after her, "Hurry! Wash, and brush your hair. Put on *both* shoes and clean clothing. We have little time!'

Not a little frightened, Mairin splashed water from a pitcher into her little silver ewer, and scrubbed the dirt from her face, hands, and neck. Stripping her clothing off she opened her trunk, and pulled from it a clean light-colored linen chemise, and a pale gold silk tunic dress which was embroidered at the neck and lower hem with blue and green silken threads and tiny pearls. The sleeves of the tunic were long and full, and just above the child's hips was a belt matching the embroidery. Mairin slipped her little feet into a pair of soft shoes that had been made of an especially finely tanned butter-soft red leather. Then taking her brush she quickly worked the snarls free from her thick hair, and neatly rebraided it with pretty green ribbons. She slipped about her neck a necklace of heavy red gold and Celtic enamelwork, and then hurried to exit her room, escorted by Dagda, who had patiently awaited her outside.

Entering the hall of the castle she went quickly to her stepmother, and knelt before her saying, "I grieve with you, my lady Blanche. I shall miss my father too." Mairin saw that the bishop of St. Brieuc sat next to his niece, his pig-sharp eyes devouring her.

Blanche St. Ronan, attired in her favorite blue, a silvery gauze veil over her golden head, glared down at the beautiful child who knelt so submissively before her. How dare the little bitch appear before her in such fine clothes! "You are to leave Landerneau this day," she said coldly. "Too long have I been forced to tolerate your presence. I did so for the deep love I bore my husband, but now that he is dead I do not have to suffer his bastard to live within *my* walls."

Confused the child looked up at her stepmother. *"Leave Landerneau?"* she said. "Madame, I do not understand you. I am the heiress to Landerneau. I cannot leave my lands."

"Heiress to Landerneau?" Blanche sneered. "You are not your father's heiress, you brat!" How dare the wench challenge her authority! Her voice rose in pitch. "You are nothing but his bastard! His get upon the filthy body of some savage Irish whore! His heiress indeed! It is my child who will be the heir to Landerneau! *My child!*"

Mairin scrambled to her feet. Her eyes were mirrors of both her anger and her fright. "I am not a bastard!" she said furiously to the seated woman. "I am as true-born a child of my father as the babe you now carry, madame, and unless that child is a son, which it is not, it is *I* who am the heiress to Landerneau! You cannot send me away! *I will not go!*"

Blanche St. Ronan struggled to rise. This was not the scenario she had planned. It had been her intention to send Mairin from Landerneau, and that was to be the end of it. That the brat dared to defy her enraged her mightily. *"You will not go?"* she shrieked. "Indeed you most certainly will go for you are not so stupid that you cannot understand what I am about to say to you. There is no proof of your mother's marriage to your father, and because of that the church has declared you bastard born. Would you dare to argue with the church?"

"The church?" said Mairin scornfully. "More than likely, madame, you mean your uncle, the fat bishop of St. Brieuc who even now sits by your side with his hands that are forever stroking, and grasping at you. I may be naught but a child, but I am not a fool!"

Blanche St. Ronan's light blue eyes grew round and bulged from their sockets. Her face was suddenly mottled red and white, her mouth flapped open like a fish gaping in the air. Clutching at her belly she screamed, "Get that brat from my sight! I never want to see her again!" And she fell back against her uncle gasping. "The bitch torments me in my grief. She will put the evil eye upon my child!" and she crossed herself dramatically.

Dagda reached for his little mistress, but Mairin brushed the giant aside, and suddenly to all those in the hall she seemed to increase in height. Her eyes, which had darkened with her anger, now appeared to flash with fire. "You may send me from Landerneau, madame, but all your scheming with your uncle will not gain you that which you actually seek. Power! Landerneau will never really be yours, and you will never find true happiness!" She raised her child's arm and pointed her finger directly at her stepmother. *"You are doomed, madame."*

Blanche St. Ronan shrieked in terror, but nevertheless she cried out, "Get the bastard witch from my sight! Never allow her entry into my presence again! I want her gone from Landerneau before nightfall!" Then she slumped into her chair, and her women clustered about her clucking sympathetically, and pressing a goblet of wine to her lips.

The hall which just moments before had been totally silent but for Mairin's young voice now erupted into a cacophony of sounds. There was not a servant or retainer there who had not known Mairin since her father brought her from Ireland five years before. Each had heard Ciaran St. Ronan speak of his beloved first wife, Maire Tir Connell, on numerous occasions. They found it hard to believe what the lady Blanche had just said. But if the church was involved they could not gainsay it. Those who might agree with the child's accusation with regard to the lady Blanche's uncle would keep silent for they were bound to Landerneau by service, loyalty, and tradition. The grieving widow could make their lives a veritable hell should she choose. With eyes lowered they turned away from the child, ashamed, but also afraid.

Her head held high, Mairin stalked from the hall with Dagda following behind her. Her heart was pounding with fright although none would have known it from her proud demeanor. She was to leave Landerneau, the only home she had ever known, but where was she to go? How would she survive? Just outside the hall she was stopped by the steward, Ivo, who said in an apologetic tone, "You are to come with me, mistress."

Confused, Mairin looked at him, but Dagda said bluntly, "Where?"

"There's nothing that you can do, Dagda," said the steward. "The lady Blanche has the church on her side, and that is the end of it."

"What does she intend to do with my little lady, Ivo?"

The steward hesitated a moment, and then he said in a low voice, "She has sold the child to a slaver bound for England, Dagda. I am to turn the demoiselle over to him now." He put a restraining hand upon the giant's arm. "What could I do, Dagda? She was my lord's wife, and now my lord is dead. The lady Blanche is mistress here now. How can I refuse to obey my lord's widow? I cannot. I am only a servant. Do you not think this tears me apart as well?" He reached down and stroked Mairin's head soothingly. "I have watched the demoiselle grow from a baby to a beautiful little girl." The steward's dark eyes filled with sudden tears. "There is nothing that I can do," he repeated helplessly.

"Take me to my father, Ivo," Mairin said, and when the seward wavered she continued, "It is my right. Would you deny me my farewells even as the lady Blanche did? I am not a bastard, but even if I were, Ciaran St. Ronan is my father."

With an unhappy shake of his head Ivo escorted them to the chapel. Mairin alone entered the silent room where her father already lay upon his bier, candles at both his head and his feet. He had been an attractive man, fair-skinned and dark-haired; and about his eyes tiny laugh lines for Ciaran St. Ronan was a man who laughed easily. Kneeling she began to speak to him as if he were resting there. Ciaran St. Ronan was handsome in death, the pain of living now erased from his strong features.

"You are with my mother again, father, and I know that you are both happy to be together once more; but I am so afraid! The lady Blanche is sending me away from Landerneau. I shall not be able to tend to your grave, or care for our people, but wherever I am I shall pray for you. Please watch over me. Dagda says he will never leave my side, but I am still fearful. Help me to be brave, father! I would not shame our name!" Her little head touched the side of the bier, and hot tears began to flow down Mairin's face. Her slender shoulders shook with the force of her sobs, but then gradually the sounds of her weeping lessened and finally stopped entirely. Drawing a deep breath the child arose slowly from the bier, wiped her face with her hands, and bending kissed the cold brow of her father. Then without so much as another glance she turned, and walked from the chapel.

"I will pack my things," she said quietly to Ivo, "and be gone from here as quickly as possible."

"She has forbidden that you take anything," the steward replied. "She says you have no right to take anything from Landerneau, that everything here belongs to her child."

"There is nothing among my things that belongs to Landerneau, Ivo. I have but my clothing, and a few trinkets my father gave me."

"I cannot allow it, my lady Mairin. You must come with me immediately. The slave merchant is waiting for you."

"The child must have a cloak, Ivo," said Dagda quietly, but the steward heard the unspoken menace in the Irishman's voice.

"Very well," he relented, "but hurry in the name of the Blessed Mother lest *she* recover from her fit, and call for me. What will happen to me, Dagda, if she takes my place from me?"

"Stay with Ivo, child," Dagda ordered his young charge, and then to the steward, "I will be but a minute." He bolted up the narrow stone staircase that led to the tiny room that had been Mairin's. Opening the door he was surprised to find Melaine there.

"Here!" The wet-nurse handed him a neatly packed bundle.

"What is it?" he demanded of her.

"A change of clothes for the little mistress, her cloak, a brush for her hair, and her mother's jewelry. I dared not take more, Dagda, else *she* find things gone. She knows everything that there is within the castle and is very possessive for her child. I can be of no use to her, however, and so I will be sent back to my village anyway. Therefore I can dare to oppose her for Mairin's sake. I do not know if what she claims is so, but she is a wicked woman to send the little mistress away."

"The child is trueborn," said Dagda quietly. "I thank you for your kindness, Melaine."

"*Kindness?* It is not simple kindness, Dagda. Did not that child suck at my breasts for almost two years? I gave her life with my milk! I love her!" Melaine's eyes filled with tears. "What will happen to my baby?" she cried.

"She will come to no harm," said Dagda. "I promised her mother that I would not leave her side until she was given into the keeping of a husband." Then with a nod to the wet-nurse Dagda turned and hurried back down the stairs to where Ivo and Mairin awaited them. The poor steward looked visibly relieved, but he paled as the voice of Blanche St. Ronan lashed out at him.

"Why is that little bitch still here? Did I not give you orders she be removed from my sight? What is that you carry, Dagda? The brat may take nothing with her! Give it to me, and then go about your duties. You, Ivo, take the wench to the slaver!"

"Would you deny my mistress her cloak, and a change of clothing, my lady Blanche?" said Dagda. "Surely you would not have it said that you were vindictive or un-Christian in your victory?"

Blanche St. Ronan flushed unbecomingly. "How do I know," she said, "that you do not steal property that belongs to Landerneau?"

"You do not," he replied calmly, "but I shall be happy to open this pitiful little bundle before all so you may check, and be certain."

"Oh, give the brat her things, and then go about your business," said Blanche St. Ronan ungraciously.

"The lady Mairin is my business," said Dagda quietly. "Where she goes, I go."

"You cannot leave Landerneau! You are bound to the land. If you try to go, I shall have you brought back and whipped for the runaway serf you are!"

Dagda threw back his head and he laughed. It was a deep and dark sound that sent a shiver down the spines of all that heard it. "I am a freed-man, madame," he said. "I came from Ireland with my mistress in answer to a dying request by her mother, the princess Maire Tir Connell. I am not bound to Landerneau, nor any other estate upon this earth. My *only* loyalty is to Mairin St. Ronan, and I will follow her unto death. If you would try to stop me, my lady Blanche, then do so," he finished, and looking into his cold blue eyes the lady St. Ronan shuddered. It would be just as well to be rid of the big man, she thought, for she did not entirely trust him.

"Go then," she said, "but do not come back begging for my favor when the slaver drives you away! It matters not! You may starve for all I care! I have gained a whole silver-piece profit for the bastard which I shall add to my coming child's inheritance."

"Blood money," said Dagda softly. "It will not bring your child luck. Rather it will bring her misfortune."

"Get out!" Blanche St. Ronan had gone white at his words.

Dagda gave her a smile that was more ferocious than friendly, and Blanche St. Ronan retreated, fleeing back into her hall. Then turning to Ivo, Dagda said, "Lead us to this slave merchant. I must have words with him."

Ivo smiled to himself and unconsciously hurried his steps as he moved from the castle out into the courtyard where the man waited for his human cargo. He wanted to see the look on the slave merchant's face when he learned that Dagda would be accompanying them.

The slaver was called Fren by the English with whom he had done business for many years, but the English no longer bought slaves in the numbers they once had. Those who lived in the Danelaw were better customers, however, than the crazy Anglo-Saxons who bought slaves only to free them. Fren was a Greek who normally would not have been inland in Brittany, but he had been approached in Brest by the secretary of a bishop who requested he come to Landerneau where the lady of St. Ronan would speak with him. Her husband was dying, she told him, and when he breathed his last, she would rid herself of his bastard daughter whom he allowed to live within the castle. The child was five, and totally useless, but she was a pretty thing and surely worth something. Fren had haggled fiercely with the lady, who had finally agreed to take a silver piece in exchange for the child.

He was secretly jubilant over his bargain. He would make a large profit on the little girl, for children, especially pretty children, were greatly sought after by connoisseurs in both Western and Eastern Europe. The lady of St. Ronan, however, could not know such a thing, thought Fren with a smile. Had she known, he thought, he should not have gained the child so cheaply. Watching as Mairin made her way toward him, her small hand tucked within the great paw of the giant who walked by her side measuring his steps carefully to fit hers, Fren was not unhappy.

The child was extremely beautiful. Incredibly so! He would certainly not sell her in England. Oh no! The little girl's value was not as a servant at all. He would carefully preserve and protect her throughout the next few months of travel for he had in mind a buyer in Constantinople who would pay him a small fortune for such perfection.

"This is the child, Mairin," said Ivo. "Are you content with the bargain, Fren? Will you turn over to me the silver piece agreed upon by my lady St. Ronan?"

Fren reached into the leather purse which hung from his waist, and unhesitantly drew forth a tarnished coin which he handed to Ivo. "I am content with the bargain."

Ivo's teeth bit into the coin, and satisfied it was genuine, he said to Mairin, "Farewell, demoiselle. May God and his Blessed Mother look after you."

"Bid old Catell adieu for me, Ivo," said Mairin.

The steward's eyes widened, but he nodded. "I will."

Fren reached out to pull Mairin toward him, but the giant by her side growled a low warning. "You will not put your rude hands upon my mistress, slaver," he said.

"Who is this . . ." Fren looked up the long length of Dagda. ". . . this fellow?" he finished helplessly. The creature was enormous, and looked dangerous.

Unable to restrain himself, Ivo chuckled. "I will let him tell you who he is, Master Fren." Then turning he reentered the castle leaving the three behind in the courtyard.

"I am Dagda," said the Irishman. "I am the child's guardian, and have been since her birth, even as I was the guardian of her mother, Maire Tir Connell, God assoil her, a princess of Ireland. The child is trueborn, but her stepmother seeks the father's inheritance for herself and her expected child. Though I am a freedman there was nothing I could do to prevent this wickedness. I will not, however, leave my little lady, slaver. *Where she goes, I go.*"

For a moment Fren was nonplussed. He had never heard of such a thing outside of the East. A man caring for a female child? "Are you a eunuch?" he asked Dagda.

The big man laughed loudly. "Nay," he said. "I have all my parts."

Strange, thought Fren, but then as he gazed upon the huge Irishman, he realized that here was a stroke of truly good fortune. This Dagda would take upon himself the entire care of the child, and keep her quite safe until he could return to Constantinople to sell her to his client. Still it would not do to appear too easily cowed. "You may come along, giant," he said pompously, "but I will expect you to earn your keep by helping me with other things. Charity is for the church and rich lords, and I am neither. Is that understood, giant?"

"It is understood, slaver," replied Dagda, and his blue eyes twinkled with amusement at Fren's attempt to control the situation.

The trader reached into his saddlebag, and withdrew from it a small leather slave collar to place about Mairin's slender neck, but Dagda's big hand stopped him. Startled, he looked up at the Irishman questioningly.

"Would you spoil her skin, slaver? It is delicate beyond anything you've ever known, and that collar will mark it."

Fren thought for a moment. The giant was correct for he had seen marks a slave collar left about the neck. Such marks could spoil the child's value, and it would really be a shame to mar such lovely skin. "Very well, Dagda," he conceded, "but she must wear it when we are in the marketplace. I will not have you slipping off with my property, and me unable to prove it."

Dagda nodded and again his eyes twinkled with the infuriating knowledge that it was really he who was in control of the situation, and not Fren. A young boy led a large horse to the Irishman, and the slave trader's eyes widened.

"You own your own horse?" His admiring gaze slid over the big beast's velvet brown coat.

"Brys was the last gift that my lady's mother gave to me before she died," came the answer. "He will be no expense to you, slaver. He is good at foraging." Vaulting into his saddle Dagda reached back down to draw Mairin up before him.

Fren scrambled onto his own horse. There was still two hours' light left, enough to travel several miles toward the coast. As they rode across the drawbridge of little Landerneau castle Mairin stared straight ahead, never once looking back, and Fren thinking it odd said to her, "Do you not wish a last glimpse of your home, girl?"

She fixed him with a strangely adult gaze, and her voice was devoid of all emotion when she spoke. "Why should I look back, slaver? That castle is my past. I look to the future."

Fren shivered. There was something about Mairin that almost frightened him. He looked over at her, but she was once again staring straight ahead. Dagda, however, had a small smile upon his lips, and when his blue eyes met those of Fren they were brimming over with mirth. The slave trader felt a bolt of irritation shoot through him. The child was his property, and yet she behaved like a queen! Then he shrugged. A quick trip to England, and then he would return to Constantinople. Once there the brat would learn her place quickly enough as the play-thing of some rich man, and there would be nothing that that big Irish giant who called himself her guardian could do about it. In Constantinople Fren had powerful friends, men who called him by his rightful name and who would destroy Dagda in a twinkling in order to possess the exquisite child. Fren smiled, showing his blackened teeth. In time, he thought to himself. Everything came in time. He had but to be patient.

Chapter 2

⟨ornament⟩

*T*hey sheltered that night on the edge of the forest where Fren loudly bewailed the lack of an inn or at least a peasant's cottage, particularly as Dagda would not let him light a fire. Fren was obviously a man used to his creature comforts.

"Light a fire," said the Irish giant matter-of-factly, "and you will attract every outlaw and brigand in the area. They are desperate men, and they would as soon slit your throat for your boots as look at you. Are you so eager to die?"

"Then how are we to eat?" demanded the slave merchant petulantly.

Dagda chuckled. "How have you ever survived all these years, Fren, trekking the world as you do with your human merchandise?"

"I do not make it a habit to travel in backwaters such as this, giant," said Fren loftily. "I travel along civilized roads with inns and other respectable accommodations. I have my own people who see to these matters."

"Well," said Dagda, "tonight I will see to these matters, and you will sleep upon the hard, cold ground wrapped in your cloak, and you can fill your fat belly with my uncivilized bread and cheese, and drink my poor wine, slaver; or you may go hungry while you stand there a fine target for whoever may be lurking in these woods."

With a nervous look about him Fren quickly plopped to the ground saying, "Where did you obtain bread and cheese, not to mention wine?"

The Irishman smiled knowingly as he cut a wedge of bread from a loaf he had pulled from his pack, and then sliced a chunk of cheese. He handed both to the slave merchant without further explanation. Fren raised a bushy eyebrow, but then he shrugged, and devoured his cold supper. It had suddenly occurred to him that were Dagda not with them he would have found himself caught in a dangerous situation for he had not realized the distance betwen Landerneau and the coast. It had not occurred to him that he could not make the round trip in a day. He ate silently, watching as Dagda slivered delicate curls of cheese which he then placed upon pieces of the soft center of the bread before giving them to Mairin. The child ate with a good appetite. He had found in his years of dealing with humanity that children were usually much more resilient than adults. Only rarely did one pine so deeply that it died. This child, however, was a survivor.

They rested. He and Dagda took turns keeping watch, and every noise in the black night set his nerves on edge. The child slept peacefully. Shortly after dawn they continued on to the seacoast village where they would meet up with Fren's two assistants and their cargo. As they rode Mairin was again silent, but Fren saw that she noted everything about them even if she said nothing. She was obviously not stupid.

It gave him personal pleasure, however, to see her eyes widen with just the slightest shock of fear when she first saw his string of prime slaves. He had some fifteen of them. Twelve men of all shapes and sizes, each one wearing a metal-studded leather slave collar, and bound together by a chain that was strung through an iron loop attached to the back of each collar. The three young women also wore collars, but they were bound together only upon the land, and then by the more humane method of a chain about their waists. Once they had set sail for England in the lumbering round boat the slave women were released. Women were considered manageable.

Fren, his party, and their horses were housed upon the open deck of the ship which carried wine and salted fish in its hold. The vessel skirted the coast of Brittany and Normandy sailing through the Pass de la Deroute with Brittany behind them, Normandy to the right, and a group of islands on their left. Mairin watched the navigator with interest as they passed Cap de la Hague, and she saw him carefully set his course across La Manche for England—the land of the Angles and the Saxons. Almost immediately thereafter it became foggy. So foggy that they could see neither where they had come from, nor where they were going.

"What are they like?" she asked Dagda. "What are the people in this England like?"

"They are brave men," said Dagda. "That I can vouch for having fought against them. Other than that, child, they are very much like people in Brittany, like people everywhere. They struggle to survive. They live. They die."

"Do they speak our language?" Mairin spoke a Celtic Breton tongue.

He shook his head in the negative. "They have their own tongue, but I understand it, and soon you will also."

"Are we going to stay in England then, Dagda?"

"Aye," he whispered to her softly, "but Fren does not know it. He has other plans for you, my little lady, but they are not plans that either your sainted mother or your noble father would approve. You are my sole responsibility. It is I who must see to your safety."

"Can we not go to my mother's family in Ireland, Dagda?"

"I had thought of that, my little lady, but it is a long and dangerous journey. Alas, I have no coin to ease our way, and we shall need money for food and for our passage to Ireland. Perhaps in a few years, but not now. First we must depart Fren's company. It should not be too difficult." Dagda had considered leaving Fren within the Forest of the Argoat, but on reflection realized that he might use the slaver to help them escape Brittany, which was no longer a safe place for Mairin, and Dagda did not doubt for a moment that had it been possible the lady Blanche would have killed the little girl. At least this way the child was alive, and in Fren's company half their journey would be completed. Dagda was not certain what he would do once they reached England, but he would think of something.

The winds were light, the fog thick, and the seas calm as a millpond. It took them almost three days to cross the water separating England from the mainland of Europe. Ashore Dagda was impressed to find that Fren had carts waiting to transport human cargo up the road called Stane Street to the city called London. Dagda would not allow his charge to ride in the cart with the women. Instead he took her up upon his horse with him as he had in Brittany. He did not want Mairin asking those women the questions she had asked him the previous night when she had awakened suddenly to see Fren and his two assistants using the three women who were docilely bent over the railing of the vessel, their skirts hiked over their hips, meekly accepting the obscene pumping of the men.

She had tugged at Dagda to awaken him, and then asked, "Are they mating?"

He nodded.

"Are they married to those women?"

"Nay, child."

"Then why are they mating with them?" she demanded innocently.

He moved them to another part of the deck, and sitting back down again he said, "What they do is wrong, my little lady. Put it from your mind, and go back to sleep," and silently cursing the lustful Fren and his two randy assistants, he cradled the child to his broad chest, encouraging her to slip once more into sleep. The sooner he could remove her from Fren's wicked grasp the better. The child was too young to be faced with such worldliness. He had to find a safe place for her.

Dagda had been to Dublin once, but nothing had prepared him for this London of the Saxons. To his eyes it was a noisy, smoky, dirty sprawl of a city; its buildings jammed too close together; its population too great. They entered it early in the morning just as the city awoke, and Fren's assistants had already found them a choice spot in the main market by the river with its great bridge.

Quickly the market became alive, and little Mairin who had never seen anything like it was goggle-eyed. To the right of their place a butcher had set up shop, putting up a standing rack from which hung newly butchered carcasses of meat. To their left was a man selling live songbirds; his stand hung with many willow cages. Next to the birdman was a fishmonger with his baskets of newly caught fish and eels. Directly across from them was a horse merchant, which was one reason Fren had chosen this particular space. The horses were always a draw, and therefore, his slaves could not be easily overlooked by the crowds.

Next to the horse seller a leech had set up his practice, and was quickly busy lancing boils and pulling teeth. Some with items for sale had no spaces in the market, but rather moved through it crying their wares. A ruddy farmer sold his milk in this fashion. A pieman with a tray of sweet buns balanced upon his head did a brisk business, as did the fresh-cheeked girls selling their herbs and flowers, and cups of fresh water.

Within the hour Fren was set up and ready to do business. True to his word he had placed about Mairin's slender little neck a heavy leather collar, fastening the lock with a click of an iron key that hung from a large ring attached to his girdle. "There!" he said with a smug and satisfied smile as he tested the strength of the collar. "You'll not be slipping off into the crowd with my merchandise now, giant. This little wench you guard so carefully for me is prime goods. Her youth and innocence paired with her rare coloring will bring me a fortune in Constantinople! She will bring me enough gold to buy me a villa in which to spend my old age."

"You would sell her to some vile and depraved pervert, slaver, wouldn't you? Do you think I am too stupid to know your evil plans? Where is your conscience?" Dagda demanded, but Fren just laughed, and Dagda felt the anger beginning to burn deep within him. It was the kind of anger that had once developed into a blood lust that had made him such a feared warrior in his youth. Fren, however, had turned away, and did not see the Irishman's blazing eyes.

The Saxons no longer believed in slavery, but they were still not above buying an occasional slave as cheap labor, and then allowing them to work off their price plus what it cost their buyer to feed, house, and clothe them. The buyer always profited under the arrangements, but slaves brought to England prayed for an Anglo-Saxon master. It was the best chance many of them had for regaining their freedom, as most of them had not been born slaves. It was also an inexpensive way to obtain help, for the price of slaves was set according to the law.

Fren had not come to England to seriously sell slaves, for the market was basically poor. Rather he came to obtain fair-skinned, fair-haired, and light-eyed Saxon maidens who would bring him a goodly profit in the teeming markets of the Levant. How he obtained such merchandise was a matter better left alone, but it was safe to say he never visited England without obtaining sufficient remuneration to encourage his return.

Dagda watched with interest, as the slaver plied his trade. Four of the men and two of the women were quickly sold off. Now Fren bargained fiercely with an innkeeper for the sale of the third woman, a young and pretty girl with thick dark brown braids.

"The wench can cook, spin, sew, *and*," here he paused for effect, giving the innkeeper a broad wink, "she's got a plump backside to warm yer bed on a cold, damp night."

"I've got a young wife," said the innkeeper. "Believe me when I tell you that she keeps me busy the whole night long."

"Don't tell me a fine fellow like yerself doesn't like a little something on the side," said Fren jovially, poking the innkeeper. "Besides, forbidden fruit is always sweetest. This girl can help in the kitchens, serve your customers, and make you a few extra coppers abovestairs, if you get my meaning. She's not a bad looker, and believe me when I tell you that she's a hot and juicy fuck."

The innkeeper let his eyes slide over the girl, and reaching out he fondled her plump breasts. The girl moved slightly into his hand, and smiled slowly and encouragingly into the man's eyes. His tongue flicked nervously over his lips as he seriously considered the wisdom of such purchase. "Is she gentle-natured?" he asked Fren. The innkeeper, who had actually had no intention of buying a slave today, was visibly weakening.

"Like a ruddy lamb," replied the slave merchant, and he turned to the girl.

"Aye, master, I be a good girl," she said with a provocative wiggle of her hips.

"I'll not pay more than the posted price," said the innkeeper, swallowing hard, and fumbling for his purse.

"I'd ask no more, sir," said Fren, his voice slightly tinged with hurt, but knowing the sale was made. The bargain was quickly concluded, and the girl went off with her new master, Fren grinning broadly as they went down the street.

One of the slave merchant's assistants laughed. "How many times is it that you've sold Gytha now? By the rood the wench makes more for you on the block than she does on her back!"

"She's good at luring the wenches for me," said Fren. "With her tales of Byzantium she has 'em practically begging me to enslave 'em. By the time we return to England next year she'll have a harvest of fair young beauties for us, you can be sure. Look how well she did for us two years ago in York. Tomorrow we'll head for Winchester. I'm eager to see the crop of girls Alhraed has enticed for us this past year. There's another fine Judas goat I own who's more than worth her keep."

The first of the morning business completed, Fren and his assistants settled down to wait for other customers. Dagda, newly enlightened of Fren's ruthlessness and business acumen, began to seriously consider the possibility of simply grabbing Mairin and making a run for it. That meek little man who had been so fearful in the forest was actually quite vicious and dangerous, and a genuine threat to Mairin. Then as she sat within the protective circle of his big lap he suddenly became aware of a tall serious-faced Saxon who stood staring at the child. The man was very well dressed, and obviously of the upper classes. He stood pondering, obviously considering something, but then as he slowly approached Fren two other men rudely pushed by him, and began shouting questions to the merchant about three of the male slaves.

The tall Saxon hesitated, but then catching Dagda's curious gaze he walked up to him and asked, "Do you speak English? Is the child for sale?"

Slowly Dagda nodded, and scanning the depths of his memory, spoke the correct English words. "What would you want with her?" His look was fierce, and extremely protective.

"My name is Aldwine Athelsbeorn. I am a king's thegn, and my estate is in Mercia. My little daughter died this past spring, and my wife cannot cease her grieving. This child reminds me of our Edyth."

"You would buy her to give her to your wife?" Dagda's heart pounded. Aldwine Athelsbeorn's face was one that concealed nothing. It was an honest face marked by life, yet kindly.

"Is the child your daughter?" the Saxon inquired, curious.

"Nay, sir," returned Dagda. Then he began to speak quickly in a low voice, hoping that Fren and his assistants would be kept busy long enough for him to make sense to the Saxon. This, he realized, was their way to escape from Fren! "The child's parents are dead, and her stepmother sold her off in order that she might steal my lady's inheritance. The child is of the nobility in Brittany, sir. I was her mother's servant, but now I am a freedman. It is a very long story. In the name of the good Jesu, sir, I beg you buy the child! I will pledge myself to your service for five years or more to repay you whatever expense you may incur. The slaver would transport my lady to Byzantium, and sell her to a lustful pervert!"

Aldwine Athelsbeorn did not even question Dagda's word in the matter. He was an educated man in a time when few were. Although the giant's words shocked him, he knew enough of the dark side of human nature not to disbelieve him. Suddenly all his previous hesitancy fell away and brushing Fren's other customers aside he demanded in an authoritative voice, "What price on the child, slaver? I fancy her as a serving maid for my wife."

"The child is not for sale, sir," replied Fren.

"Not for sale? What trick is this you attempt to play, slaver?" The Saxon's voice had risen now so that he was beginning to attract a small crowd. "If the child is not for sale, then why is she wearing a slave collar, displayed here for all to see? Is it that you seek to gain an unfair profit, or perhaps use her for immoral purposes? Speak up, man!"

Fren's face grew mottled with nervousness, and he sputtered impotently but no intelligible words could be heard.

"By our Blessed Lady Mary, that is what this rogue intends!" the Saxon shouted. Turning, he appealed to the jostling and interested crowd. "This low fellow would offer this little one, who is practically still a baby, for vile usage! Can we allow such a thing, my friends? Will someone not fetch a priest to try and bring this wicked fellow to repentance? Find me the sheriff! This villain had displayed the child in order to appeal to the evil ones, but I, Aldwine Athelsbeorn, King Edward's thegn, have found him out!" finished the Saxon dramatically.

The crowd, seeing little Mairin's innocent beauty, which Dagda, entering into the spirit of the Saxon's game, displayed by lifting the child up so she might be viewed by all, began to mutter ominously and shake their fists at Fren. The English loved their children for children were a man's immortality. Then one fellow, a bit brighter perhaps than the others, called out, "Why do you seek to buy the child, Aldwine Athelsbeorn? Are your motives pure?" The crowd's interest swung from the slaver to the thegn.

"This child reminds me of my dead daughter," said Aldwine Athelsbeorn. "I would bring her home to soothe my grieving wife. There is no crime in that."

"How do we know he speaks the truth?" cried another voice from the crowd, and looking toward Fren, Dagda saw one of his two assistants was missing.

The Saxon proudly drew himself up. "I am Aldwine Athelsbeorn, Kind Edward's thegn. In Mercia there is none who would doubt either my words, my motives or my courage!"

"This ain't Mercia! This be London!"

The crowd was becoming dangerous. Dagda's arms wrapped themselves protectively about his charge. For a minute he had thought the clever Saxon could use the crowd to his own advantage, but alas it hadn't worked. He looked to see whether or not in the ensuing uproar that was sure to transpire he might not make good his escape with Mairin. The collar about her neck did, however, pose a problem for it was too tight for him to cut or even get a grip upon so he might break it open and free her; but he would solve that problem after he brought his lady to safety.

Then suddenly amid the din he heard cries of, "Make way for Bishop Wulfstan!" and the angry crowd parted to allow the powerful and popular churchman through. "Well, Aldwine?" said the bishop sternly, but Dagda saw a twinkle in his eyes. Reaching the platform where they all stood, he demanded, "What is this all about?"

"Look at this child, my lord bishop. Does she not remind you of our little Edyth, may God assoil her innocent soul. I wish to buy this little girl to bring home to my Eada so that perhaps she will cease her lamentations over our daughter and live again. She has mourned without ceasing since the spring. The slave merchant displays the child, but then demurs on selling her to me. I believe he seeks to use the child wrongfully."

The bishop glanced at Mairin, but if there was a resemblance between this beautiful little girl and Athelsbeorn's dead daughter, he could not see it. Oh, Edyth had been about the same age probably, and she had red hair, but it was hardly the glorious color of this child's hair. Still if his friend could see a resemblance, and if he wished to rescue this pretty creature so that he might ease his wife's pain and give her a new interest, then it was a good and a Christian thing that he did.

He glared fiercely at the slaver, and did not like the look of him. "The child is displayed, which under our laws means that she is for sale," he said. "The price for a child of tender years is set at five copper pennies. You must therefore sell the child to the Thegn of Aelfleah. What is your name, man?"

"F-F-Fren, your lordship."

"Fren?" The bishop's brow furrowed for a moment. "Fren," he repeated thoughtfully, and then a knowledgeable look sprang into his eyes. "There was a slaver in York two years ago who was called Fren, and when he departed that city nearly a dozen women including two of good families were missing." The bishop's voice was soft, but beneath the softness Fren heard the ominous threat. No one could connect the slave merchant with the disappearance of those young women, Fren knew; but Bishop Wulfstan was a powerful man and he could spoil everything that Fren had worked hard to build.

He glanced at Mairin with her wonderful hair, and those perfect features on that flawless skin. For a moment he contemplated challenging the cleric's authority, then decided against it. He had not lived this long and prospered in his business by being an emotional fool. With a deep sigh of regret he allowed logic to prevail within him as it did in all his dealings. She was lovely, and she would have brought him a fortune in Byzantium. She was not, however, worth destroying a lifetime of hard work, which was what it would come to should he persist in attempting to retain her.

"If the noble thegn will step this way," Fren said loudly and unctuously, "I will take his coppers, and we will finalize the sale of the child."

With murmurs of disappointment the crowd began to melt away. The short drama was over. Eager to be rid of Aldwine Athelsbeorn and Bishop Wulfstan, Fren scribbled a bill of sale for the Saxon, took his copper pennies, and unlocking the collar from around Mairin's neck said, "She is now yours, noble thegn. Take her and depart." Then he laughed ruefully. "You have made a better bargain than you possibly know. The Irish giant is her personal guardian, but then he will tell you. If your desire for the child is an honest one you have gained a man-at-arms as well. If, however, your desire is an unholy one, the giant will undoubtedly kill you."

Aldwine Athelsbeorn looked at Dagda, and said but one word,

"Come." Then in the company of the bishop he strode off down the street, and away from the marketplace.

Safe in Dagda's arms Mairin finally spoke. "What is it? Where are we going?" She could see Fren behind them sifting some coppers from one hand to another while he regretfully watched their departure.

Dagda explained to his small mistress what had happened, and the little girl nodded her understanding. "Then I belong to this Saxon now," she said.

"He is a good man, this Aldwine Athelsbeorn. I can see it in his eyes," replied Dagda. "He will take you home to his wife. You will be safe if his wife likes you. If she cannot overcome her own grief, and your presence distresses her, I will work for the thegn until our debt is paid. Then we will depart for Ireland to find your mother's family."

"Am I still a slave?"

"Saxons do not hold with slavery any longer, my little lady. You may trust that you were free from the moment the thegn paid Fren his coppers." He chuckled. "I do not think this is quite the fate the lady Blanche envisioned for you. It restores my faith that God has seen to your safety in the guise of the thegn."

"What is this thegn, Dagda? Is he a noble like my father?"

Dagda thought a moment. "Yes," he said, "thegns could be called nobles. They are freemen with large holdings of land. They may also possess other forms of wealth. From the richness of his clothing, his cultured speech, and the fine brooch he wears, I suspect that Aldwine Athelsbeorn is a wealthy man, and perhaps more educated than most. Certainly he must have some influence, for this bishop was willing to aid him."

They followed the Saxon and Bishop Wulfstan through the streets, along the riverbank, and had Dagda not been such a big man himself he would have been hard put to keep up with them. Finally they entered a small well-kept two-story house. The building was set next to an orchard on the edge of the city itself. Two well-dressed servants hurried to escort them into the hall of the house where a fire burned taking the chill from the damp afternoon.

"Sit down, sit down," the thegn said to the bishop, and to Dagda. Then he looked to his servants. "Bring wine," he said quietly, and he turned to Dagda. "Tell us the child's story, but first I would know your name."

"I am called Dagda mac Scolaighe. Once I was a warrior to be feared, but the priests brought me to Christ, and a king in Ulster gave me his child, Maire Tir Connell, to raise. My lady Maire wed when she was fifteen to a Breton nobleman, Ciaran St. Ronan. Shortly after she bore their child she died, but before her death she put my lady Mairin into my keeping as her father had once done with her. After several years my lord remarried to a woman who hated my small mistress, and when lord St. Ronan died of the injuries he suffered in an accident, this wicked creature sold my little lady to the slaver Fren."

"Why?" The question was put to him by Bishop Wulfstan.

"The lady Blanche was expecting her own child. She feared if it were a female then it would be my mistress, of course, who would be the heiress to Landerneau, her father's estate. By ridding herself of her dead husband's elder child she opened the way for her own. She did not even wait to learn the sex of her own child. There was no one to protect my lady Mairin but me, and what power would a poor man have over a nobleman's widow? None of my lord's family was left to oppose her actions. Landerneau is remote, and so who would protest the child's disappearance?" Dagda had deliberately left out the fact that Blanche St. Ronan had managed to have Mairin declared a bastard by the bishop of St. Brieuc. Churchmen were notorious for sticking together in a situation although this bishop Wulfstan did not look like a man to be fooled. Still the man was a stranger as far as Dagda was concerned, and he couldn't be too careful with his lady's reputation. It was unlikely they would ever be involved with the lady Blanche and her uncle again. He had Mairin to protect. His story was a simple and plausible one. It was not unheard-of for a second wife to try to rid herself of children from the first marriage.

Bishop Wulfstan nodded with understanding. "This Blanche St. Ronan does not sound like an admirable woman," he noted with great understatement. "You have done a good thing, Aldwine, my friend. I think this child will prove a solace to your wife's grief. Eada is a good and gentle woman. The child's story will touch her heart." He looked at Mairin. "Why does the child not speak, Dagda? She does not look simple."

A small smile touched the corners of Dagda's mouth. "I have learned the English tongue because I fought the English at one time, but my lady Mairin, although born in Ireland, has lived most of her short life in Brittany, and speaks only Breton or Norman French. She is intelligent, however, and will learn quickly."

Aldwine Athelsbeorn looked at Mairin, and smiled his gentle smile. She was probably the loveliest thing he had ever seen. Holding out his hand to her he said in careful Norman French, "Come to me, my child. Do you understand me?"

"Aye, my lord," said Mairin, and she slipped from Dagda's lap, and walked over to the Saxon thegn.

"Mairin," he said reflectively. "It is not a Breton name."

"No, my lord, it is not," replied the child. "It is an Irish name. I was named for my mother, Maire. Mairin means little Maire in my mother's native tongue. May I have some wine? I am very thirsty."

He offered the child his cup, and she sipped eagerly from it, smiling up at him as she handed it back. "I am going to take you home with me to my wife," he told her.

She nodded. "Dagda has explained to me that your own daughter died this spring past. What was her name?"

"It was Edyth."

"Was she pretty? How old was she? What did she die of?" The questions tumbled forth from Mairin's mouth.

"Her mother and I thought she was pretty," he answered her. "She died of a spring sickness. She would have been six this summer. How old are you, Mairin?"

"I will be six on Samhein," she said proudly. "They say I am wise beyond my years. Where do you live? I hope not in this awful city!"

"*Samhein?*" He looked puzzled.

"All Hallows' Eve, October 31st," supplied Bishop Wulfstan, who now also spoke Norman French.

"I was born at the precise moment of sunset as the fires were lit," said Mairin proudly. "Dagda says it means I am blessed by the old ones. He says my head was like a flame pushing out into the world from between my mother's legs."

"God has indeed blessed you, my child," said the bishop, an amused look upon his face. He suspected his friend Aldwine had taken on more than he knew with this bright and beautiful fairy child. Reaching out the bishop patted Mairin's head and continued. "God gave you the good Dagda to look after you, and brought my old friend Aldwine Athelsbeorn to your rescue. You will be glad to know that he does not live here in London but in the countryside."

"My home is called Aelfleah," said Aldwine Athelsbeorn. "It lies in a hidden valley between the Wye and the Severn rivers on the edge of *The Forest.*"

"Aelfleah," said Mairin, feeling the strange word with her tongue. "Aelfleah. What does it mean, my lord?"

"Fairy's Meadow," came the reply.

"Is Aelfleah a Saxon word, my lord?"

"Yes, my child, it is. I think it fortunate that the first word of our language that you have learned is the name of the place which is to be your new home."

Mairin nodded at him, a serious look upon her child's face. Then she said, "Please, my lord, do you think that your lady wife will really like me? My stepmother did not like me for she was jealous of me. What of your other children? Will they like me?"

"My Eada cannot fail but like you, my child, and as for the rest of my family, there is only our son, Brand. Saxon families are usually large, but neither my wife nor I came from big families; and now there are none of them left but we three. No," he amended, "we four, for you, my little Mairin, shall take the place of the daughter we lost." Then reaching out Aldwine Athelsbeorn took the child upon his lap, and kissed her gently upon the forehead.

For the first time in many months Mairin felt safe. She had adored her handsome father, and for most of her life he had loved and spoiled her, but after his marriage to the lady Blanche everything had changed. Seeing his bride's ill-concealed dislike of his little daughter the Sieur de Landerneau had attempted to placate his new wife by lessening his attentions to the child of his first marriage, and increasing his attentions to Blanche. He had believed that if he could reassure Blanche her jealousy toward Mairin would cease. He had not been aware of the evil in his new wife's character.

The little girl, of course, had not understood, and had been frightened by this withdrawal of affection. Now suddenly here was someone who offered her the love she had lost. Looking up into the Saxon's face, Mairin touched his cheek with a delicate touch gently stroking the thegn's rough beard with her little fingers. Then she smiled at him, and seeing her face transformed Aldwine Athelsbeorn drew his breath in sharply with wonder.

Bishop Wulfstan chuckled. "I think you may have taken on more than even you anticipate, my friend. A face like that could one day gain you an earl for a son-in-law. Do not be in any hurry to match her lest you lose your advantage."

The servants brought them food, and the child ate hungrily for she had not eaten since the night before when they had been fed a cold gruel and some hard brown bread. This food was hot. A succulent capon that was so tender it fell from its bones. Her even white teeth tore at the meat, yanking it off the leg. She next ate freshly caught prawns that had been boiled with herbs, the taste of the sea contrasting strongly with the slices from a joint of rare beef that was also served. Warm, newly baked bread, a sharp, hard cheese, and sweet apples, the first of the season, completed the meal. Content, she had fallen asleep in the thegn's lap, and Aldwine Athelsbeorn had smiled with pleasure.

Early the next morning they departed London for Aelfleah, which was a good four days' ride from London. Bishop Wulfstan traveled with them for he was returning to his seat at Worcester which although it lay another day's journey from Aelfleah was in the same direction. They traveled west and had the good fortune to encounter fine weather the entire way. The roads over which they traveled had been built, Aldwine explained to Mairin, hundreds of years before by a people called the Romans.

Mairin nodded at his words. She was but half-listening. She was far more concerned with Aelfleah which was to be her new home if the lady Eada liked her. She put her mind to concentrating on that for she had learned early that she could will something to happen if she really wanted it. She also had concerns more important to her than some long-dead roadbuilders called Romans.

"Is this forest you spoke of nearby, my lord?" she questioned him.

"Yes, my child," he answered her, "but you must be careful for it is a deep and dense wood. I would not have you lost."

"I am not afraid of a forest," she answered him. "My home is, was," she corrected herself, "in the Argoat, an impenetrable and thick place of enchantment that has been there since the dawn of time. The forest is my friend. Old Catell, the wisewoman of our region, was teaching me of herbs and healing. She says I have the gift, and I do! I can see things that other people cannot," she boasted with her child's pride.

"Can you see how much my Eada and I will love you?" he asked her.

Mairin, who had been riding ahead of Aldwine Athelsbeorn upon his horse, leaned back against the Saxon, and tilted her head up to look into his blue eyes with her own deep violet ones. Mairin instinctively knew that this man would indeed love her with the unquestioning love of a father. In that instant she knew that she had found a place of refuge. "Would you really be my father?" she asked him softly, not quite able to believe her good luck.

He nodded gravely. "Yes, Mairin, I would."

"I will not forget my real father," she warned him.

"I would not expect you to, my child."

"I think you will be a good father to me," she said, and the matter was settled between them then and there.

Gently he kissed the top of her small head. As he raised his own head up his eyes met those of Dagda, who smiled, his glance one of approval. Aldwine Athelsbeorn smiled back, realizing that for the first time in many months he was truly happy. There was not a day that would go by in his life that he would not regret Edyth's loss. God was good, however, for he had given him Mairin. She needed him every bit as much as he needed her and he said a silent prayer that his wife would concur with him for he did not think now that he could part with this fairy child who had so suddenly and unexpectedly burst into his life.

At the thought of Eada his heart quickened its pace for he loved her as he was certain no man could love a woman. He was the last of his own family having lost both his brothers—the elder of a wasting sickness, the younger to the sea. His only sister had died in a childbirth that had also taken his father's only grandchild. It had therefore been his duty to find a wife as quickly as possible, his father had argued. A dutiful son, he had immediately set out to look over the marriageable daughters of the neighboring thegns who had not already been promised elsewhere.

He fell in love the first time he saw Eada in her father's hall, and he could not believe his good fortune that she was not promised to someone else, someone of importance. Particularly in light of the fact that her mother was a cousin of Earl Leofric's wife, Godiva. Eada's father, Daelwine, believed that his daughters should have some say in their choice of a husband. Although many had come to woo Eada, none had pleased her.

But if he had been instantly taken with her, Eada was equally enamored of him. Pleased by what they considered their daughter's sensible choice, Daelwine and his wife, Fearn, agreed to the match. It was celebrated with much rejoicing on the part of both families.

Before Aldwine's father died he had witnessed the birth of his first living grandchild, a boy called Brand, who was now ten years of age. Eada, who had so easily conceived Brand, bore but one more child four years later. Their daughter, Edyth. Still it had been a happy marriage, and thinking of his wife with her dark red hair, and her milk-white skin, Aldwine's loins quickened. It would be good to get home. The wind was coming from the north as they rode, its chill reminding him of the coming winter and the delightful games he and his wife played beneath the furs within their bed.

Just after the noon hour of the fourth day of their journey from London they reached Aelfleah. Warned of her husband's impending arrival by an advance rider, the lady Eada awaited her lord before the manor house. Her soft gray eyes widened with curiosity as she saw the small figure upon the saddle before her husband. Then those gentle eyes filled with quick tears for Aldwine used to carry Edyth before him in that same manner. She swallowed back her sadness. It was not seemly to greet her returning lord with the sound of weeping. She turned her glance to the huge stranger who also rode with her husband, and was that not Bishop Wulfstan? Devil take the outrider that he had neglected to warn her of that!

Her mind tumbled over the simple preparations she had made for dinner. They would have to broil a brace of rabbits in addition to what she had already ordered prepared, as well as a haunch of venison. There was yet time to send a boy to the millstream to catch a trout or two. The bishop was as good a trencherman as her husband, and the giant who rode with them did not look like he stinted himself at the table either! Blessed St. Cuthbert! Would there be enough bread? Had Byrd, the baker, baked today?

Aldwine Athelsbeorn slid easily from his horse's back, and enfolded his wife into his arms. Feeling her plump warmth made him realize all over again how much he had missed her, and so he kissed her greedily. For a moment Eada snuggled happily in his arms, and then with a laugh she struggled free of his embrace. Her pretty face was flushed with obvious pleasure. It was the first time Mairin could even remember having seen a married couple show such affection. Her father and the lady Blanche had always appeared quite formal with each other.

"Fie, my lord!" Eada scolded him lovingly. "What will his grace think of such behavior?"

"His grace," replied Bishop Wulfstan, dismounting his horse, "wishes that all married couples loved each other as truly as you two do. It does my heart good to see such a warmth in a cold world."

Now Eada turned her glance to Mairin. "And what this, my lord? Who is this pretty child you bring to Aelfleah?"

"I bought her from a particularly unpleasant slave merchant who had high hopes of taking her to Byzantium and selling her for less-than-wholesome purposes," replied Aldwine Athelsbeorn. "He was reluctant to part with her, but with the good bishop's intercession the slaver saw the error of his ways, and I was able to rescue the child."

"Ah, poor little one," said Eada sympathetically. She smiled up at

Mairin. Then her gaze moved to Dagda. "And this one, my lord? Was he also being mistreated by your slave merchant? He does not look to me like a man to be abused."

Aldwine laughed. "This is Dagda mac Scolaighe, who is the child's guardian." He quickly explained to his wife the story Dagda had told him.

When he finished Eada nodded with sympathetic understanding. "You are welcome to Aelfleah, my child," she said.

"She does not understand English, but she will soon learn from you," Aldwine told his wife. "She speaks only Breton or Norman French." He smiled up at Mairin. "My wife bids you welcome to Aelfleah, Mairin."

"Is she willing to be my new mama, my lord father?"

He looked a bit nonplussed as to what to say to her. Children were always so impatient, and as brave a man as he was, he wasn't quite certain how to broach the subject with his wife. It had somehow seemed simpler in London.

Then Eada asked, "What is it the child says about her mama, my lord? That word I could understand. If she is to stay for a while I shall indeed have to teach her English."

With a quick prayer, and the decision that a direct approach was the best way, he said, "Mairin, for that is her name, my love, wishes to know if you will be her new mama."

Eada staggered slightly and her pale face grew even paler. For a brief moment her pain-filled eyes closed. When they reopened she said in a shaking voice, "Edyth cannot be replaced, my lord. Surely you are not so callous as to believe so."

"No," he answered her, "Edyth cannot be replaced, nor will she return from her grave to us, my love. Our daughter is dead. I am not so cruel or unfeeling that I would attempt to replace one child with another as one might replace one puppy with another. Edyth does not need us anymore, Eada, but this child does. When I first saw her in the marketplace, her proud little face so frightened and forlorn, I knew then what I must do. In your heart, my loving one, you know too. God has given us another child, not to take Edyth's place, but rather to make her own place in our lives. As you have suffered, so too has this little one suffered. Mairin has asked you a question, my Eada. What shall I tell her?"

Eada looked again at Mairin, who stared back, her little face an impersonal mask. Then for a tiny second Eada saw the naked vulnerability in the child's violet-colored eyes. In that instant her heart went out to the little girl. She reached out with eager, loving arms to lift Mairin from the horse's back, saying as she did, "Of course I will be her mother, my lord husband. It is obvious that you have become her father." She gave the child a hug, kissing her upon both cheeks as she set her upon the ground. "It is easy to see she has already wrapped you around her tiny finger even as Edyth did." Then taking Mairin's hand in her own Eada led her new daughter into the hall at Aelfleah.

"Praise be to our good Lord Jesus and his Blessed Mother," said Bishop Wulfstan softly.

"Your wife is a good woman," Dagda said, the relief in his voice obvious. "My little lady will be safe with her, and for that, Aldwine Athelsbeorn, I am in your debt. You have but to tell me what you desire of me for from this moment on I am your liegeman, and you are my lord."

"The first thing we should all do," replied Aldwine Athelsbeorn, "is enter the hall and have our dinner." He chuckled at his two companions. "Well, I am hungry, my friends! As for you, my good Dagda, we will find much for a man of your many talents to do here at Aelfleah. As Mairin is welcome, so, too, I bid you welcome home." He smiled at the big Irishman. "Now, let us eat!"

Chapter 3

$\mathcal{A}$lthough Aldwine Athelsbeorn was not a man of any importance, his manor was a large one. Its lands had been collected by several generations of shrewd thegns who understood the value of owning more than less. Although the estate was somewhat isolated it was nonetheless prosperous.

Set in an almost hidden valley it was located between the Wye and the Severn rivers. Its affluence stemmed from a well-treated, contented peasantry, and from its very location which kept it safe when the nearby wild Welsh came raiding. A small river called Aldford made its way through the manor, a shallow crossing giving access to the estate from the narrow track that wound down across the hills from Watling Street.

There was a large common and pastureland for the manor's livestock on the far side of the Aldford past which the road moved on over the water through fine meadows and up to the manor house with its demesne lands. The road then branched off, the right track running on about half a mile to the village. The left track led to the manor church, and past the church the road branched again leading through fields of wheat, oats, flax, and barley as well as several arable but fallow fields. At the end of this road on the little river which had ribboned itself about the fields was a mill, and Weorth, the miller's cottage.

Behind the manor house and its fields to the left of the village was the woodland that Aldwine Athelsbeorn had called *The Forest*. It was treed with soaring English oaks, graceful beech, and sturdy pines. A tributary stream of the Aldford meandered through the forest which was peopled with deer, rabbits, fox, and other wildlife. The serfs and the peasants belonging to the manor were allowed to take one rabbit per family in each of the winter months, a generous accommodation on the part of

Aelfleah's lord. A dearth of rabbits would have endangered the domestic fowl belonging to the estate, encouraging predators from *The Forest* into the barnyard. The serfs and peasants understood this, and considered themselves fortunate to have such a kind master. Most land owners did not allow their people the freedom of their woods, and poaching brought severe retribution.

Just past the manor house on the other side of the village was an apple orchard that in the springtime was a sea of pale pink blossoms. Now the trees were heavy with the ripening fruit which in a short time would be harvested. Adjacent to the orchard was a small building where part of each year's crop was pressed for its cider. The rest of the fruit was stored in the root cellar belonging to the manor lord, to be doled out as he saw fit.

Aelfleah was self-contained like all English manors of its time. It grew its own grain, vegetables, and fruits. It kept cattle, pigs, horses, and sheep. It had an orchard, a bakehouse, a brewhouse, a church, and a mill. Cloth was woven from the raw materials produced upon the estate. Leather was tanned. Horses were shod. Farm implements and weapons were forged in the village smithy which was presided over by Osweald, the smith, a tall lean man with a thick neck and well-muscled arms. The spiritual welfare of Aelfleah was the duty of Father Albert, the manor priest.

Although the men of Aldwine Athelsbeorn's time knew nothing of fertilizing the soil, English thegns had a three-field system in which rotation of crops was practiced. One field was used for winter planting, another for summer, and the last lay fallow. Each family belonging to the estate had a strip of land in each of the different fields to farm. The land did not belong to the serf, and could not be passed on to another generation. It was merely loaned to the serf by his lord in exchange for his labor.

Although the miller, the priest, the blacksmith, the bailiff and the baker were freemen, the majority of people living at Aelfleah were serfs belonging to the manor. They could not leave the manor without the consent of their lord. The head of each family worked three days out of every week for his master. He was required to do whatever his lord might bid him, and neither he nor any in his family could marry without the lord's consent. Serfs were usually poor, oppressed and miserable. Those who lived at Aelfleah were well-cared-for, generally content and prosperous for their class.

The manor house was to all appearances typical of the time. Inside, however, major differences were apparent. Aldwine Athelsbeorn was quite eccentric in his architectural tastes. Constructed of dark gray stone, the house stood two stories high. The main floor of the building had once been a huge aisled hall subdivided by two lines of posts which supported its roof. The second story of the building had been built over part of the hall, and contained a large room called a Great Chamber which was a bed-sitting room for the lord and his family.

The only means of heating available to the house had been a firepit in the hall, an extremely unsatisfactory arrangement as the windows, although few, were not particularly tight. The smoke from the firepit had exited the building through the thatched roof of the hall which when the wind blew from a certain direction merely directed the smoke back down into the room to choke its inhabitants and cover the meager furnishings with soot. The Great Chamber had been too cold in winter, stifling in summer, and damp when it rained.

As his father's second son Aldwine Athelsbeorn had not expected to inherit Aelfleah. To earn his way in the world, he had hired out his military skills as many a hot-blooded young Anglo-Saxon did. His prowess with sword and battleax had given him his surname, *Athelsbeorn:* meaning Noble Warrior. Unlike other young men, however, he had not confined himself to England. He had instead traveled to Scandinavia, to Byzantium, and disguised as a Moorish soldier, he had even seen the Holy Land. Now that the army of the Prophet controlled Jerusalem, Christians were not readily welcome.

The world fascinated Aldwine for his was not a closed mind, and the blood of his Norman grandmother, herself a descendant of Rollo, ran thickly in his veins. He loved the color, the excitement, the sights, the smells, and the sounds of other lands, other cultures. There was a strong possibility that he would have never returned to England had not the unexpected deaths of both his elder and younger brothers recalled him. He had been about to embark for Sicily with some distant Norman cousins when his father's message came, and a sense of filial duty he thought long dead had risen within him, and he had gone.

In accordance with his father's wishes he had gotten himself a wife, and brought her home to Aelfleah, but it was still his father's house. If after his exposure to other places Aldwine found it less than comfortable it was certainly not his place to say so. His father was an Anglo-Saxon of the old traditions. He would not distress his sire in his old age with useless complaints.

What he found most intolerable was the dreadful lack of privacy. It didn't seem to bother the others of his race, and once had not bothered him. Now, however, even with the curtains drawn he could not feel at ease in bed with his wife when just beyond those curtains, his wheezing and snoring almost rocking the room, lay his father, and three body servants, and more often than not, some visitor. He knew Eada shared his feelings, but they spoke with no one else on the matter for they would have been considered odd to desire their privacy. Privacy was not Anglo-Saxon.

When Aldwine Athelsbeorn inherited Aelfleah, he immediately set about to reconstruct the house in a way considered quite strange by his neighbors. The entire main floor was roofed over, and the firepit covered, while a large fireplace was put in its stead with a well-drawing stone chimney. At the end of the large hall he had two smaller rooms built to serve as a buttery and pantry. New glass was placed securely into the windows. Aldwine did not need to remove his windows as the great lords did who carried their window glass from house to house.

Aelfleah's kitchen was located in a separate building across the herb and vegetable gardens. It was connected to the main house by means of a covered portico through the gardens which Aldwine walled in to protect from the rabbits. This allowed access to the kitchen in times of danger. Eada was delighted, for now when she planted her garden she could count on harvesting it rather than losing her crop to predators.

The Great Chamber on the upper floor was redesigned and now extended to the full length of the hall below it. One end of the second floor became a private bedchamber for the lord and his wife. The other end of the floor with its new fireplace for heating the upper story became a solar where the family might sit in privacy away from the noise of the hall. Between these two rooms ran a narrow hallway which had a small windowed chamber on either side of it for children.

Aldwine's neighbors were scandalized. They thought the house radical in its new interior. Why did a man need a private chamber for himself and his wife? What could he do behind closed doors that he could not do in an ordinary Great Chamber? As for giving children separate rooms, it was ridiculous not to mention dangerous! How was a boy to learn about women, and a girl about men if they were kept separated? Still there were those who secretly envied Eada her new privacy, and her two fireplaces, but they were wise enough to keep silent.

The furnishings in the manor house were simple yet comfortable. In the hall there was a sturdy oak highboard, and trestles. There were high-backed chairs for the senior family members, and benches for the others who came to table. The solar with its smaller fireplace had two chairs for the master and mistress of the household, a small table, some low stools, and Eada's loom. Anglo-Saxon women were famed for their beautiful cloth, and Eada was a particularly skilled weaver. The house's lighting was supplied after dark by rush and tallow torches, some candles, and bronze oil lamps that were the pride of the manor.

The bedchambers were just as sparsely furnished, with nothing more than beds and large chests which were bound in iron and used for clothing storage. Eada was the proud possessor of a round of highly polished silver which she used as a mirror. It had been her wedding present from her doting husband.

The family's personal servants slept in the solar. As the other serfs must give three days of their labor to their lord, those serfs chosen as body servants gave their lord three nights of each week sleeping in the solar on call should they be needed. When the children were young their personal servants slept with them upon a trundle which during the day was stored beneath the child's bed. The rest of the household servants bedded down in either the hall or the kitchens if they did not belong to any of the cottages on the estate.

There was a warmth and an intimacy to the manor house that had been lacking at Landerneau, Mairin thought. Perhaps if her mother had lived it might have been different, but Mairin's memories were of cold gray stone walls made habitable only by the love and the attention that her father and Dagda had lavished on her.

I can be happy here, Mairin decided. The lady Eada has easily accepted my presence at Aelfleah. It was an interesting comparison to the lady Blanche who had resented her husband's child so very much; whose only concern had been in herself, and what she considered her own. Eada, she would quickly find, was a stern but loving mother who was interested in everything that her children did. That first afternoon, however, Mairin was frightened as the tall woman with the dark red braids held out her hand to her. She strove to hide her fright, but Dagda knew her every expression.

"Go with her, my little lady," he gently encouraged Mairin. "She will be the mother you never had. A female child needs a mother."

"I need no one but you, Dagda," she bravely affirmed.

He smiled. "You need a mother, and here God has provided you with what appears to me to be a very fine one. Put your hand in hers, my child. She needs you every bit as much as you need her."

Mairin, shyly glancing up at the woman from beneath her lashes, placed her little hand in Eada's big one. They entered the house and Eada immediately called for a small oaken tub to be brought to her in the solar along with hot water sufficient to fill it. Then she led Mairin upstairs, and the child turning an anxious face saw with relief that Dagda followed. Reaching the solar, he handed Eada the small bundle he had carried from Landerneau.

"It contains her mother's jewelry," he said, "and the child's personal grooming items. The rest is of no importance, and is better disposed of, mistress. There is no need for my little lady to be reminded of what has been. It is better she face the present, perhaps even look to a happy future." Then with a courtly bow he departed the solar.

Eada spoke no language but her own and the Latin tongue which Aldwine had taught her in the early days of their marriage. She sometimes envied her husband his easy command of other languages, most of which sounded like so much gibberish to her. Nonetheless she now spoke to Mairin as if the little girl understood her perfectly.

"Gracious, child, you are simply filthy! I shall give you a good bath, and wash that wonderful mop of hair you possess!"

Lifting Mairin up onto the table she began to gently strip the clothes from her. Seeing the perfect and sturdy little body before her brought back sharp memories. Eada's eyes filled with tears which quickly spilled down her rosy cheeks. Still she did not cease in her task, and taking Mairin's garments she threw them into the fireplace where the flames caught them up with a *whoosh,* and quickly devoured them. The tears continued to run down her face though she struggled hard to master her emotions.

Mairin, who could understand Eada no more than the older woman could understand her, nevertheless comprehended grief. "Do not cry, my lady," she pleaded, attempting to brush away Eada's bitter tears. She was unaware that tears flowed from her own eyes as at last she was finally able to release her own sadness.

Seeing the child's sorrow Eada hugged the little girl to her heart. "Ah, my little one," she whispered, "my Edyth would have liked you even as I see that I am going to like you. She, too, had a good and tender heart." Then wiping the remainder of her own and Mairin's tears away, she lifted the little girl from the table, and set her in the tub.

Kneeling down she pushed up the sleeves of her gown. She first washed the glorious hair, then soaped the little body and rinsed it clean. Taking the child from the tub she put her back upon the table, and quickly toweled Mairin dry lest she catch a chill. Lifting Mairin again from the table she sat her upon a low stool before the fire. Then sitting in her own chair Eada brushed Mairin's marvelous red-gold hair until it was soft and dry, and floated like a halo of thistledown about the girl's head.

For a long moment Eada stared in amazement. Now that she was cleaned up, the child was a glorious beauty. "Sweet Jesu," Eada breathed softly. "I have never seen anyone like you before in my entire life!" Eada took one of Mairin's long curls and fingered it gently. "No wonder your stepmother was jealous of you, child." Then realizing that Mairin was apt to catch her death of cold unless she was dressed, Eada stood up and walking over to a small trunk, opened it. For a minute she gazed down and found herself again in danger of weeping, but then she bent and drew forth several garments. "These were my Edyth's," she said quietly. "I meant to give them to my brother's wife for her daughter, but somehow . . ." Her voice trailed off, and without another word she began to dress Mairin.

She slipped a long undertunic of pale yellow silk over the child's head followed by an outer tunic of copper-colored light wool which fell halfway between Mairin's knee and her ankle, and revealed the undertunic beneath. The outer tunic had wide, long sleeves with black embroidery at both the wrists and the modestly buttoned round neck of the garment. Digging back into the trunk Eada brought forth soft leather shoes that followed the shape of the foot. Although they had been made for Edyth they fit Mairin almost perfectly. Eada then girded a narrow leather belt with a bronze-green buckle about the little girl's waist. Lastly she fitted a little green ribbon band about her forehead.

Suddenly up the stairs and into the solar came a young boy. Dressed in a blue-green tunic with matching hose, he had dark red hair like Eada's. His haughty glance took in Eada and Mairin, and then he demanded arrogantly, "Where is this child that my father has decided will be my new sister?" Hostile blue eyes fixed themselves upon Mairin. "Is this *she*? I will not accept her! No one can take Edyth's place, and besides—her hair is an outrageous color!"

Like a small kitten accosted by a noisy young dog Mairin narrowed her eyes, and hissed fiercely. "Come no closer, rude boy, lest I turn you into a frog!"

Aldwine, arriving in time to hear the whole exchange, burst out laughing, and admonished his son, his face suddenly serious. "Beware, Brand! Mairin has threatened to turn you into a frog if you do not treat her in a more kindly fashion." Over his son's head his eyes twinkled at his wife.

"Hah!" the boy mocked scornfully. "She cannot do *that!*" Then he turned his gaze back upon the little girl whose glance was so fierce that he amended nervously, "She can't really? Can she, father?"

"I do not know, my son, but if it were I, I do not think that I should take the chance. It is indeed possible that Mairin knows how to turn you into a frog. She is a Celt from Brittany, and the Celts are people of magic. Yes," he considered, "she could indeed turn you into a frog, but as she is very young, she might not know how to turn you back."

Brand paled and moved closer to his father.

Eada laughed softly, admonishing her husband gently, "Fie, my lord! You must not tease Brand so."

"But I do not, lady," came the serious reply. "If I were Brand, I should be kind to Mairin who has now come to live with us. She will be a daughter to us, and a sister to him." He put an arm about his son. "I am not trying to replace Edyth either in our hearts or our minds, Brand, but she is gone from us forever. We have lost her even as Mairin has lost her mother and father. In each of our lives there is an empty space. God often works his will in a manner not fully understood by mortal men. Look at your mother, my son. There is a smile upon her lips for the first time in months. I have long prayed to our Blessed Lady to ease my Eada's sorrow. Now that prayer has been answered."

Brand's eyes turned to his mother, and he saw the truth of his father's words. The boy looked properly shamefaced as Aldwine continued, "Now, my son, greet your foster sister kindly and bid her welcome to our home. Use your best Norman French for she does not yet understand our tongue."

Brand turned to face the little girl who stood glowering at him. Her lovely hair billowed red-gold fire about her slender young shoulders. Secretly he liked the way she had defied him so bravely. Although she had not understood his words she had known by his tone and his manner that he was not being friendly. Courage was something Brand understood and admired. Looking down on Mairin he could see that she was far prettier than Edyth had ever been. In fact if he were honest with himself he had to admit that she was beautiful. He wondered if she would be one of those prissy creatures who hated getting dirty, and disdained roughhousing. Or was she a girl who liked to ride and hawk? An encouraging look from his father spurred him onward.

"I am Brand," he said slowly, uncomfortable with the language of the Normans which his father insisted he learn. "Could you really turn me into a frog?"

Mairin's eyes lightened as her anger departed. She had not understood one word of what had passed between Brand and his parents, but she knew instinctively that Aldwine had given her stature in the boy's eyes. Her mouth turned up into a half smile. "Perhaps," she admitted, aware that the doubt was a far more potent weapon than a definite yes.

Brand was not certain if he believed her or not, but as his father had warned him, it was not wise to tempt her anger. "Father says you are to be my new sister. Mairin is a pretty name. Is it Norman?"

"I am not a Norman, I am a Breton. My name is Celtic. My mother was a princess of Ireland." Her violet eyes scanned him thoughtfully. "I have never had a brother before. My father's second wife, the lady Blanche, is expecting a baby. She does not carry a male child. I know." Mairin paused a moment, and then said, "Do you have a horse? I had my own pony at Landerneau, but the lady Blanche would not let me have Parnella when she sent me away."

As the two children conversed the thegn softly translated their words so his wife might understand them. When Mairin spoke of her lost pony Eada looked at her husband with such distress that Aldwine knew just how right he had been to bring Mairin to his wife.

"I have a horse," Brand continued. "He is gray with a black mane and tail. I call him Thunderbolt. I also have a dog. She has just whelped six pups."

"Puppies!" Mairin's eyes were round with envy. "I have never had a dog," she said, the longing in her voice quite plain.

"Would you like one of Freya's?" Brand offered nonchalantly.

"Ohh, yes!" she breathed. Her small face was ecstatic.

"You will have to take care of it properly," he warned her. "I will show you how, and you must promise not to turn me into a frog, Mairin. Do you agree?"

"If I am allowed the pick of the litter," she counter-offered, "*and* I get to choose!"

"Done!" said Brand. He grinned. Mairin grinned back. They had come to an understanding with one another, and now they would be friends.

Aldwine and Eada smiled at each other over their children's heads. Each had the same thought. Edyth's death had taken something away from them, from their family. Whatever that intangible something had been, little Mairin's presence restored it. They were once more a whole family.

Mairin slipped into life at Aelfleah as if she had always been a part of it. Within weeks she was speaking the English tongue as if she had been born speaking it. Aldwine, however, would not allow her to lose her Norman French. A Norman would be England's next king. It was possible that his beautiful new daughter might make a Norman marriage.

Autumn deepened and became winter. Winter lingered until pushed aside by an insistent spring which was in its turn forced to give way to the summer. A year passed, and five more followed as easily. Those who had known Edyth Aldwinesdotter for the brief span of her life soon forgot that she had existed as Mairin's strong and healthy presence wiped from their consciousness the memory of the other child.

Brand swiftly discovered that Mairin was not a sister to sit by the fire. A fat black-and-white pony named Vychan, Welsh for "small one," came to live in the manor stables for several years, to be replaced when Mairin was ten by a dainty white mare called Odelette. Mairin was an excellent rider with a firm seat and light hands. Brand soon learned she was every bit as bold as any boy, galloping her mount at full speed over the estate, and jumping anything in her path that did not move out of the way.

"You're going to break your neck one day," he grumbled good-naturedly at her on one occasion when she had beaten him home by jumping Odelette across a narrow rocky streamed that they usually picked their way across.

Mairin had laughed at him, saying, "You must learn to anticipate your opponent, Brand, else you'll never win in life!"

Sometimes, he thought, she seemed older than he was, and he was four years her senior. As maddening as she could be he had quickly grown to love her, and she gave back that love. He was her adored big brother who took her hunting and hawking with him and who always seemed to have time to talk with her when she was troubled. She was his first love, and it pained him to think they would one day lose her to a husband.

It was Brand who had taken Mairin into *The Forest* for the first time, and shown her the paths that he knew. She in turn had shown him how to find and follow animal trails, and which mushrooms and berries were safe to eat and which weren't. He had been amazed by her knowledge of plants, and their healing abilities. Her knowledge seemed to him a special thing.

The Forest. That deep and dark preserve of ancient rumor and legend quickly became Mairin's realm. She seemed to have no fear of what lurked within its depths. There were those who dreaded the unknown, and the unseen, but Mairin was not one of them. She knew she was protected from any evil, but how she knew it, even she did not comprehend.

Eada soon learned not to fear each time her daughter wandered off, for Mairin was resourceful for all she was a child. Then, too, Dagda was never far behind his small mistress, particularly in those early days at Aelfleah. It was he who generally carried home the injured creatures that Mairin found and brought back to the manor house to treat and heal.

Then one day she used one of her special poultices to heal a kitchen serf who had punctured the heel of her hand with a knife. The wound seemed to mend itself in a miraculously short time for such a deep cut. Another injury was presented to her for treatment, and another, and suddenly it was Mairin, not Eada, who was responsible for curing Aelfleah's sick and injured.

"She is naught but a child," said Eada, amazed, "and yet she has the gift of healing."

"Then let her," said Aldwine Athelsbeorn, and he was secretly pleased. This talent of Mairin's for doctoring only confirmed his belief in her intelligence. When Mairin had first come to them he had proposed that she study with Brand.

Brother Bayhard, Brand's tutor, had not been enthusiastic about adding the daughter of the house to a schoolroom where the son and heir was so impossible to teach. In this he was supported by Eada.

"Women," he loftily told Aldwine Athelsbeorn, "have not the intelligence to understand languages, geography, philosophy, and higher mathematics. It is better that they tend to their gardens and their looms as God intended."

The thegn of Aelfleah had persisted, and Mairin had joined the schoolroom. Within days the good Brother Bayhard, who for all his high ideals was intelligent, realized that the true scholar in the household was not the son, but rather the daughter.

Having done what he could to insure that his patron's heir would not be a total dunce, Brother Bayhard concentrated his energies on Mairin. She was like a sponge, sopping up and learning everything that he might teach her. He instructed her in Greek and Latin. She learned mathematics so that she might one day oversee the bailiff should her husband not be there to do so. She learned to read and write in all the languages she spoke. Her handwriting was as fine as any monk's, her tutor proudly declared.

In his excitement at having a pupil who constantly asked him questions, who challenged answers that didn't suit her, and who in six months had learned everything that he had struggled over the last five years to teach Brand, Brother Bayhard added history to their program of studies. He quickly forgot all his previous beliefs regarding the minds of women. He was willing to admit that he had been wrong if only he might continue to teach this marvelous young mind of Mairin's.

Brand gratefully left the schoolroom at twelve, Aldwine accepting the fact that his son was no scholar. He was satisfied that the boy could read enough to understand any document that might come his way, sign his name legibly, speak the tongue of the Normans decently, and comprehend enough mathematics to know he wasn't being cheated. Brother Bayhard, however, remained to continue the education of the daughter of the house.

Eada protested Mairin's hours in the schoolroom. "You are wasting her time, my lord. She needs none of the skills you are having her taught."

Aldwine stubbornly shook his head. "We do not know what she will need," he said to his wife. "Besides, Mairin is a child who must be kept at challenging things. Surely you have noticed she grows restless when bored. Left to herself, my love, who knows what mischief she might get into."

Eada secretly agreed with his assessment, but she nonetheless pressed her own case. "Mairin needs to know how to cook, and supervise the serfs, and tend the kitchen garden. She must know how to salt meats and fish, how to preserve and dry fruits for winter, how to make soap, conserves, and candles. She needs practical skills to be a good wife."

"You will teach them to her," he said agreeably, "but she will also know the things I wish her to know. I want a fine marriage for our daughter, Eada. Mairin is not for some Saxon boy. Her beauty will gain her an important match, but when that beauty fades as does all beauty, she will hold her husband with her clever mind." He kissed his wife reassuringly and gave her a pat. "The times are changing, and it is Mairin and Brand's generation who will bear the brunt of that change."

"A Norman king is what you mean," said Eada wisely. "Oh, Aldwine, I know you have Norman blood in you, but why has King Edward chosen Duke William for his heir?"

"Who else is there?" replied her husband. "The king himself is half Norman and has no children of his own."

"But William the Bastard?"

"Would you have Harold Godwinson, that spawn of the devil himself, to rule England?" he asked her angrily. "Or perhaps another Dane or Norwegian?"

"There is Edgar Atheling," Eada ventured. "He is of the line of Cedric."

"Yes," Aldwine agreed, "but he is a weak boy. He has lived most of his life in Hungary. What can he really know of England and her people? England needs a strong king if she is to survive the coming years, and William of Normandy is that king. There is no other logical choice, and King Edward having seen it wisely designated William as his heir. He will be king, Eada. Make no mistake about it. It has been promised him, and he will have it. Those who oppose Duke William will suffer the consequences of his wrath. That is why I prepare Mairin for a Norman marriage. The Norman women may not be as free as our Anglo-Saxon women, but their men like them with wit and intelligence as well as household skills."

"My mother taught me that men did not like women who were mannish, my lord."

Aldwine laughed heartily. "There is nothing including a little knowledge that will ever make our Mairin appear masculine for she is the most feminine of creatures. She will soon surpass your talents at the loom, my dear, which is no mean feat, and her embroidery is excellent thanks to your clever tutelage."

Eada bloomed beneath his compliments. She was a simple, loving woman. In her entire life she had never been further than twenty miles from the house in which she had been born. Her entire life and world consisted of family and familial duties, first in her father's house, and then in her husband's. Housewifery was her talent, and she was justly proud of her skills. For Aldwine to praise those skills, and those of their foster daughter, was high acclaim.

Aldwine was correct in his observations of Mairin. She was as swift to boredom as she was to the pursuit of knowledge. She was nothing at all like Edyth who had been a sweet and placid girl, nor did she even try to be, which was perhaps what made it so easy for them to accept her. Eada smiled to herself. Mairin was clever at the loom. The cloth she was currently weaving was intertwined with delicate strands of gold and silver threads. It was work of the finest quality, but once having mastered the technique, Mairin became weary of it. Perhaps, thought Eada on reflection, her husband was right in having Mairin study with Brand. Eada had never known a woman who enjoyed learning, but Mairin certainly did.

If Mairin had been a happy addition to Aelfleah, so too was Dagda. His skill with horses assured his usefulness, for none of the serfs had quite his knowledge. His good nature assured he would never be lonely, for the women were drawn to Dagda like flies to manure and he adored them all, never playing favorites, and somehow managing to get away with it. The women of Aelfleah understood that Dagda's love and loyalty belonged to Mairin.

Eada could see that it was not easy for the Irishman to relinquish his authority and control over Mairin who had been his charge since her birth, but for the child's sake he had tried his best. Eada, sensing the deep love between the two, deferred to the gentle giant as often as she might.

Aldwine Athelsbeorn was a careful man where Mairin's status was concerned. In exchange for some future service to the king he had obtained from Edward a writ acknowledging Mairin as his and Eada's daughter, with all the rights and privileges thereof. She would be dowered generously. In the unlikely event of Brand's death and the absence of other heirs of his and Eada's body, Mairin would inherit the manor of Aelfleah.

Brand was now sixteen years old, and at slightly over six feet in height, he was powerfully strong. In the past two years he had developed a healthy appetite for women and with his handsome face and merry manner his advances were rarely refused.

Eada began to worry that it would soon be time to settle her son with a wife. They would have to go bride hunting, despite the fact that they were so isolated in their little valley without any near neighbors. Eada considered the possibility of visiting her family after all these years. "My brothers have daughters," she said. "Perhaps one would be suitable for our son."

Brand rolled his eyes in anguish which sent his twelve-year-old sister into a fit of giggles. Reaching out he teasingly tweaked one of her braids, and she stuck her tongue out at him. He grinned back at Mairin and said, "Actually I'd like to go over the western hills into Cymru and steal a wild Welsh wench for a wife. A little new blood might be just the thing this family needs."

"Brand!" Eada was shocked, but both Aldwine and Mairin burst into laughter, realizing that Brand was but teasing his mother.

The search for Brand's bride had to be postponed, however, for the king requested of Aldwine Athelsbeorn the favor owed to him. When he returned from Winchester the thegn brought news that both startled and frightened his wife.

His children, of course, were far more interested in the gifts he had brought them. Laughing at their greed, for even Brand still enjoyed receiving gifts, Aldwine presented them. For his son he had brought a dagger whose blade had been made in Moorish Spain. The handle of the dagger, however, was fine Celtic enamelwork. Brand's eyes lit at the sight of the weapon, and he thanked his father profusely. For Mairin there was a string of amethyst beads, "to match your eyes, sweeting," said her father as she hugged him.

"And have you forgotten me, my lord?" Eada teased her husband.

"No," he said slowly, "I have not. Are you not first in my heart, lady?" He handed her a small bolt of scarlet silk with stripes of pure gold woven into the fabric. As her mouth opened in exclamation he continued, "It comes from Byzantium where I must shortly go. I have been chosen by the king to lead a delegation to discuss new trading treaties between our two nations."

"Byzantium?" It was only a name to Eada, a fabled and faraway place her husband had once visited in his youth. She had no idea of where it really was. "Is it far, my lord? How long will you be gone?" she innocently queried him.

Aldwine Athelsbeorn put an arm about his wife's shoulders. "It is very far, my love," he said, "and *we* will be gone for as long as it takes to negotiate the treaties for the king. I intend to take you and Mairin with me."

"Ohh, father!" Mairin began to dance about the solar. "We are to go with you! How wonderful! How exciting! Will we actually get to see the Emperor of Byzantium himself? May I have a new gown for the trip? Can I take my horse, my merlin, and my dog?"

Aldwine laughed. "Yes, Mairin, you will probably get to meet the emperor, you may have several new gowns, and yes, you may take your horse. Your dog and your hawk, however, must remain here at Aelfleah."

For Mairin the opportunity of traveling to an exotic place was irresistible. Eada's face showed concern. She understood things that Mairin did not. The king was not in good health. The succession was already being haggled over despite the fact that Edward had designated his cousin, Duke William of Normandy, as his successor.

The queen wanted her brother, Harold Godwinson, to be England's next ruler, and worked constantly toward that goal. There was no royal blood in the queen's family. Her father, the late Earl Godwin, had forced her into marriage with the king, though he could not force Edward into his daughter's bed. Edward, who held Earl Godwin responsible for his elder brother's death, had not desired a wife at all. At one point he had even put the queen aside. A deeply religious man, he was more suited to the life of a monk. Indeed the royal couple's lack of children gave truth to the rumor that the marriage had never been consummated.

Norway's king also claimed sovereignty over England and he had a powerful army supporting him though his ambition was rooted in greed, not fact. If Edward died while they were gone from England war was certain to break out. What would happen to Aelfleah and its people? Then Aldwine answered her unspoken question, and Eada's blood ran like ice in her veins.

"Brand will remain in England to oversee our lands. Had I the choice, I should not leave England at all, but I cannot refuse the king."

Sweet Blessed Mother! thought Eada. If Edward dies while we are away chaos will follow. How can our son, a boy yet for all his wenching, hold Aelfleah against Harold Godwinson, Norway, and Duke William? She was certain that Aldwine could not possibly go to Byzantium at this time!

"Brand will never become a man unless we let him, Eada," Aldwine said, reading her thoughts. Her hand flew to her mouth to stifle the cry as he turned to their son. "I cannot let you take a wife at this time. The less worry you have the more your mind will be on Aelfleah. Its people, its prosperity, and its safety will be your responsibility. It is all in your keeping until I return home."

"I understand, father," said Brand, and suddenly Mairin thought her brother seemed older. "I welcome the opportunity to wench a bit more before I must settle down," he teased them. His generous mouth was turned up in a smile as he spoke, but his blue eyes were serious and thoughtful. He fully understood his duty, and the responsibility his father was placing into his hands. His entire life had been geared to the moment when Aelfleah would become his. Even if this was but a temporary thing he proudly accepted it, and looked forward to proving his worth to his father. "I will keep you fully informed, my lord," he said gravely.

"Indeed," his father agreed, "you will. Now, my son, you know the special white pigeons that are kept in the dovecote?"

"The ones with the black markings, my lord?"

"Aye," answered Aldwine. "Those birds, Brand, belong to my friend Timon Theocrates, a wealthy merchant in Constantinople. I possess six of his birds in my cote. He maintains six of our birds at his home in Constantinople. I intend to take another six of my birds with me when we depart. They are special birds, Brand, which have been taught to carry message capsules on their legs. They can bring important news far quicker than a man on horseback.

"I suspected that the king would send a delegation to Byzantium. On the rare occasions that I have gone to court to pay Edward my respects he has questioned me closely on that empire. I did not expect, however, to head our delegation. It is true that my knowledge of Byzantium is better than any of our countrymen's. In my youth I traveled widely, and the city of Constantinople was my home for over two years.

"During that time Timon Theocrates and I became close friends. That friendship has endured despite the fact that we have not seen each other in almost fifteen years. You will not remember it, of course, but Timon came to England when you were still a baby. It was then that we exchanged pigeons. They are an ancient and fairly safe way to send messages over long distances. It is rare the pigeon is injured or killed. The message arrives swiftly, and the messenger cannot gossip. Every three years Timon and I exchange additional birds, for our winged messengers can only be worked for three to five years. If they survive past then they are too old to be reliable.

"Should the king appear near death you are to launch at least two pigeons. I am Edward's thegn. I cannot stand by while Godwin's son steals England's throne and Duke William is not likely to take England without a struggle, for Godwin's brood are greedy and will not release their hold on it easily. I must be here to support the duke for in the end he will prevail over Harold. Those he believes to have opposed him will suffer the consequences of their foolish actions. I do not intend to lose my lands in the coming squabble, and you, my son Brand, are to steer clear of all factional fighting until I return.

"If Edward dies before I can reach England then you are to hold Aelfleah against all, swearing fealty only to William of Normandy. I am Thegn of Aelfleah, and those are my wishes, Brand."

"Yes, father! Like you I cannot stomach the idea of a Godwin upon the throne! I will never pledge my loyalty to them! *Never!*"

Aldwine smiled at his son's youthful fervor, and then he cautioned, "Never, Brand, declare never. If you had to choose between swearing to

Earl Harold and losing Aelfleah, I would certainly expect that you would swear. These lands are our life's blood, my son. We held them first in the days of Aethelwulf, and each generation has carefully husbanded them, some even adding to them so that today this manor is twice the size it originally was. We are one of the oldest families in Mercia.

"Godwin's family have gained too much power over the years. Particularly since they married their daughter to the king. They are overproud. I will not forget how they slighted our Earl Leofric's good wife, your grandmother's cousin, the Lady Godiva. Her ride through Coventry was a Christian act, and she was as brave as any man in battle for doing it."

"Did she *really* ride naked?" demanded Mairin with all the indelicate curiosity of a twelve-year-old.

"Yes," said Eada, taking up the story, "she did. I was no older than you at the time. She was a beautiful woman, but it was not just beauty she possessed. She had beauty of soul, and a good heart. Remember that, my daughter. A fair face will benefit you little in the end if your soul is black, and your heart hard."

"Like the lady Blanche," said Mairin softly.

"Yes," agreed Eada. "Like the lady Blanche. Oh, dearest child, I had hoped those memories would have faded by this time."

"I will never forget Blanche de St. Brieuc," said Mairin coldly, but then her eyes lightened, and she smiled at her foster mother sweetly. "Pray, lady, continue with your story of the gracious Godiva."

Eada sighed, and took up her tale. "Earl Leofric had imposed a tax upon Coventry that the lady Godiva considered unjust. When she complained to her husband demanding he rescind the tax, he refused. The lady Godiva was not a woman to be denied so she continued to badger her lord on the matter. Finally in a burst of temper the earl said carelessly that he would indeed remove the tax from the citizens of Coventry on the day that his wife rode naked through the streets of that town!

"He did not, of course, expect her to do such a thing, and considered the matter closed. I am told that the lady Godiva smiled most sweetly at her husband, and then to Earl Leofric's horror she took up his challenge. Having said it, he could not then take back his words, and naturally was most chagrined."

"Why could he not take back his words?" demanded Mairin.

"Do you not have your pride, my daughter?" Eada asked gently.

"Aye!"

"Well so do men, perhaps even more than women," replied Eada, "for a woman like a young willow sapling knows how to bend with the breeze, and retreat before a stronger force. A man rarely does."

Aldwine smiled in amusement at his wife's statement. His eyes twinkled, but he wisely held his tongue as Eada continued on with her story.

Learning of the sacrifice the lady Godiva intended to make for the people of Coventry, the women of her family living nearby came to aid their kinswoman. The good people of Coventry, hearing of what their lady intended to do in their behalf, retreated to their houses, closing their shutters out of respect to her upon that fateful day.

"The earl, now shamed by his own actions, placed her himself upon a snow-white palfrey. She was as naked as the day God had brought her into this world with only her dark red hair—the same color as mine, and how proud I have always been of that fact—to shield her nudity. I remember my child's heart swelling with pride that I could be related by blood to such a beautiful, brave, and noble woman as the lady Godiva.

"The gates of Earl Leofric's stronghold were opened by the earl. He would allow none of his own men in the courtyard that day. Three nuns, all cousins of ours, escorted the lady Godiva; one on either side of her horse to lead it, and the third who went before to ring a bell warning of their lady's approach.

"And the people of Coventry remained behind their shutters saying their beads for the lady Godiva until they could no longer hear the sound of the bells that were rung not only by the nun who led the procession, but by every church within the town's walls. One rogue dared to violate the lady Godiva's goodness. He was a blacksmith's apprentice named Tom. The wretch paid dearly for his transgression, however, for the smith took hot coals from his forge and put out both the wicked creature's eyes. From that day forth the blinded beast was known as Peeping Tom."

"And Earl Godwin made mock of Earl Leofric's wife, mother?"

"Aye, Mairin, he did. Peeping Tom was driven from Coventry by the citizens of the town. Earl Godwin's men found him wandering. They brought him to their master who kept the rude fellow to amuse his guests. Over and over again the tale was told. With each telling it was embroidered upon until both the lady Godiva and her husband were made to seem the fools for their actions.

"The story was not allowed to die for years because of Godwin and his family. They were unable to understand the kindness and goodness of heart that caused the lady Godiva to make her ride. Earl Godwin made Mercia a laughingstock at court, but in the end it did him no good.

"King Edward is a saintly man. He understood the reason behind the lady Godiva's ride. He honored Earl Leofric, and listened to his wise counsel. Had he not, we Mercians might have totally lost our influence at court. For a time the king even banished Earl Godwin from England, but alas he returned the year before he died, and his influence was stronger than ever. It was because of the king's kindness that your father swore his fealty first to King Edward. Earl Leofric's wish before he died and his son, Earl Aelfgar, inherited was that to thank the king for his kindness to the lady Godiva, some of his thegns would swear their first loyalty to Edward. Then to his son."

Eada smiled somewhat ruefully. "That is why," she continued, "the king knows your father and why we are now bound for Byzantium. Still, my lord, I should rather be with you than without you. How strange that in my old age I, who have never traveled in my entire lifetime, am now fated to leave my home. Do you realize, Mairin, that even you have seen more of the world in your few years than I have seen in my thirty-six years? I know that I shall be afraid of the sea."

"We will not travel a great distance by sea, my love," Aldwine reassured his wife. "Most of our journey will be upon land, but it will not be an easy journey. None of the other members of the delegation will be taking their families. You must travel as we would travel. It will be necessary for you to leave your women behind for I cannot bring carts and all manner of fripperies. We must cross various mountain ranges on horseback before the snows of late autumn come. There will be a few comforts, but little danger, as we will be well protected by a contingent of young men who go to join the emperor's personal guard in Constantinople. I am only sorry that Brand cannot be with us."

His words made Eada's head reel for she could not imagine any world other than her own familiar one and Brand was like her in that he found it difficult to picture that which he could not see. Yet she knew that other worlds existed, and it occurred to her that they were as safe and familiar to their inhabitants as Aelfleah was to her.

Contrary to his father's sorrow at having to leave him behind, Brand was not a bit regretful. If he never left England it would not matter a whit to him. He loved his lands, his horses, his dogs, and his falcon. When a wife was chosen for him he would do his best to love her and the children they produced. Unlike his father he was a true Anglo-Saxon. Aldwine Athelsbeorn took more after his Norman grandmother. He was curious about things that did not really concern him.

Mairin was also excited by the prospect of travel. She had only recently begun to learn Byzantium's history, and now she badgered her tutor to teach her everything about this fabled remnant of the once mighty Roman Empire. Brother Bayhard willingly complied. He was going to miss teaching Mairin, and although Aldwine Athelsbeorn had found him another position with a family whose manor was just over the Wye, Brother Bayhard knew he would never have another pupil like Mairin. He cherished their last days together.

Mairin had been at Aelfleah six years. In all that time she had never left the security of the manor. Her whole life it seemed was bound up in this place with its hills and fertile fields, the river, and *The Forest*. Her memories of Brittany had been softened by the passage of time until Aelfleah's world became the only reality for her. She loved the manor and its valley, but best of all she loved *The Forest*, and so it was difficult to say good-bye to her little realm.

It was a warm and sunny afternoon when she made her last visit to *The Forest*. The creatures had long since learned she was no enemy, and did not hide from her. She knew certain of the doe by their markings, and she had named them and their fawns. There was a particularly beautiful fox vixen she had healed several years prior. Now each year the dainty creature proudly displayed her kits to Mairin. Mairin loved the playful balls of fur with their needle sharp little teeth. Mairin would miss them all.

Brand bid his family farewell and Godspeed on the day of their departure. There was a lump in his throat, for he was of an age that considered tears a sign of weakness in a man. He would not show such public weakness before those whose safekeeping had been given over into his hands.

Brother Bayhard was not of so hearty a constitution. He wept noisily and copiously when Mairin impulsively kissed his cheek in sweet adieu. Eada and her women wept too while the horses shuffled their feet nervously at the irritating sound. Aldwine debated whether to speak harshly to his wife so they might get under way, or let her have her moment. There was but one female servant going with them, a pert young woman named Nara. She rolled her eyes comically at all the commotion which caused Mairin, who was eager for their departure, to giggle. Nara looked over at the young girl and winked.

Aldwine smiled, and spoke firmly to Eada. She sniffled, but before her tears might begin anew she was boosted into her saddle by a nearby servant. The Thegn of Aelfleah quickly signaled the start of their journey, and they were on their way. Dagda sidled his horse up next to his young mistress as they rode through the gate of the manor house, and down the dirt road across the Aldford.

Reaching the other side of the small river Mairin stopped for a moment looking back at Aelfleah.

"It is not like Landerneau, Dagda, is it?" she said quietly. "I know we shall return to Aelfleah."

Part Two

THE PRINCE'S BRIDE

Byzantium, 1063–1065

Chapter 4

*M*airin wondered afterwards if Aldwine would have taken his wife if he had known how hard the trip was to be on Eada. A voyage by sea might have been easier had the seas been calm, and the long miles between England and Constantinople might have even been covered in a shorter time. The Anglo-Saxons, however, were suspicious of covering great distances by a capricious sea when a safe land route was available to them. Consequently, as the Thegn of Aelfleah had promised his wife, they had avoided the sea as much as was possible.

It had been necessary to cross the waters separating England and Normandy, and they had done it in good time. Their party consisted of the six members of England's trade delegation to the emperor, the three women, and a troop of fifty young men going to serve in the Imperial Guard of the emperor, Constantine X Ducas. They moved swiftly across a corner of Normandy into Ile de France, through the Kingdom of Aquitaine, and finally into the Languedoc, following roads that had been built over a thousand years earlier by the Romans.

They followed the coast east from Marseilles into various small states—Genoa, Parma, Modena, Bologna—until they embarked from Brindisi across the Adriatic Sea to Macedonia. The voyage was but a day's journey in time and Eada's beads never left her hands. The whole way her fingers twitched nervously up and down the strand of white coral. Each day they traveled twenty-five to thirty miles from the break of dawn until the final light faded from the sky. At first all the bright summer days seemed the same, but as they reached Macedonia each day grew visibly shorter and Eada showed strong signs of exhaustion. By the time they reached Thessalonika Aldwine realized that his wife could travel no further at such a quick pace.

Over Eada's protests a ship was found that could take all of King Edward's delegation the final distance to Constantinople. Accustomed to the choppy northern seas, Eada was surprised by the pleasant voyage. The ship glided across the turquoise waters of the upper Aegean Sea, through the Dardanelles, and into the Sea of Marmara. While sitting upon the deck in the bright sunshine where she was refreshed by the warm breezes, Eada's strength returned. By the time they had reached the fabled city she was quite herself again.

Mairin had been pacing the small deck for over an hour. The captain had promised them that they should reach Constantinople this morning. It was a perfect day, and the Sea of Marmara was a busy waterway. They were passed by barks from Dalmatia and Croatia; feluccas from the East; great high galleys belonging to the merchantmen of Venice, Genoa, and Amalfi. There were caïques from the Greek islands. Everyone stared open-mouthed with amazement as a huge dromon of the imperial Byzantine fleet majestically swept by them.

Aldwine was familiar with dromons. Each vessel, he told them, was manned by over two hundred oarsmen, and some seventy marines. The high wooden turret mounted in the bow of each dromon projected three tubes which sprayed Greek fire. On the high deck at the stern were catapults used for hurling fiery missiles which were soaked in oil. Greek fire was the secret weapon of the Byzantines, and it was greatly feared for there was no known defense from it. The young Saxon warriors going to join the emperor's Imperial Guard were very impressed by the Thegn of Aelfleah's words.

Suddenly Mairin cried out, "Look, father! Look, mother! It is the city! It is Constantinople!"

They followed the direction of her finger, her youthful excitement contagious. Even Aldwine, for whom the sight was not a new one, stood spellbound.

The captain of their ship smiled. "She's quite a beauty, isn't she?" he said in almost reverent tones. "I've lived my entire life here, and yet always the first glimpse of her from the sea astounds me. She is truly the queen of cities."

Aldwine nodded slowly. "It has been many years since I've laid eyes upon her," he said, "but until this moment I did not realize how much I had missed her."

Constantinople, the Imperial City of the Byzantines, presented a spectacular sight to those approaching her from the sea. Like Rome the city sat upon seven hills and was entirely surrounded by great stone walls twenty-five feet in thickness that on the land side of the city rose in three levels behind a moat sixty feet in width and twenty-two feet in depth that was normally dry, but flooded in times of siege. On the sea side of the city the walls soared twenty feet high and like the land side were interspersed by watchtowers that rose an additional twenty feet above the walls. The towers held machines for Greek fire, missile throwers, and archers.

From the ship the great gilded dome of the city's most famous church, the Hagia Sophia, as well as some of its other great churches, monasteries, convents, and public buildings, was visible. Their ship sailed past several of Constantinople's walled harbors including that of Eleutherius, Contoscalion, Julian and the beautiful harborside church of Saints Sergius and Bacchus.

"There," said Aldwine, pointing, "is the Boucoleon, the imperial harbor. Only the emperor and his family are allowed to have their vessels moored there. See the lighthouse? Beyond it is the Imperial Palace."

Mairin stared fascinated, but the Imperial Palace was difficult to spot amid the gardens, and isolated summer pavilions, the various other buildings and the several churches that were spread across the terraced grounds and wooded slopes of the promontory of land that stretched south and southeast to the Sea of Marmara and the Bosporus. They rounded the point of imperial land, and once more Aldwine spoke.

"Look! To the right are the satellite cities of Pera and Galata. They are also walled, and see the chain! In times of danger it stretches from Pera across this waterway which is called the Golden Horn to a watchtower of Constantinople. When the chain is in place, no one can breach the defenses of the Golden Horn, or Constantinople."

"We are turning toward the city shore, father," Mairin said.

"Yes, my daughter, we will land at the Phosphorion Harbor. I expect there will be someone there to meet us for we are not unexpected. We are to be housed, I believe, on the grounds of the Imperial Palace."

"We will not be received by the emperor too quickly," fretted Eada. "We have not the garments! I would not shame our nation!"

Aldwine smiled. It was over two months since they had left England, but his wife had already recovered from her exhaustion. "There will be time for clothing to be made for you and Mairin, my love," he promised. "A delegation such as ours is of little import on its arrival. The emperor will greet us officially for manners' sake in due time."

Their vessel slipped safely into its dockage within the Phosphorion

Harbor. As the thegn had predicted there was a troop of imperial Varangian Guards as well as a representative of the emperor to meet them. To Aldwine's delight the official was his old friend Timon Theocrates. The two men greeted each other warmly.

"The emperor has appointed me to the delegation that is to negotiate with your people," Timon Theocrates said with a smile as Aldwine introduced him to the other members of his party.

"My friend, Timon Theocrates, Wulfhere of London, Wilfrid of York, Aethelbert of Gloucester, Richard of Winchester, and Alfred of London."

"Welcome, my friends," said the Byzantine. "Welcome to Constantinople! I know that your stay here will be a happy and successful one."

He escorted the English from their vessel to the quayside where horses had been provided for the men. A comfortable padded cart drawn by two black-and-white ponies had been brought for the women. They made their way through the Eugenius Gate into the city proper, and directly to the palace.

By tradition Byzantium's Imperial Guard was made up of Vikings from Scandinavia and, more recently, Anglo-Saxons from England. To her surprise Mairin felt a quiver race through her when an incredibly handsome young man with shoulder-length golden-yellow hair and sky-blue eyes lifted her into the cart. What was worse, she thought, was that their eyes met, hers widening in surprise, his brimming with amusement at her innocent reaction. Mairin shakily pushed his hands away from her waist where they had lingered a bit too long for propriety's sake, and the Viking chuckled wickedly. She blushed.

Eada, who had not missed any of this silent interchange, said quietly, but with firm authority,

"What is your name, guardsman?"

Instantly the young soldier snapped to attention and answered, "Eric Longsword, my lady."

"Thank you for helping my daughter, Eric Longsword," said Eada with a smile of dismissal. As the young man bowed politely Mairin, who was behind her mother, stuck her tongue out at him.

As Eada turned away Eric Longsword winked at Mairin. Once more she blushed to the roots of her hair. Why, she silently asked herself, had she encouraged that dreadful man? Why, a tiny voice asked deep within her, does it matter? She had never felt so uncomfortable with a man before. But if she were honest with herself no man had ever paid her the least attention. At home she was Aldwine Athelsbeorn's little daughter, but here . . . here no one knew her. Was it possible? Was it just possible that the guardsman had seen in her a woman? After all she would be celebrating her thirteenth birthday in less than two weeks' time! She could barely wait to arrive at their quarters so she might look into a mirror and see this great change that had been wrought in her during their travels!

Eada smiled to herself as she read her daughter's thoughts. Having never before felt such an attraction for a member of the opposite sex Mairin was most likely embarrassed and confused by her reaction. Eada realized that her daughter was growing up. It would soon be time to consider finding a husband for her.

They made their way through the city, which had no distinctly fashionable residential quarters. A middle-class merchant's house was just as likely to be flanked by that of a tenement on one side, and the magnificent villa of a wealthy man on the other. The streets were filled with peddlers who went from door to door crying their wares in singsong fashion, offering fresh bread, flowers, fruit, vegetables, songbirds in cages, and newly caught fish. All gave way before the imperial procession.

Their host, Timon Theocrates, rode at the side of the women's cart, offering them a brief history of his city. There had always been a settlement upon this spot, he told them, but many would credit the ancient Greeks with the official founding of Byzantium. Most buildings from that era, as well as those of the great Roman Empire, were long gone. They had been destroyed, the merchant explained, in the great fire of the year 532. It had burnt for five days following a series of riots.

The emperor at that time, Justinian, had razed half the original city to the ground in the wake of the destruction. He then rebuilt Constantinople, for all the magnificent buildings of the great Constantine from whom the city took its current name had been destroyed, including the revered Hagia Sophia. Justinian rebuilt it all, making Constantinople a city of unbelievable beauty and incredible magnificence. Those emperors who had followed after him had continued this building program. As time went by the Imperial Palace was enlarged, other palaces and churches built, public parks and gardens laid out, the great squares embellished with statuary.

Nara, who always had an opinion on everything, was wide-eyed and silent in awe. Eada couldn't help but gasp with wonder as their procession passed beneath the Milion Arch and into the Augustaeum, which was the main public square of the city. To their left rose the great church of Constantinople, Hagia Sophia. Directly ahead of them was the gracious Senate building. Swinging to the right, they moved around the palace wall to its main entrance, which was called the Chalke, the Brazen Entrance, for its door and roof were all gilded bronze.

The men dismounted, and the women were helped from their cart. Feeling very dwarfed by the fabulous building they followed Timon Theocrates into the vestibule of the Imperial Palace. "Look up," he instructed them and doing so they saw that the ceilings were covered with beautiful mosaics designed as pictures which showed Justinian's great general, Belisarius, returning in triumph to Constantinople after his great victories. They lowered their eyes to see that the walls and the floors of the Chalke were of fine marble in wondrous colors—emerald green, pure bright white, and deep, rich reds. There were some white blocks that were broken with wavy lines of sapphire blue.

The young Saxon soldiers were visibly awed, but it was Eada who spoke for them all when she said, "This place cannot be real. Surely we have all died, and this is God's house." She spoke slowly, in Latin, a universal tongue readily understood here in Byzantium. It had been a long time since she had used another language than her own, but all during their journey her husband and daughter had insisted she practice, else she be excluded from their new life.

Timon Theocrates, a small and plump man, beamed with pleasure at her words. He was extremely proud of his city. "I shall tell the emperor of your gracious words, lady," he said as he led them through the Chalke out into an enormous park.

Before them sprawled the vast and rambling palace grounds, which consisted of far more than royal residences. There were churches, fountains, gardens, and terraces. There was a private stadium, an indoor riding school, lily ponds, swimming pools, and storerooms. There were stables, kennels, guardrooms, servants' quarters, dungeons, and a zoo. Their Saxon troop left them to follow the Byzantine guardsmen who had escorted them from the harbor. Aldwine, his family, and the English delegation followed Timon Theocrates, who was once again speaking.

"The delegation will have spacious and comfortable apartments in a wing of the New Palace," he said. "You, my friend, and your family are to have a small house of your own set in the gardens which overlook the sea. We will go there first for your lady will want to see her new home, and immediately begin to make changes even as my good wife would do." He beamed at Eada. "Women," he said indulgently, "are ever predictable!"

They stopped before a small marble building, and Timon said, "Ah, here we are, my friends. This is to be your new home, the Garden Palace."

Before they could enter the building servants hurried out to lead them into the little palace. The richness of the decoration within amazed them. The entry hall was a square room in which columns of red onyx alternated with those of verd antique. The floor was mosaic tiles in which the central design was a golden sunburst. The rays of the sun spread outward beneath their feet against a deep blue tile sky.

"I am Zeno, the majordomo," said a pleasant-looking man stepping forward to greet them. "In the emperor's name I welcome you to the Garden Palace." He spoke in pure and unhurried Latin, and even Eada, much to her relief, was easily able to understand him.

"This is the English lord, Aldwine of Aelfleah," said Timon to Zeno. "His wife, the lady Eada, and their daughter, the lady Mairin." Then the Byzantine turned to his friend, saying, "I must leave you now to settle the rest of your delegation in the New Palace. Zeno will answer all your questions, and see to all your needs."

"When will we be able to greet the emperor in King Edward's name?" asked Aldwine.

"That information has not been imparted to me as yet," replied Timon. "I believe it has been planned that you recover from your long journey before seeing his majesty. Rest for a few days. I am certain that word will come then. No meetings between our delegations have yet been scheduled. I shall return tomorrow, and we will talk of old times." He bowed politely to Eada and Mairin. Then with a wave of his plump hand he was gone, with the rest of the English hurrying to keep up with them.

"This entire palace is yours while you are the emperor's guests in Constantinople," Zeno informed them. "Would you like to be shown to your apartments so you may first refresh yourselves? Afterwards I will personally conduct you on a tour of the building so you may be familiar and comfortable in your new surroundings." Without waiting for an answer he led them up a broad marble staircase to the second floor of the building. "Every residential building," Zeno continued as they followed him, "located upon the grounds of the Sacred Imperial Palace, is called a palace. As you can see from the size of this building it is really no more than a comfortable villa.

"I see you have brought but two servants with you. I will arrange to have you assigned our own people as well. Ahh, here we are." He flung open a pair of double doors. "Your apartment, my lord and my lady. The young mistress has a suite of rooms just down the hall. If you will step in, I shall show her the way."

"Take Nara with you, mother," said Mairin knowing her mother would be more comfortable having one of their own servants with her.

"Dagda must stay with me," said the thegn in their own tongue. "It would cause undue gossip for him to remain with you, my daughter."

"Your father is correct," seconded the Irishman.

"I understand," said Mairin. "It is all right, father. I speak fluent Greek, and unlike mother will have little difficulty getting along. Dagda can accompany me when I am outside the palace."

Zeno's view of the English was based upon the rough-and-tumble young Anglo-Saxon warriors who served in the emperor's guard. He was rather delighted to discover that well-bred English citizens were actually quite civilized. He was even more pleased to learn that Mairin could speak Greek for it was now the official language of Byzantium, replacing Latin eight years earlier when the Byzantine church had broken with that of Rome.

Now that Mairin was speaking to him in his country's language Zeno became almost voluble. Opening one side of a carved double door he ushered her into an airy, high-ceilinged room. "This, young mistress, is to be your suite." He walked across the room, opening yet another carved door. "Your bedchamber," he said.

One wall of the main chamber was practically solid windows. Walking over to them Mairin exclaimed, "What magnificent gardens, and the view of the sea is incredible, Zeno! Oh, I shall be happy in this wonderful city!"

The majordomo beamed with pride. "You belong in Constantinople, young mistress. It is a city of beautiful women, and you are surely the most lovely female I have ever seen. Forgive my boldness, but never have I seen hair or skin quite like yours."

"Such coloring is common in my land," said Mairin with more poise than she was feeling. No one, even a servant, had ever called her beautiful before. More than ever she longed to find a mirror, and see what changes her travels had wrought.

"You will want to refresh yourself after your long journey," said Zeno. "I will see that iced wine and cakes are brought to you, young mistress, and I shall personally choose the maidens who will serve you. A rare jewel should have an equally fine setting." He bowed himself from the room.

Delighted that he was gone at last, Mairin explored her new surroundings. The main room of her suite had a wonderful floor of pale gold marble. The walls were wide alternating strips of the same gold, and cream-colored marble. The ceiling was gilded. The furniture, tables, stools, and reclining couches were plated with gold, and inlaid with ivory. The lamps and other lighting fixtures were fashioned of silver, and some were inlaid with semiprecious stones. On the floor next to her bedchamber door stood a magnificent vase carved from lilac-colored jade and filled with peacock feathers.

Curious, Mairin walked into the bedchamber and gasped with delight. Upon the marble walls were wonderful paintings in bright colors showing musicians and dancers in procession about the walls of the room. Each panel of the painting was framed in gilded wood decorated with coral, lapis lazuli, and pearls, and separated from the next panel by strips of gold marble. The floors were cream-colored marble broken with undulating lines of jade green.

There was a bed upon one wall that was fashioned of wood that had first been carved and then overlaid with gold leaf. It was hung with draperies of pale green silk to match the covering upon the mattress. By the bed was a small table inlaid in ivory, and upon it stood a silver lamp that burned scented oil. As in the main room of the suite there was a wall of windows that overlooked the imperial gardens with the sea beyond.

She opened another door and saw a small hallway at the end of which was another door. Curious, she walked slowly down the short passage to discover a tiled room with a pool behind the door. It was not a large pool, and she wondered about its use. With a shrug Mairin returned to the bedchamber to discover something that she had somehow managed to miss before. A *mirror*, and what a mirror! It was not a mere polished round of metal, but real glass, and large enough that she might see her entire self in it!

Fascinated, she studied her image for a long minute. Then with a sigh she turned away. There was no change at all that she could see in herself. She turned to find her mother entering the room.

"What is it, child? You look so disappointed," Eada said.

"I thought surely there would be some change in me, mother," Mairin replied.

"You change each day, my dearest. You are growing up."

"No. I look just the same as I did when we left England. Yet Zeno, the majordomo, said I was beautiful. Am I beautiful, mother?"

Eada hesitated a moment, but then deciding honesty was the best course she answered, "Yes, my daughter, you are very beautiful."

"But I look the way I always have!" despaired Mairin.

"You have always been beautiful, Mairin," laughed Eada. "I remember thinking that the first time I saw you. You are simply used to yourself, and you are not a prideful child. Some of the differences you feel, however, come from the inside and are not necessarily visible; like the confusion you felt today when that young soldier aided you. He looked at you as a young man looks at a lovely girl. Since no one has ever viewed you in that light before, he made you feel very aware of yourself, and of him also." She smiled. "It is a normal state, my daughter, and I fear it will get worse before it gets better."

Mairin made a face at herself in the wonderful glass mirror. "Oh, mother," she said, "I don't know if I want to grow up! It feels so strange to be me, and yet not to be me!"

Eada laughed again. "I felt the same way when I was your age," she admitted, "but alas, my dearest, there is no stopping time. It moves on-ward no matter how we feel about it." She put an arm about the girl, and gave her a loving squeeze. "Zeno has arranged to bring several skilled seamstresses here into the palace this afternoon, and what do you think I found awaiting us in our apartment? Bolts and bolts of the most beautiful fabrics! They are a gift from the wife of Timon Theocrates. Imagine! What generosity! She has never laid eyes upon us, and yet she has shown us great kindness. I do not know how we can repay her, but fashionable gowns we shall have when we meet the emperor! Come, and pick what you would have."

The next few days were busy ones for Mairin and her mother. Although Anglo-Saxon England was noted for the fabrics its women wove, they could not compare their own cloth with what had been sent them. There were brocades in clear jewel colors of ruby, emerald, sapphire, amethyst, and topaz. There were delicate silks that had been woven with gold and silver threads so that in one light the fabric appeared a solid color. In another light it was a shimmering waterfall of metallic glory. There were silks as sheer as an early-morning mist in ethereal hues of blossom pink, sea green, pale peach, dawn gold, and aquamarine.

If Mairin appreciated the pure beauty of the fabrics they had been gifted with, her mother recognized the skill and imagination that had gone into their making. Neither had ever owned such stunning garments as were created for them by the imperial seamstresses. Even the simple, practical Eada was not loath to admit her pleasure in such fine feathers. Her initial fears of meeting the fabled Emperor of Byzantium faded as her new clothing gave her equally new confidence. A confidence seen by and highly approved by the entire English delegation.

"I did not approve of a woman and child coming upon this mission," admitted Wulfhere of London, "but seeing you so splendidly gowned, Eada of Aelfleah, I think it is a good thing that you are with us. You lend an elegance to us, and in this magnificent city I cannot think that a bad thing."

"It is good for the Byzantines to see one of our women, and a child of our people," seconded Aethelbert of Gloucester. "It makes us seem more human to them. Besides," and his blue eyes twinkled merrily, "little Mairin's beauty has them quite in awe, and that cannot be a bad thing either."

His companions nodded for Aethelbert of Gloucester spoke a truth. The city of Constantinople was famed for the beauty of its women. There were blonds with skin like white roses, and brunettes who were tawny and golden. There were blue eyes, dark eyes, eyes of green or hazel. Nowhere in the city, however, was there anyone with hair the fiery red-gold of Mairin's tresses, a color which sharply contrasted with the creaminess of her skin.

Such hair and skin were usually complemented with light eyes, but Mairin's eyes were purple, sometimes amethyst in hue, and at other times a deep violet, depending upon her mood. Added to the perfection of her features her beauty seemed unreal for Mairin was one of those rare creatures who appeared lovelier with each viewing. She was a child teetering upon the brink of womanhood, yet in this great city her unusual beauty was being extolled to such an extent that word of it had even penetrated the emperor's court.

Constantine X was a member of the Ducas family, and had been elected to his imperial throne in 1059. His predecessor, Isaac I of the Comnenus family, had been an excellent emperor who had sadly reigned only two years. His death was a misfortune for Byzantium because the two emperors before him, Michael VI and Constantine IX, had been weak men. Neither had distinguished himself to any great extent although in the last year of Constantine IX's reign the Byzantine church had broken with that of Rome.

Constantine X was a charming if ineffectual man but if his government was lackluster and undistinguished, the arts and those associated with them flourished greatly under his reign. He loved beauty and upon hearing of Mairin's, he scheduled his audience with King Edward's trade delegation far in advance of when he had actually planned to receive them. He was enormously curious to view the English child, and was quite frank in making that admission to his favorite cousin, Basil.

"I wonder if she can be your equal, my princely cousin," he teased. Basil Ducas was called the most beautiful man in Byzantium.

"Then I should have to marry her so we might create a race of beautiful and perfect children, sire," came the prince's quick reply. Basil Ducas might be handsome, but he was also highly intelligent.

The emperor smiled. "What will Bellisarius say should you take a wife? Surely he will resent a rival for your affections. He is very possessive of you, Basil."

The prince frowned, but even in annoyance his features remained attractive. "In my thirty years, Constans, I have had both beautiful men and beautiful women as lovers. Bellisarius knows that someday I will marry. I must have heirs, cousin. However, you are correct in one of your observations. Bellisarius is possessive of me. Too much so, I think. Still I would not distress him for he is the greatest actor of our age, and he amuses me more than most. When we finally part he will cost me far less than my last paramour. Do you remember Helena Monomachus, and how she attempted to pass off her blackamoor's bastard as mine? She almost cost me a fortune until she spawned her baby with its dark skin, wide flat nose, and kinky hair. In the entire history of our family, Constans, there has *never* been a nose like *that!*"

The emperor smiled at his cousin's words, and then he said, "Do you think that the little English girl can be as fair as they say, Basil? I have never heard so much chatter about a child not yet a woman. They say she cannot go out in the city any longer for crowds follow her. They attempt to touch her hair for they cannot believe it real. Some have even said it is not hair, but a flame that surrounds her head." The emperor's pale blue eyes were quite curious.

The prince laughed heartily. "Poor child," he said sympathetically. "Next the unwashed masses will attribute miracles and disasters to her tresses. Well, we shall see for ourselves this afternoon, won't we?"

Mairin was in a frenzy of excitement. She had never seen an emperor before. She had never even seen her own king, but she was absolutely certain that the saintly Edward of England would pale in comparison to the splendor of Byzantium's ruler. Mairin stared at her full-length image in the pier glass.

She was wearing a tunic dress made of lilac-colored brocade worked with both gold and silver threads. The tunic dress was wide-sleeved over a close-sleeved undertunic of gold cloth. Both garments had high, round necks, but where the undertunic was floor-length, the tunic dress ended just below the kneeline. She didn't know why, but she felt she looked quite distinctly older in her new garments.

If only her mother hadn't insisted that she wear her hair unbound so that it fell about her shoulders in a cloud of vibrant color. It was so babyish! She sighed deeply. After all, she was to be thirteen years old tomorrow! At thirteen years of age girls married, but Mairin knew very well that her father had not yet made any matches for her. Whenever she attempted to broach the subject, he would smile tenderly at her and say, "It is too soon, my angel. I will not give you to just anyone. For you, my Mairin, it will be a very special man." What made a man special? she wondered.

"Look between your eyebrows, child," said Eada coming up behind her daughter. "There is a distinct frown groove there. Whatever can you be thinking of that has caused you such distress?"

"Must I wear my hair loose, mother?"

Eada swallowed back her smile. "Yes," she said firmly. "You are a maiden, my daughter. Among our people it is the custom for a maiden to wear her hair loose, or in braids. I thought you would prefer wearing it loose today. I have brought you this to make your coiffure a tiny bit more elegant." She placed a filmy gold silk veil atop Mairin's head which she then set firmly by means of a dainty gold-and-freshwater-pearl circlet.

Mairin's eyes widened with delight. "Ohh, mother! It is beautiful!" She flung her arms about Eada. "Thank you! Thank you!" She preened before the mirror. "I look older, don't I, mother? I mean I don't look like a *child*, do I?"

"You look every inch the young lady you are, my daughter," said Eada.

The young girl looked away from her own mirror image to gaze at that of her mother. Then she said feelingly, "You are so beautiful in your Byzantine garments, mother. Forgive me for I have been so concerned with myself I did not stop to look at you."

Her gaze swept admiringly over the beautiful grass green silk dress embroidered with gold threads, pearls, darker green peridots, and golden beryls worn over a silvery-green undertunic. Eada's dark red hair had been fashioned into an architecture of ornate braids brought up over the outside of her gold wire cauls, and fastened with a jeweled band about her forehead.

Eada smiled at her daughter with newly found confidence. "Yes," she said with great understatement, "I am pleased with how the women aided me in my dressing. Nara is learning a great deal from them. When we return to England I intend to give her to you as your serving woman, but we chatter too much, child! Your father and his delegation await us. They will no doubt have grown impatient by now. We must hurry!"

King Edward's trade delegation was to be received in the Great Hall of the Imperial Palace. To the surprise of the Anglo-Saxons the emperor had sent them each a beautiful silk robe of deep blue and yellow silk that they were instructed to wear. The entire group was escorted across the palace grounds by royal eunuchs who explained that the women would wait at the back of the audience chamber until called upon. The emperor was most anxious, confided the head eunuch to Eada, to see the child with the hair of fire. Here the eunuch reached out almost shyly to quickly touch a lock of Mairin's lovely hair. Eada hid another smile.

Not having been repulsed, the eunuch now chatted with the foreign woman. "The emperor will be seated upon the Throne of Solomon today, and never, my lady, have you seen such an object. Do not be afraid of anything that happens for you will be quite safe," he finished mysteriously. Eada and Mairin both wondered what he could possibly mean.

The Great Hall of the Imperial Palace was the most magnificent place any of them had ever seen. The walls of the room were pure white marble. Each section of marble was separated from floor to ceiling by a wide band of pure gold. The pillars in the hall were dark red marble broken by undulating ripples of golden color and the vast space was lit by a huge gold candelabrum which hung from great copper chains that had been silvered. The marble floors of the room had been strewn with fragrant roses, pungent laurel and ivy, sweet rosemary, and other herbs. As the delegation walked forward trampling the greenery beneath their feet, the perfume from the crushed essences swirled into the air filling the room with its exotic bouquet.

At the eunuch's signal Eada and Mairin had stopped. From their vantage point they had an excellent view of everything. Before them at the end of the hall they could see the Emperor Constantine X already seated upon his throne. He wore a long, tight-sleeved tunic of white silk over which was a royal purple silk cape opening on the right side. It was decorated with embroidered squares of golden cloth both front and back. Heavily jeweled scarlet satin shoes were upon his feet. The imperial crown he wore was a hemispherical and close-fitting cap bejeweled with precious gems and large pearls, some of which hung down in the back to the nape of his neck.

About him stood the Imperial Guards, most of whom were from the noble families of Byzantium. The rest were sons of the wealthy who were considered loyal. Around the hall were posted the Varangian Guards.

To her delight Mairin saw that Eric Longsword was near enough that she might attract his attention with her beautiful clothing, and then snub him as he stood dumbfounded with admiration. But Eric Longsword refused to take his blue eyes from some spot directly ahead of him, much to Mairin's annoyance. She turned her gaze back to the delegation, and was amazed to see that the carved and jeweled golden lions that made up the armrests of the emperor's throne were moving!

"*Mother!*" she whispered, and clutched at Eada.

To the eunuch's delight both women were now wide-eyed. The lions on the emperor's throne were not only moving, they were opening their mouths and roaring most realistically! Atop the throne were birds made of silver and colorful enamels with bejeweled eyes. They, too, were a part of the throne's decoration. As the birds began to flutter their wings, to trill and to sing, the emperor and his throne began to rise upward until they hovered close to the decorated ceiling. From some hidden place within the room a choir began to sing extolling the many virtues of God's chosen empire of Byzantium.

The eunuch was almost beside himself with glee at the look upon their faces. "It is not wonderful?" he chortled to them. "Is not Byzantium the most wonderful place upon God's earth?"

Stunned, they watched as the emperor and his throne now descended to the floor again. The delegation was led forward by the band of eunuchs, and the Anglo-Saxons made the prescribed bow of three prostrations to the Emperor Constantine X. They could not hear what was said from their place in the rear of the hall, but King Edward's trade delegation was obviously well received. Then suddenly their eunuch escort received some unseen signal, and Eada and Mairin were led forward.

Constantine X found himself as surprised as his guests usually were, for the reputation that had preceded the English child had not exaggerated her beauty even the tiniest bit. If anything she was lovelier. He could not remember ever having seen such purity of features in any person. His gaze flicked swiftly from the child's father to her mother. They were handsome people, but it astounded him that they had created the exquisite creature that now stood before him.

Leaning back he murmured to his cousin, "Well, Basil, what think you? She is more than your equal though I would not have believed it possible."

"Nor would I," came back the soft reply. "She is pure perfection, Constans."

"Sire," said the eunuch in charge of their presentation, "may I present to you the lady Eada of Aelfleah and her daughter, the lady Mairin."

Mother and daughter bowed thrice to Byzantium's ruler, who said, "We welcome you to Constantinople, my lady. Your beautiful child's reputation is, to our amazement, truth."

"True beauty, sire, does not show. It is goodness of heart and true Christian charity," replied Eada quietly. "I would wish that for my daughter, and I hope she will be remembered, if she is remembered at all, for those qualities rather than the beauty of her face."

Aldwine was surprised by the length of his wife's speech, but pleased by the wisdom she spoke.

The priests standing below the throne nodded their heads and murmured their assent at Eada's words. The church was an enormous power in Byzantium. Their goodwill was paramount to the success of the English negotiations. Eada's speech had pleased them, and they would now look with favor upon the diplomatic efforts for new trade between the two countries.

"Come to me, my child," the emperor commanded Mairin, "I admit to being as curious as any of my subjects with regard to your incredible hair." He smiled encouragingly at her, and offered her his hand.

Shyly Mairin moved up the steps to the emperor's throne. Although his attire and his surroundings were incredibly magnificent, Constantine himself was a friendly-looking man of medium height with tired blue eyes. He was not an unattractive man, but neither did he have any distinguishing features save a too-long and somewhat narrow nose that almost ended in a point. His hair was bobbed, and he had bangs across his forehead. Its color, like his neatly trimmed beard, was a graying brown.

Constantine smiled again as he cupped Mairin's face in his hand and looked into her purple eyes. With his other hand he removed her circlet with its veil, handing them to a servant. Then he caressed her beautiful red-gold hair, and capturing a lock between his thumb and first two fingers he gauged its texture. "It is as soft as thistle-down. If my daughters had had your beauty, and this hair," he acknowledged, "I could have ruled the entire world, my child."

Mairin blushed at so unexpected, and extravagant, a compliment.

The emperor chuckled and released his hold upon her. "I think you must be magic, my child. Certainly such loveliness is an enchantment of

84

sorts." He drew a ring from his finger. It was a large diamond that blazed an orange-gold fire deep within the stone. "Take this in remembrance of me, my child," he told her. "It is said to be a perfect stone. If that indeed be the truth, then it belongs with a perfect beauty. When you are an old woman you may show this jewel to your grandchildren. Tell them that once in your youth you captured the heart of the greatest ruler in all Christendom, and it was he who gave you this token to remember him by."

Overwhelmed, Mairin stammered her gratitude, backing nervously down the steps to where her mother awaited her. She was trembling, and to her surprise she thought she might cry. She didn't remember leaving the emperor's audience chamber, becoming only fully aware once they were back out in the gardens. The diamond ring was clutched tightly in her hand.

"You are a very fortunate girl," Eada told her. "You should feel honored to have gained the emperor's attention."

"Perhaps now you will understand," said Aldwine to his wife, "why I have not yet made a match for Mairin. I know that all these years you have believed it mere paternal pride upon my part, but it was not. Mairin is special. Her beauty makes her so. It is true we have raised her as our own, but her lineage is far nobler than ours. Her birth mother was royal. I will have a fine husband for her if we are clever, and patient, and willing to bide our time."

"A Norman husband, you mean," said Eada quietly.

"Aye! A Norman, and why not? With William our next king, the Normans will be favored. It will not hurt our daughter to be the wife of a powerful and wealthy Norman lord. Her beauty will help us to secure a great name. It cannot hurt our son either. Perhaps we will find him a Norman wife. Brand has but one great love, Aelfleah. A Norman wife with a fat dowry may help him to add to our lands one day. Somewhere there is a rich man with a beloved bastard daughter he wants respectably wed. We have a good name and much land. I shall see both our children well settled."

"I never realized before how ambitious you are, my lord," said Eada with faint disapproval in her voice.

"The times are changing, my wife. England will never again be as it was. Those who do not see that are doomed to extinction. I do not want to see my line end; my lands lost to strangers who will not love and care for our people as we do. If we are to survive, Eada, we must change with the times."

"I will not let you give Mairin to anyone who will make her unhappy, my lord."

"I think, lady, that you know me better than that," he chided her.

Eada sighed so deeply that a shudder ran through her frame. "I am no longer certain of anything," she said. "We are so far from England. I miss Brand. I miss Aelfleah." Then catching hold of herself she looked up at him smiling wryly. "I do not think this traveling agrees with me, my lord. I was happier with myself when I was naught but the wife of a simple Mercian thegn."

He put a protective arm about her. "Perhaps you would have been happier had I left you at home, Eada, but it will be at least two years before we can return to England. I could not have borne being apart from you for so long a time. I know it was selfish of me."

"It is the city that frets me," she said. "It is so big and crowded! So noisy and dirty! What will I do while you and the others negotiate your treaties? I am not comfortable to sit idly."

Mairin, recovered and listening to this exchange between her parents, spoke up. "We will explore the city, mother. There is so much to see and do here! We shall not be bored for a minute, I promise you!"

"How can we move about the city when the very sight of your hair draws crowds?" replied Eada irritably.

"I shall braid my hair up, and hide it beneath a coif, mother."

Eada smiled, and gave her daughter a hug. "You know," she said, "I believe you are right. I should have seen it myself. You are growing up, Mairin."

Her cheerful words belied the ache in her heart, and Aldwine knew it. Perhaps he had been thoughtless in taking her from her safe and familiar world. He let his eyes roam over the imperial gardens and across the Bosporus to the green hills beyond. It might be possible to rent a villa away from the city, away from the palace, somewhere where Eada would feel more comfortable.

Aldwine looked to his daughter. Tomorrow was October 31st, Samhein, Mairin's birthday. He wondered where his daughter would light her fire, for Mairin still observed the four high holy days of the old Celtic religion. It was a part of her past that she refused to relinquish although she had become an Anglo-Saxon maiden in every other way. Neither Aldwine nor Eada had felt that they had the right to interfere, but here in Constantinople the thegn of Aelfleah wondered how his daughter would accomplish what she considered her duty to the old ways. Amid all the excitement of the trip he wondered if she even remembered.

Mairin did indeed remember. Though she had been raised a Christian she respected the ancient religion of her people. The feast of Samhein marked the end of the Druidic calendar, and it was considered the most powerful spiritual night of the year. It was believed that on Samhein night the gates between the human world and the spirit world were wide open, and either might visit the other. The Christians called it All Hallows' Eve. At the very moment that the sun dipped below the earth's horizon the Samhein fires leapt skyward, symbolizing that light of the human spirit which never dies. It was considered a time for thanksgiving.

Being born on Samhein had been considered a wonderful omen among Maire Tir Connell's people. The baby had been thought to be blessed by the old Gods. Perhaps she was, thought Dagda with a quiet smile as he watched Mairin preparing the wood for her fire. Aldwine Athelsbeorn might have been surprised, but Dagda was not when Mairin had announced that she had found a perfect spot in the Imperial Palace gardens facing west in which to light her Samhein fire.

Dagda had been even less surprised when Mairin drew a small leather bag from her tunic holding three wooden chips. She reverently placed them atop the carefully laid fire.

"Oak?" he asked her, knowing the answer she would give. Oak was sacred to the Druids.

"From the grove in *The Forest*. I did not know how long I would be gone from England, but I have brought thirty chips of oak with me. The fire just wouldn't be right without oak, Dagda."

He nodded. It was like Mairin to remember small details.

"I wonder," she mused, "if Constantinople has ever seen a Samhein fire before."

"It is said that our people came out of the darkness and across the steppes to the north of here to migrate across the face of Europe. I have never, however, heard of Celts in Byzantium."

"There are Celts in Byzantium now," she said softly. Her eyes fixed themselves upon the horizon where the sun, now tired from its journey across the sky, prepared to sink away into its molten bed of scarlet and gold.

Dagda knelt by the small lamp that they had brought with them. He had the harder task. He must keep his own eyes upon the sun while putting fire to the girl's brand at the proper instant. She never doubted for a moment his ability to do it, and as always Dagda's timing was flawless. The lamp touched the torch. Without even gazing downward Mairin knew it was lit. As the sun collapsed below the horizon she touched her fire to the wood, and the flames leapt upward.

There was not a sound to be heard at that moment in the imperial gardens. Not a leaf stirred upon any of the trees. It was as if the whole world had suddenly gone silent. Even the waters of the Marmara were still. Dagda and Mairin stood respectfully, eyes closed as they prayed. Then suddenly the fire crackled with a loud snap and several noisy pops.

Dagda opened his eyes, and looked at the girl. "In all my years," he said, "I have never known such silence as when you light your fires. Especially this night. Your birth-time remembrance."

She smiled up at him. "I have never really understood it, Dagda, but there is something about the fires . . ." she said, then paused and shrugged. "I cannot explain it," she finished.

"It is in your blood," he told her. "It was not so long ago that we Celts worshiped the Mother and the Father, and all of their children. We still know despite the Christian teachings that there are spirits belonging to the trees, the waters, the animals, and all living things. The Christ did not forbid us those spirits, but those who rule this church are a jealous lot who demand a single dedication of their followers. It is best to nod our heads in agreement, then go our own way, my lady."

Above them the sky had quickly grown velvety dark. A royal-blue evening punctuated by one bright cold star directly overhead. Mairin watched the orange blaze of her Samhein fire, and her mind drifted easily away in the almost hypnotic swirl of the flames. She drew a long deep breath, and with the expelling of air from her slender frame she felt herself beginning to drift slowly upward and away from her body. In just a moment she would be free to soar above the fire as she did each year.

For an instant she remembered the first time she had done it. She was barely a toddler, and her father had been so proud that she possessed the power of the old ones, a power that had grown with the aid of Dagda, and old Catell; a power that allowed her to see truth or falsehood within others. It gave her the gift of healing, and sometimes offered her sight beyond that of most mortals. That part of the gift she feared, for since leaving Brittany she had had no one to teach her and Dagda's knowledge was limited. Mairin wisely kept her fears to herself for though she worked her powers only for good there were those who knowing her secrets would fear her. They would call her enchantress, or witch. Then as her sweetly soaring spirit was about to attain freedom from her mortal body she was drawn sharply back by a harsh voice saying, "In the emperor's name!"

Mairin's eyes flew open and her demeanor was that of a young doe startled. Into what she had imagined her own private and secret domain had come a troop of Varangian Guards. Angrily she said, "How dare you intrude upon me!"

"Nay, wench, 'tis you who intrude. These are the imperial gardens, and you trespass," came the quick reply. "Identify yourself! You do not, I suspect, have the right to be here."

Before she might reply a man stepped from the shadows and said quietly, "This is the lady Mairin, captain. Daughter of the English trade envoy. I am surprised that you did not recognize her by her fiery hair which is the talk of the city. She is permitted to be here. You may go."

"Your pardon, lady," said the captain of the Varangian Guards. "I but did my duty." He saluted her smartly. Then turning, he led his men from the area.

Mairin turned to look at the man who had championed her. Dagda, she noted, had disappeared, but she knew he was not far. "Thank you, my lord," she acknowledged her knight. "Have we met?" She wondered who this man might be that the captain of the Varangian Guards had obeyed him so swiftly, and without question. The flames from the fire lit his image, and looking closely at him for the first time Mairin felt her breath catch sharply in her chest. The man before her was the most incredibly beautiful man she had ever seen. Handsome, she thought, was a word one usually applied to a man, but this man was more than that. The only word that might indeed apply was "beautiful."

"I am Prince Basil Ducas, the emperor's cousin," said her protector, "and no, we have not met formally, but having seen you yesterday I knew that we must meet."

"Y-you saw me yesterday?" The stumbling words sounded stupid to her own ears, and she was furious with herself.

"I was standing just to the right behind my cousin's throne," he answered. "I am not surprised you did not see me. The Throne of Solomon is a fascinating contraption particularly when one is seeing it for the very first time." He was endeavoring to put her at ease. "Tell me," he asked her, "why are you burning this fire?"

"It is a Samhein fire, my lord. When my people worshiped the Mother and the Father it was their custom to celebrate four great feasts each year. *Imbolc* which notes the lengthening of the days, the drawing to a close of winter, and the coming of spring. *Beltaine* which celebrates the planting and a return of life; *Lugnasagh* on August 1st to give thanks for a successful growing season and the harvest; and tonight, *Samhein,* our year's-end festival."

"These are not Christian customs," he said. "I thought that the Anglo-Saxons were of the Christian faith."

"The Anglo-Saxons are, my lord, as are my people, the Celts. There is no harm in what I do. It honors the customs of my Celtic ancestors."

"I was given to understand that your father, Aldwine Athelsbeorn, is an Anglo-Saxon lord."

"Aldwine Athelsbeorn is my adoptive father, my lord. My father was Ciaran St. Ronan, a nobleman of Brittany. My mother, Maire Tir Connell, was a princess of Ireland. Both are Celtic peoples, and I revere their ancient customs. Besides, Samhein is my birthday. Dagda says that I burst into the world with a head like the Samhein fire." Her eyes were twinkling as she spoke.

"And who is Dagda?" he asked.

"Dagda is a mighty warrior that my kingly grandfather entrusted with the care of my mother. When she died shortly after my birth she put me into his keeping. Where I go, my lord, he goes."

"Your hair is like the flame," the prince murmured, his voice low. "You are the most beautiful girl I have ever seen."

Her cheeks grew warm, but whether from the heat of the fire or the heat of his words she knew not. "I thank you for your compliment, my lord," she said slowly. "Byzantines use the word 'beautiful' with ease it seems. It is a word I have heard often since arriving in Constantinople." Dagda stepped back into the circle of the fire, and Mairin finished, "I must go now, my lord. Thank you for your kindness."

The prince was not so easily dismissed. "Let your dragon tend to the fire," he said. "I will personally escort you back to your parents in the Garden Palace."

Her mirth bubbled forth. "Dagda, a dragon?" she giggled.

"Does he not guard the fair maiden, and keep her safe from the evils of the world?"

"I do, my lord," said Dagda quietly in his deep voice. "I would give my life for my lady."

The prince nodded, saying, "I will see her safe, Dagda." Then taking Mairin's hand he led her away from the fire into the evening darkness of the garden which was now half-lit by the rising moon. Her slender hand was warm. He could feel her trembling slightly as they walked. She was very young, he thought, and very innocent. He believed she had never been approached seriously by a man before. Something about her reached out and touched him and he remembered his careless words to the emperor only yesterday that if she were as beautiful as he was then he should wed with her, and they would create beautiful children.

Perhaps it was not such an idle remark after all. He must eventually marry, and there were none among the women he had known all his life who attracted him enough that he would marry one of them. In his thirty years he had many lovers both male and female. He was fonder of his current inamorato than most of those who had come to his bed, but the actor was extremely jealous of anyone who took the prince's attention. Basil smiled to himself in the darkness. He did not think Bellisarius would like Mairin.

"Have you seen much of the city?" he inquired as they walked along.

"Not a great deal, my lord. The people follow me seeking to touch my hair. I have promised my mother I will braid it up and hide it beneath a veil so we may visit in the city. My mother is lonely for England and I feel I must divert her from her sadness. She is a gentle lady who has never before traveled so far from her home. I think she is overwhelmed by the greatness of Constantinople."

"But you are not overwhelmed?" He found that as interesting as he found her. One moment she was a giggling child, the next she spoke with wisdom beyond her years.

"I find it exciting," she told him. "London frightens me for it is smoky and gloomy, but Constantinople is bright and wonderful."

"Yes," he agreed. "It is a colorful place. I was born here. I shall show you and your mother my city," he promised. "Shall we begin tomorrow? There is much to see and it will take many months for me to complete the task. Perhaps when I am finished you will not want to return to England."

They had reached the Garden Palace. He quickly raised her hand to his lips, and kissing it bid her good night before disappearing swiftly back into the darkness.

For a long moment Mairin stood in the flickering torchlight of the villa's entry. His quick departure left her with the feeling that perhaps she had imagined the whole thing. She stared at the hand he had held so securely and kissed before leaving her. Her heart was hammering. The dancing flames of her Samhein fire had shown her the perfect and flawless features of the man. His sculptured cheekbones that had caught at the shadows, a long straight nose, and narrow lips. She had not been able to tell the color of his eyes which were spaced perfectly alongside his nose, but his fringe of beard and his curly hair were definitely dark. His voice, deep and creamy, had reached out to her and touched something deep within her soul. She had entered this world on Samhein. Was her meeting with Basil Ducas the beginning of another life of sorts? Though it was not cold, she shivered.

Chapter 5

True to his word the prince arrived the next day. Eada quickly realized that the attraction for Basil Ducas was Mairin, not a burning desire to show them Constantinople. He did so nonetheless with enthusiasm, and Eada's head was quickly filled with more history than she had any wish to know.

"He exhausts me," she said to her husband one evening when they had been in Constantinople for over six months. "He is an enormously learned man, and Mairin enjoys his company greatly."

Aldwine chuckled. "One good thing has come of it for you, my love. You do not have time to miss England."

"That is true," agreed his wife, "but I would wish for a week of peace from this prince and his marvelous but tiring city!"

"You cannot allow Mairin to be unchaperoned with Basil Ducas," her husband said.

Eada glowered at him. "I know my duty as a mother, my lord," she snipped. "As long as Mairin enjoys his company I shall accompany them." She looked at Aldwine and her blue eyes twinkled. "Did you know, my lord, that Constantinople, like Rome, has fourteen districts; and because one of Rome's districts lies across the Tiber River, one of Constantinople's fourteen districts lies across the Golden Horn in Pera? Are you aware, my lord, that Constantinople has fifty fortified gates and thirteen miles of walls; and because of its enormous grain reserves and cisterns, can indefinitely sustain siege? Did you know, my lord, that the great chain across the Golden Horn protects Constantinople from attacks by sea?"

He laughed, and Mairin, joining them, chimed in, "Do you know, father, that the aqueducts guarantee the populace an adequate supply of clean water at all times; and that unlike the cities in Western Europe

Constantinople has underground sewers to carry off the city's wastes? Unlike our towns in England, father, the streets are lit at night! There are free hospitals for all, father, and even women doctors! There is a city fire brigade, and almost a million people in Constantinople!"

"All this is quite fascinating," he agreed with them, "but I suspect that the prince is far more interested in you, my daughter, than in all the statistics and facts he has fed you in order to be with you."

"Father!" Mairin's cheeks grew pink, but Eada was instantly alert.

"What have you heard?" she asked him. "What has the prince said to you, my lord?"

"Nothing yet, but he has asked to speak to me privately, and comes this very day to do so." Aldwine Athelsbeorn looked at his daughter. "Well, Mairin, what say you? If he asks for you in marriage shall I give you to Prince Basil? Could you be happy here in Constantinople? Your mother and I cannot stay once our trade negotiations are agreed upon. It will take several more years to settle everything, the way these Byzantines do business. We would be here that long."

"Mother has taught me that a woman has but two paths in life. My choices are the church or the marriage bed," said Mairin. "I have no calling to the church, and therefore will marry as pleases you, father."

"No, Mairin," he said quietly. "I would have you marry one day, but if I could I would give you some choice in the matter. Think what it is I say to you, Mairin."

"Duke William will be England's next king, and so if I return to England I must of necessity marry a Norman," Mairin answered. "The Normans are a proud people and my dowry is not a large one. I have no lands in England. Should the prince want me for a wife it would probably be a better match than any other I receive. There is little I have to offer a well-connected Norman husband."

"You have your beauty, Mairin," said Aldwine. "There are men who would seek to possess you despite your lack of fortune."

"I would be loved," she said. "Is it so very much to ask, father?"

"I cannot answer you, my daughter. I love your mother. Ciaran St. Ronan loved Maire Tir Connell, but for many, marriage is an arrangement whereby a man adds to his wealth and to his lands. Still if a man and a woman respect one another, friendship which often leads to love may grow between them."

"You speak like the Anglo-Saxon you are, my father," she answered. "The Normans do not respect and appreciate their women as do the English. I may be young, but I know that women for them are objects of beauty and lust, a means by which they may get their children. You are clever, but your choice is no real choice. A nameless, faceless Norman who will marry me for my beauty while looking upon my small portion with scorn, and treat me as a possession. Or Prince Basil who is kind, and would behave toward me with honor. Of course it is the prince I would choose. Could I find a more worthy husband?"

Eada shook her head. "You get ahead of yourselves," she worried. "The prince has only asked to speak with you, Aldwine. No prior mention has been made of Mairin. Do not give our daughter ideas she should not have."

Aldwine Athelsbeorn smiled. "If the prince wished to speak to me about something else then he would have said it. He said he wished to speak to me about something of a private nature. What else could it be but Mairin?"

"I have heard gossip," Eada said. "Gossip about the prince, and the actor, Bellisarius."

"Street talk." Aldwine dismissed his wife's words. He knew more than she, but how could he explain it to his simple, innocent Eada?

"The actor lives in the Boucoleon Palace as does Prince Basil," replied Eada sharply. "The servants may gossip, but there are grains of truth in their chatter, my lord. Bellisarius' name is mentioned often in connection with the prince."

"He is this empire's greatest actor. The emperor honors him, and Basil is his friend," said Aldwine. "Such friendships are common here. They do not prevent a man from marrying, and cleaving to his wife. Remember, Eada, that I lived here in my youth. I know. There is nothing unusual in their friendship for Constantinople."

"You have always behaved as if Mairin were yours alone," said Eada with a trace of bitterness, "but I love her too! I want her happy, and such talk disturbs me, my lord!"

"Oh, do not quarrel on my account!" begged Mairin. She put her slender arms about Eada. "Dearest mother, if the prince seeks to have me for his wife, I would be content. He is kind, thoughtful, and amusing. He would make me happy I know."

Eada smoothed an errant lock of her daughter's fiery hair from her forehead. "You are so innocent of the world, my darling," she said softly. Then putting the girl gently aside she said firmly to her husband, "Grant me this, my lord. If the prince does indeed seek to wed with our child let them wait six months' time. If at the end of that time they still wish to wed, so be it."

Aldwine thought a moment then said, "Has Mairin yet begun her woman's flow?"

Eada flushed. "Nay, my lord."

He nodded. "Then I will consider your terms. If the marriage cannot be consummated I see no need to hasten it."

Eada sighed with relief. Anything could happen in six months' time. Perhaps her husband was wrong. Perhaps the prince did not seek to wed Mairin, but came on another mission.

When Prince Basil arrived at the Garden Palace, Eada and Mairin were discreetly absent. Eada wished there were anyplace else that they might be. Together mother and daughter walked in the gardens of the Imperial Palace. They admired the flowering trees and the springtime flowers that were set amid the tiled fountains and the many fishponds. When a slave came to fetch them quickly back Eada's heart sank. She knew it meant that the prince had asked for Mairin in marriage. Had it been otherwise they would have dallied the afternoon away until Aldwine joined them.

The two men sat within the courtyard garden of the small palace. Both were smiling. Zeno was pouring wine into four delicate golden goblets. Aldwine hurried them forward with a broad wave of his hand.

"Come, my wife! Come, Mairin! I have news!" He waited until the two women had seated themselves on the cushioned stools by the two chairs in which the men sat. Then he said as if it were the greatest surprise to him, "My dear, Prince Basil has asked for Mairin to wive! Of course, I have agreed. He does us a great honor. One I would have never expected. What think you, Eada?"

"It is indeed an honor, my lord," said Eada slowly, "but our daughter is not yet a woman. She is too young for the marriage bed."

"Your husband has explained Mairin's innocence to me," the prince said in reassuring tones. "I have agreed that the marriage not be consummated until she is a true woman. The marriage, however, will take place on May 1st. Mairin will then come to live with me at the Boucoleon Palace."

Eada gave her husband an anguished glance; her soft eyes were questioning. She was too well mannered to defy Aldwine, or demand answers of him in the prince's presence. "It will be as you and my lord agree," she said, "but if I might be permitted to ask, why such unseemly haste? It is scarce three weeks until May 1st."

The prince smiled at Eada. When he did his astounding turquoise-colored eyes grew warm with emotion. "I fell in love with Mairin the first time I saw her, my lady. For six months I have been with her almost every day as we toured the city. You are a charming chaperon, but I would be alone with Mairin. Away from prying eyes.

"How can I tell her of my love for her when a hundred ears, her mother's being the chiefest, listen to every word that I say to her? In the last six months I have composed a hundred love songs yet not once have I had a private moment in which to sing them to her. You have only my word, lady, but ask anyone in Byzantium. You will be told that the word of Prince Basil Ducas is an honest one. I promise you I will cherish and adore Mairin. I will let no harm or hurt come to her. I will honor her all my days if you will but trust me to do so."

"You have defeated me, my lord," Eada said with a sigh. "What can I possibly say in the face of such a declaration?"

"Give us your blessing, my lady." He smiled at her again.

"I give it," she said, resigned.

Aldwine Athelsbeorn arose from his chair drawing his wife up to her feet as he did so. "Come, Eada," he said leading her from the garden.

Basil and Mairin were alone for the first time since Samhein when he had taken her from Dagda and returned her to the villa.

"You say nothing, Mairin," he noted quietly.

"Neither you nor my mother have given me the opportunity, my lord," she replied.

"Are you content to be my wife?" He took her chin into his hand, tipping her face up to his.

"I am, my lord," she answered, "but if I were not?"

"I should still have you," he said quietly and she saw a hint of ruthlessness in his beautiful face.

"I do not love you yet, my lord," she pressed him.

"That I will teach you, Mairin. Have you ever loved a man? Perhaps there is some unforgotten sweetheart in England you remember with fondness."

"There is no one, my lord, nor has there ever been. I do not know how to love a man in any sense." He saw the truth of her words in her violet eyes.

Then gently his hand caressed her face, enjoying the rose-petal softness of her skin, the velvety outline of her lush mouth. Mairin felt as if she had been touched by lightning. Her eyes widened slightly. A small smile touched the corners of his lips; he saw quite plainly that he was indeed the first with her, and he suppressed a shudder. She was even more perfect than he had dared to imagine. He would take her and mold her into exactly what he wanted her to be. Never had he hoped for such good fortune in a wife!

In his apartments in the Boucoleon Palace were many rare and beautiful things for Prince Basil was a collector of beauty. He had the largest and best assemblage of ancient Grecian pottery in the known world. There was not a piece less than a thousand years old, and all of it was without blemish. The statuary he had gathered together was also ancient and free of disfigurement of any sort. He possessed a collection of loose gemstones all of which were flawless.

As a Christian he could have but one wife. Mairin with her perfect beauty would be the unmatched centerpiece in all of his collections, an unrivaled ornament to be envied, coveted, and admired by all who saw her. Looking down into her lovely face he felt a shaft of desire race through him. Who knew when he would be able to have her? Anticipation only whetted his appetite for her. Raising a slender finger he touched her temptingly delicious lips. Mairin's mouth was moist, and parted just slightly. Beneath the modesty of her high-necked tunic dress he could see the rapid rise and fall of her chest as he stimulated her. His wonderful turquoise eyes locked with hers. Slowly with mesmerizing motion he rubbed his finger over the tender sensitive skin of her mouth. "Has any man ever kissed you? Not your father, or brother, or a relative, but a sweetheart?" he demanded of her.

"No," she answered him a bit breathlessly. "I have told you, my lord, that I have had no sweetheart." His powerful glance made breathing hard.

"Then I shall be the only man to plunder that ripeness, Mairin. It is a very sensuous mouth you possess, my perfect little love. It tempts a man to rashness." Leaning forward he touched her tips with his own. Innocently the sweet flesh yielded beneath his assault, and only his experience with passion prevented him from taking her then and there within the garden.

Within Mairin something seemed to explode, sending an ooze of burning languor through her veins, causing her heart to race madly. It made her want more of the unknown passion that his eyes promised. She knew that he could see her desire, but in her innocence it never occurred to her that she should hide it.

"I have promised your parents that I will not consummate our union until you are fully a woman, Mairin," he said softly, "but there are other ways in which we may pleasure each other while we await your flowering. There are many things which I will teach you about giving and receiving passion. You will not be afraid of me, will you my perfect love?"

"No, my lord." She tried to draw a breath, but her chest felt like it was encased in bonds of iron. Her head was whirling. If the truth be known she was a little afraid of this man's sudden and open desire for her, but it seemed wrong to her to even admit it when he was being so gentle with her.

He saw it, and attempted to reassure her. "Desire between a man and a woman is a good and natural thing, Mairin. You are only afraid because it is new and unfamiliar to you. That is the proper emotion for a pure and innocent virgin such as yourself. I will never knowingly hurt you, Mairin. Believe me, and trust me, my perfect love."

She swallowed. A blush suffused her cheeks. "I do trust you, my lord."

His hand cupped her chin again, and smiling at her he kissed her once more. "On the first day of May you will become my wife, my perfect princess."

"Beltaine," she said. "The feast of planting, of flowering, and of planning for the harvest to come. It is the traditional day for marriage among the Celts."

"Then you are satisfied that we be wed that day?"

"Yes, my lord. That in your ignorance of my people you have chosen that day is to me a portent of good fortune."

"You will live in the Boucoleon, Mairin. It is not, of course, my personal palace. I only have apartments there as do many others in the emperor's family and favor. This summer I shall build for you across the Bosporus a palace set like a perfect gemstone in the green hillside above the sea. There we shall consummate our love and there our children will be born, and we will one day die after many blissful years together. Does that please you?"

"Oh, yes, my lord," she said, a smile lighting her features for the first time. "The Imperial Palace with all its buildings and grounds is very beautiful, but I should prefer my own home. A place where we may be private with ourselves and our family."

"You do not seek the glory and the intrigue of court life, Mairin?"

"No, my lord, such things are not for me. I am happiest with my home and my family."

"Surely there are other things that pleasure you, Mairin. You are far too intelligent not to have other interests. I would learn all about you, and what you like."

"I like music, my lord, and it is said that I have a gift for healing. I know much of herbs."

"An inborn gift for healing is a special one," he noted.

"There is little else I can tell you. My life has been a simple one. England is a beautiful land, but its beauty is a natural one. It has not the magnificence of what I have seen in Byzantium. There is a great deal I can learn here! Your libraries hold the wisdom of the ancients. It will take me a lifetime to penetrate even a portion of it."

"You read?" That knowledge seemed to surprise him.

"Do you mind?" she worried.

"No," he said slowly, "I am just a little surprised. I did not think Anglo-Saxon women knew such things."

"Mother says that men do not like women with knowledge for it is not feminine. My father believes women need enough learning to read and write, and be certain that the bailiff isn't robbing them. So I sat with my brother, Brand, in his schoolroom, and Brother Bayhard soon learned that if Brand was no scholar, I seemed to be. He always said that it was sad I was not the boy."

"You enjoyed your studies?" Basil was absolutely fascinated by this totally unexpected side of Mairin. He would not have expected such a thing of her, for when compared with Byzantium's enlightened empire England was a half-savage country.

"Yes," she answered him, "I must be honest with you, my lord, I did enjoy my studies."

"I will find you a tutor!" he said excitedly. "When we are married you shall spend part of each day in study, my love. As long as such things please you, you shall do them. In Constantinople we do not disapprove of women learning. Indeed we encourage the pursuit of knowledge."

He could barely contain his delight. He had never considered the sort of woman who would make him happy. He enjoyed all beautiful women, and that, he realized, had been his problem. He had never looked beyond the beauty of a woman's face and form which was probably due to the fact that many women of his own generation and social standing were indolent, indulged beauties who rarely troubled themselves to be anything other than exquisite ornaments. Those few who looked beyond their paintpots and dressmakers were rare creatures usually lacking in great beauty or fortune who were wise enough to realize that they needed more, and therefore sought it. They usually ended up in the church, or became scholars of renown with little time for husbands and families.

Mairin on the other hand was that virtually nonexistent creature. She had been blessed with extraordinary beauty, and had a mind susceptible to, and capable of, learning. This, he realized, was precisely what he had been seeking in a woman. He intended molding her as a sculptor might mold his clay. She would be not only the most beautiful, but she would become the wisest woman in Byzantium. *His creation*. His instincts told him that she was virtuous. He would love her and provide for her so totally that she would never be tempted by another. She would be a shining example of perfection to other women. Beautiful. Learned. Virtuous. Remote. And his alone!

"Come to me," he said, and he drew her into his lap. She was cradled by one of his arms while his other hand reached out to turn her face to him. His eyes! The unbelievable color of a Persian turquoise looked possessively at her. "I love you," he said. His voice was almost harsh. "I will teach you to love me. There will never be anyone else for us but the other. I will give you happiness beyond all other women. *Now kiss me!*"

He suddenly seemed so fierce that she felt shy. Her face colored with his words. Catching her lower lip between her teeth she attempted to turn away from him. He forced her gaze back to his.

"Obedience is the first rule of marriage, Mairin. You are young, unschooled, and a virgin. I expect shyness. I will permit you this lapse, but in the future, I will expect perfect obedience. Now give me your lips, and kiss me."

He was very masterful, she thought. Yet his tone, and his talk of obedience, seemed so severe. Still he was to be her husband. She had agreed to it, and it was a fabulous match. Mairin pushed her doubts away. Blushing, she raised her mouth to him and her eyelids fluttered closed. At his touch her heart raced madly for this was no gentle kiss. This time his lips took fierce and total possession of her, molding themselves against her innocent, soft flesh with a burning unmistakable proprietorship that left her quite breathless.

"Ohhhhh," she gasped softly when he finally released her. Basil chuckled, noting the sudden dawning of new knowledge within her violet eyes. Gently he tipped her from his lap, and standing up he turned without a word and walked from the room. Mairin stood rooted to the floor. His earlier gentle kisses had left her feeling somewhat giddy and tingly. This last kiss had sent the blood to pounding in her brain, her stomach churning with a wildness that she didn't understand. If this was love, then it was incredible!

Eada and Aldwine hurried back into the room, both speaking at once. Mairin smiled and nodded, but she only half-listened to them. Her mind was far too occupied with Basil, and his extravagant promises of their future happiness. Messengers, her father was saying, would have to be dispatched to England informing the king of her marriage. Brand must be told too.

Prince Basil would speak to the emperor to formally request his permission for the marriage to take place. It was unlikely that the emperor would object to his cousin's happiness for the Byzantines were remarkably democratic in their attitude toward marriage. A rich man was never looked down upon for taking a bride from another social stratum as long as she suited him and was a good wife.

Constantine X was pleased to give his royal blessing to the match. It meant that his cousin was committed to having a family, and the more of them that there were, the stronger. The emperor, however, had one concern.

"Have you spoken to Bellisarius yet of your impending marriage?" he asked Basil.

"There was no need for me to say anything until I had your blessing, my liege," was the smooth reply. "I shall speak to him this night."

"He will not be happy with your decision, Basil. He is an intense man," warned Constantine.

"There is no need for him to distress himself. I love Mairin, but I love Bellisarius too. Why should I send him away merely because I marry?"

"Will Mairin understand such a thing, Basil? Will Bellisarius, for that matter?"

"She need never know, Constans. I intend to build her a palace in the hills across the Bosporus. She wants her own home. As much as she enjoys the city she prefers country living, and will come rarely to Constantinople I suspect. Bellisarius on the other hand detests the country, and never leaves Constantinople. I think I may safely keep my wife and my current lover apart. Don't all men?"

"A *wife?*" Bellisarius Phocus, Constantinople's greatest actor of the century, looked upon his princely lover that evening with shock. "You are taking a wife on the first day of May? Sweet Jesus, Basil! How could you

102

be so cruel? 'Twas on the first day of May last year that we met! I shall never forgive you, Basil! *Never!*" A single tear slipped down his long, elegant face to catch within the fringe of his perfectly barbered beard.

"So that is why the day had sweet memories for me," the prince exclaimed. Then he put a friendly arm about his lover. "I would not intentionally hurt you, Bellisarius, but the date is now set. It cannot be changed."

"But why must you wed?" The actor's golden brown eyes filled with tears. "Do you not love me?"

"Yes, I love you," said the prince indulgently, "but you cannot give me children. Bellisarius. It is my duty to my family to have children. Besides, Mairin is exquisite. In beauty she is every bit my equal. I could not resist her, and already I love her."

"I have heard her hair is a most noxious color," the actor retorted sharply. "*Orange!* How can a girl with orange hair hope to equal your beauty, my sweet prince?"

"Her hair is a red-gold. It is as if a fire burns atop her sweet head. She is pure perfection in face and form. An innocent virgin. Best of all, Bellisarius, she is intelligent!"

"She is an Anglo-Saxon, Basil!" he protested. "They are barely civilized! Have you seen that trade delegation of theirs? Long hair, and unkempt beards, and the most appalling clothing!"

Basil laughed. "She reads, Bellisarius. She can do simple mathematics. She writes a fine hand. She speaks several languages. What say you to that?"

"That I should like to meet your paragon. Perhaps we might find we have something else in common besides you."

"Oh, no, my darling," the prince chuckled. "You most certainly will not meet Mairin. I will not have you shocking her by letting slip our relationship. She would not understand such a thing. Perhaps when she is older, and has learned our ways, it will be different, but not now. I am building her a villa across the Bosporus, and neither of you shall be distressed by the sight of the other."

"How thoughtful you are of us both," sniped Bellisanus dryly. "How fortunate it is that I understand the necessity of your marriage even if your bride should not understand that which is between us." He eyed Basil jealously. "I do not think it is as simple as you think, my prince. What you and I are to each other has never been a secret. What makes you think that someone will not speak to the girl, and divulge our relationship to her? Are you without enemies? What of the girl's parents? When they learn of your eccentric tastes, will they still release their treasure to you? Are they so eager to have a prince for a son-in-law that they will put aside their barbarian scruples? I wonder."

"Be warned, Bellisarius," said the prince in low tones. "I want this girl! Should you attempt to spoil it for me I shall leave you."

"You will leave me anyhow," said the actor. "I know it!" His voice had a slightly hysterical edge to it.

"No," said Basil softly. He caressed the actor's curly blond head reassuringly. "No, my darling, I shall not leave you. A man can love more than one person at a time, Bellisarius, as I love you and Mairin. Each of you serves a different need for me, and I must have you both. You have always known that unlike you I am able to love both women and men. That eventually you would have to share me with a wife. You have never been jealous before. Do not pout now, my love," he cajoled, and quickly kissed the actor's lips.

Bellisarius eagerly returned the kiss and sighing said, "You will break my heart yet, my lord prince, but then I knew it the moment our eyes first met, yet even knowing it I still loved you."

Basil smiled into Bellisarius' eyes. "Trust me," he said softly. "I will make everything all right for all of us. You know that I can, don't you?"

"I almost feel sorry for your bride, Basil," said Bellisarius quietly. "I wonder if she realizes what a ruthless man you really are."

But Mairin in the flush of first love only saw what she wanted. The prince had swept her off her feet with his declaration of devotion, and his passionate possession of her innocent lips. His kisses had thrilled and excited her beyond anything she had ever known. She unquestioningly believed all he said, and longed for the day when her body would be ready to receive the full homage of a man's love.

Already she had grown in height, and was now taller than Eada. Her breasts, only buds upon her smooth child's chest when they had first come to Constantinople, suddenly swelled and rounded, pushing the cloth of her tunic dresses outward. The garments had had to be altered as they quickly became too tight. Mairin found herself assailed by a variety of new moods that had her edgy one minute, and ecstatic with joy the next. If she had been a beautiful child she was quickly becoming an equally beautiful woman.

Dagda silently noted the many glances his young mistress elicited as she moved unawares through the pattern of her days. Women, of course, were envious. Men, however, gazed longingly at Mairin. Twice Dagda saw the young Varangian guardsman Eric Longsword staring after Mairin with open lust in his eyes. Finding himself observed, the light of desire would depart the guardsman's eyes to be replaced by a flat blue stare.

The empress, Marie Irene, came from her palace to meet Mairin. She was a deeply pious, reclusive woman whose life had been devoted to prayer and good works. Her dark eyes scanned Mairin's face anxiously. Then she smiled, obviously pleased by what she had seen. She patted the girl's hand in a motherly fashion.

"You are a good little maid, I can see it," she said in a whispery voice so low they had to strain to hear her. "I shall make special offerings to the blessed Saint Anne, mother of our Blessed Lady Marie, that Basil has at last found a wife. You know, of course, that the chief duty of a wife is to bear children, my dear?" Her pale face with its dark eyes peered into Mairin's blushing countenance.

"My daughter is not yet old enough to conceive and bear children, gracious majesty," said Eada.

"She will be soon. I can see womanhood already dawning in her beautiful eyes. Listen to me, my child. It is hard to be a woman, to yield yourself humbly to the base and carnal desires of a man, but it is your duty as a wife to do so. Your mother has undoubtedly told you of the shameless way in which children are conceived. It is God's punishment upon us for Eve's sin that we be humbled so, and must be tolerated. You can do your soul great good, however, if you will simply concentrate upon your beads during the degrading act." The empress peered anxiously at Mairin, fearful that perhaps she had shocked the poor innocent with her bluntness.

Mairin swallowed back the urge to laugh. Sex was not a taboo event among the Anglo-Saxons who harking back to a more primitive time entered into it with joyous abandon. Eada and Aldwine's marital happiness was no secret. Brand and Mairin had on several occasions unwittingly caught their parents in a lusty embrace. They had always been free to ask their parents about matters pertaining to the flesh and Eada answered with honesty and with love, confiding to her daughter that though such delights might first prove awkward, they were nonetheless pleasurable.

The empress's words were therefore astounding. Still Mairin knew that she must be polite to the anxious empress whose motives sprang from genuine caring. She instinctively knew Basil was a man of deep passion. He had even admitted to finding her innocent enthusiasm for his kisses preferable to women who bore their lords' embraces in silent submission.

She could not imagine why the empress had taken it upon herself to address her in such a solemn fashion.

"I thank your gracious majesty for even taking the time to come and see me let alone offering me your sage advice," she said politely. "I will remember your words."

Eada beamed with pride. She had taught her child well, for Mairin's manners were flawless, and her tact commendable. Honored that the empress Irene Marie had taken the time to personally welcome Mairin into the Ducas family, Eada could not, however, imagine why the older woman thought it necessary to impart such gloom to Mairin. The thought of concentrating upon one's beads during supreme passion was too amusing for words.

Led by the empress other members of the Ducas family now came to pay their respects, and each brought a gift for Mairin. Not all of them were wealthy, nor of the noble branch of the family. They took great pride, however, in being related to the emperor, and being again in the spotlight by virtue of Basil's marriage to the beautiful foreigner. The prince's father was dead, but his mother came immediately after the empress.

Ileana Ducas was a tiny, elegant woman with a somewhat forbidding mien. She had her son's coloring, but where his hair was wavy, hers was straight. It was severely fashioned into a knot at the base of her neck. Basil's turquoise eyes were warm, but his mother's were flat and expressionless, lighting up only when she spoke of her only child. She was magnificently attired in bright scarlet silk heavily encrusted with gold embroidery. Even the empress had not been as grand.

She brought Mairin jewelry, a marvelous necklace of gold filigreed squares encrusted with amethysts. "To match your eyes," she said dourly. "My son said your eyes were the color of amethysts, but they look more violet to me. You are very young, but I suppose I should thank you for taking my son away from the hedonistic life he has persisted in living these past years. I do not approve of his companions. I trust you will be a good wife to him, not some silly little fool who worships the ground he walks upon, and permits him to continue his licentious behavior. Give me grandsons as quickly as possible! It was my misfortune that among all my babies only Basil lived. Children settle a man even more than a wife." She peered at Mairin. "You are old enough to have children, aren't you?"

"Not quite," said Eada protectively.

"Then why does he marry her if not to get himself sons?" demanded

Ileana Ducas irritably. "My son should be having children, not consorting with them."

"We love each other," Mairin exclaimed innocently, "and I will shortly be old enough to consummate our marriage."

"*Love?*" The older woman laughed harshly, but then she sighed. "Love, my dear, is pure illusion though you will not believe me now. In time you will learn that the only reality in this world is that which you can hold within your two hands. I know my son. He loves you for your perfect beauty, and your innocence. The latter you will lose quickly enough living in Constantinople. Guard the former as carefully as old Empress Zoe did, else you'll lose Basil entirely one day."

At the distressed look that passed over Mairin's face Ileana's own features softened sympathetically. "There, child, I have grown bitter with age, but I am not as unkind as I seem. I only seek to prevent you the pain that I have suffered." She smiled a wintry smile. "I shall endeavor to be a good mother-in-law, and not interfere, Mairin. If you should ever need my help, or my counsel, however, do not be afraid to come to me. I have only Basil's best interests at heart, and since I know you do too, we shall be friends and allies. There is no need for history to repeat itself," she finished.

When Eada and Mairin were once more alone Mairin exclaimed, "What a strange woman Basil's mother is! At first she frightened me but as she spoke I realized that I felt sorry for her, yet I do not know why."

Eada shook her head. "Perhaps her husband was not as kind to her as Basil is to you. A woman's whole world is her man and her family. To be treated unkindly by the man you love is a great sadness, but to bear babies that die is the deepest pain of all. May you never know such sadness, Mairin."

Mairin took her mother's hand and in a gesture of affection pressed it to her heart. Since Aldwine and his wife had taken her for their daughter, Eada had lost two babies. One had been a little boy who lived but a day. The other was a child so new in the womb that it had been impossible to tell whether it was a boy or a girl. The loss was doubly hard as it had been many years since Eada had last conceived a child. They had accepted the fact of her barrenness once. That she suddenly conceived again had been considered a small miracle rendered worthless with the unexpected loss of both infants. After that there had been no more children. Mairin knew how Eada had grieved for those lost babies, and perfectly understood her adoptive mother's words.

"I will try to be friends with the lady Ileana, mother."

"Yes, that would be best, Mairin. When your father and I have returned to England Basil's family will be all the family you have. It is important to your future happiness that you find friends among members of the Ducas clan."

Mairin's wedding drew nearer. The imperial seamstresses worked frantically upon the wedding gown. The high-necked underdress with its long tight sleeves was made of cloth of gold, and molded to her figure. Over it she would wear a tunic dress of gold silk that was sewn all over with amethysts, diamonds, and pearls. Mairin's hair would be unbound to indicate her virginity, but atop her head would be a crown of delicate gold filigree, diamonds, and freshwater pearls. The seamstresses sewing the gown were very excited and on the day of Mairin's final fitting they stared open-mouthed at the future princess dressed in their creation.

Eada sighed. "I have never seen anything so beautiful," she said to her daughter.

Mairin said nothing. She stared dreamy-eyed at her glittering reflection, and dreamed of the day when she would belong to Basil. Across the Bosporus building had begun upon the palace that was to be their home. Set into a green hillside the domed and columned building was of cream-colored marble. Marble steps flowed down the terraced hillsides to a small sheltered harbor with its marble quay. Each level of terrace was planted; an orchard of flowering peach, apple, and almond trees on one level, roses on another, sweet herbs on another, colorful garden flowers and spicy herbs upon another.

In the weeks before her wedding Mairin watched the construction from afar peering through a spyglass that the prince had brought her. The palace and its grounds would not be ready for months after the wedding, but the day before the marriage was to be celebrated Mairin could no longer bear only tantalizing glimpses of her future home.

"I must go across the water and see it!" she exclaimed to the prince who had come to pay his usual morning visit. "Oh, Basil, you must let me go!" With innocent artfulness she flung herself into his arms, and looked winningly up at him. *"Please!"*

He let his hands smooth down her young body. He noted the childish thickness was suddenly gone. Her waist was quite defined. He rested his fingertips at the base of that supple waist, and pulled her closer to him, feeling as he did a new fullness in her breasts. She had not a grown woman's shape yet, but her youthful body was beginning to change quite rapidly. His lips teased at hers, and she boldly kissed him a quick kiss.

Basil laughed. "So, my beauty, you would see the fine setting I am creating for you."

"Yes! Yes! Yes!" she insisted. Her sparkling eyes were the color of amethysts now. They were always lighter, he observed, when she was happy. If he could only always keep her as happy as she was this very minute.

"Then, my perfect princess, we shall go across the water this very morning. I will show you the palace that is being built for you. A testament of my love for you, Mairin. I adore you, my beauty! There has never before been anyone like you in my life, and there never will be. You are unique, and you are mine alone!"

He looked down into her eyes, and Mairin once again felt herself filled with tumultuous mixed emotions. Did all brides feel as she felt? Surely not for there was no man in the world quite like Basil. In that moment she felt that she must surely love him, for what else were all these emotions that rolled within her? Shyly she touched his face with its soft curly fringe of dark beard. "I love you, my lord," she whispered, "and you have made me so very happy."

He smiled tenderly down at her. "Ah, my perfect little beauty! In your girlish innocence you have no idea how very happy I can really make you. In time I will show you. For now I am content that your love for me has begun to grow. I am content that after today you will belong to me forever."

The prince sent his servants for a barge after politely requesting Eada's permission to take Mairin across the water. He led his bride-to-be from the Garden Palace down to the Boucoleon Harbor where only imperial vessels were allowed to dock. Smiling, Eada watched them go. Basil had invited her to accompany them, but she believed Mairin needed this time alone with the man she would marry tomorrow.

Eada liked Basil. He seemed a good man. He was ever gentle and considerate with Mairin. Had he been pretending, Eada knew she would have sensed it. He had gone out of his way to reassure Eada that he would not consummate his marriage to her daughter until Mairin had begun her monthly flow, and was fully a woman. Eada believed he would keep his promise though she concluded her daughter's flowering was an event not far off. Recently Mairin's body had begun to rapidly develop. Her waist was quite defined, her hips rounding, the buds of her breasts swelling, a soft down of peach-colored fuzz beginning to sprout along her arms, legs and private parts. Mairin would soon be a woman grown.

And yet there was something undefinable about Basil Ducas that disturbed Eada although she could not quite put her finger upon it. She had tried speaking to Aldwine about it, but her husband had always had a blind spot where Mairin was concerned. From the moment he had brought her home from London he had said no mere Saxon would do as a husband for Mairin. Now he had done even better than some minor Norman lordling. He had found a prince of Byzantium for his precious daughter and he would hear no word of dissent where Basil was concerned. Eada could only hope that her female intuition was being oversolicitous in this particular situation. She loved Mairin every bit as much as her husband did, perhaps even more.

The barge carrying Mairin and Basil swiftly crossed the water. The prince was enchanted by his betrothed's excitement over the new palace and its gardens. Color stained her fair skin as the barge touched the marble quay. It was immediately made fast by a slave who leapt from the vessel to tie it to one of the marble columns sunk into the sea next to the quay. The slave then offered a hand to Mairin who eagerly jumped from the boat. Coming behind her Basil led her up the terraced hillside to the main building.

"The rooms are just now being laid out," he told her. "There is no decoration upon the walls yet. We will have beautiful public rooms for entertaining and dining. Our own private apartments with their baths, and room in a separate wing for our many children. Do you know," he said, taking her into his arms, "how very much I desire you, my perfect one?"

"I think, my lord, that I must desire you also. I ache and long for things I do not even yet know or understand," she answered.

"Soon," he murmured against her soft hair, "soon you will be a woman, Mairin. Tomorrow night I will take you to my bed, and I will begin to prepare you for that time. In doing so, I will give you pleasure."

"Will that give you pleasure also, my lord?"

"I will teach you to give me pleasure, my perfect beauty," he assured her nuzzling his lips against her ear while shivers of hunger sped down her spine.

Her fragrance was haunting, he thought, as he held her, her red-gold head against his shoulder. The warm lilac essence wafted about her, and aroused his senses. Bellisarius was a charming lover, but this beautiful young girl aroused him more than any lover he had ever had. That he could not possess her fully only made the situation of their impending nuptials more piquant. The self-control he would evince until the time

Mairin became a woman would in the end only make that first possession more pleasurable. He actually looked forward to his self-denial.

Mairin snuggled against him feeling safe and loved. It amazed her that this handsome and sophisticated man should have chosen her as his wife. Constantinople was a city of beautiful women, and yet he had picked her. Mairin was no fool. She understood how great her beauty was, yet she knew she lacked all the other traits she so admired in the women of Constantinople, traits she had assumed he would want in a wife. She wanted to make him happy, but she was not certain how to go about it. She knew that as long as Eada remained in Constantinople she would help her to solve these mysteries.

His hand smoothed down her head. "What are you thinking of, Mairin? You are so still and silent against me."

Shifting her position so she might look up at him she smiled and said, "I so very much want to make you happy, my lord. I was thinking on it."

A spasm crossed his face. It was so quick that she wasn't even sure it had been there. He felt as if a powerful hand had just tightened its hold upon his heart. Dear sweet Jesus! How innocent and how very, very sweet she was! Then he realized that he did indeed love her deeply. Not simply for her great beauty, but for the pure and good heart that she seemed to possess as well. "How fortunate I am in you," he said quietly. "You do not have to make any special attempt to please me, my perfect love. Your mere being gives me pleasure. The knowledge that tomorrow you will be my wife offers me the greatest happiness of all. Ahh, Mairin! We will have the most beautiful and perfect life together. I promise you!"

Chapter 6

"*Mother! I am bleeding!*" Mairin looked down at the crimson stains upon her thighs. Then with dawning realization she cried out, "Mother! *I am a woman!*"

For a brief moment Eada closed her eyes in resignation. It had been bound to happen, but why, oh why, now? Why the night before Mairin's wedding? There could be no possibility of consummating the marriage until Mairin's first flow was over, but she had hoped her child would have a little more time. Hiding the emotions that assailed her she briskly went about the business of showing her daughter how to cope during this monthly occurrence. Eada could see she was pale, her fair skin clammy.

Mairin complained of pain in both her belly and back. Eada tucked her into a soft bed, feeding her a warm, medicated drink. Then Eada sat by Mairin's bedside until her daughter fell into a deep sleep. Satisfied that her child was comfortable she hurried off to find the prince.

To her surprise Basil was very sympathetic. "There is no reason," he said, "for our plans to change, my lady Eada. I know that younger women have married and borne children, but Mairin is more innocent than most. She has not the sophistication of a woman of Byzantium. There are some men to whom it would not matter, but I am not like them. I want to introduce Mairin slowly to the pleasures that can be between a man and a woman. I have no great need to immediately possess myself of her maidenhead. I want her to savor and fully enjoy her awakening before we consummate our union."

"Can you consummate that union?" The words were out of her mouth before she realized it. Horrified, Eada clapped her hand over her mouth, her face crimsoning.

The prince laughed, amused by her regretted boldness. "Yes, I most certainly can consummate my marriage to your daughter, lady."

"My lord, I do beg your pardon, but I have heard rumors," Eada apologized. "I cannot help but be concerned for my child's well-being. Eventually we will return to England, leaving Mairin in a strange land. We may never see her again. I only want her happy, my lord."

"She will not be discontent with me, lady. I will give her all she needs to be happy," he said quietly. "I love Mairin, and whatever you have heard about me has nothing to do with my devotion to your daughter."

Eada knew that she must be satisfied. "My lord," she said, "I have committed a terrible breach of good manners with you. I swear I do not seek to be an interfering mother-in-law."

"To seek the well-being of a child is no sin, lady," he interrupted her. Then he said reassuringly, "The words that have passed between us this afternoon are private ones. I shall not allude to this conversation again if you will not."

"My lord is most kind," Eada replied. She was relieved that Aldwine should not know of this incident. Curtsying to Basil she hurried from the room.

The following day dawned clear and warm. The bright sun shone down upon them from a sky of pure turquoise. Mairin followed the ancient custom and had risen early to gather flowers from the gardens before the dew was even off them. She still felt somewhat shaky, a condition brought about by her new status as a grown woman. Her wedding, however, was to be a small, quiet affair. If the bride was slightly subdued no one would gossip. Indeed she suspected her apparent modesty would be applauded.

As Basil was not an immediate member of the royal family, his marriage was not a dynastic one. His title had come to him through his mother. The wedding ceremony would take place not at the great domed basilica of Hagia Sophia, but at Hagia Eirene, a smaller church opposite it.

In early afternoon the prince and a band of musicians came to escort the bride and her parents to the church. The musicians, garbed in scarlet, gold, green, and peacock blue silks, played merrily upon pipes and drums.

With her long, thick hair unbound to show her maiden state, the bridal crown glittering upon her head, Mairin was led from the Garden Palace by her parents and Dagda. The bride was escorted to the church which lay across the Imperial Gardens. The groom and his musicians went ahead of them. Within the church a soft golden light permeated everywhere. The sunshine coming through the beautiful windows reflected off the pale yellow walls and Mairin's beautiful white-and-gold bridal garments.

Although the church in Constantinople had separated from the church in Rome several years earlier, Mairin could see little difference between the two other than language. One church used Greek, the other Latin. As the bride and groom stood before the priest, their crowns were joined together by a slender gold ribbon signifying the bonds of matrimony that would join Mairin to Basil. Three times the priest led the bridal couple around the altar. The invited guests consisted of Aldwine, Eada, Dagda, Eada's serving woman, Nara, Princess Ileana, the Emperor Constantine, the Empress Irene Marie, Timon Theocrates, and his wife, Eudoxia. The members of the wedding chanted joyful matrimonial hymns, and threw rice at the couple to insure the bride's fertility. Then they slapped the prince upon the back in congratulation. When the religious ceremony was over Basil and his bride led their guests back to the Garden Palace to be served bride cakes and wine.

It had been a simple wedding, and health was drunk to the newly wedded couple. Noticing that Mairin was tired, the prince called for a litter. They were wished well and sent quietly upon their way. Dagda and Nara had already gone on ahead to the Boucoleon Palace. Eada had promised her daughter that Nara would be hers when she wed. As for Dagda, Aldwine Athelsbeorn understood that he would serve Mairin and her new husband for he was first Mairin's loyal man.

Mairin lay back in the litter, and for a moment her eyelids drooped. Walking by her side Basil smiled. She was so very beautiful. He took her hand in his, and her eyes opened.

"What kind of a bride am I to fall asleep?" she scolded herself.

"A tired one," he laughed. "It has all been very exciting, my beauty."

She heard his emphasis upon the word "all," and realized that her mother must have told him that she was at last a woman grown. Mairin was relieved. She did not think she would know how to broach such a personal subject with a man even if that man was now her husband.

"Lie back, and rest," he said gently. "We are almost home, and will speak then."

She understood he did not wish to discuss their private life aloud before the servants. Nodding she said, "Yes, my lord."

The Boucoleon Palace overlooked the imperial yacht basin. Its wharf was decorated with fantastic statues of lions, dragons, griffins, and other beasts both mythological and real. The palace was constructed of the finest marbles with mosaics of pure, blazing colors. It sat within a landscape of pavilions and fishponds, fountains, and gardens. Its peaceful setting was misleading for within the Boucoleon twenty thousand people lived and worked as courtiers, soldiers, priests, servants, civil servants, and entertainers. In the workshops of the Boucoleon artisans manufactured high-grade silks—a state monopoly—dyes for fabrics, and weapons of excellent quality.

It was here that Mairin would live until her own home was completed. Prince Basil's apartments overlooked both the gardens and the sea. The little wing of the palace in which they were to live had its own private courtyard and entrance. The prince helped his bride from the litter, and carried her across the threshold of her new home. Blushing, Mairin hid her face in his shoulder. Her heart hammered with excitement and not a little fear, but to her surprise he settled her upon the bed in the bedchamber saying, "Rest now, Mairin. I will join you later for supper." Then he was gone.

She was too tired to argue. The cramps that had earlier assaulted her belly now returned with a vengeance. She even felt queasy. "If this is being a woman," Mairin muttered, "I think I should just as soon not be one!" She turned onto her side, but she was no more comfortable in that position than she had been upon her back. "Nara!" she called out. The serving woman appeared almost instantly.

"How may I serve you, princess?" asked Nara, very aware of her own elevation in status.

"Go to my mother. Tell her I would have some of the elixir she fed me yesterday for the pains in my belly. Tell her also I would know how it is made so I may brew it myself in the future."

"Yes, my lady, I will go immediately, but may I suggest in the meantime that you try some of the red Cyprus wine?"

"Pour me some," Mairin ordered. Then she asked, "Do you get pains, Nara, when your link with the moon is broken?"

The servant smiled. "I used to when I was yet a girl, but I don't now."

Mairin looked puzzled a moment. "I don't understand," she said.

"Well," said Nara with a wink, "once a girl's had a bit of a taste it eases things up for her."

"A taste of what?"

Nara suddenly realized that although Mairin might have been taught the basics of passion by her mother she actually knew little, and had no practical experience. That was how it should be for a proper young lady. The saucy servant, however, had backed herself into a corner. There was no help for it. She must tell the truth.

"Well, my princess, what I mean to say is that once you're coupling regular like with your husband, the pains should go. At least they did with me."

"But you're not married," replied Mairin. Then she blushed crimson as Nara's words sank into her brain. "Ohhh!"

"I'll go right to your mother, my princess," said Nara quickly as she scooted through the door of the bedchamber.

Of course! Nara had a lover! How could she have been so stupid? Perhaps she should be shocked, but she wasn't. At home in England the village boys and girls often coupled before the marriage banns were announced from the church pulpit. Although she knew that Nara's confession wasn't quite the same she found she was not put off by her serving woman's admission. She wondered if her mother knew of Nara's indiscretions, and decided Eada did not. Still, she thought, it could not hurt to have someone so obviously knowledgeable in her service. At least until the time that she herself gained such wisdom.

Then as she awaited Nara's return she remembered that it was May 1st! She had known it this morning, but somehow with the excitement of the wedding she had forgotten. She had to light her Beltaine fire! Particularly on this the most important day of her life! It was her only real link with the parents who had given her life. How else could she share her happiness with them?

Frantically she looked about the room. Everything was totally strange. She had never been in Basil's apartments before today. She had no idea where Nara had placed her cache of oak chips. A knock sounded upon the door, and she bid the knocker admittance.

Dagda entered bearing in his hands a shallow enameled copper dish. "I know you are tired, my lady, but I knew you would not forget Beltaine. The bedchamber terrace faces partly to the west. You may celebrate your fire in privacy there."

He held out the bowl to her, and she set up within its flat bottom the makings of a fire in miniature. "Let us go outside," she said smiling, and he saw the relief in her eyes. "I almost forgot, Dagda, and when I remembered I couldn't find the oak," she admitted.

"I have it safe," he said.

They stood together before the little flame, once again celebrating their ancient heritage. Mairin, her soul soaring free, saw two brown eyes peering from a long, lean face, and knew with some primitive instinct that the owner of that face hated her and therefore her happiness. With a little cry of horror she returned to herself.

"What is it?" Dagda demanded, his familiar face looking anxiously into hers.

"Nothing," she said, not wishing to share her vision with him. She was without a doubt unsettled by her first woman's flow, and now felt foolish. "I am all right," she told him patting his hand, and felt guilty seeing the hurt look in his eyes, for they both knew she lied.

The fire died quickly now and Dagda left her. Returning to the bed-chamber she sipped the wine that Nara had poured her, and awaited the servant's return. Nara had run the entire way. Mixing Eada's potion with fresh wine, Mairin drank it down and quickly fell asleep. When she awoke her pain had gone. Fortunately her gown was so encrusted with jewels it had not wrinkled. Bathing her face in rosewater she appeared fresh and lovely as she joined her husband for their wedding supper.

It was a dainty repast that had been placed before them—a plate of mussels that had been poached in white wine and herbs; a silver platter with two pigeons roasted golden, and set upon a bed of saffroned rice dotted with raisins. A leg of baby lamb rubbed with garlic, and surrounded with tiny white onions, a bowl of artichokes braised in oil and tarragon vinegar, black olives in their own oil, goat's cheese in brine, and soft, fresh white bread.

Feeling much better, Mairin ate with a good appetite. The servants cleared the table of the main meal, and set a bowl of fruit before them. It was then Mairin realized that she was alone with her husband. Slowly she chose an apricot from the bowl, and bit into it.

Sensing her thoughts he reached over to touch her cheek. "I love you," he said, "but I am also aware that your mother died at fifteen, weakened by childbirth. I do not want that happening to you, my perfect one."

"Has my mother not told you that my woman's flow began just last night?" She blushed as she said the words, but Eada had said a woman must be forthright with her husband. She had been certain he knew, yet his words confused her.

"She did," he answered her gravely, "but that will not change the way I feel, Mairin. I am not some ravening beast who must instantly consummate my marriage to you. Tonight is but the first of many nights for us.

There is time for us to love, but not until you and I have learned to know each other better. I know that such an attitude is rare among men, but it is how I feel. I do not wish to lose you to childbirth as your father lost your mother. Can you understand that?"

She nodded feeling strangely relieved. It had been very exciting to be courted by a prince, to be chosen by him to be his wife. She was quickly realizing, however, that she actually knew little about this man who was now her husband. She found that she was glad that he wanted to give her time to acquaint herself with him. "I do not know you at all, do I?" she said thoughtfully.

"No," he answered her, "you do not. When you do, I do not think that you will be too disappointed, my love."

Mairin suddenly laughed. "But what if I am?" she teased him.

"I shall have to see that you are not," he told her with a chuckle. He liked her gentle mockery of his confidence. When she grew up she was going to be a magnificent woman. He saw now though that she was pale again, and so he suggested that she retire.

"But where will you sleep, my lord?"

"I have arranged with Nara to have the couch in our bedchamber made up for me, Mairin. It is not necessary that the world know our business. We have but three personal servants. Your Nara and Dagda, and my body slave, John. They will be silent unless they wish their tongues removed. Our lives will be our own."

So their life settled itself into an easy pattern. He had promised her a tutor, and he found her one. Master Simeon was a learned and elderly Jew who came several days a week to teach her philosophy and history, higher mathematics and the natural sciences. There was a particularly skilled young eunuch named Peter who came to instruct her upon the lute. He taught her the music of Byzantium. She and Basil rode in the hills behind and outside the city walls each day. They swam naked together in a pool within their private garden.

For the first few months of their marriage they slept separately though neither was shy of the other's nudity. She easily became used to him, and his being there. An easy affection sprang up between them. He soon began to wonder how he had ever existed without her for she was loving, and amusing. As she grew surer of his love for her he found she was less shy, and very quick-witted which greatly delighted Basil. After a short time her tutors became lavish in their praise of her intelligence. He shared with her their plaudits drawing her into his arms as he had done a hundred times before to give her a kiss of congratulation. He grew prouder each day of his beautiful and brilliant wife.

This time, however, something happened. Afterward neither of them was ever certain just what it was, but when Basil's mouth touched Mairin's their senses ignited simultaneously. Her slender arms wound around him as she pressed the length of her body against his, suddenly needing his warmth. Beneath his lips hers softened. What had begun as an innocent kiss of congratulation became a kiss of unexpected passion as his tongue slid easily past her teeth into her fragrant mouth. Mairin murmured contentedly, rubbing against him like a kitten. Her little tongue shyly teased at his. Suddenly he was pulling her sleeping chemise from her unresisting body, and laying her back upon the bed.

For a long moment he looked down upon her. Then he sighed deeply. She was unbelievably lovely, and really quite perfect with her creamy fair skin, and her delicate coloring. It wasn't just her innocence that aroused him. It was that aura of the unknown that surrounded her. All loves were unfamiliar for a time, but Basil sensed that his wife would always retain something of her own that she would never share with another. He wanted her very much, but it was still too soon. He had always planned to familiarize her with other paths to pleasure, and at this moment the time seemed right to begin her instruction. Though her eyes were tightly shut she neither struggled against him nor forbade him. Indeed she showed no fear of him, her calm acquiescence encouraging him onward.

Removing his undertunic he seated himself cross-legged above her. He began with gentleness to lightly stroke her breasts. After a few minutes the feathery touches caused her eyes to open, and she looked up at him. His fingers were now slowly encircling her rosy nipples with delicate, teasing caresses that as delicious as they felt were also becoming pure torture. Mairin made a small sound of obvious pleasure that brought a smile to her husband's lips.

"You like this," he said, making it a statement.

"Yes," she answered. "Why have you not touched me thusly before?"

"You were not ready," came the reply.

"What makes me ready now?" Her voice was a trifle breathless.

"I don't know," he said honestly. "You just are, my darling." His dark head dropped down to quickly kiss her lips. Then stretching out beside her he leaned over and his warm tongue began to slowly lick at the nipple of one breast. After a moment she shuddered. His hand began to fon-

dle her other breast, cupping and kneading and stroking at it as he continued lapping at the now tight little bud of the first breast.

The warm wet on her flesh. The knowledge that it was his tongue
touching her ignited something deep within Mairin. A heat that seemed
to center itself between her thighs. She shifted anxiously, but when he
lifted his head from her breast she whispered, "Oh, please don't stop, my
lord!"

With a smile he transferred his mouth to her other nipple, closing his
lips over the sensitive skin and drawing firmly upon it. She gasped with
surprise! Then her fingers threaded themselves into his hair, and she held
him hard against her, her voice crying urgently.

"Yes!"

He played with her for some time in this fashion. The soft globes of
her tender breasts were wonderfully responsive to his touch. So much so
that he wondered if the rest of her body would be as responsive. His hands
began to feather downward over her slender torso. Her quivering, aching
breasts silently cried out for the return of those hands. Her flat belly
shrank beneath the fingers that gently kindled little flames within its
depths, and smoothed hot desire over her perfumed skin. She could not
suppress the pained moan that escaped her.

"Oh, Basil, my love! 'Tis so very sweet. How I burn! Oh, kiss me!"

Slowly he pressed his lips against hers. She kissed him back with intense passion, her mouth pressing firmly upon his. Her pointed little
tongue running quickly along his mouth to plunge within and stroke fervently at his own tongue. Her hands reached up to caress his lean body.
Frantically her fingers sought him, sliding over his shoulders and down
his back to caress his tight buttocks. Her innocent touch caused an ex-
plosion of his own passions. Shifting his body so that they lay side by side
he took her slim hand and drew it down to his manhood. Without any
hesitation her fingers fastened about the smooth warm shaft. She fondled
him gently and lovingly. To his great surprise, for he had not believed
himself so deeply roused, her touch caused his seed to spurt almost immediately over her warm hand. He groaned, half-shamed, but Mairin was
delighted.

"I have never seen a man's seed before," she said, her own passion
ebbing as her curiosity took over. "Imagine that a child comes from
that!" Sitting up she released her hold upon him, and examined the
sticky liquid.

There was nothing he could do but laugh and ruefully he did. "I'm afraid I have sinned by spilling my seed where it will not take root," he said.

"Is this the first time you have done such a thing, my lord? I thought that a man's seed could only be expelled into a woman's womb. I see now that it is not so."

"No, it is not so, my love. A man can release his seed anywhere when he is aroused. Only in a woman's womb will it take root, however, and grow into a child."

"Tell me of other places where a man might release his seed, Basil. I want to learn to give you pleasure as you have given me pleasure."

For a moment he considered her request, but realized she was still too inexperienced. "I would make no mystery of it, my darling," he said, "but I should prefer demonstrating to you all these delicious things. You must be patient, however. For now, I prefer to end our lessons. We must bathe for we are invited to take our evening meal with the emperor."

Mairin pouted. She lacked the wiles that would have helped her to get around her husband. "I will be glad," she said, "when we are in our own home, and separated from Constantinople by the Bosporus. The emperor and his meals are most inconvenient!"

"By late winter," he promised her. "The water supply for our palace was not as near as I had anticipated. An aqueduct is being built, but it takes time."

"I want to be alone with you," Mairin complained, and he smiled.

She was suddenly very much in love with him, and jealous of every minute he spent away from her. He had given her a taste for passion. Mairin wanted to drink deeply and often from that well. She took to lingering in her bath, and even purchased a slavegirl who was a skilled masseuse. Zoe spent several hours a day ministering to her mistress's body so that it would be flawless for the prince. Mairin found that she craved Basil's touch. She sought all sorts of ways to attract his attention, for the more he petted and caressed her, the more eager she was for his loving.

Basil did not disappoint his bride. Although he still believed her too young to completely consummate their union she was anxious to learn everything else that could give them pleasure. He knew that the time was drawing near when he would be unable to restrain his desire for this beautiful girl. If Mairin in her innocence craved total fulfillment, Basil ached with his knowledge of what their passion could be.

When she was not at her lessons with Master Simeon or Peter the Musician, and Basil not at court attending on his cousin, they were in each other's arms. Her breasts had thrived with his attention. They were now perfect smooth globes of lush flesh in whose deep valley he enjoyed slipping his hard length, being careful to remove it just before his crisis. She was not shy of playing with him. Indeed one day as they fondled each other she bent her head down and boldly took him into her mouth.

When he gasped with surprise she released him, and looking up asked, "Is such a thing forbidden?"

"Only by fools and hypocrites," he answered her, and gently pushed her head back down so she might continue pleasuring him. When she had driven him almost to the brink he bade her cease. Then laying her upon her back he slipped between her slender legs drawing them up and over his shoulders as he loved her in the same gentle fashion.

As his tongue plied its tender torture the gates of knowledge opened just a bit wider for Mairin. Until now she had believed that even their eventual consummation could be little better than the delightful pleasures they gave and received of one another during their long evenings together. Now in this blazing moment she knew how ignorant she really was of what lay ahead. She felt suddenly out of control. Unable to stop herself she soared amid the very stars and moon for what seemed like an eternity. Then once more she found herself within the safety of his strong arms, and he looked down upon her, smiling.

"I cannot wait much longer to possess you, my love," he whispered to her. "You have become life itself for me, Mairin."

"I don't want to wait either," she returned. "I love you, my prince. It has been eight months since our marriage was celebrated. I am now fourteen, and ready to be a woman, but let us wait just a few weeks longer. We will be moving into our palace soon. I do not want to consummate our marriage here in the Boucoleon, Basil. I want to consummate it on that first night in our own home. Would it not be a favorable omen for our future happiness to conceive our first child, our son, in our own home?"

Her words touched him. As deeply as he desired her the idea of celebrating their first passion for one another in their own palace pleased him. He caressed her cheek with the back of his hand. His turquoise eyes were warm with his love and his admiration for her. She was indeed the perfect wife for him. Her sense of tradition was instinctive and admirable.

"I shall see that our home is habitable as quickly as possible," he promised her. "In the meantime we shall keep from one another. It will put a fine edge upon our desire, Mairin. You are a skillful and natural student of passion, my love. I want our consumption to be so perfect that you will remember it all of your life with joy."

"But I cannot do without your touch, my lord! You are necessary to my very survival!" She flattered him artlessly.

"Tonight I shall satisfy all your lustful little cravings, my love, but come the dawn I shall take myself to another room and there remain, until we enter into our own home. I want you as hungry for me, my beautiful bride, as I am at this very moment for you!"

He took her into his arms, and kissed her. "You are delicious," he murmured against her mouth. "I think I am mad to make such a sacrifice as separating myself from you."

"Perhaps," she teased him, "it would be better if we began our celibacy now, my lord."

"Oh no, my fair enchantress, you shall not escape me this night!" he laughed. Then sweeping her up into his arms he carried her to their bed, and they lay naked together.

Ardently they caressed one another with hands and lips. He suckled upon her breasts and she sighed with contentment as the now familiar darts of excitement raced through her eager body. Then his hand was stroking the soft insides of her half-parted thighs. She quivered as for the very first time his fingers moved up to slip between the tender folds of pink flesh.

He felt her stiffen with resistance, and his voice soothed her. "No, Mairin, do not be afraid. I would only explore your sweetness a bit." A gentle finger rubbed her, and then was delicately inserted into her trembling body. "Ahh, my love, how I wish I might pierce you with my love-shaft instead of a finger," he whispered to her.

He moved the finger rhythmically within her and as her fear dissolved she felt a new excitement. Her body would not stay still, and she thrust her hips up to meet the movement of his hand. "Oh, Basil! It is good!" she sighed as suddenly a hot melting feeling suffused her entire being.

He bent his head, and kissed her passionately. He was pleased that this first serious penetration had not frightened her. He had learned what he needed to know. Her maidenhead was lodged tight, and would, when the consummation of their union took place, require all his skill and patience to breach. Raising himself up he said, "As always, my love, you are perfection. How I adore you!"

Her spirits soared. She loved and was loved. She was desired and she desired in return. During the next few days there was a glow and an excitement about her that had not been there before. Eada saw it, and unable to help herself, questioned Mairin.

"Are you happy, my child?"

"Oh, yes, mother!"

Eada debated with herself a moment. Then she said, "Have you yet . . . ?" She hesitated, but Mairin read her mother's thoughts.

"Not yet, but I am ready, and Basil agrees, mother. We have decided to wait, however, until we move across the water into our own home. I want my son conceived beneath his own roof where he will first see the light of day."

"I have not yet spoken to you on what you should expect, my child," said Eada. "I would not have you unprepared now that your time is near."

"I do not think there is anything I have not already learned, mother. It is true we have not yet consummated our union, but Basil and I have played at all manner of bedsport these past months. I have found everything quite wonderful," Mairin said somewhat smugly.

"But has he warned you of the pain?" Eada asked her daughter.

"Pain?" Mairin looked somewhat startled. "What pain? There has been no mention of pain!"

Eada smiled softly. How just like a man, she thought, to stress only the pleasures of an initial encounter. "You could, Mairin, experience some pain upon first becoming a woman," she told her daughter. "It is nothing to be fearful of for it is quite natural, and to be expected. There will also be a slight bleeding when the virgin shield is pierced. It only happens the first time. After that there will be neither pain, nor bleeding. There should only be pleasures for you and Basil for you love one another."

"Is there still pleasure for you and father?" Mairin asked boldly. Then she blushed, and lowered her eyes.

Eada laughed. "Yes!" she said, and her blue eyes twinkled. "Even after all these years there is yet pleasure in the coupling for your father and me. We love each other, Mairin. There is the difference. One cannot sustain joy where there is no love. May there always be love between you and Basil as there is between your father and me."

"Oh, there will be, mother!" said Mairin with the deep assurance of every bride who can see no further than tomorrow. "He says that his every thought both waking and sleeping is of me! I am so very fortunate that he loves me!"

"You love her?" Bellisarius' usually controlled voice sounded strangely high-pitched in the prince's ears as with his habitual restless energy he prowled about the magnificently furnished anteroom of his private apart-

ments in the Boucoleon Palace. As Byzantium's most famous actor of the times it was his privilege to be housed there at the emperor's expense.

"Dear God, Basil! Why do you not simply take a dagger and stab me through the heart? When you announced your intentions to marry you swore to me that you would never stop loving me even if you did intend to wed to beget heirs for your family. In the eight months since that day you have not once visited me as my lover. Still I remained loyal to you for I have never known you to lie.

"Now you come to me and you tell me that you love the bitch! You have but come today to bid me farewell! *I love you!* Does that mean nothing to you at all? You are cruel! *Cruel!*" He flung himself upon a couch that was covered in red satin and cloth of gold. Clutching a green-and-gold-striped pillow to his chest he stared darkly at the prince with a look that was part anger, part jealousy, part hate.

"I am not like you, Bellisarius," Basil said quietly. "In my entire lifetime I have had but two male lovers. My first lover was as you know my cousin Eugenius Demertzis. We were both only thirteen and fearful of approaching a woman lest we be rebuffed. We experimented upon each other until we had enough confidence to tumble my aunt's slavegirl. Until you all my other lovers have been women. I have always enjoyed women. You are not like me. You have never loved a woman nor are you even capable of it. How many times have you admitted to me that the idea of making love to a woman repels you? Sometimes I believe you are a female soul caught within a man's body."

"Then why did you become involved with me?" demanded the actor petulantly.

"Do you remember when we first met, Bellisarius? I had been involved with three women, and had discovered that each of the bitches had been playing me false while filling her jewel chests with my very generous baubles. Then to add insult to my injury Helena Monomachus attempted to pawn her bastard off upon me. I was angry. Maybe even bored with the female of the species. Perhaps I felt I needed a change, and a male lover was certainly a change. Besides, I liked you." He reached out and patted the actor's shoulder comfortingly. "You are my best friend, Bellisarius. Please, I beg you, try to understand my feelings. Mairin is everything I have ever sought in a woman. Oh yes, she is young, but she has such promise! Sometimes in the night I awaken, and fear that I shall not be able to keep up with her one day." He smiled to himself. "May God help me, but I am so in love with her! Can you not comprehend that, dear Bellisarius?"

"Love?" The actor sneered bitterly, his face a vicious mask. "You do not know how to love, Basil. You know only the pleasure in possessing a new toy, which is precisely what your precious bride is to you, my prince! Once the novelty of fucking her has worn off you will seek another pretty diversion! Poor little girl! I actually feel sympathy for her though I have never met her. They say she is a sweet thing, but when you have drained her sweetness away you will discard her for another new toy even as you are discarding me, Basil, and I hate you for it!"

"You are wrong! I love her!" said Basil, stung by Bellisarius' unkind words. "We have not yet even consummated our marriage. I believed her too young when we married, but now she is ready for love. In three days' time we will consummate our love in our own home."

Seating himself beside Bellisarius he flung his arm about the actor who shrank rather pointedly from this casual embrace. "Oh, come, my friend! Be happy for me! There are many who seek to be your lover. You cannot deny that to me of all people! How many times did we laugh over your lovesick swains? Tell me truly, Bellisarius. Have you not been approached at least a hundred times over these last few months?"

"Of course I have been approached," sniffed Bellisarius, "and by men of greater importance than you, Basil. I am greatly desired." He preened, unconsciously arching his neck, a faint smile upon his face which faded as quickly as it had come. "I, however, remained true to our love. You have not! I never even allowed myself one tiny tryst."

"I am sorry," said the prince. "You are my friend, and I never meant to hurt you. I thought I could love you both, but I cannot," he finished honestly.

"And so you chose *her* over me," Bellisarius said. Suddenly there was a note of deep sadness in his voice as if he had resigned himself to the prince's words. "Why?" he asked plaintively.

"I could not help myself," said Basil. "I know now that I was hers from the very first moment I saw her."

Bellisarius sighed. It was a sound of such infinite pain that Basil felt tears pricking at the back of his eyelids. "All the love I have for you cannot bind you to me if you do not wish to be held, my prince. You have broken my heart as you will one day break hers, but I am no fool. Loving you as I do I want your happiness even if it means that you are leaving me." He arose from the couch. "Come! We will drink a last goblet of wine together. Then you must go, and return to your innocent wife." With slow mincing steps he walked across the room. A silver tray with goblets and decanters sat upon a round marble-and-gold table with great claw feet of green agate. "She has never known about us, has she?" he said thoughtfully.

"No," answered the prince. "Mairin is a true innocent. A love such as is sometimes shared between two men is not within her scope of knowledge. She would be shocked by it. She was not brought up here in Constantinople where such things are not considered unusual."

Bellisarius had reached the table. He nodded as if in agreement with Basil. Upon the first finger of his right hand was a large ruby. His body shielding the tray with its goblets and decanter from the prince, he flipped open a secret catch upon the dark red stone revealing in its hollowed interior a fine black powder. Skillfully he spilled half the powder into each of the two silver-chased goblets, quickly pouring atop it a blood-red Grecian vintage. The powder instantly dissolved, disappearing into a swirl of sweet wine. The actor swung smilingly about to come forward with the two goblets.

Gracefully he offered one to the prince. "To what shall we drink?" he said. "Since it is to be the last toast we shall ever share between us it should be a special one."

"Let us drink that we each find true happiness," said Basil, "for, dear Bellisarius, it saddens me to think that I have caused you any pain. I would have you as happy this very minute as I am."

Bellisarius smiled broadly. "Suddenly I am, my prince," he said, and raising the goblet to his lips he drank it down. Basil followed suit.

When the cups had been placed upon the table again the actor said with sudden and surprising venom in his voice, "Your precious princess will soon learn of how easily you betray someone you claim to love, my prince! She will shortly know the terrible pain you have visited upon me, and she will be forced to live with that pain for the rest of her life which I pray will be a long one! When we are found together, Basil, there will be those only too willing to reveal our relationship, and all its attendant gossip, to your wife. For me the greatest revenge I will have upon you both is the knowledge that she will never, ever be completely certain that you really loved her! You see, my prince, you will not be alive to either comfort her, or to deny the rumors!" He laughed a sharp high cackle of mirth. Then he staggered suddenly and fell to his knees.

As he did Basil felt a cruel, sharp pain knife through his own guts. "*Bellisarius*," he cried, "*what have you done?*" Then he, too, fell to his knees to find himself facing the actor whose face was a mask of vengeful triumph.

"*Done?*" Bellisarius was fast growing pale. "I have done nothing more than to insure that you will always be with me, my darling! She cannot have you for you are mine, Basil! Mine for now and all eternity! *Mine!*" And so saying he fell forward into the prince's arms quite dead. His weight tumbled the weakened man backward onto the magnificent thick red-and-black wool carpet.

Basil's whole body felt numb. Unable to move he lay upon his back, Bellisarius clasped within his helpless embrace, his blond head as if in sleep upon the prince's chest. As his murderer's words penetrated his befogged brain Basil felt his own heart slowly coming to a stop. With a last burst of energy he cried out but one word, "*Mairin!*" and then he died.

For several long minutes there was silence within the beautiful room. Then slowly the door to the antechamber opened, and a young boy hurried in. Seeing the bodies upon the floor he stopped, gasping, then bravely he made his way to where the bodies lay. Being careful not to disturb them, he reached into his tunic and drew out a small mirror which he placed first beneath the prince's nostrils, and then the actor's. The glass remained clear.

The boy sighed, and rising left the room to hurry off through the maze of corridors that connected the various sections of the palace with one another. Reaching Basil's apartments he smoothed his tunic neatly, and boldly entering, asked to speak with the princess.

"She is with her lady mother," said Nara, thinking this boy seemed of little importance. "She cannot be disturbed."

"I must speak with her!" the boy insisted. "*I must!*"

"Well you can't, my lad, and that is that," replied Nara bossily.

Suddenly the boy who was no more than ten began to cry. "My master is dead, and the prince with him," he sobbed. "I do not know what to do. I thought the princess could help," he sniveled, wiping his nose with the back of his hand.

"*What?*" Nara screeched. "What is this you say? Dagda! Dagda, come quickly!" She reached out with a strong hand yanking the boy into the center of the room where he suddenly found himself facing a giant with shoulder-length white hair. The boy quailed with fright.

"Don't be afraid, lad," said Dagda, his deep kindly voice belying his fierce appearance. "What is the matter, and who are you?"

"I am Paul. I belong to Bellisarius, the great actor. I have just come from my master's apartments. He and Prince Basil are lying upon the floor. Both are quite dead, sir."

"Lord have mercy upon us all!" cried Nara, only to be silenced by a look from Dagda.

"You are quite certain that they are dead, lad?" Dagda gently questioned the boy.

"Yes, my lord. I took my mirror and held it to their nostrils. There was no fog upon the glass. It was my master's bath time. I only entered the room to remind him, for if the water was not the proper temperature he would beat me. I was not spying upon them!" The boy now began to tremble in fear as he realized how very serious a matter this really was.

"Why did you come here, lad?" said Dagda.

"Is not this the apartment of Prince Basil and his wife, sir? It is Prince Basil who lies dead with my master. Where else would I have gone?"

"Woman!" Dagda pierced Nara with a cold look. "Keep your wits about you and your mouth shut until I see this tragedy."

Nara nodded, very frightened.

Bidding the boy remain where he stood by Nara, the Irishman ran back through the corridors to Bellisarius' apartments. Looking quickly about to be certain he wasn't observed, he entered. Dagda knew the rumors of the prince's relationship with the actor. He also knew that it had ended with Basil's marriage to Mairin. Now as he saw the two men clasped in their obscene and deathly embrace, his lip curled scornfully.

Then he began to assess the situation more clearly. It became important that the bodies be moved so that the scandal not hurt Mairin. Pulling Bellisarius off the prince, he wrinkled his nose in distaste as the actor's cloying perfume rose to assail him. He moved Basil's body over to the red-and-gold couch and laid it back amid the pillows. It was the best he could do. At least the two men weren't entwined in that perversion of an embrace any longer. With a sigh he departed the room, hurrying through the palace corridors to the rooms of the court physician, Demetrios.

Over the many months he had lived in Constantinople Dagda had made friends with Demetrios. The two played at chess in the evenings. Now Dagda needed that friendship. Unhindered he entered into the physician's chambers, and finding his friend alone quickly explained his need. Demetrios followed Dagda back to the apartments of Bellisarius. Shaking his head at the futility of it all he moved to examine the two bodies.

"Poison," he said quietly, sniffing first at the region about the prince's lips, and then moving across the room to check first the dregs in the cups and the decanter. "It's not in the decanter. It was put into the cups itself."

"What is it?" demanded Dagda. "Do you know? How was it administered, and by whom?"

"I can't be certain of what it is," said Demetrios, "except probably some particularly virulent and highly distilled form of nightshade for which there is no antidote. It worked almost instantly, Dagda. That I can tell for there is virtually no distortion of the bodies. It would have been either powder or a liquid. We'll never know now as we will never know whether it was a suicide pact between the prince and his lover, or a suicide and murder. We cannot even know which one of them initiated it."

"The prince was not the actor's lover any longer," said Dagda. "He was faithful to my mistress from the day they wed. They were looking forward to leaving the Boucoleon for their own home across the water in just another day or two."

"Then it is likely that Bellisarius, learning of this, and having been ignored by Prince Basil these last months, lured him here with the intention of murdering him, and taking his own life," said Demetrios.

"Will you swear to it?" demanded Dagda. "The prince's death will break my lady's heart for she loved him with all her being. She never knew of his prior relationships. Not in her wildest imaginings would she believe that Prince Basil would have loved a man. It is not our way."

The physician nodded with understanding. "There is no need, my friend, to distress the poor lady, any more than she will be. I will attest to the fact that Bellisarius murdered Prince Basil before taking his own life. I cannot stop the gossip that will ensue, Dagda, and believe me there will be gossip. The prince's previous relationships are well known. Though your lady has been fortunate to escape the rumors until now, she will no longer have that luxury. There will be those who will not believe that Bellisarius murdered the prince. They will say that the two men, lovers still, decided to die together rather than be separated, which they would have been when Prince Basil and his wife left Constantinople. This is a cruel court."

"I must go and tell my mistress," said Dagda.

"She does not yet know?"

Dagda shook his head in the negative, and for a moment his shoulders slumped wearily. "She is like my own child," he said. "Her mother gave her to my care upon her deathbed. I have protected and cared for her all her life, but I cannot keep her from this pain, Demetrios. Even now I feel as if a sword is piercing my own heart."

"Let me come with you," said the physician. "The princess may need a sedative for the shock, but do not fear, my friend. She is young and healthy, and time will heal this terrible wound even as it heals all others. Tell me though, is she with child?"

"No," said Dagda. "Of that I am certain."

"What a pity. Sometimes a baby gives a widow an even greater reason for living."

Quickly the two men made their way back to Mairin.

"Where have you been?" demanded Nara. "The princess is just now coming from her bath. She has asked if *he* is back yet. Are they really dead? What happened? If she sees this boy she will want to know who he is. What am I to say?"

"You are to say nothing, Nara," said Dagda, and he turned to Paul. "You will now serve the court physician, Master Demetrios, boy. You will say nothing of this matter to anyone. Nor will you speak of the prince's past relationship with your former master. Do you understand?"

"Yes, my lord," said the boy, his dark eyes large and frightened. He considered himself lucky to have gotten off so easily. It was not unusual for slaves who had witnessed sensitive matters to be blinded, have their tongues torn out, or be otherwise maimed or killed to silence them. He could not suppress a shudder, which both men saw.

"You will not be harmed, Paul," said Demetrios. "You have but to be discreet. I have need of a bright boy like yourself. I shall teach you to grind medicines for me."

"We must tell her," said Dagda, and the physician nodded.

"Shall I fetch the lady Eada and our lord Aldwine, Dagda?" asked Nara.

"Yes," he answered her. "Tell them that the prince has been murdered. They must come quickly for their daughter's sake."

"Dagda!"

They turned to find Mairin standing in the doorway between the bedchamber and the anteroom. Nara gave a little shriek, and ran from the room.

"Dagda, what is this that you say? Where is my husband?" Mairin was paler than he had ever seen her. "Where is Basil?" Mairin repeated.

There was no easy way. "He is dead," Dagda said quietly.

"*No!*" She reached out to cling to the doorframe for her knees felt weak, and she wasn't certain she was capable of standing by herself any longer. "*You lie!*"

His eyes filled with tears which he quickly blinked back as he said quietly to her, "Have I ever lied to you, my child? Would I willingly hurt you?"

"No!" This time her voice became a whimper. "Not dead, Dagda. *Please, not dead!*"

With a groan of pain, for his own heart was breaking, Dagda took Mairin in his arms. Holding her protectively within his embrace he begged her, "Weep, child. Weep!"

Mairin pulled from his grasp. Her violet eyes were dark with her anguish. She was ashen in color. She opened her mouth to speak, but no sound issued forth. Then without warning she crumpled unconscious to the floor.

Chapter 7

"My son is dead! It is your daughter's fault!" Ileana Ducas accused. Her dark eyes were spilling over with pain. "Oh, Basil, I loved you," she wept, "but you never really understood how I adored you. Now you are gone!"

"My *daughter's fault?*" Eada was outraged! "It was not my daughter who administered poison to Basil. It was his lover!"

"If your daughter had truly made my son happy he would not have returned to Bellisarius! What kind of a woman was she to drive him into the arms of another man? What terrible things did she do to Basil that he sought solace elsewhere?"

"Mairin loved Basil, and he loved her," said Eada in a quiet voice. "She is innocent in this matter. You, I am told, are not. Whatever Basil was, you as his mother are partly responsible."

"What do you dare imply?" demanded Ileana coldly.

"I imply nothing, princess. It is common knowledge in Constantinople that your late husband kept half a dozen young boys for his pleasure. He openly consorted with men of such foul reputation that even the church could not ignore it, and so they excommunicated him. Did you blame yourself for your husband's behavior as you attempt to blame Mairin for Basil's behavior? Did you think that because we are strangers here we would not eventually learn your family's history? Had we known it before our daughter's marriage to your son took place there would have been no marriage.

"In our land passion such as Basil shared with Bellisarius is considered illicit, ungodly, and shameful. Even with all my years I did not know of such things until my husband was forced to explain them to me.

"How dare you come into my home and accuse my poor child of causing your son's demise. In the four days since Basil's death Mairin has lain unconscious. She is devastated by what has happened to her husband. Her husband, who was murdered by his male lover! Where is my child's crime, princess? She is as innocent as a newborn lamb! Would that Basil, may God assoil his tormented soul, have been so innocent! Beware lest anything happen to my daughter because of your wanton disregard for her happiness. I shall lay a curse upon your family that shall not be lifted until after our Lord's second coming!

"Now get from my sight! Never again do I wish to lay eyes upon you! You but remind me of the terrible suffering Mairin has been caused. May God and his Blessed Mother help you! If she does not regain consciousness I will kill you with my bare hands! I swear it!"

Ileana Ducas' composure left her as she stared horrified at Eada. Never before had she noticed how big the Saxon woman was. But how could she not see it now as Eada towered over her, her long dark red hair unbound, and swirling about her in her passionate rage; her blue, blue eyes flashing with menace. Ileana believed Eada when the Saxon threatened her with death. With a shriek she turned and fled the furious woman.

"Good riddance!" Eada ground out through clenched teeth as her husband put gentle calming hands upon her shoulders.

"I do not think she will be back," said Aldwine. "You have quite frightened her, my love. It reminds me of a time not so long ago when the women of our people were as fierce fighters as the men."

"Fiercer," said Eada emphatically.

He laughed softly, turning her toward him to hold her against his chest. It was that familiar gesture of comfort that caused Eada to burst into tears. "No, no, my love," he soothed her. "Do not cry. I bring good news. Mairin awoke a short while ago. Before she might remember and question, Demetrios gave her a calming draught. She is now sleeping a natural sleep."

"Th-thank God!" Eada sobbed, and cried all the harder.

Aldwine Athelsbeorn allowed his wife to vent her relief. When her weeping finally eased he said, "When Mairin is strong enough to travel, I want you to take her home to England, Eada. I do not want her remaining in Constantinople. Everything she knows here would be a reminder of Basil. He saw her when she first arrived, monopolized her time, and then quickly married her. Our daughter had no time to make other friends, have other memories of this city.

"For her Constantinople is Basil, and Basil Constantinople. If she remains she will pine away. I have no doubt she loved him, but I will not allow her to waste her life mourning him. He was a charming man. His intentions toward her were good, but he was not worthy of her, Eada. Prince or no, he was not worthy of her!

"I should not have given my consent to their marriage. My ambition for Mairin blinded me. I must bear the greater responsibility for the pain she has been caused, but I will not let her be pained further.

"This is not the city I remember as a youth. Perhaps, though, my young eyes saw only the beauty of Constantinople. Now I see its decay. It will soon be spring, Eada. Take our daughter and travel with the troop of Varangian Guards who are returning to England for home leave. I will make all the arrangements."

"But what of you?" she asked. "Can you not come home with us? Surely under these circumstances you can leave the delegation in other hands, Aldwine. Your work here is almost done. You have said it yourself!"

"That is true, my love," he agreed, "but hammering out the last bits of a trade treaty is perhaps the trickiest part of all. It is what I was sent here for, and I cannot go until it is done. The latest messages from Brand say that as the king grows weaker, the queen continues to agitate for the succession of her brother. I would prefer that you and Mairin were safely at Aelfleah should Edward die. Brand has done well, but in my absence he will need your guidance should he be forced to defend our holding."

"But if the king dies," fretted Eada, "how will you return to us?"

"It will be easier to reach England without the burden of two women," he replied. "It took us over two months to reach Constantinople, Eada. I can cut that time in half traveling without you. Send me word of the king's death, and I will be home within the month. I swear it!"

"I dislike being apart from you, my husband, but it is now our daughter for whom I must be concerned. When Mairin is able to travel we will leave."

It was not until the second week in April that they departed Constantinople. At first when Mairin had fully awakened she could not remember anything of what had happened since her arrival in Constantinople. She was once again half-child, half-woman. That, said the physician Demetrios, was not a good thing. Pain blocked her memories of Basil and their marriage and her avoidance of the truth could have resulted in an even worse trauma. Mairin had to be made to remember so she might face her anguish honestly and overcome it.

The emperor insisted Demetrios move into the Garden Palace so he might treat Mairin, who at first could not understand why the physician was there. Then the dawning knowledge within her that almost eighteen months had passed since her arrival in Constantinople, months that were blank to her, frightened her into cooperation with Demetrios. Slowly the memories began to return. With them came the pain.

Mairin, her hair braided up and covered, was accompanied by Eada and Demetrios as she began to revisit all the places she had first seen with Basil. One afternoon they entered into Hagia Eirene. Looking around her in the soft golden light Mairin unexpectedly burst into tears. Confused, she could only look to her mother for reassurance. Gathering her daughter into her arms Eada crooned reassuringly. Then suddenly one evening several days later as they all sat at the evening meal Mairin looked up and said calmly to Demetrios, "My husband is dead, isn't he?"

About the table they all froze, shocked with the suddenness of her question.

Regaining his senses first Demetrios answered her, "Yes, highness. Prince Basil is dead these two months past."

"How did he die?" she asked, her voice still frighteningly calm.

"He was murdered. Poisoned by his old friend the actor Bellisarius, who then took his own life."

"Why?" The single word was sharp.

There was a deep silence within the room. Then Eada said, "Dearest, does it matter now? Poor Basil is dead and buried. You are a widow. I thank God you have at last remembered it! It is time to begin to forget once more. To start your life anew."

"Why did Bellisarius kill my husband?" demanded Mairin again, a hard edge to her voice now. "I want to know! I want to know why my husband is dead!"

Aldwine Athelsbeorn looked at his daughter seeing suddenly that the child he had so dearly loved and protected was gone. It was an adult face that looked directly at them. It was adult eyes that questioned, and demanded answers to those questions. "Tell her the truth," he said.

"No!" Eada whispered, her eyes brimming with tears. "Do not pain her further! How much more can you ask her to bear?"

"Do you want her mourning him forever?" demanded Aldwine angrily. "I do not! I want her to be free to renew her life, and go forward. She cannot if she does not know the truth."

"Yes! Tell me the truth," said Mairin fiercely.

"Once, before you were married," began Demetrios, "your husband and Bellisarius were lovers. There are some men who cleave only to women. There are some who can cleave only to other men. Then there are men like your husband who first enjoy women, but occasionally need the diversion of a male lover. When Prince Basil married you he had fallen in love with you. In marrying you he deserted Bellisarius.

"To our knowledge, never in the months of your marriage did the prince visit his former lover. We can only guess why he went the day of his death. We believe it was to tell Bellisarius that it was indeed finished between them. Certainly Bellisarius must have felt betrayed and hurt by the prince's words. Perhaps he was even angry. We must assume that Bellisarius hid his true feelings. Unknown to the prince he poisoned two goblets of wine, and then cajoled your husband into a farewell drink. Both died swiftly, and relatively without pain."

Mairin nodded as if the physician's explanation was totally plausible and acceptable to her. "Thank you," she said. There was a frightening remoteness about her.

"Will you not weep for your husband, princess?" questioned Demetrios gently.

She shook her head. "No," she said. "I cannot weep for Basil. Your explanation of his death is pure conjecture, Demetrios, for you were not there. You cannot be certain that my husband deserted his lover upon our marriage. My marriage was never consummated. I shall spend my life wondering if Basil's reasons for it were honest. Did he really love me? Was his concern truly for my well-being? Or perhaps having gained possession of his perfect princess was he repelled by her? I shall always wonder when I remember our short time together where he went each time he left me. Was he really where he said he had been, or was he with Bellisarius? I shall always wonder if he really meant to leave Constantinople for our own home, or if it was to merely be a gilded prison for me. Was the thought of being separated so terrible that Basil and Bellisarius died together rather than be parted?

"Basil said he loved me. In my innocence I believed him. There are other things I will remember. I will remember his kisses, and his hands upon my body. Having this new knowledge you have given me, Demetrios, I will wonder if he truly enjoyed the innocent lovemaking that we shared. Or whether each time he touched me he but held back his disgust, and wished I were the actor. Perhaps one day when my pain is not so great I will weep for my husband, physician. I may even forgive him, but now is not the time. I cannot waste my precious tears upon a man who has brutalized my innocence and destroyed my dreams."

Demetrios nodded his understanding. "Someday you will love anew, princess. When you do, these memories will fade in their importance for you. It is then that you will weep for Prince Basil. As for me my task is finished. You have faced the truth, and can heal. Now leave Constantinople, and return to your England. You will find happiness again one day."

"Yes," said Mairin, "I want to go home to England. I shall never leave Aelfleah again."

"You will leave Aelfleah when you marry to go to your husband's home," said Aldwine.

"*Marry?*" said Mairin bitterly. "I will never marry again, father! *Never!*"

The thegn silenced his wife's impending protest with a look. He put an arm about his daughter, gently hugging her. "We need make no decisions now," he said. "In time you will change your mind, Mairin. Basil's death has left you a wealthy woman. That wealth will buy you a good match."

"I want nothing of Basil's wealth!" she cried.

"Do not be foolish," he replied sharply. "As his legal widow that wealth is now yours. Wealth will buy you a secure future."

"Give it to his mother! I want nothing but to go home and live out my days in peace!"

"Take your daughter to her bed," said Aldwine sternly to Eada. "She is hysterical, and obviously still not herself."

In the end, however, the thegn compromised with his stubborn daughter. He took from the prince's treasury enough gold to give Mairin a dowry worthy of a princess. He took for his child all the fabulous jewelry that her husband had lavished upon her. Everything else he gave at Mairin's request to Princess Ileana. Everything but the palace that Basil had built for his bride across the Bosporus. That Mairin ordered torn down, and the land donated in Basil's memory to the church.

"Why do you simply not sell it?" Eada asked her daughter.

"Sell a monument to a love that never really existed?" she said scornfully and bitterly. "No one should ever live in it, mother. It is curst!" That was the last she spoke of it, but her final days in Constantinople were spent on a terrace overlooking the sea where she watched for hours with grim satisfaction the destruction of the palace that Basil Ducas had built for her.

She shed no tears as she and Eada left Constantinople. Indeed having

landed thegn, and she the daughter of another. They would be social equals. Certainly after her period of mourning had expired her father would want her remarried. Marriage or the convent—that was a woman's only choice. That red hair of hers didn't betoken a spiritual celibate. He would wager she could keep a man hotter than hellfire itself on a cold winter's night. He had wanted her from the first moment he had seen her. Eric Longsword grinned to himself. He would allow nothing to stand in his way for despite what Mairin said about life, he didn't intend to be denied his pleasure.

They traveled west across Europe. This time Eada did not grow ill and tired. Their pace was brisk for they were anxious to reach England quickly. Most of the returning soldiers had been away for years. They would visit with their families before returning to the emperor's service, but others, aware of the danger facing England, would stay to aid their families in the coming power struggle.

Each day the sun stayed longer, extending their travel time.

They reached the Italian kingdoms, and traveled swiftly through them along the incredibly beautiful and rugged Mediterranean coastline. Finally they arrived in the Languedoc to traverse roads that followed the great rivers of the various French kingdoms. Then one day they topped a rise in the duchy of Flanders to see before them in the sunshine of an early June afternoon the sparkling blue-gray waters of the English Channel. The Saxon soldiers gave a mighty cheer.

"It is so clear you can see our homeland!" Eada cried happily. "If we embark tonight we can be in England by morning!"

Mairin laughed for the first time in months. "Oh, mother! How father would tease you if he could hear you now. He was so proud to have shown you some of the world, and you cared not. You just want to go home! Well, so do I!" She flung an arm about Eada's shoulders, and hugged her.

Eada turned her head and looked into her daughter's face.

"Why, Mairin, my child, you sound happy for the first time in weeks. If you are, then I thank the Blessed Mother for it!"

"I do not know if I am happy, mother. I do know that with each mile we have traveled away from Constantinople I have become less bitter about what happened. I do not think the doubts and the sorrow will ever leave me," she sighed. "At least I no longer hate Basil for what happened, and I am as glad as you are to be returning home."

"Perhaps young Eric Longsword has something to do with your lightening mood," noted Eada. "He is a handsome rascal, and as merry as a drunkard in his cups. I have seen him seek out every opportunity to ride by your side."

Mairin smiled. "He thinks to court me, mother. I have not encouraged him. I do not really like him. Once we reach England we will go our separate ways. I shall not be bothered by him again."

"He would not be a bad catch," mused the practical Eada. "His father has almost as much land as does yours. Of course you'd have to have several sons fairly quickly to cement your position. The men of the Danelaw are not above taking several wives despite their professed Christianity."

"Having their sons is no guarantee of keeping your husband in the Danelaw," said Mairin wisely. "Has not Harold Godwinson put Edyth Swansneck aside? Is she not the mother of his only three sons?"

"Yes," acknowledged Eada, "he did indeed put poor Edyth Swansneck aside in order to marry the earl of Mercia's sister."

"The murder of whose first husband Harold Godwinson neatly arranged. He thinks by taking Edyth of Mercia to wive he can bind Mercia to him," snapped Mairin. "Thank you, no, mother!"

"You could do worse than Eric Longsword," said Eada calmly.

"I have no intention of remarrying, mother."

"Do you wish to enter holy orders?" Eada asked, knowing the answer.

"Of course not!"

"Then you must remarry, Mairin. There is nothing else for a woman. It does not have to be Eric Longsword, but you must eventually take another husband."

"Why can I not stay home with you and father?" demanded Mairin.

"Aldwine and I will not always be here. You know it. Whoever Brand takes to wive will not welcome another female in a house that will one day be hers. What will happen to you if you don't remarry?"

"Could I not have a little house for my own, mother, and live by myself?"

"What nonsense you prattle, Mairin! Who would till your lands, and hunt for you? Who would protect you in times of danger? Do not tell me Dagda, for one day he will not be here either. You have been hurt deeply by what happened in Constantinople, and rightly so. But do not let that brief encounter with Basil Ducas destroy your life. He loved you, Mairin. I know it as your mother. He would not want you to stand paralyzed with fear for the rest of your days.

"You do not have to remarry immediately. Perhaps it is better you don't until this matter of the English succession is settled. Your father and

I have spoken on it, and we are sure there will be a war. There is no escaping it. You are a wealthy woman. There will be many suitors for your hand one day, Mairin."

"Suitors seeking my gold," said Mairin with a knowing chuckle.

Eada nodded. "Yes," she said honestly, "but I know you will find the right man to love. A man who will love you in return as well as loving your wealth."

"Perhaps," Mairin allowed, "but Eric Longsword is not that man. When I first met him he made me feel things I had never known existed within me. He was the first man who ever looked at me through a man's eyes as a grown woman. I have come to know him as we have traveled these last weeks. I find that there is something about him that makes me nervous and uncomfortable. He resists the natural flow of things in such a way that is discordant to me. I particularly do not like the possessive way in which he looks at me. As if he owned me, and I were already in his possession. I could never marry a man like that, and I will not."

Eada nodded. She never discounted Mairin's feelings. Her daughter seemed to have an instinct about people. How sad that instinct had not warned her of the danger of falling in love with Basil. Eada smiled wryly to herself. When was love ever logical? Eric Longsword was a very eligible young man, but if Mairin was not of a mind to encourage his suit there was nothing lost. There would be no difficulty in finding her a husband provided that all the eligible young Anglo-Saxons and Normans did not get themselves killed off in the coming war of succession.

They embarked late that afternoon, having found to take them several coastal vessels that traded back and forth between Flanders and England. The winds were right, and promised to hold. Although there were no cabins to shelter them from the night air, the weather was fair and the June night would not be cold. Their cloaks would be enough to keep them warm out upon the water.

The horses were led blindfolded into the hold of the vessel for they would not otherwise go willingly. Nara purchased a newly roasted capon, fresh-baked bread, a small wheel of soft cheese, wine, and a basket of just-picked cherries to take with them for their supper and morning meal. With luck they would reach England by dawn.

The winds lessened only slightly at sunset. Guided by the bright stars above, they moved steadily through the night toward their destination. Mairin could not resist standing in the bow of the round boat with the wind at her back peering deeply into the darkness ahead. She remembered back to the first time she had crossed these waters. She had been a frightened little child and, despite Dagda's comfortable presence, lonely and afraid of what might lie ahead. She remembered how the slavers had used their female cargo for their own gratification. How Dagda had protected her from the sight.

The second time she ventured upon these waters she was on her way to Constantinople. Mairin closed her eyes, but still tears managed to squeeze themselves from beneath her thick eyelashes to run down her cheeks. Oh, Basil, she thought. I loved you! I believed that you loved me. Though it would pain me to learn you didn't, perhaps I could learn to accept it. It is the doubts. The not really knowing that haunts me. Did you love Bellisarius more than you loved me? So much that you could not bear to be parted from him? I shall never know! Dear God, I shall never know! She shuddered, then stiffened as she felt an arm go about her.

"Are you cold?" Eric Longsword asked pulling her against him.

"No." She waited a long moment. Then she said, "Take your hands from me, Eric Longsword. You have not the right."

"Then give me the right, Mairin. Come dawn we will be in Engand where you and I are equals. I want to pay you court. I want you to become my wife." His arm remained.

To his surprise she struggled against him, finally pulling away. Furiously she faced him, her violet eyes almost black with her anger. "How dare you, Eric Longsword? My husband is dead but four months! How dare you accost me while I yet mourn? But since you have, my answer is no, and no again a thousand times! I will never marry you! *Never!*"

He burst out laughing. The sound echoed eerily in the stillness of midchannel. His arm snaked out to yank her back against him. Her fists beat an angry tattoo against his hard chest. Looking down into her face he growled, "A woman with spirit! I knew that flaming head of yours crowned a woman of spirit. By God, you'll breed me up a race of strong sons, won't you? Think of the fun we'll have making those sons, Mairin! That half-man you were married to couldn't have possibly tapped your passion as I will!"

Mairin tried to squirm free of his iron grasp. She was angrier than she could ever remember being in her whole life. Then she felt him hard and hot pushing against her thigh, through the very fabric of her gown and her chemise. "Release me at once!" she commanded him, but he had seen the slight widening of her eyes as he had pressed against her. He believed he was well aware of the reason for it. Though she might deny it, she desired him.

Lowering his blond head he pressed kisses upon her face. Mairin quickly turned her head away from him so that his mouth found itself facing the side of her head. Tightening his grip so that she could no longer successfully struggle, he ran his tongue with deliberate slowness about the inside of her ear, whispering warmly to her, "You'll fight me, won't you, Mairin? You'll bite and you'll claw, but it won't do you any good. You will sweetly sheath my sword. I will pierce you to the heart until you're begging me not to stop. Then I will pour my seed into you. I like a woman who fights me! Christ, you've made me hot! I could take you now right here upon this very deck! Then you would have to marry me, wouldn't you?"

She could feel his big hand crushing her breast, and for a moment she panicked. Then the anger poured back into her veins, and bringing her knee up hard into his sensitive sex she brutally unmanned him. His arms fell from about her as the air was expelled from his lungs. She stepped quickly back to see her opponent, his blue eyes bugging from his head, gasping in shock to breathe, unable to even howl his terrible pain. She added to his misery by drawing back her hand and hitting him across his handsome face as hard as she was able.

"Don't you ever dare to lay hands on me again, Eric Longsword," she hissed at him through gritted teeth. "If you do I swear I shall take the first weapon that I can lay my hands upon, and I will kill you!" Then turning on her heel she strode away from him down the deck of the ship to the stern end where her party lay sleeping.

Eric Longsword rubbed his injured parts with a gentle hand, and gradually a grin began to turn his mouth up into a smile. She was absolutely wonderful! She was just what he had always sought in a wife. She was strong, and spirited, and intelligent. He wanted her and he intended to have her at any cost. He was not such a fool as to believe that the daughter of Aldwine Athelsbeorn would not have a number of suitors for her hand. Many of those suitors could be easily discouraged. He might even have to fight for her but he would win.

She was the most beautiful woman in the world. He was certain, of course, that she now possessed great wealth from her first husband, which would help his family become more powerful. There was no reason for her father to deny his suit. Mairin would have little to say about it for women seldom did. He knew from talking to the servant, Nara, that there was an elder brother who would soon be marrying. No man wanted a houseful of women. She was as good as his even if she didn't know it.

It would not hurt to have her family on his side. With this in mind he intended escorting her to Aelfleah even though it was greatly out of his way. He would meet her brother, make friends with him, and then when her father came home he would return and ask for her. If the brother was his friend, and her mother liked him, then she would have little recourse. She would be forced to obey her father's wishes.

The pain was subsiding slowly from his lower regions. He was now able to take long deep breaths which helped even more. He licked his lips in anticipation of eventual victory, thinking as he did so that she had nice breasts. They had just filled his hands. He wondered what they looked like. Were her nipples large, or were they budlike? He could feel himself pulsing again at the thought of what she looked like without her clothing. Then he shook himself like a wet puppy. He was behaving like a boy who had yet to fuck his first woman. It had been a long time since any woman had made him feel like that.

The winds had blown steadily all through the night. Now as the sun rose behind them to the east they could see the harbor of Dover before them. Their vessel was made fast to the dock, and they eagerly disembarked to await their horses. It was then that Eric Longsword joined them, a smile upon his face.

"No land smells like England, does it, my lady Eada? It is good to be home at last!" He looked at Mairin. "Did you sleep well, *princess?*"

"Quite well, Eric Longsword," said Mairin with false sweetness.

He grinned back, his blue eyes dancing with mischief. The bastard was laughing at her. He is so very sure of himself, she thought furiously. He will soon learn that I am the one thing he may want but cannot have.

"I am going to escort you to Aelfleah, my lady Eada. There are not enough Mercians among us to assure you safe passage," he said. "The roads in England are not the safe roads of Byzantium. Lord Aldwine would want me to do this, as would the emperor."

Eada smiled back at him. "You are kind, Eric Longsword. I know we take you greatly out of your way."

"My friends and I have been away from home so long that another two or three days will not matter." He smiled toothily at her. "We are in England, and that is what is important to us. Had you been able to tell your son precisely when and where you would arrive he could have come with his own men to escort you. I cannot leave three women alone with only a single man to guard them. We will dispatch one of the Mercians to ride ahead of us to inform your son of your safe arrival, and of by what road we come."

"I feel safer knowing that you will be with us, Eric Longsword," said Eada. She was always more comfortable knowing that someone was in charge.

"Oh, mother, we need not ask Eric Longsword to accompany us," said Mairin. "We have over a dozen Mercians to travel with us. The weather is good so the roads will be clear. We will be following well-traveled roads almost the entire way, and can probably join with a merchant's party going to Gloucester from Dover. I am certain that Brand will meet us somewhere along the road. Surely Eric Longsword desires to reach his home so that he might comfort his parents over the loss of his elder brother, Randwulf. I am certain that his mother is particularly eager to see him."

Eada looked indecisive. Poor Eric's mother to have lost her elder son. Mairin was absolutely right when she said the lady must be anxiously anticipating the safe arrival of her surviving son. A dozen Mercians would be more than enough protection. Particularly when Dagda was with them for he was as good as another six men.

He could see her wavering. Eric Longsword quickly drew a breath and said, "I will send a messenger to my own family when I dispatch one to your son at Aelfleah, my lady, but I insist upon escorting you. I would never forgive myself if anything happened to your party."

"Let it be," Dagda said softly to Mairin, who was preparing to speak once again.

She compressed her lips tightly together in annoyance, but she remained silent. When Eric smiled triumphantly at her she longed to slap his smug face. "Do not leave my side," she replied quietly to Dagda. "I was forced to fight off that pompous fool last night. I do not want to have to do so again."

"He dared to accost you?" Dagda was outraged.

"He is bold. Obviously the blood of his Viking ancestors runs thick and fast in his veins. He would make me his wife," she finished.

"He is not your equal," said Dagda bluntly.

"I do not want him," said Mairin, "but it is hard to convince him of that fact. He does not understand why I would refuse the offer of the heir to five hides of land. After all, I am a widow, and ripe for the taking."

"Have you told your mother?" The horses had now been unloaded. Dagda checked Thunderer's saddle girth as he spoke.

"I have not had the opportunity yet, but I would not distress her, Dagda. Perhaps once we reach Aelfleah I will be able to say farewell to Eric Longsword forever."

"Not if he really wants you," replied Dagda grimly. He boosted her into her saddle. "I may have to kill him."

She gathered the reins into her hands. "It will not come to that. Father will not force me into marriage with Eric Longsword. He seeks a far better match which he assures me my widow's wealth will guarantee."

They stayed in Dover long enough to celebrate morning mass at the church of St. Mary in Castro. Eada insisted that having come safely the great distance from Constantinople and across the waters from Europe that they should all give thanks, and receive the sacrament. The poor parish priest faced with so many confessions heard those of Eada, Mairin, and Nara. Then looking at the men before him asked, "Do you repent of the sins you have committed?" When they cried with one voice, "Aye, father!" he absolved them making the sign of the cross over them. Then he began the mass.

They journeyed west, keeping south of London. To Mairin's surprise the weather held as they crossed the North Downs with its low hills and lonely heaths. They passed through Guildford with its castle belonging to Earl Harold, and onward across Lambourne Downs through great stretches of countryside broken but infrequently by small villages or an occasional manor house.

It was necessary that several of their party ride ahead to find lodgings each night for the few inns along their route were not fit for ladies. They were forced to rely upon the hospitality of distant relations where they could find them, monastery or convent guest houses, or strangers who were of their own class.

Then one afternoon as they were crossing the Cotswolds Brand and a band of Aelfleah retainers met them. It was Mairin who seeing her brother and his men spurred Thunderer forward racing to be the first to greet him. Reining her mount in before him she laughed at the look of total surprise upon his face.

"You're a beautiful woman!" he exclaimed.

"You needn't sound so surprised, brother," she answered him. "Remember I shall be fifteen at Samhein." Her glance swept over him. "You have grown handsome," she noted. Then lest he grow overproud she added, "Your beard hides your spots."

"The girls don't seem to mind," he teased her back.

"The part they're interested in doesn't have spots I hope," she laughed.

Brand chuckled. "Don't let mother hear you speaking so boldly, little sister," he cautioned.

"I am a widow, Brand. It is only natural I know such things."

"I am sorry about your husband, Mairin, but I am glad you have returned to England. I should not like to have lived the rest of my life without you. I have missed you, troublesome creature though you are."

She felt the sting of tears. It was the closest Brand had ever come in his life to saying he loved her. Her own features softened showing her deep love for him. Reaching out she caressed his cheek with her hand. "Oh, dear brother, I missed you too. I am very glad to be home with you!"

Catching her hand before she might withdraw it he kissed it lovingly, his warm gaze locking onto hers. Then he said, "I had best find mother."

Before they could turn their horses about, however, Eric Longsword rode up. His look was black as he said, "Who is this man with whom you behave in such shamelessly familiar fashion, Mairin? Remember, you are to be my wife!"

"What is this?" Brand demanded.

"*This* is a fool," replied Mairin furiously, "who presumes much! How dare you remonstrate with me over my behavior, Eric Longsword? We are not promised. I have already told you I will not marry you!"

"I am Brand Aldwineson," said Brand to his sister's antagonist. He successfully fought back his urge to laugh, for the young man before him was surely in love with Mairin, who could not countenance it.

"You are her brother? Of course!" The anger left his handsome face. "I am Eric Longsword, late of the Emperor Constantine X's Varangian Guards."

"You are not Mercian," said Brand.

"No, my home is near York. My men and I felt it best to escort the lady Eada and her daughter home. There were but a dozen Mercians among us."

"I am most grateful to you, Eric Longsword," said Brand. Then catching his sister's black look he continued, "But now that my men and I are here to see my mother and sister's safe passage, you will be able to go on your own way home. How long have you been away?"

"Seven years. I left England when I was fifteen."

"Then you will certainly be anxious to be on your way," said Brand smoothly. "Now you will excuse me, as I see my mother. Come, Mairin!" They moved away from Eric Longsword.

Eric smiled, but felt a deep-seated anger burning within him. The young puppy had dismissed him as if he had been a servant, and not an equal. An excess of pride obviously ran in the blood of Aldwine Athelsbeorn's children.

"Brand!" Eada had dismounted from her horse, and held out her arms to her beloved son.

"Mother!" He slid from his own beast, hugging her. As he did he felt again like a small boy, for smelling her familiar lavender fragrance seemed to bring back so many memories. He had not realized until this very moment how much he had missed her.

Her eyes searched his face anxiously, but then she smiled warmly at him. "You have become a man," she said. "I am so proud of you!"

"Father?"

"He will not come until the treaty is totally agreed upon, but it was best Mairin return home, and so here we are."

"Now don't go blaming our return all on me, mother," laughed Mairin. "You have been longing to return to Aelfleah since the moment we rode through its gates last!"

"I cannot deny it!" came the heartfelt reply. Both of her children laughed at Eada's obvious relief. At that moment Eric joined them, and Eada said to her son, "You have met Eric Longsword, Brand? I do not know what we would have done had he not been kind enough to escort us from Dover. He has managed to find us decent lodging in the most desolate of places. I hope you will offer him our hospitality at Aelfleah, my son."

"Eric Longsword is always welcome at Aelfleah, mother, but surely he will want to leave us now to return to his own home."

Eric smiled with false joviality. "Your home is but another day away while mine is several days' ride. I have released my men, for I would not impose upon your generosity too greatly. As for myself I shall be glad to partake of your kindness. As anxious as I am to see my own parents, another day or two will not matter after seven years. By now my messenger will have reached them at Denholm. They will know at least of my safe arrival."

Mairin almost shrieked with her frustration. She had hoped to be rid of Eric Longsword today. There was nothing she could do now that would not have been rude, and so she was forced to bear his company further. Strangely he did not trouble her for the next few days, being far too busy with Brand.

They arrived at Aelfleah, and Eada wept with happiness at the joy of seeing her home again. Within a day it was as if she had never left. She immediately became involved with the running of her household, shaking her head and clucking about all the things that had not been done properly since her departure.

Mairin quickly realized that she had nothing to do. Aelfleah was Eada's, and would one day belong to Brand's wife. Slipping from the house she hurried off to refamiliarize herself with *The Forest*. In all the months in Byzantium she had never once thought of it, but now suddenly all the memories of her childhood were rising up to assault her.

Within *The Forest* nothing seemed to have changed, and she felt comforted for a time. To her delight the dainty fox vixen was still alive, and although skittish of her, seemed to recall Mairin. When she had left Aelfleah she had been an innocent child. Now she was a woman. Well perhaps not a *real* woman, but no one knew that but herself and her mother. To all intents and purposes she was indeed a woman. A woman without her own home. Her parents were correct. It irritated her slightly to have to admit it. She would never be respected in England unless she had a husband, and her own home.

Mairin sighed. It seemed so unfair that in order to have a proper place in the world she needed a husband. Why couldn't a woman have her own place? No one, she knew, would have an answer to that question. She wasn't even certain she could think of an answer. So, she thought, I must remarry, but to whom? Not Eric Longsword! That much she knew. He was arrogant, ill educated, and she suspected had a mean streak within him. No, she couldn't. Nay, wouldn't marry Eric.

That evening it rained, a steady gentle rain that gave every indication of continuing all night. The excitement of being home had finally caught up with Eada. Exhausted, she had taken to her bed almost immediately after supper. Brand had without warning slipped away also. Mairin suddenly found herself alone in the Hall with their guest. Before she might excuse herself from her place by the fire he came to stand next to her, saying, "Your brother has given me his permission to court you."

"Brand does not have that right," she answered.

"As long as your father is away he is the head of this household, Mairin."

She looked up at him, her eyes devoid of emotion as she said, "Why do you wish to court a woman who cannot stand the sight of you? Have I not made myself clear, Eric Longsword? Do you think, perhaps, that I play the coy maiden with you? You waste your time with me. I will not accept your suit! Surely you understand that?"

"You must marry again," he said obdurately.

"I know that, but I will not marry you. I loved Prince Basil, and he loved me. I do not love you."

"The prince loved Bellisarius," he replied cruelly. "Even a woman's intelligence can understand that, and you, I am told, are more intelligent than most women. The prince and his lover chose to enter death's kingdom together leaving you behind. How can you still offer your loyalty to a man who so betrayed you? It matters not to me whether you love me or not. I will wager, however, I can teach you to love me if you must have love to be content." He pulled her to her feet, and holding her tightly against him looked down into her face as he said, "You fill my senses, and you intoxicate me, Mairin. Indeed I believe you have cast an enchantment upon me. I desire you as I have never before desired a woman. I will have you, or no man will! You are mine!" His mouth then descended fiercely upon hers, and he kissed her soft lips with a bruising passion.

She was stunned by the suddenness of his attack. When she tried to struggle against him she realized he had learned from their last encounter, and pinioned her in such a way that it was impossible to defend herself from him. She shuddered with revulsion as his lips moved slowly over her lips. He called himself a man, yet Basil's kisses had been far sweeter. Unable to bear another moment of this insult Mairin resorted to the only weapon left available to her. Forcing her arms from his iron grip she quickly reached up, and with all ten fingernails raked his face deeply.

With a surprised yelp he released her, his blue eyes glittering. For a moment they stood staring at each other. She could see that he was bleeding. Then turning from him she forced herself to walk slowly from the Hall. The look she had seen within those blue eyes bespoke murder, and she was hard pressed not to show fear.

"Hellcat," he called after her, "you have marked me as your own by that impetuous act!"

Stopping she turned to face him. "When you ride from Aelfleah tomorrow, Eric Longsword, do not return. There will never be a warm welcome awaiting you here from me. I will kill myself before I ever become your bride! No! I will kill you!"

His dark laughter echoed about the room. "Woman," he said, "you but whet my appetite!"

Part Three

THE HEIRESS OF AELFLEAH

England, 1065–1068

Chapter 8

While Mairin and her family had been in Byzantium Earl Harold had conquered Wales in the name of King Edward. Gryffydd, the King of Cymru, as the people of Wales called their land, was murdered. Technically Harold's hands were clean of the deed for Gryffydd's own men had lured him into ambush to brutally slaughter him. It was whispered, however, that the earl had made it known he would reward those who saw to Gryffydd's death. Harold had then forced Gryffydd's queen, Edyth, into marriage. Edyth's father had been Aelfgar, Earl of Mercia. Brand had seen that his father knew all of this.

Several weeks after their return to Aelfleah, they learned that Harold had arranged to have built a hunting lodge at Portskewet in Wales in the hope of entertaining the king. When it was ready, Caradoc, the son of the dead Gryffydd, brought a force of men to Portskewet on August 25th, St. Bartholomew's Day. They totally destroyed the lodge, killed the retainers there, and made off with all the wealth meant to impress the king.

As if Harold did not have enough trouble grasping at the slippery succession, all the thegnes in Yorkshire and Northumberland met in hastily called session. With one voice they outlawed Earl Tostig, Earl Harold's youngest brother, choosing in his place to be their earl the younger of Earl Aelfgar's sons, Morkar, whose loyalty was to Harold. Then they killed all of Tostig's retainers that they could find, both Danish and English, seizing all of Tostig's weapons, gold and silver.

Again there were the soft voices suggesting Earl Harold did not care that his brother, and his brother's family were forced to flee England to take refuge in Flanders with William of Normandy's father-in-law. Tostig had been a great favorite with King Edward and now that he was gone,

155

the ailing king had no diversions from his wife and her retainers, all of whom lobbied for Harold Godwinson to be named England's heir.

"He has no royal blood," the dying king maintained, and refused to make any public preference.

Just before Mairin's birthday, on October 27th, the eve of St. Simon and St. Jude's Day, the king granted Harold's request that his brother-in-law, Morkar of Mercia, be granted Tostig's earldom. The northerners had anticipated Morkar's confirmation while waiting for the king's decision. At Northampton they pillaged the area, indulging themselves in a bout of burning, killing, and cattle stealing before returning to their own homes.

One afternoon a messenger arrived at Aelfleah in the form of a traveling monk. He brought word that Eric Longsword's family, loyal to Tostig, had suffered in the uprising. Both his parents had been killed and his lands confiscated. Eric had gone with Earl Tostig to Flanders. He would, however, eventually return to England when his earl did. As Thegn of Denholm, he was offering for Mairin's hand in marriage.

Brand laughed. "The man is bold," he noted, "but he is also a fool to think I would allow my sister to wed with one of Tostig's outlaws. Thegn of Denholm, indeed! The lands are no longer his nor, I doubt, will they ever be again. He would be wise to return to service with the emperor in Byzantium."

"Poor man," said Eada sympathetically. "I will pray for his parents."

"Good riddance!" said Mairin. "I know I must marry again, but at least we shall not be troubled by that pompous fool any longer."

"Any candidates?" teased Brand.

"I think father means me to marry a Norman lord, and you a Norman lady, brother."

"Harold will be England's next king, sister. Even I see the way the wind blows. If Edward will not change the succession then Harold will forcibly take the kingdom."

"And Duke William will take it away from Harold," Mairin replied. "I agree with father, Brand. England cannot go on like this. Edward is the first Anglo-Saxon king of England in many years and he is actually half-Norman. England's rulers have been Danish, Norwegian, Swedish. The northmen are forever squabbling over our land. It is time for change. We need a strong ruler, and I do not believe Earl Harold is that man.

"I do not trust a man who out of ambition puts aside his wife of many years to marry an enemy's widow because he feels her brothers will be of service to him in his battle for England's throne. Such behavior does not speak well of Harold's loyalty. We cannot be certain that he was not behind the uprising in York that unseated a rival brother. Look who is put in his place. Morkar! A mere boy! A boy who can be used and manipulated. Earl Harold will never bring peace to England, Brand."

"And you think William can?"

"Yes, I do. William is strong. With him upon the throne I do not believe outsiders will ever again attack us. That has been one of our greatest problems. We have been prey to all those seeking new lands. As for our people I believe that they will welcome the eventual peace that comes with the advantage of having a strong ruler."

"You do not think the Normans who come with William will be seeking new lands? His army will be made up of a host of younger sons all eager to make their fortunes. I do not like Harold Godwinson, but at least he is English. I am not certain I want some foreign-born king ruling over me."

"Duke William is a fair man. Father has always said so, Brand. He will not confiscate the lands belonging to those who support him. Only those who rebel against him."

"Nonetheless," said Brand, "for the first time in my life I am glad to live in this backwater on a small and not very tempting estate. With luck father and I shall be able to stay put until after the fighting, and then simply pledge our loyalty to the winner."

Mairin chuckled. "Brother Bayhard always said I was the more intelligent, but I do not think it so, Brand. I think father would very much approve our staying clear of factional fighting."

"We are safe for now, Mairin. Father's first loyalty is pledged to King Edward. I can pledge no loyalty other than what my father ordains. As long as the king lives, and father remains in Constantinople, Aelfleah is safe."

King Edward enjoyed a happy Christmastide at Westminster, during which time the great church he had spent his reign building was hallowed. This was done on the Feast of the Holy Innocents, December 28th. Shortly thereafter the king fell mortally ill. He died on Twelfthnight, January 5th. When word of his death was brought to all the four corners of England there was other news as well. The king had been buried immediately on January 6th, after which the mourners had allowed Harold Godwinson to crown himself king of England.

It was mid-January when word of this finally filtered into Aelfleah.

The following dawn Brand and Mairin released the last two of Timon Theocrates' black-and-white pigeons with a message capsule attached to a leg of each bird. The simple note was written in Mairin's clear hand. *Edward is dead. Harold crowned. Come home.*

If either of the birds got through to Constantinople Aldwine Athelsbeorn would return by the spring.

Meanwhile like every other manor in rural England, Aelfleah anxiously awaited the outcome of Harold Godwinson's piracy of the English throne. It was not long in coming.

Duke William protested that Earl Harold had broken a pledge made two years prior supporting William's claim to England's throne. Harold ignored the Norman ruler. It was a serious and foolish breach, for among the kingdoms in Europe a man's word was neither given nor taken lightly. Those who might have been sympathetic toward Harold now questioned his honesty. William prepared for invasion while obtaining the support of the Holy Roman Emperor, Henry IV, and the pope.

On the night of the 24th of April there appeared in the sky what some called a long-haired star, and others called a comet. For seven nights it blazed so brightly across the skies of Europe and England that it could even be seen during daylight. Tides were abnormally high and there were great showers of shooting stars on at least three nights. Both women and animals gave birth prematurely in the hysteria surrounding the phenomenon. Some felt the comet portended the end of the world. Others interpreted it as God's obvious displeasure with Harold Godwinson's usurpation of England's throne. They said the comet was being used to light William of Normandy's way to victory over Harold. The pope obviously agreed for he publicly declared his support for Duke William, and excommunicated Harold.

The comet disappeared as quickly as it had come, but Harold's troubles were just beginning. Suddenly his brother, Tostig, arrived on the Isle of Wight where he was greeted warmly, and given ships, money and provisions. Meanwhile Harold gathered about him a huge army with which to repel William when he came. All of England waited poised.

At Aelfleah, however, there was a celebration to welcome home Aldwine Athelsbeorn. He had wisely stopped at Duke William's court first and sworn his fealty. Since Edward's death, Aldwine was free to pledge his loyalty to whom he chose.

"You English are always swearing me fealty," said the duke wryly, "but once you gain the safety of your own shores you deny me."

"Am I the only Englishman to swear to you since the death of King Edward?" the Thegn of Aelfleah asked.

"No," said William, "you are not."

"And do you distrust the others also, my lord?"

The duke chuckled. "I can see why my cousin Edward sent you to Byzantium. You are clever, Aldwine Athelsbeorn."

"I am also a man of my word, my lord. Norman blood runs in my veins also, but even if it didn't I would still think you the best king for England. There is no advantage to my having come here for my holding is isolated and unimportant. Although I have always been happy with Aelfleah, I doubt any among your followers would want my poor lands. I am not a man of ambition, and I seek nothing of you, my lord. I might have hurried home through Flanders, as did my five companions, but I chose to come and swear my loyalty to you, and if you will accept it, I will never betray you." Then the thegn knelt, bowing his head in submission to the duke.

William of Normandy nodded almost imperceptibly. Looking down at the bowed head his hard, handsome face softened a little, and he said, "I accept your loyalty, Aldwine Athelsbeorn, and that of your son and family. I am grateful for it. I shall need good friends when I come to England. Rise now, and go in safety."

The thegn rose to his feet, and bowed again to the duke. "I shall look for your coming, my lord," he said. "When will I see you again?"

"I plan to be crowned in London by Christmas at the latest, Aldwine Athelsbeorn. You and your family are invited to my coronation."

When the Englishman had departed the duke turned to his single companion, saying, "Well, Josselin, what do you think?"

"He seems sincere, my lord William, but one can never really be certain. If, heaven forfend, you lose in your battle to Harold Godwinson, I suspect he would as quickly swear his fealty to Harold."

"That, my young friend, is called survival," laughed the duke. "I shall find lands for you in England, Joss. When you must defend your own holding we will see how firm your ideals are. I will wager you quickly learn the fine art of compromise yourself."

The younger man smiled. "I have decided upon a motto for my crest," he said. "What do you think of *Honor Above All*?"

"That you set your descendants an overly hard task," replied the duke. "Do not, my young friend, feel that because of the circumstances of your birth you must strive harder."

"Haven't you, my lord?"

"Touché, Joss. Perhaps I have at that, but there comes a time when a man must stop berating himself for something that was not of his making. It is true that you and I were both born out of the bonds of holy wedlock, but both of our fathers loved our mothers, and they recognized our births. Neither of us has really suffered the stigma of bastardy other than that occasional taunt from someone not even worthy of our notice. If Raoul de Combourg had been married to your mother when you were conceived, could he have loved you any more? I think not."

"Still," said Josselin de Combourg, "the circumstances of my birth have made it impossible for me to reap any gain in Brittany. My younger, legitimate brother is my father's heir. I pledged myself to your service over twenty years ago, but were you not bound for England in the spring I should yet be landless. A man without lands is nothing, my lord William."

The duke nodded his agreement. "If there were no English throne, Joss, I should find an estate somewhere with which to reward you for your loyalty to me all these years. I owe you much. Had you not been my messenger and bolstered Matilda's confidence during the years I courted her, during the years that the pope refused us permission to wed, I do not think she would have had the strength to wait. There were others who would have seen her wed elsewhere. In England you shall make your fortune, my good and true friend. I shall need you there for I have not many friends such as that humble thegn, Aldwine Athelsbeorn.

"He is not a man of the court, but my cousin Edward wrote that in a world where so many men are not what they seem, Aldwine Athelsbeorn was exactly as he appeared. An honest man. He is also a skilled negotiator. We may eventually make use of him, but for now I wish him Godspeed in the last days of his long journey home."

Aldwine Athelsbeorn did not know of Duke William's blessing upon his journey, but the same day that he left the duke's court he embarked for England. Within three days he rode across the little Aldford river and through his own gates. He had seen as he came from the coast the open preparations for the coming war, but in Aelfleah's valley there were only preparations for the spring planting. The meadows held a bumper crop of lambs who gamboled in the spring sunshine. There was peace here, and he was relieved.

A young lad had seen him as he crossed over the river, and dropping his hoe the boy ran toward the manor house shouting as he ran, "The lord comes! The lord is home!"

Eada ran from the house, and seeing her, Aldwine spurred his horse. He leapt from the big beast's back as they met and caught her up in his arms, kissing her soundly. Mairin came from *The Forest* with a basket of new herbs and roots but upon seeing her parents, she dropped her basket and ran to greet her father, almost colliding with Brand who had hurried from the fields where he had been supervising the serfs. Hugging, laughing, and weeping with their joy they moved into the house. Eada called for food and drink to be brought to her husband.

"What news?" demanded Brand, unable to wait even though his mother sent him a reproving look.

"Preparations for war, of course," replied the thegn. "It's evident everywhere. I stopped in Normandy to pledge my fealty to the duke."

"Do they prepare for war in Normandy, father?" Mairin asked.

"Aye, and God help England if they resist."

"But it is said that Harold Godwinson has a larger army than the duke," said Brand. "How can the duke hope to beat such great numbers?"

"Harold Godwinson is a fine warrior, but William of Normandy is a better one, Brand, and he is a leader to whom men flock. From all over the French kingdoms, from Brittany, from Flanders, from Aquitaine and the Languedoc men are coming to join his army for he inspires loyalty. He has endless monies and great resources, and in the end he will prevail. I but pray it is sooner than later for the sake of England and her peoples."

"What will you do, father," said Mairin, "if Harold Godwinson calls for the *Fyrd* to be raised? How can you not go?"

"Once again I thank God for Aelfleah's isolation. But if we are called, I shall find myself too ill from my long journey, and unable to answer Earl Harold's request. As for you, my son, you will then be forced to remain here protecting Aelfleah as I will be unable to do so. Remember, Brand, there is nothing dishonorable in refusing to commit a foolish act even if everyone else around you does. There are those who will speak of honor and duty in this matter, but having pledged my fealty to Duke William, it would be dishonorable for me to fight against him. Our duty, Brand, is to your mother, your sister, our people, and to Aelfleah."

All during the summer of 1066 England waited for the invasion to come. Though William of Normandy was more than ready the winds would not cooperate and blew steadily from the wrong direction. Earl Harold had indeed called for the *Fyrd* to be raised. They learned it from a traveler passing through the valley. No one, however, had come to Aelfleah. In the invasion hysteria they had been overlooked. Along the coast facing Normandy the English army waited and waited for the attack that never came.

The army that had been raised from the *Fyrd,* which was a local militia under the command of its various thegns, grew restless. Many had come from a great distance and as the summer wore on the local people grew tired of feeding the great horde of men who did nothing but eat, drink, wench, and polish their weapons. Then messages began to arrive for the waiting thegns from their wives. It was harvest time, and there were no harvesters.

The coming of Earl Tostig on the Isle of Wight caused momentary excitement particularly when he sailed into the Humber with sixty ships. Mercia's young Earl Edwin came with a large land force, and drove Tostig off. Aldwine Athelsbeorn, hearing of the battle, smiled grimly and said, "Englishmen fighting Englishmen. This is what Harold Godwinson and his brothers have brought us to. There will be worse to come, you may be certain. Tostig has gone to Scotland, but you can be sure we have not heard the last of him."

In September Harold Godwinson was finally forced to disband his army. It was obvious that William of Normandy would not be coming to England this year, and the harvest would not wait any longer. The good weather was almost over, and the winds had kept William at bay all summer. Soon the waters that separated England and Normandy would be too unpleasant to navigate and only the heartiest fisherfolk and traders would venture out upon that choppy sea.

Just as the army returned home the King of Norway, Harold Hardraade, decided to press his tenuous claim to the English throne. Joining with Earl Tostig, he swept down the Yorkshire coast. Young Earl Morkar sent to his brother, Earl Edwin, for help. This time a call to arms arrived at Aelfleah.

"We must go," said Aldwine Athelsbeorn.

"But why?" Eada demanded. "Did you not say you would not answer the fyrd?"

"I said I would not fight William of Normandy, but this is not William. It is that damned savage Norwegian, and Tostig! How can I refuse Earl Edwin's call to aid his brother? I am a Mercian, and it is Mercia's earl who asks my help. Brand and I must go."

Brand was beside himself with excitement. He was past twenty, but had never had the opportunity to participate in a battle. Joyfully he prepared his weapons, sharpening his sword blade, honing his spear, while his mother grimly checked his chain mail to be certain that it was in good order.

Mairin took Dagda aside. "Go with them," she begged. "I know that it has been many years since you have smelt the winds of war, and I do not ask you to fight, but stay near them, Dagda. Bring them safely home."

Dagda did not ask her what she saw in the runes she had cast although he had seen her spread the stones upon their velvet cloth three times. He knew he would come back safely because Mairin would have warned him if he needed to take extra care.

In the days following their departure the women of Aelfleah manor completed their chores as if in a daze. It had been many years since their village had been touched by war. The old women shook their heads and told terrible tales while the young women fretted for the safe return of husbands and lovers. They arose at first light, and sought their beds shortly after sunset. Each found comfort in sleep. Mairin did not.

At York a great battle was fought, and the Norwegians triumphed. There was terrible slaughter of the English forces. Dagda gathered together those of Aelfleah's people who were alive and recalling his old battle skills, he circumvented the Norwegians and led them all home to their quiet valley. Seeing the look on Eada's face as he gave her the body of her only son for burial, he realized the futility of war, and wept with her.

As they stood by Brand's grave he said to Eada, "If it is any consolation, I can tell you that Brand was as brave and noble a warrior as any I have ever seen. It was an awful battle for his baptism of fire. More skilled men than he lost their lives."

She nodded silently, and he knew his words had brought her a small measure of comfort. He was grateful she did not ask the circumstances of her son's death, for Dagda did not think he could relate the truth to this gentle woman.

Mairin, of course, had asked him, and he had told her that as Brand knelt over his injured father he was struck from behind by a helmeted warrior who then disappeared back into the thick of the battle. He told her of the look of total surprise that filled Brand's blue eyes in the instant of his death.

"You cast the runes thrice," he said. "Did they not warn you of this tragedy?"

"You know how hard it is for me to see things relating to those closest to me," she answered him. "I asked the runes if father and Brand would return home. Thrice I asked, and three times the runes said they would return. It did not occur to me that Brand would be dead, and father mortally wounded. If I had been more specific I might have warned them."

"Then it was their fate," replied Dagda. "You are not to blame. How could you have known?"

Aldwine Athelsbeorn lay dying in his own bed. He called for Eada, Mairin, Dagda, the priest from the village church, and as many of his people as could crowd into his bedchamber. Gathering the last of his strength he told them, "My son is dead, but my daughter lives. It is she that I designate my heiress. It is she to whom I leave all my worldly goods, my lands, and whatever wealth I have managed to accumulate. Do you swear to me that you will give her your fealty?" He fell back against his pillows, and for a moment his eyes closed. Then they opened and focused sharply on the people about him.

A chorus of "Ayes" echoed throughout the room.

"Father," he continued, "will you swear to any who ask that it was my last wish that the lady Mairin be my heiress?"

"Aye, my lord," said Father Albert. "I will so swear upon the blessed body of Christ crucified, and upon the tears his holy Mother Mary shed."

"Mairin, my daughter, will you keep my fealty to Duke William?"

"Aye, father." The tears coursed down her cheeks. The knowledge that she was losing the wonderful man who had rescued her and who had become her parent was incredibly painful.

"And you will care for your mother?"

She nodded, reaching out to take Eada's hand, unable to speak now.

He fastened his dimming gaze upon Eada. A weak smile lit his face. "Ahh," he said, "you are as beautiful now as the day I first saw you in your father's hall. Protect Mairin. Love each other after I am gone as you have loved each other in my lifetime."

"Do not leave me, my lord," Eada wept. "What is there for me without you?" She was visibly paler.

"There is our daughter, Eada! You cannot leave her to fend for herself. She needs you! It is not God's will that you come with me. You have been the best, nay, the most perfect of wives. Never have you disobeyed me. This is the hardest task that God has ever set for us both—to go on without each other—but surely it is meant to be else he would not ask it of us. If you love me you will do this for me." He fell back again amid the pillows of his bed, ashen, his breathing now rasping painfully.

"*I love you,*" she whispered. "There was never anyone but you, and though it pains me I will obey you, my lord, in this last thing."

He smiled faintly at her. Then he said, "I love you too, my true heart, but I must go. Brand awaits me. He is even now calling to me."

She saw the life flee from his eyes, and she fell upon his chest sobbing. For over twenty-five years she had shared his life, and now he was gone. She was alone. Then she felt Mairin's hands gently drawing her away, and held in her daughter's embrace she realized that she was not alone. The greatest gift that Aldwine had ever given her was on an autumn day long ago when he had come home from London with a giant of an Irishman, and the most beautiful girl-child that had ever been born in his keeping. Now he had put them into each other's keeping. She looked up at her daughter saying, "How do we go on, my child? I feel that you are wiser than I."

Mairin sighed. "I suppose," she said, "that we begin at the beginning, mother. We will bury father next to Brand, and then we will continue as we have always done. The harvest must be completed. None of what has happened today will prevent the winter from coming this year. If I am to feed and protect our people we must gather in all the foodstuffs that we can." She turned to the priest. "Father Albert, we will bury my father tomorrow after his people have paid him their respects. You will put in the church book that on this Michaelmas Day, in the year 1066, Aldwine Athelsbeorn joined his Lord and that it was a sad day for all his people of Aelfleah."

Those at Aelfleah did not learn until weeks later that on the same day that Aldwine Athelsbeorn had died, William, Duke of Normandy, had landed at Pevensey. Several days later the decisive battle for England was fought at Hastings, and Harold Godwinson was killed along with his brothers Leofwine and Gyrth.

In London Archbishop Aldred and the townspeople attempted to place the child, Edgar the Atheling, the last in the line of Wessex kings, upon the throne. Earls Edwin and Morkar swore fealty to the child. In the end, however, the archbishop, the young Edgar Atheling, Earls Edwin and Morkar, and the influential citizens of London, capitulated to William of Normandy. They gave him hostages, and swore their loyalty to him. William in return promised to be a good king to them, but he also allowed his men three days' plunder to punish the English for their resistance to his claim of sovereignty.

At Aelfleah none of this was known, for the very isolation that had protected the manor over the years also made it the last place in Earl Edwin's domain that news arrived. On St. Hilda's Day, the eighteenth of

November, Mairin was returning from the woods with a party of young girls with whom she had been nutting. Having taken on her father's heavy responsibilities she had found little time for levity and had needed this respite from more pressing manor business. She rarely had time to ride Thunderer, who was restless from inactivity. Now as they came laughing and chatting from the woodland they saw a party of armed and mounted men just coming across the ford in the river. The village girls stopped. Eyeing the men warily they then looked to Mairin for direction.

"Stay by me, lasses," she ordered them. "There is always safety in numbers."

They clustered about her like a group of chicks to a hen. The horsemen approached them. When the strangers had drawn level with them they stopped, and one man, better dressed than the others and obviously the leader, said, "Is this the manor of Aelfleah?"

"Who seeks to know, my lord?" Mairin answered him.

The knight's eyebrows lifted slightly in surprise. Although he had spoken in English she answered him in perfect and unaccented Norman French. He had spotted her immediately as the leader of this pretty pack of females, deciding that if she belonged to the manor she would warm his bed this night. It was obvious, however, that she was not a serf. "I am Josselin de Combourg, the new lord of this manor," he said, "and who, my beauty, might you be?"

"I am Mairin Alwinesdotter, the heiress to the manor of Aelfleah, my lord. As that obviously puts us at an impasse of sorts, may I suggest that you come into the hall where we may speak further on this."

"William of Normandy rules in England this day," said the knight.

"Thanks to a merciful God, my lord," she answered him piously. "The fealty of this manor has always belonged to King William. Will you tell your men to stable their own horses? My people will help them. Then they may come into the hall for refreshment." Dismissing him momentarily she turned back to the girls who accompanied her and said, "Take your nuts to the granary to be culled and stored. Then return quickly to your homes." Returning her attention to the knight, she smiled up at him disarmingly and put her hand upon his bridle. "Come, my lord, I will show you the way."

Josselin de Combourg did not know whether to be amused or angry. He wisely decided upon the former emotion. The exquisite beauty so calmly leading his massive mount up to the door of Aelfleah's manor house possessed great presence in the face of his news. Who was she? The king had said nothing about an heiress to Aelfleah. Learning that both Aldwine Athelsbeorn and his only son had been recently killed, and that Aelfleah was near the border between England and Wales, William had given the manor to his friend. Hastings' victor would not take the estates of the Saxon thegns who had sworn fealty to him, Aelfleah was already loyal to him. Its strategic location made it imperative that it remain in loyal hands.

Mairin was furious, but knew she must remain calm in the face of this sudden danger. How dare William of Normandy offer her inheritance to this knight! What did he think would become of her and Eada without lands? Were they to be robbed of their home as well as Aldwine and Brand? It was obvious that William of Normandy was a callous man, but Mairin had no intention of sitting calmly by while someone else re-arranged her life for her yet again. The lady Blanche had done so to her, and she had been powerless to prevent it. Bellisarius had done so when he killed Basil. This time she would fight! She would not let others rule her or Eada or Aelfleah and its people!

She ushered Josselin de Combourg into the Hall. Eada, who had been working upon a tapestry, arose and came forward to greet the guest. "Welcome to Aelfleah, my lord," she said in her gentle voice. "I am the lady Eada, widow to Aldwine Athelsbeorn."

Josselin was feeling distinctly uncomfortable now. The sweet-faced woman before him had not been overlooked by the king. Indeed she had been put in his charge, but try as he might he could remember no mention of a daughter. What was he to do with her? Was she also his responsibility? She had not the gentle look of her mother.

"There is a widow," William had distinctly said. "If you fancy her then marry her though she may be a bit long in the tooth for you. If she is not to your tastes you must nonetheless protect and shelter her as if she were a member of your own family. Aldwine Athelsbeorn's fealty to me demands that I see to the comfort and safety of his widow. Perhaps she will prefer returning to her brother's hall. If so, give her passage. Perhaps she will want to remarry. If that be the case then see that she is dowered. Perhaps she will require nothing more than to remain at Aelfleah for the rest of her days. If that be the case you must treat her with kindness and give her an honored place at your table, and in your hall."

Josselin had agreed for it was the honorable thing to do. The confrontation with the daughter had complicated things immeasurably. Drawing a deep breath he said in response to Eada's greeting, "I am Josselin de Combourg, my lady Eada."

"The *new* lord of Aelfleah manor," said Mairin sweetly.

Josselin frowned at Mairin though it did not disquiet her in the least.

"I do not understand," said Eada, with a confused look in her eyes.

"What is to understand, mother? William of Normandy has rewarded my father's fealty to him by dispossessing his heiress and his widow of their lands! Tell me, my lord de Combourg, will my mother and I be allowed to keep our personal possessions when we are driven from our home? Must we go today, or will you give us till the morning to gather our things?" She stood glaring at him defiantly, her hands upon her hips.

Strangely he understood her anger for had he found himself in a similar situation he would have felt anger too. He could not, however, countenance her rudeness before the servants. "I am certain, my lady Mairin, that your gentle mother has taught you better manners than you show me. Obviously your doting father did not beat you enough to reinforce those lessons."

"Do not dare to speak of my father, may God assoil his good soul! My father was a kind and gentle man with a care for everyone from the lowliest to the highest! He would not dispossess innocent women of their home and chattels!" Mairin's ire now overflowed; there would be no turning back. "My father," she finished coldly, "did not have to resort to physical violence to control the people about him. Whatever we did, we did for the pure love of him!"

She stood defying and embarrassing him before the serfs without entirely knowing the true circumstances, yet all Josselin could think of was that she was the most beautiful woman he had ever seen. He wanted to kiss her. He wanted to carry her off to some secret place and make love to her. Her hair . . . that red-gold mass of living flame that crowned her hot head, was incredibly alluring, even intoxicating. He shook himself like a wet terrier to clear his head. "Be silent, Mairin Aldwinesdotter!" he roared at her.

Eada, who had been afraid, suddenly wanted to giggle. She swallowed hard to stifle the sound. The look on the knight's face was one Eada had seen many times in connection with her daughter. She found it very funny that Mairin had so easily conquered their conqueror.

Josselin turned to her. "Might I have some wine, my lady? I find I have a great thirst." He looked back to Mairin. "*Sit down!* No, not in the chair, but on the stool at its feet."

She glared at him outraged. There was something in his voice that warned her that for now she had gone as far as she might dare with him.

Compressing her generous mouth into a tight line she did as he bid her. Eada poured the wine into a goblet, and having served the knight, she seated herself in her own chair, placing a restraining hand upon her daughter's head in an effort to calm her.

Josselin seated himself in the other chair. Looking at the two women he began to speak. "It is true that King William rewarded my many years of service to him with these lands. Had his loyal friend Aldwine Athelsbeorn lived, these lands would not now be mine. Aelfleah, although isolated, is nonetheless in a very strategic position, my lady Eada.

"From the tops of the hills that rim this valley to the west one can see Wales. The Welsh are a volatile people who have a history of running disputes with the English. The king wants peace now. I have been charged, therefore, with the task of building a castle atop these hills. One of several in fact that the king intends building to protect the border region. With the raising of that castle I hope to be able to keep the king's peace in this part of England.

"I do not believe that the king was aware that Aldwine Athelsbeorn had a daughter. I have served William of Normandy for twenty years and while he may be considered a hard man, he is a just lord, and not a man to steal from widows and orphans. If you are surprised by my arrival, I am no less surprised to find you, Mairin Aldwinesdotter. As for you, my lady Eada, the king has charged me with your care. There is no need for either of you to leave Aelfleah. It is your home."

"But, my lord," said Eada in her quiet voice, "will not your wife resent this manor's former mistress and her child within her house? It is not, alas, a big house."

"I have no wife, my lady. My duty, and lack of lands, has kept me from seeking a mate all these years. I am happy to have you remain to chatelaine this manor as you have always done."

"I will go to the king!" Mairin burst out. "If he is indeed as you say, a man of principle, then he will return my lands to me."

"And will you build the king's keep?" he mocked her.

"If that is the price I must pay, yes! Do you think I cannot do it, my lord? I love Aelfleah, but more important, it was my father's parting gift to me. It is my dowry. What man will have me without a dowry? In Saxon law a woman may inherit if there is no male heir to do so. This manor makes me a valuable and worthy bride for some man of influence. Without it I am nothing! Let the king give you other lands. You cannot have mine!"

"So you would sell yourself to the highest bidder, lady?"

"You disapprove, my lord? How strange, for when the time comes for you to choose a wife you will seek to make the best possible match. You will not choose a wife for her sweetness of character, or her intelligence, or her housewifely skills. You will seek the richest woman you can find who will have you, and favor your suit, no matter she may look like a dead codfish, and be just as cold in your bed!"

"Mairin!" Eada looked horrified. Saxon women were noted for their blunt speech, but even Eada wondered if her daughter had gone perhaps too far this time.

"Oh, mother, do not chide me! This man would rob me of my inheritance. Then he dares to look down his long Norman nose at me in scorn. Aelfleah is mine! I will not relinquish it! I am going to the king!"

"No," said Josselin de Combourg, "you are not!"

"What, my lord? Do you fear he will hear me favorably, and so you seek to prevent my going?"

"Lady, you would not know it hidden safe here in your little valley, but England is yet chaotic. There are pockets of resistance everywhere. Roving bands of malcontents are terrorizing the roads, making travel nearly impossible without an armed escort, which I cannot give you right now."

"I do not need your help," Mairin sneered.

"Oh, but you do if you are to reach the king in safety."

"Then, my lord, you should let me go for perhaps I will be killed along the way, and then there will be no one to contest your claim to *my* estate!"

Anger darkened his handsome face, a dull red spread across his wind-bronzed skin. "The day your father swore fealty to King William, Mairin Aldwinesdotter, I stood next to my lord. The king invited your father and his family to his coronation. He will be crowned in London at Christmastide. You, my lady, may go then to plead your case with the king. I will not prevent your going. Indeed I will personally escort you to insure your safety. For now, however, I am charged by my lord with the responsibility of building his castle. Until this matter between us is settled you will continue to run the manor as you have done since your father's death.

"Now, lady, I am hungry, and so are my men. Let there be peace between us for the time being. Your hall is smaller than I would have thought. Will there be room here for my men?"

Mairin was somewhat stunned by his easy solution to their problem. For a moment she attempted to decide where the trick in it was, then seeing Eada frown she quickly said, "Your men may have the hall, my lord. It is true the house is not large, but we do not keep many servants. Those we have sleep either in the kitchens or in the solar above."

He nodded. "I will want a tour of the house," he said.

"My mother will be glad to show you," she replied quickly.

"No," said Eada, "you must do it. I will hasten to the kitchens to see that the cook prepares enough food for our guests. Remove my belongings from the master chamber, Mairin, and place them in Brand's room. Then have linens upon the bed changed."

"Nay, lady," he said gently to her. "Until the king decides it I am not fully master here. With your permission I will sleep in your son's chamber. I will not dispossess you from your place."

For that Mairin liked him. Arising she said, "Come, my lord, and I will show you the upper floor. Then the kitchens." She led him up the stairs and into the solar with its brightly burning fireplace. Then down the little passageway, pointing out the two smaller chambers where she and Brand slept, and on into the master bedchamber where her parents slept.

"This is a most unusual design for a house," he noted, and she smiled proudly.

"My father designed this house. It was not like this in his father's time, but my father was not the eldest, and did not expect to inherit. He traveled widely in his youth. In Byzantium, he said, people built their homes to afford themselves privacy from their noisy relations, their children, and their servants. When Aelfleah became his he redesigned it to be like the houses he had seen in his travels."

"I like it," said Josselin de Combourg.

"Do not like it too much, my lord," said Mairin mockingly. "It will never be yours."

The knight chuckled, and thought how very different this Saxon girl was from the women of the Norman court. He was not himself a Norman. He was a Breton. His father was Raoul de Rohan, the Comte de Combourg. His mother, Eve, was the daughter of a wealthy cloth merchant. His father had been married for many years to a noblewoman who had given him two daughters but after her death he had seen Josselin's mother and fallen in love with her.

The disparity in their social positions was considered too great to countenance a marriage. So despite the birth of his first son, Raoul de Rohan gave in to his family's pleas and remarried a suitable wife, who, quickly producing their required heir, died in childbirth. The comte refused to remarry to suit his relations this time. He married his mistress, and moved her and Josselin back into his castle. It was Eve who raised both of her lord's sons, but it was the younger, Guéthenoc, who was his father's heir.

The Comte de Combourg loved both of his sons, but perhaps he loved Josselin a bit more. Still he knew that he could not continue to favor the elder over his legitimate heir. So following the custom of the times he sent Josselin at the age of eight to be raised in the house of another nobleman. Wanting him to have the best possible chance in life, he placed him at the Norman court of Duke William. There he knew his son would be safe from the usual taunts that dogged the heels of even the noble bastard-born. Duke William himself had been born of a union not blessed by the church.

He told his son that William's father, upon seeing Herleve, his mother, washing her linen in a local stream beneath the castle walls, found out that she was the daughter of a wealthy tanner. He had courted her and she had borne a son even as Josselin's own mother had borne him. Duke Robert had then traveled to the Holy Land on a pilgrimage, and died there. Before he had gone, however, he had made his liegemen swear fealty to his young son should he not return. William had inherited his dukedom. That was the part that Josselin didn't understand.

"How can William, bastard-born even as I am, be Duke Robert's heir, yet I cannot be yours, father?"

"Because his father had no other child, either son or daughter, who might inherit, Josselin. He had no wife."

"But I was born before Guéthenoc, father. If you loved my mother then why did you marry the demoiselle Elisette, Guéthenoc's mother? You are married to my mother now, and I am your eldest son. Should I not be your heir?"

"Had Duke Robert returned he would have probably given in to the pleadings of his family to get a legitimate heir even as I did, Josselin. Your mother, like Herleve, was not of equal birth with me. Since Guéthenoc was born healthy, and poor Elisette died, I decided to no longer be separated from Eve. I had an heir my family could accept, so I married to suit myself this time. It was blind luck that brought Duke William his domain but at his court there will be few who make mock of you for your birth, my son. You have no need to be ashamed. You are Josselin de Combourg, the much-loved son of Raoul de Rohan. I hope you will take pride in it."

He had taken pride in his heritage, but he nonetheless strove harder than all the other little pages at the court of Duke William. So hard did he strive that his extra efforts brought him the attention of the young duke who was but nine years his senior. Fascinated by the serious little boy who worked so desperately to please, William sought his history. Learning of it he was strangely touched and took the child into his personal care. He understood the demons the boy faced because of his birth. He also knew that no matter how much his parents loved him it would not erase the stain of bastardy. Was not he, the ruler of one of the most powerful dukedoms in Europe, referred to as William the Bastard?

Josselin grew up under the guidance of the duke, whose favor did not deter the boy from continuing to exert himself in all of his duties. When he was fourteen William sent him to the court of Baldwin of Flanders on a very important mission. He was the duke's gift to the lady Matilda, Baldwin's daughter, whom William of Normandy had singled out to be his wife. There were innumerable difficulties involved in the marriage plans, not the least of which was the bride's resistance.

Matilda announced quite loudly to one and all that she would not marry a bastard. The other courts of Europe tittered at the insult. The duke refused to accept her rude answer, and went to Flanders to woo her himself. It was said that he accosted her as she came from church, beating her publicly for her slander of his person. Duke Baldwin's daughter suddenly found herself very impressed with his passion, his pride, and his sense of command. Intrigued by this bold man who had dared to lay rough hands upon her before her father and his court, she abruptly changed her mind and agreed to marry William.

The pope, however, forbade the marriage saying Matilda of Flanders must marry elsewhere. Now the lady would hear of no other for her husband but William of Normandy. She refused to even consider another match.

It was at that point young Josselin was sent to Flanders. He was now a big handsome boy of fourteen. His mission was to stay by the lady's side as her page. To tell her all he could about Duke William. To keep her amused and to bolster her spirits when she became afraid or discouraged. To make certain that she would not change her mind again. Josselin did his job well for the petite blond Matilda became even more obdurate in her refusal to marry anyone but Duke William of Normandy.

Finally Baldwin of Flanders agreed to the match despite the pope's objections. His strong-willed daughter was making his life a veritable hell. He had had enough. Let Normandy have her. The pope was far away, and would eventually relent. Matilda and William were married. It was an extremely happy and fruitful marriage. William adored his wife, and was never unfaithful to her. It was a rarity of behavior for a man of both his times, and his position.

In all of this Josselin de Combourg's loyalty to his lord and his lady was not forgotten. He had gained the valued friendship of them both, and it was that which had brought him to Aelfleah. William knew that he might count upon Josselin de Combourg to keep the peace in this little corner of England, and to raise up a castle that would help to insure that peace.

Mairin led him back downstairs, showing him the buttery, the pantry, and the kitchens. He was extremely impressed by the covered portico that separated the main house from the kitchens, by the kitchen garden that lay to one side of it, and the herb garden that lay to the other side. The household well was in a corner by the kitchen and safe within the walls where it could not be poisoned by an enemy. It was a shame that he could not incorporate the manor house into the castle, but the castle would have to be located upon the crest of the hill where it could look down into Wales.

"How is it," he asked Mairin as they returned to the hall, "that a Saxon girl speaks fluent and accentless Norman French?"

She looked up at him, and he saw that her eyes were a wonderful violet color. "I am not Saxon-born although I have been raised as one, my lord. My father was a Breton, my mother Irish. When I was orphaned Aldwine Athelsbeorn and his wife took me as their own child."

"Then you are not really his daughter?"

"I was formally adopted by my Saxon father, and formally recognized as his heiress should there be no male heirs of his blood, my lord. King Edward did this for my father in return for a favor. That is why my father went to Constantinople several years ago as the head of the king's trade delegation. It was the price the king requested in return for agreeing to my adoption. I am, according to Saxon law, the daughter of Aldwine Athelsbeorn and his wife, Eada. My claim to Aelfleah is quite legitimate. I speak not only Norman French, but Breton, Latin, Greek, and of course English. I can read and I can write. I am knowledgeable in mathematics, logic, history, geography, and philosophy. My mother says an educated woman is anathema to a man, but both my father and my husband encouraged my learning."

"You are married?" Josselin asked. Of course she was! She was far too beautiful not to be.

"I was," she said quietly, and for a moment a shadow passed over her features. "My husband is dead."

"Did he die like your brother and father fighting the Norwegians, or was he with Harold Godwinson at Hastings?" he queried her, seeking knowledge of this man who had loved her.

"Basil was a prince of Byzantium, my lord. He died in Constantinople at the hand of an assassin. The taking of his life was a needless waste for he was a good man."

"Forgive me, Mairin Aldwinesdotter. I did not mean to cause you pain by bringing up unhappy memories."

"Excepting his death, my lord, the memories I have of my husband are happy ones."

"You had no children?"

"We had only been married a few months when he was struck down," she answered. "That is why I returned home to England with my parents. There was nothing left for me in Constantinople once Basil was gone. Now you would take my home from me, but I am not some meek creature who will sit quietly by and let that happen, my lord." Her look was a bold and defiant one.

Josselin couldn't help but chuckle. He quickly saw that his reaction to her words annoyed her greatly. She was not a tiny woman like the Duchess Matilda, but neither was she big. She was rather of medium height, and fine-boned, which gave her a delicate look. Still he towered over her, being very long like his father, and having a medium frame. This lankiness coupled with a youthful face that belied his thirty years had been of great advantage to him in the past for it had given him the appearance of a half-grown youth which was why he had been so successful in his endeavors for William. Those who did not know him thought him a mere boy. They were therefore less careful in their speech. He was relieved that in the last few years his face had gained some maturity, but even now he thought that had he an older visage, Mairin would not be defying him.

In the weeks that followed Mairin could not fault Josselin's courteous behavior. It did not, however, stop Mairin from reminding him at every turn that Aelfleah was hers. To Eada he was gentle and kind, which caused her to remark to her daughter, "It is fortunate you are not married to that good knight, Mairin. If you were he would beat you black and blue for your wicked tongue. I am not certain that I should not encourage him myself in such an undertaking."

"I say nothing that is not truth, mother."

"Nonetheless he is in a difficult position, and you are making it no easier for him."

"I simply do not wish him to become too attached to Aelfleah since it will never be his," was the proud reply.

"Be careful, Mairin, that you do not say something that you will one day regret," Eada warned. Then she went about preparing the clothing that they would take to London when King William was crowned.

Josselin de Combourg had brought with him to Aelfleah an engineer. Master Gilleet of Rouen would oversee the actual building of the castle. It would be a costly endeavor and the bulk of the expense would be borne by Josselin de Combourg himself. Once the king confirmed his ownership of Aelfleah manor and its lands, Josselin would have the right to tax the inhabitants within his domain to help pay for the castle. But for now it was fortunate that the knight was a rich man.

His beautiful mother, Eve Drapier, had been her father's only surviving child. It was expected that she would make a very good marriage, being her father's heiress. Reluctant to lose his child to another man, her indulgent father delayed his choice of a son-in-law. It was then the Comte de Combourg had seen her, and fallen desperately in love with her, an emotion that Eve Drapier reciprocated with equal passion.

After that there had been no more talk of marriage, for Eve's father had been wise enough to understand his daughter's heart. Besides, her new status reflected upon him. It was no crime that the beauteous Eve was the comte's mistress, and the mother of his eldest, albeit illegitimate son. When the cloth merchant had died he had left all of his wealth to his only grandson, knowing that to advance himself in life the boy would need gold to help him overcome the slight stigma of his noble illegitimacy.

Since only a rich man could afford to bear the expense of building a king's castle, the man who held such a castle commanded great power. Particularly if like Josselin de Combourg his loyalty was total and unquestioned. That he had been chosen for this task was a great honor for the king had friends of unquestioned birth in greater families who were themselves great noblemen. Josselin de Combourg was but a simple knight in rank. Few, however, were jealous of the young Breton for he had always been careful not to make enemies. He was considered, despite his birth, a part of the king's inner circle.

The king, too, had been careful. The castle to be raised would not be large, nor was a town to be built with it. It would be little more than a border keep. There would be no jealousy among the king's friends over this gift. Possibly in the future Josselin might find himself ennobled should he again render valuable service to his liege. For now, however, he remained a simple knight whose task was to build a castle.

It was much too late in the year to begin the actual construction of the castle. The site would be chosen, and the buildings raised to house the workers who would be coming to Aelfleah in the springtime. Josselin asked Mairin to ride with him and Master Gilleet that he might familiarize himself with the land, and decide upon the right location.

"Why must you build at Aelfleah?" demanded Mairin irritably. "The Welsh have never bothered us."

"You cannot count upon the fact that in the past you have escaped their detection, my lady Mairin. The king is asking that castles be raised in several spots along the border."

"You will draw them right to us," Mairin grumbled. "Logic dictates that the castle be placed upon the heights. There it will sit like a wart upon a nose. A beacon drawing every Welsh outlaw and raider right to Aelfleah! Why do you think this manor is so prosperous? It is because few know we are here."

"I cannot put the castle in the valley," he said.

"I am aware of that!" she snapped at him. "I wish you didn't have to put a castle anywhere upon *my* lands."

"Lady, given the choice, I should far rather be a lover than a warrior," he teased her.

The engineer accompanying them chuckled.

"I have seen evidence of neither a lover nor a warrior, my lord," she snipped, and he burst out laughing.

"Which skill do you prefer I demonstrate first?" he chortled as she blushed fiery red.

"Ohh, you are insufferable!" she fumed, kicking her horse into a canter to escape his laughter. She was uncomfortably aware of his masculinity. Admittedly he was an attractive man although he had not the elegant beauty of Basil, nor the handsome prettiness of Eric Longsword. Rather Josselin de Combourg's face gave the impression of severity. Still when he smiled the precise features softened.

He had a long yet roundish face that matched his long body. His tawny dark blond hair was cropped short close to his head, and cut in a bang that only partly covered his wide, high forehead. His nose was big, the nostrils flaring just slightly at the base above the full lips that ran practically the width of his squared and sharply sculpted jaw. His eyes glinted a green-gold from beneath thick brows and heavy eyelids giving the mistaken impression that he was contemplating sleep when he was, in fact, always alert. He was, she decided, a dangerous man.

Catching up with her he apologized. "I should not tease you, my lady, not when our situation is so confusing. Yet I find I enjoy it. I cannot believe you have not been teased before by a man who was as totally enchanted by your beauty as I am. Can we not be friends? I do not believe us enemies."

"I am not certain what we should be to each other, my lord," she said, turning to look directly at him. "My experience has been somewhat limited where men are concerned. I was half-child, half-woman when I arrived in Byzantium and attracted the attention of my husband. I had never had a suitor until Basil. The only men I have ever known well have been relatives or Dagda, who is like my family to me. I have always been sheltered by the men in my life. My Breton father oversaw the years of my early childhood. When he died, Dagda, who had been my mother's servant, looked after me. Then came my adoptive father, and my husband. Now once again Dagda sees to my safety.

"In Constantinople Basil did not allow me to be part of the court for he considered it corrupt, and felt it would spoil me. I have lived all my life surrounded by those who would shelter me from a world I have never had the opportunity to really know. The only thing I am able to judge you by, my lord, is your motives, which seem to be to take my lands from me. Without my lands I am worthless. Even a serf has more value than a landless noblewoman. Each of us claims Aelfleah. Should this not make us enemies, my lord?"

"No, no," he protested, realizing suddenly the one thing he did not want was her enmity. "The king is fair, and he is just, my lady. When he learns of your existence, and of your status as your father's heiress, he will surely compensate you for Aelfleah. You will not be worthless!"

"My lord, I do not wish to be compensated for the loss of my home. I wish to keep it," she answered him. Though her words were serious her voice was gentle. Then she laughed, almost ruefully. "You and I shall not settle this matter between us, my lord. Neither of us wishes to give up what we rightfully consider ours. Let the king who has unwittingly placed us both in this quandary settle the matter."

"And if he gives Aelfleah to me?" he inquired mischievously.

"He won't," she said with infuriating certainty.

"And in the meantime," he asked her, "shall we be friends?"

"Yes," she answered unhesitantly, "and Master Gilleet shall continue to plan for the king's keep. It matters not, my lord, whether you or I build it. I know now it must be raised to help keep the king's peace."

He smiled at her words. "It requires a great deal of gold to build a castle, my lady Mairin. I was chosen because I am a wealthy man."

"I am a wealthy woman," she answered him airily. "Remember, Josselin de Combourg, I am the widow of a prince of Byzantium. My jewelry alone could have financed your king's war with Harold Godwinson."

"Do not boast so, lady," he cautioned her.

"Do you not believe me? You have but to ask my mother."

"I do not believe you capable of lying, my lady Mairin. If your wealth is as vast as you believe it you must take care. There are those who would desire your wealth more than yourself. You could easily become prey to some unscrupulous knight and so you must be discreet. The happiness you knew with your prince was brief. The unhappiness you might face with the wrong man could be endless."

"Would that make you unhappy?" she heard herself asking him.

Reaching out he drew her horse to a stop beside his. "Yes," he said quietly. "To see you possessed by another man would make me very unhappy." It was in that moment he knew that he wanted her more than he wanted Aelfleah. Or her fortune. Or even the king's favor.

Mairin, her eyes widening slightly with this unexpected revelation, knew it too. "My *lord*," she whispered half-afraid, "what is this that is happening between us?"

"I do not know," he said honestly. "You are surely an enchantress, Mairin of Aelfleah, to have so quickly captured my heart." Reaching out he took her hand, and raising it to his lips, kissed it.

His mouth was like a burning brand upon her cool skin. The heat coming through the soft kid of her riding gloves. She felt as if her heart had caught within her throat, and for the longest moment she thought her bones were melting. She even believed she might fall from her mount's back, and disgrace herself. Yanking her hand from his grasp she said, "I cannot think when you do *that*, my lord!"

"Josselin," he answered her hoarsely. "My name is Josselin, enchantress. Say it!"

Mairin gathered her reins back into her hands, and gently nudged Thunderer forward again. "Josselin, we are almost at the crest of the hill.

I believe I know a perfect site there for the king's keep. Do not look at me that way! Master Gilleet is almost upon us now. Would you have him gossip?"

"Tonight, enchantress mine," he warned her. "You will not escape me so easily again. I vow it!" His heart was beating erratically within his chest and he was uncertain he could even breathe when she looked at him with those huge velvet eyes of hers. *Witchcraft!* It had to be witchcraft, for when else had he been so suddenly affected by a woman?

The engineer joined them. Together they rode to the top of the hill, where Mairin pointed out a large, almost square piece of land that was surfaced in solid rock.

Master Gilleet was delighted, for a castle built upon a foundation of solid rock would never fall. "We will allow the walls to follow the slightly irregular shape of our foundation," he said, extremely pleased as he walked about making mental measurements. "Your serfs can spend the winter building housing up here for the workers. With any luck by March we shall be able to begin the digging for the walls, my lord. Look to the west! The view is unobstructed for miles in all directions. This will be an important castle despite its small size."

They smiled at his enthusiasm, their eyes meeting over his head. When the engineer was satisfied with his inspection of the site he remounted his horse. Turning their horses once more toward Aelfleah they began the descent into the valley. A wind had sprung up, and the sun was beginning to slip behind the horizon as they reached the manor house.

"The day was so fair that I forgot it is December," said Mairin, dismounting her animal to hurry swiftly into the building. Standing before the blazing fireplace in the hall she pulled off her gloves and held out her hands to the warmth.

"With you every day would be fair," he said quietly coming up behind her to place his hands upon her shoulders and draw her back against him. "The day I arrived at Aelfleah I saw you coming from the woods with a group of young girls. I thought that you were the loveliest creature I had ever seen." He brushed his lips against the crown of her head, savoring the soft texture of her hair against his lips, inhaling the haunting fragrance of her in his nostrils. His arms slipped down to encircle her narrow waist, to bring her even closer against him. "I thought to myself that if you were a serf I should have you in my bed that very night," he finished with brutal honesty.

She stiffened at his words, and attempted to pull away from him. "But I am not a serf, Josselin."

He maintained his firm grasp on her, and she thought she heard humor in his voice as he said, "No, you are not a serf, Mairin. You are the heiress to Aelfleah, and I find to my own amazement that I have fallen in love with you. I have made love to women, but I have never loved one."

"Do you not love your mother?" she said infuriatingly.

"That is different," he said. "You know it is!"

"How?" she demanded, feeling incredibly elated by his words. This is what she had been waiting for all her life, and until this moment she had not realized it! Still she would follow the advice he himself had earlier given her. Could love really happen this quickly? How could she be certain? She must be wary.

"How?" He echoed her question. "I am not certain that I can explain. I want to be with you. Not just today. I want to be with you always. I want your children to be our children. I would grow old with you," he finished desperately, wondering if she understood him.

"Not too quickly, I hope," she gently mocked him.

He turned her so that they faced one another. "I have never before opened my heart to a woman," he said quietly.

"Basil loved me for my beauty," she said seriously. "He adored perfection and in Byzantium my type of beauty was unique. He was not unkind to me. I believe I loved him in my naiveté. You, I think, love me for my lands, my lord. No, do not be distressed," she said, putting a gentle hand upon his arm. "My innocence was lost these many months past. I am no longer certain that I believe in the kind of love that is yet sung by the bards in the halls on long winter nights." She sighed deeply. "Perhaps it is better I do not believe in love. Then I cannot be disappointed, can I?"

"Do you say then that I lie, Mairin?" She could hear the hurt in his voice.

"Nay, Josselin. I believe that you believe you love me."

"But you do not."

"I cannot help but wonder how great this love of yours for me would be if I were not the heiress to Aelfleah."

He nodded slowly. He could understand her dilemma. In his heart he knew that he had loved her from the first moment he had seen her. "I am not certain how to prove my love for you, Mairin, but I will try."

"Kiss me," she said, and when he looked startled, as if he had not heard her correctly, she laughed and repeated, *"Kiss me!"*

He needed no further urging and dipped his tawny head to meet her luscious mouth with his own. To Mairin's great surprise the touch of his cool lips upon her sent her senses reeling. His mouth was hard, and instinctively her mouth softened and opened slightly beneath his. Her arms moved up, and about his neck as she pressed herself against him. They kissed for what seemed like an interminable time. Then she broke off their embrace, and throwing back her head, said,

"There is an obvious solution to this problem, Josselin. You could marry me. I am not so great a fool that I do not realize I must have another husband. Depending upon the viewpoint, we each have a legitimate claim to this manor. Would not such a marriage settle everything between us?" She pulled his head back to hers and nibbled upon his lips a moment. "I have not the widest experience but I like the way you kiss. We could be content together."

She had totally surprised him. One moment she was so innocent and lacking in guile that he feared for her, and then suddenly she was all the wisdom that women had accumulated throughout the ages. He had often heard William proclaim the female of the species a deep and great puzzlement. Now faced with Mairin's outspokenness he wondered if any man ever truly understood a woman. She could chide him for loving her because she believed it was her lands he loved best, and with her next breath she was proposing marriage between them because she claimed to like the way he kissed her. How he wished he might marry her this very night! If she had enchanted him, he wanted to stay enchanted forever.

He was filled with joyous laughter, but mastering his emotions he said to her, "The king did not know of your existence when he awarded me the lands of Aelfleah, but I cannot marry you without his permission. He may wish to place both you and your lands in the hands of one of his great lords. I am but a humble knight, Mairin, the nobility-born bastard of Raoul de Rohan, the Comte de Combourg."

"The Comte de Combourg? He was my father's dearest friend! You are his son?"

"*His bastard*," he repeated, wanting to be certain that she understood him.

"William of Normandy is bastard-born," she answered him with a wave of her hand. "My stepmother declared me a bastard though it was not true. It matters not to me, Josselin de Combourg, but to find that you are the son of my father's friend. I was only five and a half when my Breton father died, but I remember his best friend, Raoul de Rohan. He came to the Argoat twice each year to hunt with papa within our forest. When papa died my stepmother had the church declare that I was not true-born so that her daughter might inherit my lands. Then Dagda and I came to England. Aldwine Athelsbeorn saw me, and brought me home to his wife who was grieving the loss of their own daughter, Edyth. The rest you know. An heiress I may be, Josselin, but I have no great name either here in England or in Brittany. My lands are not so vast that a great lord might covet them. Surely the king will agree to our marriage. It is the perfect answer!"

"I cannot wed you without my lord's permission," he repeated.

"Yet you say you love me. Perhaps you really do, Josselin de Combourg. A greedy man would wed me and bed me before he next saw the king, and only then ask for royal permission. You seek my lands, but you refuse the easy solution."

"When the king first knighted me I could not decide upon a motto for my future family. Only recently have I made that decision. The words I will emblazon upon my shield will read, *Honor Above All*. I have tried all my life to live by those words. I cannot change now even for the love of you, Mairin of Aelfleah."

"I could not be happy with you, Josselin, if you did. Men like to believe that honor is something belonging only to them, but women, too, have their honor. When my stepmother sent me from my home she dishonored not only my father's name and memory, but my mother's name and memory as well. One day I will right that wrong."

"Have you proof that she testified falsely against you? If you do the king will see that your lands in Brittany are returned to you."

"I have the proof," she answered him. "I always did. But Dagda said we were safer leaving Brittany for my stepmother would not rest until my lands were her child's. Even if it meant committing murder. I have lived most of my life an Englishwoman and so I do not seek my father's lands, Josselin, because I have Aelfleah. Yet I do want to clear my mother's name."

All the while she had spoken she had stood within his embrace. Now he gently released her, and set her back so he might look into her face. His eyes gleamed with love. "You are everything I have always sought in a wife," he said, "and now I know why I have never loved another. To have loved any woman less than you would have rendered valueless the love I have for you. If it be necessary I will do battle for you. Only you will be my wife. I will have no other!"

Chapter 9

William of Normandy had declared all along that he would be crowned in London on Christmas Day. He was not, however, able to enter the city of London itself until just a few days before his coronation. Hastings had not been an automatic entrée to all of England, and there were yet strong pockets of resistance against William.

Josselin de Combourg and his party did not arrive in the great city until December 24th. Mairin told him of the small house located on the edge of the town owned by Aelfleah manor and they immediately realized how providential such a dwelling was for the city was filled with those who had come to see the new king crowned. Since housing was at a premium, they were fortunate the little house had not already been confiscated to shelter some Norman lord. They found William at the archbishop of York's London residence.

"Ho, Josselin de Combourg!" The king's usually stern features were relaxed this day. "Have you so quickly subdued the manor I gave you that you can come to see me crowned?" He held out his hand in friendship, and Josselin grasped it with a smile.

Then he turned to greet those closest to William. His half-brother, Odo, the bishop of Bayeux. William FitzOsbern, the king's steward. Robert, Count of Eu. Robert de Beaumont, William de Warenne, and Hugh de Montfort. "There was nothing to subdue, my lord. I was welcomed at Aelfleah. Had it been necessary for me to subdue the manor it would now be done. I would not miss your greatest hour of triumph."

"Then you are welcome, and those who come with you also," said William. "You may present them to us, Josselin."

Josselin drew Eada forward. She had worn her very best winter gown for this occasion, but now she wondered if the fine-spun indigo blue wool was suitable, or if she looked like the bumpkin she felt. At least, she thought, my garnets are the best to be had.

"My lord, I present to you the lady Eada, widow of your loyal ally Aldwine Athelsbeorn."

Eada curtsied low, her skirts blossoming upon the gray stone floor about her, her dark red head dressed with its coronet of braids bowed in perfect homage. She did not realize just how pretty she looked or that her sweet smile reminded the others in the room of the wives they had had to leave behind in Normandy.

"I am pleased to learn, my lady, of Aelfleah's gentle submission to this good knight. You need have no fears of being uprooted from your home for I have charged Josselin de Combourg with your care."

"I thank your majesty," said Eada. "Your loyal knight has been kind to both me and my beloved daughter."

"*Your daughter?*" William looked genuinely puzzled. "I was not aware that you had a daughter, my lady."

The other men in the room now found themselves interested by the exchange going on, and the bishop of Bayeux could see that Josselin's eyes were bright with humor as he answered the king's query.

"Sire, may I present to you the *Heiress of Aelfleah*, the lady Mairin Aldwinesdotter. Therein, my liege, lies a problem that only you can solve for we both claim the lands in question. She by the legitimate right of inheritance. I by right of your majesty's conquest of England."

The king was decidedly curious. "Come forward, Mairin of Aelfleah," he said, "and let me see you."

Mairin moved from her place beside Josselin, coming forward to stand before the king. With a deliberate motion she pushed back the richly furred hood of her nut-brown woolen cloak to reveal her extraordinarily beautiful face framed by its red-gold hair which was barely restrained by finely carved gold hairpins studded with pearls, small emeralds, and crystals. The soft hiss of admiration that echoed through the room did not distract her in the least. She curtsied, but the king could see there was little submission in the gesture, only politeness.

William stared hard at her for a long moment. He could not ever remember having seen such a lovely girl. She was extremely well dressed. Her deep green silk tunic was buttoned modestly at the neckline with small pearls, and fell just below her knee and was worn over an undertunic of rich yellow wool. The sleeves of her gown were long and wide and embroidered with gold and blue metallic thread bands along the edges.

About her waist was a girdle of gold plaques enameled in scarlet, blue, and green, and around her neck she wore a thick gold rope necklace with a circular pendant of rubies and pearls. In her ears were small pear-shaped pearls, and upon her fingers were several rings.

Slowly he let his eyes travel the length of her, realizing she was almost his height. Unlike his wife who was extremely tiny in stature, Mairin could look him directly in the eye. His life had frequently depended upon his ability to make quick judgments. Looking at Mairin he saw before him a well-to-do young woman, and realized that his gift to his loyal Josselin was perhaps greater than he had intended. He could not, of course, take it back now.

Focusing his gray-blue eyes his gaze met that of the girl. It was a proud gaze, but beyond it he saw the worry. She feared for herself. For her mother. And for the lands which were the greater part of her value to a future husband. She had every right to be worried, he thought. I have casually given away her inheritance to a stranger seemingly without care for her. That is not right. Still I have given my word to my old friend that the manor is his. "Well, Mairin of Aelfleah, we do indeed have a problem," he said. "What say you?"

"Your majesty could give me in marriage to Josselin de Combourg, for Aelfleah is my dowry. It would seem, my lord William, a fair and sensible solution," she answered him boldly.

The men about them chuckled, eyeing the young knight with amused approval.

"You are not promised, lady? I cannot believe that."

"I am a widow, sire. My husband is dead these past ten months."

"Who was he?"

"Prince Basil Ducas. He was the Emperor Constantine's cousin. I was married to him while my father was in Constantinople negotiating a trade treaty between England and Byzantium. I hope your majesty will continue to honor that treaty, for it is greatly to England's advantage. With my husband's sudden and unexpected death I returned home to England with my mother. As I was in mourning and England was on the brink of war, it was not a propitious time to consider another marriage. Then my father and brother were killed fighting Harold Hardraade."

He nodded. "You would be willing to marry Josselin de Combourg? He has told you of his birth?"

"Yes, sire, he has been forthright with me, and I with him."

"What is it that you must confess, lady? I cannot believe that anyone so fair should have a stain on her soul."

"Josselin has said that I must tell your majesty my entire history before a decision can be made regarding our fate, and the disposition of the manor of Aelfleah. I have agreed."

"*Honor Above All*, eh, Joss?" said the king in a gently mocking tone.

"Yes, my lord."

"Very well then, Mairin of Aelfleah, say on."

"I am not the natural-born daughter of Aldwine Athelsbeorn, and his wife, Eada, sire. They adopted me as their child when their only daughter died. It was all quite legal, and within the Anglo-Saxon code. I was designated my adoptive father's heiress should there be no other heirs of his blood. When my brother, Brand, was killed at York I became Heiress of Aelfleah.

"I was born in Brittany. My father, Ciaran St. Ronan, was the Sieur de Landerneau. My mother, his first wife, Maire Tir Connell, a princess of Ireland, died shortly after my birth. When I was a small child my father remarried. My stepmother was with child when father was killed in an accident, and she arranged with her uncle, a bishop, to have me declared bastard-born so that I could not inherit my father's lands. An hour after my father's death she sold me to a passing slave trader who brought me to England where Aldwine Athelsbeorn saw me, and purchasing my freedom brought me home to Aelfleah. I was just six years old. That is my history, my lord William."

"You make serious charges, Mairin of Aelfleah. Not only against your father's widow, but against a bishop of the holy church," said the king. "I realize that you were a child when these things transpired, but could you still not have proved your claim if indeed you were legitimate?"

Mairin turned, and beckoned to Dagda, who came forward to kneel before William. "This is Dagda, my lord. He was my mother's servant, and has protected me all these years. The explanation to your question is his to make. May he speak?"

"Rise, Dagda," said the king. "You have my permission to continue your lady's tale."

The big Irishman arose, and in his deep, commanding voice said, "I have the proof." He reached into his tunic to draw forth a folded piece of yellowed parchment which he carefully opened and spread out for the king to read. "These are the marriage lines of the lady Mairin's parents, sire. They were entrusted to me by my lord St. Ronan shortly before he died. In the days following I kept them on my person for safety's sake. Had I dared to show this proof of my lady's true birth I believe that neither the widow of St. Ronan nor her bishop uncle would have hesitated to kill the lady Mairin, for they meant to have the St. Ronan lands at any cost.

"Aldwin Athelsbeorn knew the truth and agreed with me that she must be protected. We did what I believed was right, sire. It is hard for any child to be bastard-born, but it is harder for a maiden than a lad."

The king nodded in agreement. "So," he said, "Mairin of Aelfleah is also an heiress in Brittany. What say you, Joss? Would you stay in England, or would you go home to Brittany?"

"Sire." It was Mairin who spoke. They looked at her in surprise.

"My lady?" The king gave her leave to speak for the urgency in her voice startled him.

"I do not want my lands in Brittany, sire. My half-sister is innocent of the wickedness her mother committed. She should not suffer for it. I am the heiress of Aelfleah. It is enough!"

The king looked as if he might argue the point with her. No one could ever have enough lands, but of course a woman wouldn't understand that.

Then the king's brother, Odo, the bishop of Bayeux, said quietly, "This is a scandal not worth making, William. The lady Mairin has been careful not to mention names, but I know of whom she speaks. We have many good Breton knights who have helped contribute to your victory. The pope himself has aided you. I think we would be wise not to incur any enmity.

"The cleric in question is long dead of his own vile excesses. As for the *lady*, she has no dowry of her own. Having bartered the lands in question to gain her own daughter a respectable match, she lives in retirement, a pensioner in her eldest brother's house. It is hardly an enviable position for a woman yet young. The lady Mairin shows a generous nature in true Christian fashion, my brother. Can we expect any less from you who are as loyal and good a son of the church?"

William of Normandy snorted with amused affection. "Now," he said, "I know why mother put you with the church, Odo."

The handsome young bishop smiled. "The church," he said in a pious tone, "is in the blood of this family even as is conquest."

The king laughed, and flinging up his hands said, "I cannot argue with you, Odo. We must settle this question of the manor of Aelfleah, its heiress, and its new lord whom I appointed not knowing of its heiress."

The bishop lowered his voice, and softly advised his half-brother, "The lady wears her jewelry casually as if she is accustomed to wealth although her foster father was not a wealthy man. She has obviously inherited from her first husband. How much she possesses, William, that is the question. The manor involved is not enough to raise jealousy among your closer friends and more powerful allies. Since Josselin is well liked, I do not believe anyone would deny he deserves your generosity. And you cannot afford to lose such a loyal friend. As for the heiress, beauty such as the lady Mairin possesses can be a dangerous liability. We must chance that the monies possessed by the lady are not so great as to cause dissension among your supporters later on."

"What you are saying, Odo," the king replied in as soft a voice, "is that the solution is as the lady Mairin has suggested. That they marry with one another."

The bishop nodded. "Now," he said. "Today before any thought can be given to it by those who might be envious. After your coronation tomorrow Josselin and his bride will leave London to return to Aelfleah. Once out of sight they will be forgotten by those who otherwise might question your decision, and envy de Combourg his good fortune."

William nodded. Then he said to Josselin, "You are not precontracted to any other woman, Joss?"

"No, my liege. There is no one."

"Not even one you might prefer over Mairin of Aelfleah, or someone with whom you have discussed the possibility of marriage? Speak the truth to me as you always have, Joss. If you cannot be content with this lady, or your heart is elsewhere, I will still see you well rewarded for your long service to me."

"I can be content with this lady," came the quiet answer. He looked to Mairin whose radiant smile set other hearts within the room racing.

"And you, Mairin of Aelfleah," said the king. "Will you accept my choice of a husband for you, and surrender to him your lands in dowry?"

"I will accept your choice of a husband for me, my liege, but I would retain my own lands, and swear my fealty to you even as did my father."

William looked surprised at her bold words. He had heard that Anglo-Saxon women were outspoken and independent. He was not certain that he approved. "What is this?" he said. "You would haggle with me, lady?"

"Saxon law," she said, "allows me possession of my own property, sire. Norman law does not. Have you not agreed to honor the laws of this land? If my lord husband should fall in defense of you, and our children be but babies, how can I protect them without another husband? What man will have me without a dowry? I pray that God will give my lord Josselin and myself many years together, but I must plan ahead."

The king shook his head. "The lands must be in the hands of those who can defend it, Mairin of Aelfleah. You are but a weak woman. I will, however, strike a bargain with you. Render the manor of Aelfleah to Josselin de Combourg to be his in his lifetime. It will revert to your ownership should he die and you be either childless, or your heir be a minor. That, and half your wealth to your husband."

"I agree, sire," she answered him, and her violet eyes twinkled. "I suspect if I don't you will have everything of me before I know it. Only let your scribe draw up the papers before the marriage ceremony."

Again William shook his head. "You must learn to trust me, lady," he told her sternly. "You will be married here and now before me, but when you leave to return home the proper papers will be in your possession." The blue-gray eyes stared hard at her, and Mairin bowed her head in submission. It was far more than she had hoped for when she so daringly bargained with him.

The king looked at his brother and said, "Will you waive the banns, brother bishop?"

"I will!"

"Then perform the ceremony, my lord of Bayeux. All of you here with me will be witness to the fact that on this twenty-fourth day of December in the year of our Lord, ten hundred and sixty-six, Josselin de Combourg, a Breton knight, and a loyal servant of William of Normandy, took to wive the lady Mairin Aldwinesdotter, heiress to the manor of Aelfleah—in the presence of their king, and of her mother, the lady Eada of Aelfleah; Robert, Count of Eu; William FitzOsbern; William de Warenne; Hugh de Montfort; and Robert de Beaumont."

Josselin took her hand in his; and together they stood before Bishop Odo as he united them in holy matrimony. Afterward the king ordered that a health be drunk to the newlyweds, who then raised their goblets to toast their king. Mairin was feeling very giddy after two goblets of strong red wine.

Her mind fled back several years to her wedding day with Basil of Byzantium. How different it had all been on that bright spring day when hope itself had perfumed the air, and she had believed in a love that would last past mortal life into eternity itself. Now, she thought, I have made a marriage of convenience, and given Aelfleah into the keeping of a stranger. I wonder if he really loves me, or if now that the manor is his I will become just another of his new possessions.

"You must follow my brother's example, Josselin," the bishop was saying, "and have a large family. Our own mother gave birth to five living children, and I have two half-brothers, the sons of my father's second wife, Fredesendis. Families are important. A man's strength comes in part from the strong familial ties he has as well as those he makes."

Josselin nodded. "My lady and I will found a whole new branch of my father's family here in England. God willing, our name will have honor. What say you, Mairin? Will you give me at least half a dozen strong sons?" His arm tightened about her waist.

"*What?*" She looked startled. Though she had heard her name, she had not comprehended his question.

The young bishop chuckled indulgently. "You have the look of a maiden wed for the first time," he said. "Your new lord asks if you will give him a large family. You had no children from your first marriage?"

"We were but wed eight months, my lord bishop."

"Time enough for a man to plant his seed," the bishop remarked casually.

"My daughter was overyoung to be wed," said Eada, coming to Mairin's rescue. "The prince adored her! He insisted upon their marriage for he feared that someone else might see her, and seeing be unable to restrain his desire."

"Ahh," said the bishop, understanding lighting his gray eyes. "It is well known that maidens wed too young do not easily conceive. How old are you now, my lady?"

"Sixteen this October past, my lord."

"You are certainly old enough now! Do well by your lady, Josselin de Combourg! By autumn next I predict she will have given you a fine son!"

"Sons for a new England," said the king. "Yes, my lords and ladies, 'tis just what we need. Strong sons for a strong England!"

Another toast was raised, this time to the future sons of Josselin de Combourg. Mairin wondered as the cool wine burned its way down her throat if she would be able to walk or for that matter even stand if Josselin took his arm from about her waist. "Do not release your grasp of me, my lord," she murmured to him. "I think that I am drunk."

He chuckled. "The king will not tolerate a poor vintage in his wines. Those of us who serve him grow quickly used to it."

"It might be better had we eaten earlier, but we have had nothing since we broke our fast after the Mass this morning," she said. "I do not know if my legs can still function."

"Let us find out," he said, and then, "My liege, will you give us leave to depart? Aelfleah is several days' journey away, and we only arrived this morning. My lady is tired, and so am I. If we are to depart tomorrow after the coronation I think some rest is due us now."

"Rest? On your wedding night? What of those strong sons for England, de Combourg?" teased Hugh de Montfort.

"Fie, my lords," scolded Eada, but the king and his friends could not restrain their laughter. Mairin blushed a rose color, realizing the implications behind their words.

"My liege, my lords," laughed Josselin good-naturedly, "my wife and I will take our leave of you now." His arm still about Mairin, he led her from the king's residence. Finding herself the only woman in a roomful of men, several of whom sent her admiring looks, Eada curtsied to the king and hurried after them.

"A most handsome woman," observed the Count of Eu. "What a pity she cannot stay."

"Perhaps in the spring we should visit this Aelfleah," said Hugh de Montfort, "to see how our friend Josselin gets on."

"Do you think the widow will give you a warm welcome, Hugh?" teased Robert de Beaumont.

"A widow is still a woman, mon ami," laughed de Montfort, looking out the window to see the newlyweds mounting their horses.

"Just sit upon Thunderer," Josselin instructed Mairin as he boosted her into her saddle. "I will lead him."

"Are you all right, my child?" fretted Eada anxiously.

"The wine," Mairin said weakly, feeling her stomach beginning to roil ominously.

Eada shook her head, and turned to her new son-in-law. "She has never had a strong head for wine. She usually waters hers. The king's wine was a particularly fine one. I enjoyed it, but I fear Mairin will be ill from drinking it."

Josselin's mouth quivered with humor. He had just married the most beautiful woman anyone had ever seen. His bride, however, looked close to vomiting. It was not, Josselin decided, a particularly romantic wedding night. He gazed over at Mairin, and saw that she was indeed very pale. A faint sheen of perspiration moistened her brow, and her violet eyes were closed. He wondered if she felt as awful as she now looked.

She did. Mairin had never realized before how very much like a ship a horse could be. Her head was beginning to ache fiercely and with every step that Thunderer took she felt closer to disaster. She wondered if she could reach home without getting ill, but between the rocking motion of her horse and the stink of the narrow streets she was not certain. The smell of the river at low tide did not help, but by some miracle the icy cold air of the late December afternoon kept her from losing control. She opened her eyes gratefully when her mount finally stopped and Josselin lifted her down in front of their London house.

His green-gold eyes shone with sympathy as he said, "I fear we must postpone any celebration of our nuptials, my lady wife. I would show you off proudly tomorrow at the coronation. To do that I think you will need a long night's rest."

"My lord, I am sorry," she murmured, and he laughed ruefully.

"Enchantress," he said, "I truly do love you, and I do not think that either of us could overcome your being sick amidst the heights of passion. England's strong sons can wait another night for their creation."

Mairin chuckled weakly. "My mother said you were a good man, Josselin de Combourg. I suspect she does not know the half of it. I think I will like getting to know you better."

He grinned back at her. Then picking her up he carried her into the house and upstairs to the bedroom, where he set her down. "I will sleep downstairs tonight, Mairin," he told her, kissing her quickly upon the forehead. Then as he left her he said, "I will send your mother to you," and he was gone.

"Go to your daughter," he told Eada when he had returned to the downstairs hall. "I will sleep here tonight."

As Eada disappeared up the stairs Dagda moved to the fireplace and put light to the kindling he had arranged earlier. Carefully he fed the little blaze until it was burning brightly. Then he added two dry logs. The wood crackled sharply, the flame leaping and casting dark shadows upon the walls of the room. After moving a long table within the little hall, he filled two goblets of wine from the decanter upon the dusty oak surface. He handed one to Josselin.

"Now, my lord," he said, "I will toast your marriage to my lady Mairin. Long life to you both! Many children! Peace!" and he quaffed the liquid down in a single gulp. Then he placed his goblet upon the table. "I am fifty-eight years old," he began in his deep voice. "My father I do not remember. My mother was a large woman with a great capacity for almost anything but her many children by as many men. We were allowed to run wild. I stood over six feet tall at the age of twelve, and I had not yet stopped growing. I fought my maiden battle at twelve and a half. I killed two men, and for the first time in my life I found approval, adulation, acceptance. By the time I was seventeen, my lord, I was the most vicious and most feared warrior in Ireland. My name was a curse that mothers used to frighten unruly children into good behavior.

"At twenty-six I was captured by a group of monks. I was lured to them by stories of their hidden wealth. *Monks!* They knew me, and for what I stood. They had decided to save my immortal soul." Dagda chuckled with the memory. "So they stripped me of my chain mail and my weapons. Then, when I was naked as the day I popped from my mother's belly, they put me into a small windowless cell. 'You are to be reborn, Dagda,' they said to me, 'and this cell is your womb.'

"How I hated those monks at first, my lord, for hate was the only emotion I could understand. I cursed those kindly old men who twice each day brought me food, but otherwise left me alone with my thoughts. I vowed if I could but get free I should destroy their monastery about them.

"Finally after many weeks the hate and the anger drained out of me. One morning as an old monk brought me my food I found myself weeping, and begging his help. Without weapons and my hate I had become again the child I once was. Those good monks began the reeducation of that child. They taught me that although physical force is sometimes the answer, more often than not problems can be solved without violence. They taught me to use my brains to reason, and to solve dilemmas rather than fight mindlessly over them.

"They put me in charge of the helpless creatures, the small beasts of their farm, who needed the protection and care of someone stronger. One day I found myself reassigned to the monastery's hospital caring for those who were ill and dying. It was these things that taught me the value of life over death, my lord. I would have been contented to stay there forever.

"After two years with the monks I was told I was to be given a new task and was sent to the court of King Rory Tir Connell who ruled in the northwest of Ireland. The King's old wife had given her husband five living sons and four daughters, all of whom were grown. She was a grandmother near fifty when she again conceived, but she died giving birth to Maire Tir Connell, your wife's mother. She was placed in my custody to raise, for Rory Tir Connell, angered by his wife's death, refused to even look upon the babe."

Dagda's eyes teared from his memories, and for a moment he was silent. Then he continued his tale. "Never in my life had anyone loved me, my lord, nor trusted me as implicitly as did my princess. The heart I had so long denied bloomed warm within my chest so I gave my life to her care. It was I who chose her wet-nurse, making certain the wench was healthy. It was I who fretted over her first steps. It was I upon whom she bestowed her first smile. My name she first spoke. I watched her grow from infant to little girl to woman. I saw the pained looks of the young men who came to court her only to be sent away. I knew before she did that she was in love with Ciaran St. Ronan and I was overjoyed the day that they wed. Never for a moment did I imagine that their love for one another would end in her death.

"When she died shortly after birthing my lady Mairin I felt as if I should have died myself. The princess, however, knew me as well as I knew her. She placed her child's well-being and safety into my hands as the monks had once placed her life into my keeping. She knew I would not fail her, and I have not.

"When Ciaran St. Ronan died I protected my lady Mairin from that unholy bitch, her stepmother. When Aldwine Athelsbeorn took my lady into his home, and made her his daughter, I gave him my fealty. Now I offer my loyalty to you, my lord. Be warned though that should your interests ever conflict with those of my lady Mairin, I will serve her first. I felt that you should know this."

Josselin was fascinated by this recitation, for he had wondered about Dagda's presence in Mairin's life. He had immediately liked the Irishman because he was obviously honorable, loyal, and one to be trusted.

"I can only hope, Dagda, that my interests and those of my wife never conflict. It is obvious that you could be a formidable opponent," replied Josselin with a warm smile.

"I have not raised my sword to kill in many years, my lord. I went with Aldwine Athelsbeorn and his son to York, but the thegn, knowing how I felt, let me remain in the background caring for the wounded. Seeing the battle brought back many memories to me, my lord, but I felt no great longing to take up my sword and kill. The blood lust is long gone from me. I value life far too much now."

Josselin nodded. Somehow he understood Dagda's feelings, and he admired his fortitude. Dagda had no need to prove himself. "The king has charged me with the task of building a castle at Aelfleah," he said. "What would you say to overseeing the workers that Master Gilleet brings us in the spring? My engineer must contend with the problems of the construction, which are great. I must have someone I can trust who can see to the workers, and you are a man who is liked and respected, at Aelfleah."

Dagda nodded, and a smile creased his strong features. "Yes," he said, "I should very much like to be a part of building your castle, my lord. There was a time in my life when I was a destroyer. For many years now I have been a nurturer, but never have I had a part in creating."

"Have you no children then, Dagda?"

The Irishman chuckled, then nodded. "The care of my lady never left me time for a proper wife. There have been several women both in Ireland and at Aelfleah who have occasionally and most generously shared their beds with me. I am said to have fathered eight sons and some six daughters in my years in England. Since they have all had the disconcerting habit of looking very much like me there is simply no denying them. With your permission, my lord, I should like my eldest son, Edwin, to aid me in my task for you."

"Choose whom you will, Dagda. I will leave such decisions with you for you know the people of Aelfleah far better than I."

Dagda, satisfied with the arrangement, realized he was quite hungry. He had earlier gone to the neighborhood cook shop, purchasing a roasted capon, a loaf of bread, a small hard cheese, and for Mairin and her mother he had bought some apples and pears. After carving the bird, he sliced the bread and cheese, making three plates of food. Having served his new lord, he took a plate to Eada.

"The lady Mairin is already asleep," he said with a smile as he returned to the hall.

"The lady Eada says that my wife has no tolerance for wine," Josselin remarked.

Dagda chuckled. "I have known few Celts," he said, "with such little tolerance for spirits, but my lady is indeed one. Wine unless watered has always made her ill. Sometimes she vomits it away, and other times not, but the sickness is always followed by sleep. Neither of her parents was that way."

"What were they like? Her parents?" Josselin asked.

"Her mother was beautiful," Dagda said. "She had a voice like a lark, and she laughed easily. She was slow to anger, and usually managed to find some good in everything. I think that is why God must have taken her so young. She was surely one of his favorite children. He could obviously not bear to be parted from her.

"As for her father, he was kind and loving to my princess. He was that rare man, one with a genuinely good heart. He adored his first wife, and was devastated by her death. He would not have married again, I think, had he not felt so strongly the responsibility to sire a son. He certainly did not expect to die when he did. He was far too young."

"How did he die, Dagda?"

"An accident. He fell from his horse into the moat, and contracted a fever and illness immediately thereafter. In a few weeks he was dead, and his lady wife had managed by trickery and fraud to expel lady Mairin from her home. She was a wicked woman, my lord, with a face like an angel but a heart as black as any daughter of the devil. Had I known what she was to put her hand to I think I might have arranged an *accident* for her. So great was her lust for the lands of Landerneau that the lady Blanche cared not what happened to an innocent child."

"The lady Blanche?"

"Blanche de St. Brieuc—may God curse her!—my lady Mairin's step-mother. But that is long over with, and God and his Blessed Mother protected my lady." He took up the leg of the capon and bit into it.

Blanche de St. Brieuc! Josselin felt the blood drain from his face. He lowered his head so that Dagda might not see it, and slowly chewed on a piece of bread and cheese. Could it be the same Blanche de St. Brieuc? It had to be! There were not two women of the same name within that family to his knowledge, and Dagda's description certainly fit her. The woman Josselin had known indeed had the face of an angel. He found it difficult to believe that she was so wicked, but the evidence could not be denied.

His Blanche. He choked on a piece of bread at that thought causing Dagda to pound him on his back and hand him his goblet. Josselin nodded his thanks through watery eyes. The Blanche he had known had lived in the house of her eldest brother. She was a widow with a daughter, but he had never seen the child for the girl lived with her betrothed husband's family. Blanche had been very pleased with the match she had obtained for her offspring, for the little girl's rich lands had netted her a husband, a younger son of the powerful Montgomerie family.

Blanche had spoken little of that first marriage, indicating delicately that she had been forced to it by her family. She had said her husband was a terrible old man, and that only his sudden death had saved her from a life of unspeakable horror. She had never mentioned her lord nor his estate by name. Josselin had thought the memories were too painful for her, but now he realized her reluctance stemmed from the fact that she did not want him discussing her with his own father, who had been her husband's close friend.

She had blinded him with those limpid blue eyes of hers, with her soft voice and an even softer hand laid upon his arm when they had walked in her brother's garden. She had given subtle hints of how it might be between them.

Joss had been flattered by her attention for he was naught but a landless bastard, noble though his blood might be. He had even thought that someday when he had his lands, and a place of honor in the king's service, he might be fit to court her; to make her his wife. He did not love her, but then he had never expected to love his wife. How many men did? A man married for lands, for position, for the gold his wife could bring him. In bringing him all those things she brought them to his family also. Strong alliances made strong families.

Such had been his thoughts until the day he crossed the Aldford River at Aelfleah and saw Mairin coming from the woods surrounded by her maidens. He had loved and lusted after her on first sight. She was his beautiful and exquisite enchantress who haunted his thoughts. God had surely been looking after him when he saved Josselin from such a venal and genuinely wicked woman as Blanche de St. Brieuc by giving him Mairin of Aelfleah.

Chewing more slowly, he washed down his meal with the wine Dagda kept pouring. He decided that it was not necessary for Mairin to know of his brief connection with her stepmother for it was unlikely that either of them would ever again see Brittany, and Blanche would certainly not come to England. He had had a lucky escape, and there was no sense in distressing his wife unduly.

When he had finished his meal Dagda whisked the plates away and fetched two straw-filled pallets from a cupboard in the fireplace wall which he placed before the fire. The two men wrapped themselves in their cloaks, and slept undisturbed during the night. Josselin's first hazy thoughts as he awoke to the sounds of Dagda building up the fire were to wonder where he was. He quickly remembered. Shivering from the cold December morning, he heard the bells outside ringing in Christmas Day.

"What time is it?" he mumbled from the tangle of his heavy cloak.

"Dawn, my lord. I've already awakened my lady and her mother."

Josselin sat up. "How does my wife feel this morning, Dagda?"

"Weak, but her stomach has settled, she says. I've already taken her some bread and toasted cheese, fruit and watered wine."

Josselin arose from his pallet. "That sounds like a good breakfast provided there is some capon left."

Without another word Dagda placed the requested food before him, and Josselin raised a dark eyebrow. "Are you as magical as your mistress, Dagda, that you know my desires before I even voiced them?"

Dagda chuckled, a rumbly noise that had a warm sound to it. "There is no sorcery here, my lord. Our larder is scant. I merely provided you with what we had. Eat now. I must draw enough water from the well in the courtyard to heat so that my mistress may wash herself. It will first be necessary to break the ice away from the surface."

Josselin gobbled his food hastily but he was very hungry and barely satisfied by his meal. Then he hurried up the stairs to see Mairin, passing his mother-in-law on her way down as he went. She gave him a smile and a cheerful "Good morning" which he returned. He liked Eada. She was a warm, good and sensible woman.

Mairin sat in the large bed which was hung with dusty velvet drapes of a long-faded color. It looked nonetheless like a comfortable bed, one Josselin would have enjoyed spending his wedding night in, but that would have to be delayed until they returned home to Aelfleah. He had no intention of exercising his husbandly rights along the road in some inn or in a stranger's house. He wanted her in their own bed where he might enjoy his possession at their leisure, and not have to worry about rising early to be on their way once more. The king had always teased him about being too fastidious.

His eyes took Mairin in with a long, assessing look that brought a delicious pink hue to her cheeks. She was wearing her chemise, and he could see a pair of tempting lovely breasts through the sheer silk of the garment. "Good morning, wife," he said as he sat down beside her on the bed. She moved to raise the coverlet up to shield herself from his gaze, but he stayed her hand with his own. "No," he said softly. "I have been denied your company, enchantress. Do not, I beg you, deny me my right to at least look upon your beauty." Reaching out he gently cupped one of her breasts with his other hand, rubbing the nipple provocatively with a slow, teasing motion.

Every inch of her tingled at his touch. She thought her desire must be obvious. It had been so very long since she had been touched with love. When she faced the fact that in order to keep Aelfleah she would have to wed Josselin de Combourg, she had also thought that she would hate his lovemaking. She had believed she loved Basil and she had certainly loved the desire he had raised within her. She adored his touch. She had never been afraid when he taught her the many ways two lovers could please one another without consummating their passion. When Eric Longsword had touched her she had hated it, and foolishly, she had assumed that she would hate the touch of all other men. How wonderful to find that it was not so!

She almost purred with her pleasure, and seeing the look of contentment upon her beautiful face Josselin laughed aloud. "Oh, my sweet enchantress, how you tempt me! I wish we were not expected at Westminster for the king's coronation. I wish it were not necessary to leave as soon as possible in order to be admitted. I should like to climb into bed with you this minute, pull the curtains tight, and satisfy your charming, and obvious longings." Reluctantly he took his hand from her breast. "God, Mairin, do not look at me that way! It makes me want to ravish you!"

"I do not mean to be so shameless," she murmured ingenuously, "but it has been a long time since a man touched me. I did not believe I should enjoy another man's touch after Basil's death. Have I shocked you, my lord?"

"Lady, you have delighted me with your desire. I promise you that when we return home to Aelfleah I shall satisfy all those hot little passions of yours. Is there no end to your surprises, Mairin? A beautiful wife with prosperous lands who is eager for her husband! The king has given me more than he realizes. If the truth were known I should this day be the most envied man in England!" He took her hand, turning it over to kiss first her palm, and then the sensitive skin upon the inside of her wrist.

She felt her pulse leap wildly, but whether it was his words, his kisses, or a combination of both, she knew not. "My lord, if this be a honeymoon then I hope it will last our lifetime," she murmured, "but now I must dress if I am to be ready in time."

"May I help?" he teased her mischievously, and was surprised once more by her honesty and openness.

"My lord, if you touch me again I shall not be responsible for my actions. If you could send my mother to me I would be grateful."

She swung her legs over the bed, and stood up.

He stood also, and taking her by her slim shoulders he looked into her violet eyes, feeling his breath catch within his chest. "Do you want me, enchantress, as much as I want you?" he half-groaned, feeling his senses fill to overflowing with her elusive scent and the heat of her body.

"Yes," she whispered huskily, "I want you, my lord husband. Not merely for the children you will give me, but for the pleasure we can give each other. Basil always said that children grew up, and left their parents but that a man and a woman began and ended together; that they taught one another passion in the beginning, and despite their duties to family and country they should not lose that passion because in the end it would once more be for them as it was in the beginning. Their love and their passion for one another would sustain them in their old age. Oh, Josselin! I suddenly realize that I want you to love me!"

"*You want me to love you?* But, enchantress, *I do!* Have I not said it? I love you!"

They stood for a long moment gazing at one another. Then Eada's step upon the stairs brought them back to reality. "Josselin," said the older woman as she entered the room, a steaming basin in her hands, "Dagda has heated some water for you downstairs. Mairin and I will hurry, and be ready as quickly as possible."

There was nothing for him to do but return to the hall, but before he went he stole a quick kiss from his wife which brought a smile to her lips and those of her mother, particularly when he whistled his way back down the stairs.

"You are fortunate," said Eada. "Did I not say he was a good man?"

"You are thinking of father," said Mairin, who had quickly seen the sad look that crept into Eada's eyes.

"I miss him," said Eada softly. "I spent practically my whole life with Aldwine. Now I am alone. It is a strange feeling, my child. I go through the days thinking that something is wrong, that something is missing. Then suddenly I realize what it is. It is your father. He is gone, and I feel for the first time in my life less than whole."

"But you are not alone, mother! You have me, and you have Josselin. One day you will have grandchildren too. We need you!"

"Then you do not want me to return to my brother's hall? I may stay at Aelfleah?"

"Stay at Aelfleah? Aelfleah is your home, mother! You are its mistress."

"No, Mairin. You are now its mistress, and Josselin de Combourg is its lord. Aelfleah is mine no longer."

Mairin flung her arms about her mother and hugged her hard. "Once," she said, "my home was stolen from me. I was sent away from the place I loved and knew best. Then you opened your heart and your home to me. You took me for your daughter even though at the time your heart was breaking for Edyth whom you had carried within your womb and raised for five years.

"I do not remember the woman who gave birth to me, mother. It is you who raised me, who rejoiced with me in the hour of my small triumphs, who wept with me over my small misfortunes that at the time seemed so enormous to me. It is you who nursed me when I was sick and scolded me when I was wrong but too stubborn to admit to my faults. Faults which you always forgave. It is you who are my mother. To send you from your home, from a place you love, would be a great sin. But more important, I love you, mother! I want you with me for as long as God will allow."

Eada looked with tear-filled eyes at Mairin. Her hand went to her mouth to stifle her cry of happiness. When she had recovered herself she said, "I will mourn your father and Brand all my days, but surely God blest me when he gave me you for my own true child, Mairin."

The two women hugged again, and brushed away each other's tears. Then with a smile they began to help each other wash and dress for the coronation. They would wear the gowns they had worn yesterday when they had been presented to the king. The only other garments that they possessed were the more serviceable ones that they had worn traveling down to London. No one would notice, they knew, for they were not important. It was very unlikely that they would be close enough to see the king again except at a distance. After the ceremony they would return to the house to change their clothing, and be on their way back to Aelfleah that day.

They were not expected to join the feasting afterward where there would be more male guests for there were few Norman ladies of rank in England yet. It was still considered too dangerous due to the continued unrest in the countryside. Norman women were considered by their men to be ornamental and useful only for the breeding of children, or the making of alliances. Even the queen had not yet set her dainty foot in England.

It was a cold Christmas Day, gray and overcast with just the hint of snow in the air. The streets of London were festive, and filled with both Normans and Saxons of all ranks on their way to the great Cathedral of Westminster, built by the late King Edward, and only a year ago consecrated to God's service. William had thought it the most appropriate place to be crowned. Most guests were on foot, but here and there were parties of mounted guests who rode even as did the little group from Aelfleah. They had not come to London unescorted, but Josselin was not certain of the temper of the city and had left his men camped on the far side of the London Bridge where there was less likelihood of trouble.

Now as they drew nearer to the great church the pace slowed even more in the press of the crowds. The noise was fearsome. They had been promised a place within the cathedral itself, and leaving their horses with Dagda they joined those on foot to enter Westminster. Josselin could see no one that he knew, but he managed to secure a place for his wife and Eada toward the rear of the great church on the edge of the large crowd where they would have a fine view of William as he passed by.

William of Normandy entered the abbey of Westminster with a firm tread to be hallowed as England's king according to the ancient British rite. He was crowned and the unction performed by Aldred, the archbishop of York. The late King Edward had been forced by the Godwin faction to remove the legal prelate of Westminster, and replace him with a priest named Stigand whom the pope had disavowed.

It was not a long ceremony, and when it was over Archbishop Aldred presented William I, King of England, to the people, speaking in the English tongue which was quite an innovation. Then Geoffrey, the bishop of Coutances, speaking in his native Norman French, also presented the king to all his subjects.

Unfortunately the mercenary troops guarding Westminster heard the second round of shouts marking the king's acclamation and thought a rebellion was starting. They promptly set fire to some of the surrounding houses. This error in judgment was quickly corrected, but not before two homes had burned to the ground, and some half a dozen others had been damaged. Horrified, the king gave immediate orders that reparations be paid to the householders. Then he thanked God upon his knees before the main altar that no one had been hurt in the melee.

Torn between the women in his care, and a possible danger to his liege lord, Josselin had hesitated a moment when the furor arose. Then Mairin had hissed at him, "Go to the king, my lord! We will be safe here." He left them without even looking back. When the confusion had settled William noticed his Breton knight, and smiled briefly at him.

"I am all right, Josselin. Go back to your beautiful wife and to those lands of yours, and help to keep England safe for us. I have been crowned king this day, but if I am to keep my crown then I must unite this country into one. Marriages such as yours, and men like you upon the estates will help me to make England strong." He held out his hand to the younger man, and Josselin de Combourg, kneeling briefly, kissed it. Rising, he left the king's presence. William smiled after him, and turning to his brother, Odo, said, "Let us depart for Barking, brother, and receive the homage of my subjects good and true."

The bishop grinned back at his brother and replied, "Let us depart for Barking, William, because it is a cold day, and at Barking there is food and hot mulled wine awaiting us. Perhaps even a warm maiden who might be half as lovely as the flame-haired wench you so casually gave to de Combourg. Ahh, I envy the man! If she's as fiery as her hair you'll be lucky if that border keep gets built. She'll exhaust him in the nights, and he'll have nothing left for the days! You would have done better to give him an ugly wife so he would spend all his time out upon the walls driving the workers." And the bishop laughed uproariously.

"Odo, you are far too worldly for a man of God," said the king, a slightly disapproving tone to his voice.

"But, William," replied his brother wisely, "you needed a bishop in the family."

A small, frosty smile touched William of Normandy's mouth for the briefest moment, and then he said two words. "To Barking!" and turning, left Westminster.

Odo of Bayeux, a knowing look upon his own face, hurried to catch up with his older brother.

Josselin had shepherded his wife and mother-in-law from the great church. He knew that once the king had left, the crowds would thicken again. He hoped to get quickly away and back to their own house so that they might change their clothing and depart. Despite the disturbance Dagda was exactly where they had left him.

Mairin grinned as he boosted her into her saddle. "Can you imagine anyone forcing *him* to move?" she said to her husband.

"What happened?" demanded the big Irishman. "My heart was in my mouth when those mercenaries began firing the houses."

Josselin explained, and Dagda nodded. "Undisciplined fools!" he muttered as he climbed upon his horse.

Making their way back through the city, they reached the house where the two women quickly changed from their finery into their more practical traveling garb. The clothing was serviceable, dark and plain to the eye, for despite their armed escort, Josselin did not wish to attract any attention. His objective was to return to Aelfleah as easily and as swiftly as possible. Checking that the coals in the fireplace were completely dead, Dagda took the remaining food and locked the small house behind them. They rode over the London Bridge to meet with their armed escort.

The weather was bitterly cold, and light snow fell intermittently. The damp seemed to creep right through their fur-lined cloaks. Mairin rode with her head tucked as deeply into her hood as she could get it. Even so her cheeks felt frosted with the icy air. A year ago she and Eada had celebrated a quiet but happy Christmas with Brand, and two years ago she had been in Byzantium at Christmastide, and in love with Basil. She felt a tear glaze her red cheeks.

Why am I weeping for *him*, she thought? It was bad enough that he deserted me for a lover, but a male lover? He did not really love me for all his beautiful words! Then she thought of the tender initiation he had given her into the sensual world of passion, and of the exquisite arts of love he had taught her. Surely he had felt some love for her. She wondered if Josselin would enjoy having her practice upon his body those delicious arts in which Basil had instructed her. She very much wanted to make love to Josselin, and she wanted him to make love to her. This husband, she mused, would not leave her a virgin.

They rode until just before dark when they were forced to accept the hospitality of strangers, a Saxon thegn and his family. The thegn had not fought at Hastings having been ill at the time, and his sons were too young to have gone in his stead. Now he and his wife thanked a merciful God that it had been so for several of his neighbors had died at the hands of the Normans. Their women and children had been cast out into the winter cold to wander the roads. At least half a dozen girls of good families had been debauched by their Norman conquerors, and they were not faring well. It was a tragedy repeated all over England. Basically the king had been merciful, but there were those who had boldly defied him even after his victory over Harold Godwinson. To them he showed his wrath.

Their hosts were anxious for the latest word, and eagerly listened to the accounts of the coronation. They nodded their heads approvingly as Eada told them of how the archbishop of York had presented William to his subjects in the English tongue. The thegn almost wept openly when Josselin told him that he would be confirmed in his lands provided he swore his fealty to William. Relief was evident upon his face for he had feared that like his neighbors he would lose his lands.

"The king is not like that," said Josselin firmly. "Though I am not a

Norman I have served him for many years. William of Normandy is a just man. A harsh one I will admit, but a fair and an honest lord. You have but to be loyal and honest to him in return."

"But can he hold England?" the thegn questioned. "I hear there is yet restlessness in the north, and Exeter as well."

"King William will hold England you may rest assured," replied Josselin. "You cannot harm yourselves or your family by giving him your fealty."

The following morning they took leave of their hosts, and continued upon their way. For a few hours the sun made a brave attempt to shine, but the cloudy lemon disc was quickly overcome by the gray as they hurried slightly north and west toward Aelfleah. They traveled onward for several more days, stopping only at night to shelter, and once during the mid-day to rest the horses, and eat. At last the landscape around them began to look familiar, and they knew that they were near the end of their journey.

The valley with its fine manor house looked so peaceful and welcoming as they rode down the eastern hills to cross over the Aldford river. The stableboys came running to take their weary mounts, and within the house was warmth, and decent food and wine.

"And a hot bath!" said Mairin gleefully.

"Oh, yes," echoed Eada fervently, "but you first, child. I must see to the removal of my things from the master's bedchamber. It now belongs to you and Josselin. I will sleep in your room from now on."

Mairin was about to protest, but then realized her mother was right. The master's chamber did belong to Josselin now, and she was Josselin's wife. Mairin might be uncomfortable at first in the chamber she considered her parent's, but she would get used to it.

"I will see to the evening meal then, mother," she said quietly as Eada hurried up the stairs, Nara in her wake.

"Has the king then confirmed my lady Mairin as heiress to these lands?" asked Nara.

"Not quite, Nara," said Eada with a small smile. "The lady Mairin and my lord de Combourg were married in London in the king's very presence, by the king's own brother, the bishop of Bayeux! What think you of that?! Josselin de Combourg is now master of Aelfleah, and lady Mairin is its mistress. Now open the chest, girl, and hand me out those clean sheets for the bed!"

Rendered speechless for once Nara aided her mistress to clean and freshen the bedchamber so that the new lord and lady of Aelfleah might take their rest.

When she was satisfied that the room was ready for its new inhabitants Eada instructed Nara. "Have Kene help Dagda bring water upstairs for your lady's tub." Then she hurried back down the stairs again for in the back of her mind she remembered Mairin saying something about supper. As she reached the hall, however, Eada stopped suddenly. Her daughter was now mistress of this house, and it was her duty to plan the menus. Eada had always hated having to decide on what to have for the evening meal. It was one chore she would not regret giving up. With a chuckle she helped herself to a goblet of wine, and sat down before the fire.

Chapter 10

❦

$\mathscr{I}$t was night and the manor of Aelfleah had settled down to rest. Outside the narrow windows of the lord's house the snow, which had been threatening to fall for several days, was silently drifting down through the pitch black night to quietly blanket the sleeping earth. In the hills above the valley a wolf howled his lonely cry and was taken up by another of his kind who hunted nearby. They were doomed to failure this night and would go to bed hungry, for all the other creatures had taken shelter from the storm.

Mairin had bathed earlier in the large oaken tub that had been set before the fireplace in the solar. It had been refilled with boiling water after the evening meal and left to cool. Now with everyone else abed Josselin was to be bathed by his wife. It fascinated him that although she was a widow, Mairin had not been in the least embarrassed by his nakedness when he had first pulled his clothes from his body. Indeed she had seemed to assess him, or was that his imagination? He was uncomfortable to think she was weighing and balancing his attributes against others she had seen in such a state of nature.

"You are very long," she noted innocently while looking at him up and down. He had just stripped the last of his clothes off.

"Is there any particular part to which you refer, lady?" he teased her devilishly.

"Everything about you is long, my lord. Your face, your arms and legs, your trunk. Indeed I have never seen such a long man."

"Is there nothing else of great length that takes your fancy, lady?" He leered wickedly at her.

He could see her seriously considering his words for a long moment. Then suddenly she turned fiery red as what he really meant struck home.

"Oh, knave!" she scolded him as he laughed. "Get into the tub, my lord, before the water cools too much! I am not certain that a cold bath would not be more suitable for such a randy fellow!"

"Oh, Mairin, my sweet enchantress of a wife! I admit to being as randy as a young billy goat for you! You are the most beautiful woman I have ever seen! We have been man and wife these six nights yet I have been unable to bed you. Do you know how very much I long to lie with you? To caress your beautiful body? To possess you fully?"

She smiled, and began to gently soap his broad shoulders. "Tonight, my lord, we will both satisfy our desires for each other. I will give you pleasure such as my first husband taught me, pleasures that delight a man. In return you will make love to me, and give me children. I very much want children!"

She had no idea of the effect her words had upon Josselin. The blood pounded in his ears and with a suddenness that surprised her he reached up and pulled her into the tub with him. Wrapping his arms about her he kissed her with a ferocity that left her totally breathless. She felt his tongue push into her mouth. She welcomed that first penetration of her person, slowly stroking at his tongue with her own even as Basil had instructed her. Cradling her in his lap he tore away the delicate linen of her shift, the only garment she had been wearing, and flung the two pieces from him. She was vaguely aware of water sloshing over the side of the tub and onto the floor as he drew her hard against his chest.

Their tongues were cavorting wildly, one about the other, licking at each other, at lips and cheeks and ears. She flung her head back exposing the column of her throat to him. His tongue darted along the silken length of the skin while a hand fastened itself about her breast. With unhurried movement he kneaded the flesh within his fingers slowly, until he felt her bottom grinding into his lap as her passion began to rise.

She turned her head to bury her face into his neck. Then reaching up she fastened her teeth into his earlobe, and bit gently, worrying it as a puppy might worry a piece of cloth. Next she pushed the tip of her tongue deep into his ear, teasing at him with little flicking motions.

"Ahh, enchantress," he groaned, "unless you desire our first coupling to be here in this tub, then you must cease this sweet torment."

"I did not know one could couple in the water." She looked into his face seductively, saying sweetly, "I was quite happy bathing you, my lord. 'Twas you who drew me into the tub, and totally destroyed my chemise. Are you not ashamed?"

"No," he said softly, his green-gold eyes bright with his desire.

"Let me up," she commanded him weakly, his look seeming to drain the very strength from her bones.

Reluctantly he released her, and helped her to arise. Mairin stepped quickly from the tub and knelt to finish her task of bathing him. The ends of her long hair were wet, but she did not feel them for her skin was still damp too.

Josselin had glimpsed her fully when she had risen and he had almost lost his breath in wonder at her beauty. He had felt himself hardening with the mere sight of her. She was so very beautiful, *and* she was his.

With a pounding heart and lowered eyes so she might hide her thoughts, Mairin finished bathing Josselin. She poured several buckets of rinse water over him and he stood up, his aroused state no longer a secret. Her breath had grown quite shallow as she observed the hard, pale column of his manhood springing from the dark blond curls between his lean thighs. Here before her was the weapon which would destroy her virginity, and how eager she found she was to face that destruction. Rubbing him dry with a rough piece of linen she said huskily, "We must get into bed, my lord, lest we catch a chill."

Without a word he took the cloth from her, and gently rubbed her damp smooth skin which was almost dry from the warmth of the fire. His hands lingered in the region of her breasts, tracing the shape of them, encircling the nipples until they stood hard. Kneeling he stroked the cloth down around her navel across her plump, pink mound. His fingers followed the slit carefully, caressing gently. He felt her shudder. Wordlessly he picked her up, and carried her down the hall that ran between the solar and their bedchamber, depositing her carefully upon their bed.

The flickering candlelight cast black shadows upon his fair body as he stood above her looking down upon her beauty. When she held out her arms to him he could not resist the invitation and he lowered himself to the bed to wrap himself about her. His length pressed itself against hers, and she sighed. He smiled for her open pleasure was enormously flattering. He had never known a woman who admitted to enjoying a man's attentions. Indeed he found it delightful for it seemed to intensify his own desires. He swept his hand down her back to cup her buttock, and was somewhat surprised when she did the same.

"Your skin is soft for a man even where it is hard with muscle," she murmured.

It was not quite what he expected. All the women he had ever known lay quiet while he had his way with them. Mairin seemed to want to actually participate in their passion. It was startling, but it definitely had possible advantages. "Your skin is soft too," he answered, suddenly seeing the humor in their situation.

They lay together caressing and learning each other's bodies. To his surprise he found he wanted to be very gentle with her even though she was a widow. He could not remember having ever taken as much care with a woman as he now took with Mairin. Straddling her, he reached out to play with her breasts. Then bending forward he took a nipple into his mouth, and began to suckle upon it.

Mairin felt the warmth of his lips clamping about her skin, and involuntarily her body arched upward. The pull and tug upon her tender breasts was deliciously maddening. Threading her fingers through his tawny hair she kneaded at his scalp like a cat. Then she felt his teeth, nipping lightly at her sensitive flesh, to be followed by his tongue rubbing where his teeth had mildly scored her. It was all so marvelous to be loved again, Mairin thought, and she wanted to love him back. She wanted him to feel the same wonderful feeling that his mouth, and tongue, his hands and his teeth engendered in her.

Josselin's tongue swept down the valley between her breasts to her navel, leaving a trail of tingles behind it. "You are delicious, enchantress," he growled at her. "I want to kiss and caress every inch of you!"

"No, no!" she said. "Not yet! Let me love you a little, my lord."

"Love me? Isn't that what you're doing, dearling?"

"Nay, husband, *you* are loving me. *I* would love you now. Oh, please, Josselin! Lie upon your back, and I will love you a little."

Amused he complied to her rather strange request, curious as to what she would do. Kneeling upon her haunches Mairin leaned over him, kissed him sweetly and swiftly. Then her little tongue began to bathe him, sweeping down his neck, over his shoulders, and across his chest to his nipples. She licked and nibbled at them, and Josselin was assailed by the most incredible feelings.

He had never been touched by a woman in such a manner. He had believed a man mounted a woman and had his pleasure of her. He, however, had learned early that he gained more pleasure of his partner by caressing her a bit before the coupling. He had never had any complaints. Now, however, his wife was showing him another side of a woman. He was not, however, certain whether she should do these lovely things to him even though he was enjoying every moment of her attentions.

Then suddenly to his immense consternation Mairin's red-gold head dipped low, and he felt her take him into her mouth. With a groan of total surprise his first thought was to reach for her, and draw her away from him, but he could not do it. Rhythmically she drew upon his manhood sending shocks of burning passion through his entire system until he was certain he would burst. In that moment he regained enough of his senses to order her away.

"Cease, enchantress!" he managed to gasp. "Though I would flood you with my seed, at least let it be where it can take root!"

Mairin raised her head up and said, "But did I give you pleasure, my lord?"

He nodded, and then asked, "Did your prince teach you such things?"

"Yes"—she smiled—"he did. I asked him if such a thing was forbidden, but he said only by fools and hypocrites."

Josselin laughed weakly. "I think, lady, that I follow in large footsteps," he said. Then reaching up he pulled her back down to him, feeling her breasts crush against his chest as their tongues began to play once again. He could taste himself within her mouth, and he found it arousing.

He inflamed her. This man who was her husband excited her greatly and she wanted him very much. How strange, she thought hazily. I thought I should never love or trust again. Though I knew it not at the time, I was naught but another beautiful possession to Basil. I cannot help but wonder if he ever really wanted me. Would I have been enough woman for him? Why did Basil wed with me? Was it that he wanted no one else to have me if he could not? With Josselin things were much simpler. We have wed for the sake of Aelfleah. He is a normal man, and he wants me because I incite genuine lust within him. He says he loves me, and perhaps he believes it himself. Maybe he even does.

He was stroking her breasts again. His warm hands cupped and fondled her while his fingers played with the tight buds of her nipples. Gently he pinched the sensitive flesh, pulling it out to roll the tender tips between a thumb and forefinger. Mairin murmured softly with pleasure.

I want him! she thought. I want to be taken and totally possessed by this man; I want my virginity to end. *Sweet Holy Mother!* He doesn't know! Mairin suddenly realized she hadn't told him that she was still a virgin! She hadn't even thought of it seriously until this very minute! It had not mattered, considering all that happened since he had come to Aelfleah.

She was a widow. In light of their love play she knew that he would assume her to be totally experienced. How many virgins had experienced the various kinds of passion she had with Basil? And then came to their marriage beds still virgins? Could a man really tell if a woman was a virgin? It was something she had never considered before. What was she to do? This was hardly the time for them to discuss it.

Josselin was burning with desire for his beautiful wife. Her provocative actions had aroused the most incredible lust within him. He had never felt this way before. She was the most exciting female that he had ever known. He didn't know whether to be delighted by this knowledge or not. Passion was not, after all, a quality one expected in a wife. Then feeling her warm, silky body atop his, he could no longer resist. With a groan he rolled her over so that it was he who mounted her.

"Enchantress, I will wait no longer! You have kindled a raging inferno within me that I am not even certain possessing you will ease."

"Josselin . . ." she began, but he silenced her with a kiss, and she felt him seeking between her thighs. She pulled her head away from him desperately. His kisses were like a drug which always left her feeling dizzy with pleasure. "You don't understand!" She made another attempt to tell him.

Gently he put his hand over her mouth. "No, enchantress, *you* don't understand. I am hot to have you, my adorable flame-haired wife, and I will without further delay!" His legs straddled hers and his big hands firmly parted her thighs. One hand reached forward, a slender finger slipping between her nether lips to gently rub at her little jewel. He knew the action always excited a woman.

A soft hiss escaped her. His touch sent a tiny flame of desire racing through her which was followed by several others in quick succession. Her body was both weak with her longings, and tense with her imaginings of what was to come. *I must tell him*, she thought dreamily, but it was too late. His mouth closed over hers again, and she could feel the smooth head of his manhood probing her unresisting flesh to finally press forward just within her passage.

I must be gentle for it has been a long time since she last received a man, he considered thoughtfully. She is so tight! So very tight! Ahh, sweet Jesus! How I want her!

She tried to relax, willing her young body to be warm and welcoming, but she was suddenly afraid. Pain! Eada had said there was pain. He was going to hurt her, and she had to stop him! He had to know that she was a virgin! They couldn't do this thing! She panicked completely, all her sweet memories of pleasures fleeing before her fear. To his great surprise Mairin struggled wildly against him, twisting this way and that, almost unseating him in her terror. Her fists beat against him with serious intent.

At first he thought it some new game she played. Catching at her hands he yanked her arms above her, and began to once more press forward within her. "Why, enchantress," he demanded of her through gritted teeth, "do you play the virgin with me?"

Bosom heaving with her exertions Mairin managed to sob, "I am a virgin, my lord! *I am!*"

He was about to laugh, then he unexpectedly found his progress within her delicious body impeded by some barrier. Thinking he had imagined it, he drew back, gently advancing only to find himself again prevented from any further progress. Amazement written upon his features he looked down at her questioningly. "What sorcery is this, enchantress?" he demanded feeling the insistent throbbing of his manhood, and the need to complete what they had started.

"None, my lord," she sobbed. "Basil did not consummate our union. I was too young. There was no time!"

"No time?" The words exploded in his brain. There had been time enough to teach her a courtesan's tricks, but none to honestly consummate a marriage? What the hell kind of man had Basil of Byzantium been? Why had he not made Mairin completely his wife? Josselin's head was beginning to throb. Why was he so angry? he wondered. Mairin was a virgin. No other man had even known her. None ever would. She was his, and his alone. He could feel himself aching with his need to finish what had begun.

"Enchantress," he groaned, "I will try to go gently, but I cannot stop now!" He began to move once more within her, pulling back to begin a tantalizing, rhythmic motion that left her gasping with pleasure. Then when she did not expect it, he burst through her maiden barrier burying himself as deeply as he could inside her, saddened by her sharp cry of pain, yet glad to have been the only man to have heard it.

Her own cry echoed in her ears. The pain seemed to be everywhere. It spread up into her chest, and down almost to her knees. Was this pleasure? It couldn't be! And then as quickly as it had claimed her the pain was fast receding from her body like a tide. A different feeling began to grow, a feeling of such enormous proportions that she was almost as frightened of it as she had been of her other fears. Still it was not unpleasant, only unfamiliar. Reaching out she clung to Josselin, some primitive instinct leading her onward now, her lips moving against the side of his face.

He had lain for a long moment atop her, willing himself still so that she might regain herself. Then feeling her arms about him, her soft mouth kissing him, he could no longer restrain himself, and began to drive within her with a sweetly sensual rhythm that he knew would bring them both to eventual fulfillment. Her sharp little nails began to claw him, but at the same time he felt her make the first tentative movements of her own in answer to his body's call. Very quickly they were moving together as one, and her face soon told him everything he needed to know.

I have died, she thought. I have died of pure pleasure! She was very conscious of him. He was big and hard, and throbbing with an unbelievable heat inside of her own pulsing body. She ached with his loving, and at the same time she soared like a falcon. Up. Up. UP. Surely she could go no higher! Yes, her bemused brain told her. I have died, and it is magnificent. Then she was whirling downward into a warm darkness that suddenly claimed her.

With a groan Josselin loosed the flood of his seed into her eager virgin's body. In his entire lifetime he had never known such fulfillment with a woman! She was perfection, and she was his wife. Rolling his weight off of her he wrapped his arms about her, holding her close. "I love you, Mairin," he said simply, smiling against the tangle of her hair as she sighed softly and replied, "I think I love you too, Josselin."

He managed to pull the fox coverlet over them before they fell into an exhausted sleep, and they slept for most of the night. In the cold, gray light of dawn Mairin awoke. She was aware of an incredible feeling of well-being such as she had never experienced. She heard the sound of his breathing next to her. Mairin turned her head slowly and saw that he lay yet sleeping, one arm flung over his head, the other across his eyes. He looked vulnerable in sleep. She wondered what his life had been like when he had been a child. His father had obviously accepted him despite his bastardy. Who are you, Josselin de Combourg? she wondered with a little smile. Who are you, you who are my husband and my lord?

"Good morning, my lady wife," his voice said, piercing the quiet. His eyes were still closed.

Mairin chuckled. "How long have you been awake, my lord?"

"Since before you awoke, enchantress."

"And you lay there while I contemplated you?" He nodded, and she chuckled again. "Thou art a villain at heart, my lord," she said, but she was smiling, her eyes light with laughter. "Have I properly fed your vanity now?"

"What were you thinking as you looked upon me?" he said.

"Despite our marriage and our coupling I was realizing how little I know you, Josselin de Combourg. I was wondering what your childhood had been like."

"It was happy and it was unhappy," he said, fascinated by her thoughts.

"Why?" she probed.

"You know the circumstances of my birth, Mairin. I lived at Combourg from the time of my birth until I was four years of age when my father remarried. My mother and I were then sent to my grandfather's house. I was happy in both places. I was well loved by my parents, and by my grandfather. My much elder half-sisters, Adelé and Bruis were kind, and spoilt me.

"My father visited my mother each day while we lived away from him. Then his young wife died in childbed delivering my half-brother. At first there was much consternation that Guéthenoc might not live, but a strong, healthy wet-nurse was found for him, and he thrived. By then mother and I were back at Combourg. This time my father would not listen to his relations, and he wed with my mother. I was six then, and it was then my life began to change.

"Of course my mother was anxious to prove to my father's family that she was fit to be his wife and the chatelaine of Combourg. She lavished great and loving care upon my younger half-brother. Guéthenoc was, of course, by virtue of his legitimate birth, my father's legal heir. My mother would allow nothing to discomfit Gué. Knowing no other mother my half-brother adored her unquestioningly. When he was two I was sent to William of Normandy to begin my formal education for my father would educate me as he had been educated."

"And you were unhappy to be sent away," said Mairin.

For a moment Josselin's eyes grew distant and sad. Then he answered her, "Yes, I was unhappy. By that time my mother was more Gué's mother than she was mine. It has been that way ever since. She was a wonderful mother to me for six years, but today there are those in Brittany who believe her my half-brother's natural mother for she behaves that way. I am considered my father's motherless bastard.

"I would be lying if I said to you that I did not resent it. I do, yet I feel guilty. My family has never denied me their love or support. By making my own way I learned my worth, and that is important for a man. Still each time I see my half-brother with my mother I ache. Her eyes light with pride for his meager accomplishments. They turn away from the sight of me for my presence embarrasses her. Nothing I can ever do will wipe away for her the stain of my bastardy."

"And your father?" Mairin queried curiously.

"My father has always been kind, but he has never allowed me to forget that I am his bastard, and not his legitimate son. Still he has provided well for me, considering. It was he who opened the doors to William of Normandy's court for me, and in the years in which I was yet young he oversaw with honesty the inheritance that my maternal grandfather had left me. He has never denied my paternity, acknowledging me publicly as his son. No, my father has treated me well, considering my birth."

"How old are you?" Mairin asked him. "I am your wife, and yet I do not know the simplest things about you."

"I am thirty. My birth date is August 3rd. I know that you are sixteen for Eada has told me, but when is your birthdate?"

"October 31st, Samhein eve."

"Samhein? Do you keep the old ways, Mairin?"

"I light my fires," she said warily. "I have done so all my life. Dagda taught me, for my mother's people did."

"It is a pagan rite, Mairin. I do not think the church looks kindly upon such behavior."

"Pah!" she snapped at him. "What do you really know of it, my lord? Do you understand why the fires are lit?"

He had to admit that he didn't.

"Then I will explain it to you," she said, "but do not think to forbid me for I will not obey you in this one thing! Samhein is the start of the new year when the earth begins the slow cold death of winter that must always precede its rebirth in the spring. Do you find that un-Christian?" Mairin had conveniently neglected to mention to her husband that Samhein was also the time when it was thought that the barriers between life and death were the lowest, and it was believed that the spirits moved most freely between the two planes. "Imbolc on February 1st celebrates the lactating of the ewes, a certain sign of the returning spring. Beltaine, May 1st, is a spring festival of fertility, of conception, and was once in our past the traditional day for Celtic marriage. Lugnasagh which is celebrated on August 1st is a feast to commemorate the sun, and the energy represented by life in all its diverse embodiments. Is any of this wrong, my lord?"

"It does not sound so," he considered slowly, "but what does Father Albert think of all of this, Mairin?"

Mairin chuckled. "Father Albert comes from Cymru—Wales—and the Welsh are a Celtic people. The fires are not unusual here in this part of the country. As long as the Mass is well attended the clergy tends to look the other way."

"It is not so at the Norman court, my lady wife," he told her. "The king is most orthodox in his beliefs, and seeks to cleanse away any heresy on the part of the clergy. In this he is firmly supported by the pope."

Mairin raised herself upon an elbow, and looked down into his face. Her flame-colored hair hung like a curtain from her head down one side of her body: "Do you usually speak on such weighty matters as religion with the women who share your bed?" she asked him teasingly. "Is it a Norman court custom?"

One breast was hidden by her arm and the curve of her body; the other, however, was quite visible. Turning himself Josselin clamped his mouth over its nipple, and tugged upon the soft flesh. She gave a little shriek of surprise, and pulled herself into a half-sitting position against the pillows, but instead of releasing his hold upon her he simply moved with her.

"Two," said Mairin mischievously, "can play at this game, my naughty lord." Reaching down she took his sex into her hand to play with it. Beneath her skillful touch he began to grow rigid. Her fingers moved gently and provocatively along the firm length of him. She knew from the sudden nip of his teeth against her now hard nipple that she was exciting him even as he excited her.

They were both intent on their play, and intense in their exploration of each other's bodies. He loved the feel of her skin beneath his mouth, against his body. She reciprocated his passion, adoring the sensation of the hair upon his legs and his chest pressing against her tender skin. If she continued fondling him he would lose his control, he thought. He released his hold upon her breast with his mouth, and pulling himself up so he was level with her, he tasted of her mouth while her hand continued what his lips had begun.

There was so much sweetness, Mairin thought, as she felt his arm about her shoulders, his other hand cupping and squeezing a breast. His thumb rubbing against the sentient swollen nipple. Her shapely hands slipped up and down the sensitive back of his neck, caressing one moment, fingernails raking gently the next. It seemed so natural when he covered her body with his own and with an easy motion entered her. Tenderly he moved upon her, remembering she was but newly deflowered.

"Ahh, enchantress," he murmured, "you fill my senses and take my breath completely away."

His words filled her with almost as much pleasure as did his ardent body which now strove to again bring her perfect fulfillment. Instinct instructed her to wrap her legs about his trunk, and she gasped with surprised delight as she felt him drive deeper within her. She now knew to move with his rhythm, and was amazed at how well their bodies fit each other. She could feel the control that she was attempting to maintain beginning to slip and cried out softly to him.

"Ohh, Josselin, my husband, is it always so sweet?"

"Blessed Mother," he whispered back, "I hope so, enchantress!"

She was beginning to soar wildly again. The feeling was strangely reminiscent of the spiraling flight of the seabirds she remembered seeing on her short voyages; of gulls who, catching at a whorl in the current of the winds, followed it upward winding and whirling until the gyre ended to drive back down to the earth in one great swoop.

Again and again he drove himself within her and with each thrust of his loins she seemed to crave him more until she thought she should perish from the pure pleasure she was receiving. She wondered if he, too, was being pleasured. Then, just as the night before, without warning she plunged down into honeyed darkness, hearing as she slid away his triumphant cry of ecstasy, feeling the warmth of his seed as it once again flooded her womb.

When she once again found herself breathing in what seemed a normal manner, she discovered that she was cradling him within her arms, her hand gently stroking his head. "How can it be like this between us when we are little more than strangers?" she questioned him.

"Hardly strangers now, Mairin," he laughed weakly. He drew away from her so he might sit up and look upon her. His hand reached out to caress the curve of her jaw that led to her chin. "No, enchantress, not strangers. Perhaps we know little about each other in the formal sense, but our bodies have certainly become old friends in a very short time."

"Our souls too, I would venture to guess, my lord."

He nodded. "Yes, my lady wife, I believe it to be so."

"It is strange but I am happy," she told him. "In my whole life I can only remember being really unhappy once, but what I feel lying here with you is an entirely new emotion for me. I realize now that what I feel is true happiness. We are fortunate, my lord."

"Aye, Mairin, we are fortunate to have found each other in this topsy-turvy world in which we live." He drew her into his arms so that her head rested against his chest.

Beneath her ear she could hear the strong, steady beat of his heart. Her nostrils were filled with his now familiar male scent. He did not smell as her father or Brand had smelled. It was different, yet comforting. It was early still. The pale gray morning light barely managing to creep through the narrow windows and illuminate the room. Other than the wind there was no sound to be heard, which indicated to Mairin that it was still snowing outside, and so she dozed within the circle of her husband's arms. She was at peace in Josselin's love.

He held her against him as if she were the most delicate and rare of creatures. He felt her body relax to slip into sleep, and his heart swelled with an emotion that he found he could not identify. This was his wife, and with her he would found a proper and respected family. His children would never suffer the sting of illegitimacy that had dogged him all of his life. That had caused his own mother to abandon him in favor of his father's legitimate son. No! His children would be legal, and they would be loved by both their parents. She stirred slightly in her sleep, and he wondered if his seed had already taken root within her lovely body, if perhaps already his son had been created, and was even now beginning to grow. Only time, of course, would give him the answer to that question. In the meantime he intended to use her often to insure their success in having children quickly.

He found himself drifting back to sleep without realizing it until he awoke once more to find her stretching herself beside him. She had thrown the fox coverlet off and was preparing to arise when suddenly he saw the brownish stains upon the insides of her thighs. Reaching out he touched them lightly, and their eyes met, the passion flowing fiercely between them. Raising himself up he leaned forward, and placed several soft kisses upon the dried and bloodied smudges, and then looked up at her once again.

"Merci, enchantress," he said meaningfully, charmed by the delicate color that tinted her cheeks.

Pulling a chemise from her trunk, she drew it over her head, and hurried out into the solar where the servants had already started a fire. The big tub had been removed, but there was a basin of warm water waiting upon a brick shelf that had been built within the fireplace. Carefully she reached around the flames of the fire, and placed it upon the table.

Wringing out the soft cloth floating in the basin, she sponged away the evidence of her lost innocence, and then returned to the bedchamber.

Josselin still lay within the bed, and he watched her curiously as she dressed. A fur-lined jupe went over her chemise to be followed by a linen skirt and a matching tunic of violet-blue, long sleeves widening from the elbow to the wrist, and which she belted with a belt of purple and gold metal disks. Lastly she pulled on a pair of soft shoes that buttoned up the front.

He watched in fascination as she brushed out her wonderful long hair with smooth, vigorous strokes, braiding it with violet-colored ribbons and looping it up so that the braids did not hang too long. Standing, she gave her skirt a little shake to remove the wrinkles and then looked over at him.

"You will be late for the Mass if you do not hurry, Josselin."

"You are the most beautiful woman I have ever seen," he said.

"Ah, my lord, do not harp upon such a thing. Beauty can be a pleasure for the recipient of such a gift, but more often it is a curse. If you love me then I would hope it would be for me, myself, and not for my beauty. If I lost that beauty then what would be left, and would you love me still?"

"Your beauty is but a part of you, my lady wife. There is far more to Mairin of Aelfleah than her extraordinary beauty. I hope to spend the rest of my life learning the many facets of the rare jewel that my lord William has entrusted to me."

"Blessed St. Cuthbert, my lord, how such flattery trips with honeyed ease from your tongue! You are, I think, a man to beware of, Josselin." She walked to the bed, and yanked the warm fox coverlet from him. "Arise, my lord! Would you set a bad example for the manor folk?" He grabbed for her to pull her back into their bed, but laughing, Mairin eluded him, turning as she fled through the door to thumb her nose at him.

She could hear his laughter as she hurried down the stairs into the hall where Eada was already waiting. The older woman turned to bid her daughter a good morning. As she did she peered closely at Mairin. Seeing nothing but happiness in the girl's eyes, she smiled with poorly disguised relief. Mairin's eyes twinkled as she hugged her mother.

"Are you all right, my child?" Eada would not be convinced by her daughter's radiant looks. She needed a verbal confirmation.

"I am fine, mother, and in answer to the question in your eyes, yes, I am at last a woman!"

"You told him, and he was gentle?"

Mairin nodded. "Yes" was easier than explaining that she had neglected to tell Josselin of her virginity until it was almost too late. "He is a good man, mother. You were right."

"Can you love him? I know it will never be as it was with Basil, Mairin, but I pray for your happiness."

"I loved Basil with a child's love, mother. I believe I can love Josselin, but it will be with a woman's love. With Basil I lived an unreal fairy tale in a golden and fabled city. I realize now that once the novelty of my beauty and innocence had worn off, Basil would have sought elsewhere for his amusements. I was a diversion to him. With Josselin I will forge a strong bond of love, and building upon that, mother, who knows what we may accomplish together. I know it would have never been that way with Basil."

Eada was more than satisfied with Mairin's answer. "Then," she said teasingly, "I may look forward to a peaceful old age."

"You will never be old, mother," said Josselin, coming into the hall, and hearing her. He went directly up to her, kissing her upon her cheek. "May I call you mother, my lady?"

Why was it she cried so easily these days? Eada wondered, feeling the tears sting her eyelids. "Yes, my son," she told him, "you may call me mother." She hugged him hard. "Now, my children, we will surely be late for the Mass," and she moved swiftly past the carved screen that divided the hall from the entry of the house where a servant was waiting with the outdoor cloaks.

"How handsome you look, my lord," Mairin complimented him.

"I would not disappoint the manor folk," he teased back, and she stuck out her tongue at him.

He was wearing blue chausses that she thought rather ill-fitting. They should have been better shaped to his legs, and she resolved then and there to go over his wardrobe, and make what he needed. His darker blue tunic which fell to just below his knee was embroidered on the neckline with silver threads, and had long wide sleeves. It was belted with a slightly wide girdle with embroidery that matched that at his neckline. As they would be going out, he wore boots that extended halfway up his leg to his knee.

As they put on their heavy fur-lined capes Dagda came in from the outside saying, "A wolf came down from the hills last night, my lord. Its tracks are everywhere about the house."

"It did not carry off any of the livestock, did it?" Josselin inquired.

"Nay. The animals were all safe within the barns because of the storm, but the beast must be hungry to have come so close to the manor."

"Be certain that the manor folk know of the wolf," said Josselin. "Starving wolves have been known to attack small children and carry them off. We will go hunting when the storm is over."

Outside it was still snowing. They walked the short distance between the house and the manor church where Father Albert said the morning Mass. Inside the church it was cold, and the wind caused the tallow candles upon the carved wooden altar to smoke. The stone floor was icy and the bitterness spread through their clothing as they knelt to receive the host from Father Albert.

It snowed on and off for the next few days, and afterward there was a week of gloomy days when the skies threatened again to loose a torrent of snow.

When they could they rode about the manor visiting the cottages to ascertain the well-being of their people. Josselin believed, to Mairin's delighted relief, that unhappy peasants were poor workers. Like Aldwine Athelsbeorn, Josselin de Combourg sought to care for his people. The smiling faces as they left each cottage told Mairin that Aelfleah's people were well-pleased with their new lord.

Sometimes Egbert, the bailiff, rode with them. He pointed out to his lord the few repairs that needed to be made here and there. They inspected the granary to learn that there had been some small losses due to a larger-than-expected population of field mice. Weorth the miller reassured his lord and lady he had recently acquired a large young tomcat who had a vigorous capacity for both the female cats who lived in the mill— all of whom were now fat with expected kittens—and for the mice whose population had already been halved.

"May yer lordship be as successful with the lady Mairin so that we may have again at Aelfleah a large family of children," the miller said boldly.

"Be silent, Weorth!" ordered the bailiff, but both Mairin and Josselin laughed. The look that passed between them told the miller and the bailiff that any lack of children at Aelfleah would not be for want of trying on the part of their lord and his lady.

On the days when the cold or the weather made it impossible to be out-of-doors, Josselin spent long hours in the hall going over the manor records while Mairin and her mother sat by the fire sewing new clothing for him. Most of his garments were worn, and the workmanship was not of the best quality, which was not surprising. Josselin had had no family to see to his clothing. When he had been a child page at the Norman court his mother had yearly sent two tunics, one for cold weather, the other for milder days, and a small assortment of shirts to be worn under his tunics, two pair of chausses, a pair of boots, and a cloak. As he had grown older, however, these small gifts had ceased coming. He was considered old enough to fend for himself by the time he was thirteen, and he had.

Young bachelors, however, had to depend upon strangers to sew for them when they could afford it, usually women servants anxious to earn an extra penny or two. It was also necessary that they purchase their own cloth, and their limited incomes naturally limited such purchases to the least costly fabrics. Eada and Mairin, both expert seamstresses, complained more than once as they viewed the sorry state of the wardrobe that Aelfleah's new lord possessed. Raiding the storage room of the manor house they brought forth linens that they themselves had woven, fine wools, and cottons, brocades and silks from Byzantium. They measured him carefully, making him stand for what seemed to Josselin hours. Then they cut and stitched until suddenly the cloth began to assume shapes. He saw a fine new wardrobe appearing before his very eyes.

At first he was embarrassed by this sudden largess, but Eada took him aside saying, "You are the lord of Aelfleah, Josselin. All that belongs to this manor belongs to you. Your old clothing was in such a bad state of disrepair that mending it was even beyond our skills as needlewomen. It is necessary to make you new clothing. We would have done the same for my husband and Brand. Who else should do these things for you?"

"I like him better without clothing," said Mairin saucily, and to her delight her husband blushed which made her laugh mischievously.

"Mother," he said to Eada, "your daughter does not render me proper respect."

"You should beat her then," replied Eada seriously, but her bright blue eyes were laughing.

"Do you really want to spank me, my lord?" demanded Mairin tantalizingly, sliding her arms about her husband's neck and looking up at him in a provocative manner. The tip of her tongue darted over her lips, moistening them.

He could feel the tightening in his loins as her teasing body and her suggestive words taunted him. "I think you need a good spanking to instill within you a proper reverence for my position as your lord and master," he growled back, "and I am of a mind to administer it now!"

"Then you will have to catch me, *my lord!*" she mocked, pushing him so hard that he fell back. She made her escape running across the hall and up the stairs, shrieking with pretended horror as he pursued her, roaring with equally feigned outrage.

Behind them Eada, and Dagda who had also been seated by the fire honing knife blades, smiled at one another, their silent thoughts quite in accord with each other.

Mairin fled down the hallway to their bedchamber, but before she might bar the door behind her he was in the room.

"You're a poor tactician, wife. Not being swift enough to outrun me, you should have given yourself at least one other route of escape." His green-gold eyes glittered wickedly as he stalked her into a corner. Reaching out he easily captured her, drawing her from her useless sanctuary.

"You're not *really* going to spank me?" she said.

"Oh, but I am," he replied, backing over to the bed where, as he sat down, he pulled her into his lap and over his knees.

Mairin was unbelieving. Then she felt him yank her skirts up to bare her bottom. She cried out in a shocked tone, "Josselin!" as she felt a hard arm clamp across her back to prevent her struggles.

For a moment he viewed with satisfaction the tight little hillocks of her pure smooth flesh. Then his hand descended with a satisfying smack which left the clear pink imprint of his hand upon her heretofore unblemished skin. Mairin shrieked more with surprise than any hurt for the blow had been only noisy, and not severe. "I will have your respect, woman," he said, his voice a parody of an outraged and offended husband. Then he laid two more spanks upon her squirming bottom, and turning her over demanded, "Are you chastened now, lady?"

"Oh, oh!" she cried, squeezing out two false tears from beneath tightly closed eyes. "Thou art a brute, my lord, to abuse me so!"

"What now? You would criticize your lord's behavior? I think I must chastise you further, lady." He stood, lifting her up into his arms as he did, and dumped her unceremoniously upon their bed. Then before she might escape him he flung himself upon her, pushing her long skirts before him, and burying his dark blond head between her thighs. That he immediately found the mark was instantly evident.

"Ohhhhh!" she squealed. "Ohhhhh, Josselin! Oh, how you punish me!"

His skilled tongue moved over her quivering pink flesh with unerring accuracy, and though he held her down tightly, his hands clasping her hips, she squirmed most deliciously beneath his marauding tongue. "Sweet," he murmured against her body. "You are so sweet, my enchantress!"

"Ahhhhh, Josselin, my lord," she whispered breathily, "I am well punished by you this day, but you will have to continue to discipline me in future quite regularly lest I forget my place again."

"Shall I correct your wayward behavior like this?" he asked her, worrying the bud of her womanhood with a flickering tongue.

"Ahhhhh, 'tis cruel torture, my lord," she cried, "but do not stop I beg of you for I would be all that you want me to be! Ahhhhh! Ohhhhh! Ohh!" And suddenly fulfilled, Mairin's body relaxed as a wave of warm, honeyed pleasure swept over her.

With a growl of lust that came from deep within his throat, Josselin pulled himself up, and mounting her, plunged his aching manhood into her welcoming passage. Like one possessed, he drove himself into her over and over again . . . withdrawing and thrusting . . . withdrawing and thrusting until she raked his back bloody with her nails and they bruised each other's mouths with hungry kisses. At last when neither of them could any longer sustain the pleasure, their juices poured forth and mingled wildly, leaving them weak with the force of their passion.

And after a long while it was Mairin who, recovering her senses, said in a shocked tone, "It is not two hours past the noon hour yet!"

Josselin laughed weakly. "Lady," he said, "what has the hour to do with it?"

"Should we be making love now? In the daytime? It seems somehow indecent."

"I know of no rule of either God or man that forbids a husband and wife from enjoying each other whenever it suits them." He rolled off her, but quickly took her hand in his, and kissing it, held it.

"Do you remember your parents making love in the daytime?" she asked him.

"Before they were married, aye, but once they had wed, she became very proper. Not so proper that she didn't have another baby. It seems so strange. My sister, Linette, is legitimate, and I am not. I hardly know her, for mother was not anxious that her precious daughter be exposed to her bastard." There was a hint of bitterness in his voice.

Mairin squeezed his hand. "We will love all our children, Josselin. I never knew my half-sister, but Brand was all the world to me. I loved him dearly. I would have our children love each other too in that way."

She was magnificent, this beautiful girl he had married! He had never known such kindness of heart in any woman, and he marveled at her sweetness. What had he done to merit such good fortune? he wondered. He wanted to shout aloud with his joy.

"I must write to my father," he said, "and tell him of our marriage. It is past time I did so, but I have not a fine hand. Can Father Albert do it for me?"

"I will do it for you," she answered him, standing up and smoothing her skirts down demurely. "If, my lord, you can compose yourself, and come back to the hall with me."

"Very well, lady, I will come with you, but from now on I shall keep a strict accounting of your behavior, and each night we will settle matters between us."

"And your behavior, my lord?" she asked, her mouth curving into a mischievous smile. "Shall I also keep a strict accounting?"

He nodded. "I am a fair man. You will have your chance to plead your case." He stood up, and settled his own clothing so that it had a semblance of neatness. Then reaching out he swiftly swept her into his arms. "You're a saucy wench, Mairin, my wife."

"A saucy wench for a bold knave, my lord," she answered him pertly, and pulling his head down kissed him hard.

"Not so quickly," he laughed as she moved to pull away from him. Then he kissed her slowly, and sweetly, his mouth moving sensuously on hers, his tongue running softly along her lips.

Why, she thought, *why is it that when he kisses me I feel as if my veins are filled with honeyed wine?* She managed to pull her head away from him. "Don't," she begged weakly.

"Why not?" he demanded. "I like kissing you."

"I like it too," she admitted, "but it makes me want you very much."

He chuckled. "I find that extremely acceptable behavior in my wife." He held her tightly against him, his hands rubbing up and down her back in a suggestive manner.

"We shall never get anything else done if all we do is . . . is . . ."

"Fuck," he supplied cheerfully, and then he laughed. "The word may be Anglo-Saxon, Mairin, but I know it. It means *to plant,* and that is just what I want to do with you. Plant my seed in you deep and sure, and see you ripen with child." The hooded eyes blazed down at her with passionate intensity. "I don't think I shall ever get enough of you, enchantress mine."

"Nor I of you, my lord!" she whispered. "Do you know how very much

I crave you? I wonder if I should not be ashamed of such a fierce desire." Reaching up she touched his cheek softly, and Josselin shuddered with his feelings.

Then he loosed her, and shaking himself said, "You are right, Mairin. We shall never get anything done if we do not leave this room." Without another word he took her by the hand and they descended back down into the hall where Eada sat still placidly sewing, and Dagda yet honed on several knife blades.

Mairin picked up the tunic she had been working on, and began once again to add embroidery to the neckline. Josselin returned to the high board where he studied the manor books. Every once in a while, however, their eyes would meet, for neither could help but look at the other. Their ardor excited and thrilled them and they felt they could not get enough of one another.

When the evening meal was served, they ate automatically, tasting little, anxious for the time when they might once more leave the hall and escape to the private world of their bedchamber. The letter to Raoul de Rohan was momentarily forgotten. Eada and Dagda cast amused looks at each other. Finally when Mairin and Josselin, with much yawning and complaint of fatigue, had left the hall, Eada said, "I think, Dagda, that we may look for an heir to Aelfleah by Michaelmas. I confess that I long to hold my grandchild in my arms!"

The Irishman rumbled with humor, but there was a touch of nostalgia in his voice. "She is like Maire Tir Connell if she but knew it. My princess was as hungry with her passion for Ciaran St. Ronan as Mairin is for her husband."

"Pray that that passion does not result in the same end," fretted Eada.

"No," said Dagda. "My princess was always delicate in her health. Mairin has always been strong, and she is broader across her hips than the princess was. Mairin has her natural mother's face, my lady Eada, but she is more like her father in build. There's a look to her. She was meant to breed up babies, and she wants to have them. My princess was joyful to be bearing Baron St. Ronan's child, but she was also secretly fearful. Such fears can take a toll on a woman. Mairin is not that way. Maire Tir Connell was a fairychild, delicate and elusive. Her daughter is made of sterner stuff. Have no fears for her safety, my lady Eada. She will not only survive whatever life offers her, she will thrive."

Chapter 11

꧁❦꧂

The winter had seemed long, but now suddenly the winds were blowing from the south. The snows upon the ground began to turn to mush, the drifts pitting first, then melting down into nothing more than icy puddles of dirty water. The earth began to thaw and warm. Everywhere there was mud. Soft and oozing in the sunshine, freezing again in the dark of night. The tips of the tree branches, tight dark nubbins throughout the winter, now began to grow lighter and burgeon with newly revived life. In a meadow by the river the lambs, born so improvidently during the harshest part of winter, gamboled within sight of their mothers, scampering and bouncing with each other amid the faint new green of the longer days.

Early each morning as the sun began to rise, and again each afternoon when the chill of evening began to creep into the air, Master Gilleet would climb up the western hills to the castle site. He would push his staff into the ground to check the gradual retreat of the frost from the bosom of Mother Earth. Already in these final days of the late winter the serfs belonging to Aelfleah had begun to build the barracks that would house those coming to erect the castle. It was still too early to till the fields and plant.

One week Dagda and Master Gilleet went off to Hereford, to Worcester, and finally to Gloucester seeking laborers, diggers, and carpenters. They returned successful each time. Aelfleah's population doubled, and then tripled as the barracks filled with workers. The stonemasons had already arrived from Normandy. A blacksmith's forge was constructed on the site for Osweald, the manor smith, so that he would not have to travel back and forth with his work between his own smithy and the castle site.

Egbert the bailiff sought among the cottages for new kitchen helpers.

He took younger girls than he normally might have for simpler tasks, and promoted other servants earlier than he usually did. They would need everyone they could get. The responsibility of feeding the vast army of workers needed to build the castle was a great one.

Weorth, the miller, added two young boys to his staff, and ground extra grain daily into flour. He couldn't remember ever having worked so hard. Aelfleah had always been a quiet, peaceful place. His responsibilities, inherited from his father who had once been Aelfleah's miller, had always been minimal. Now he worked from dawn to dusk falling into his bed so exhausted that his young second wife complained bitterly that he was neglecting her.

Byrd, the manor baker, a little wiry man whose mother had been a wild Welsh hill girl, ruled the ovens with a twinkling eye and a merry jest for everyone. The extra work was no burden for him for he loved being busy. Covered in flour up to his elbows he worked kneading the dough into loaves, whisking them to the ovens to bake and out again when they were done. Then his helpers would trek the bread up the hill to the building site where the camp cooks were busy over their fires, and glad to see Byrd the baker's loaves which were tasty and filling.

Then almost overnight the winter was gone, and the land began to quickly green. Master Gilleet and his staff began to design the castle while the moat was being dug. It was not to be a large castle for Josselin de Combourg was not a great lord. Its main purpose was one of defensive vigilance although there would be comfortable living quarters designed within the castle for the lord and his family. Although Mairin resisted the idea of eventually leaving the manor house the thought of living again within a castle was intriguing. It seemed a long time since Landerneau.

The king returned to Normandy in March taking with him those whose presence might encourage rebellion. Namely young Edgar the Atheling, Waltheof, the Earl of Northampton and Huntingdon, and the brothers Earls Edwin and Morkar. He left behind him as co-regents his brother, Bishop Odo, and his seneschal, William FitzOsbern, whom he newly created Earl of Hereford. The bishop would rule southeast England as far west as Winchester. FitzOsbern would oversee the Midlands from the marches of Wales to Norwich. Northumbria was to be overseen by a thegn named Copsi who had been a relative of the Godwin family. The southwest of England had not yet submitted to William, and was still loyal to the dead Harold Godwinson whose mother and sister were residing in Exeter.

As the days grew longer and warmer, Aelfleah's peasants were able to work the fields which were planted in barley, oats, wheat, and rye. The orchard flowered profusely in a copious haze of pinkish-white blossoms. Within *The Forest* the streams ran swiftly, and completely free of ice. Taking her basket into the woods Mairin found marvelous large mushrooms which she brought home, instructing the cook to cook them with oil, pepper, and some of their precious salt. This way the mushrooms could not give rise to the illnesses that encouraged black bile.

Then it was summer. The grain stood tall and began to ripen. A messenger from the north sheltered with them one evening and told them that Copsi had been murdered by Oswulf, the son of the ex-earl of Bernicia, in a feud that dated back between Godwin's family and the old Northumbrian ruling house. Then came a summons to Josselin to come with his men and aid the king's brother. Eustace of Boulogne, a Picard, had seized Dover Castle, and was holding it against Bishop Odo.

Mairin burst into tears. "No!" she said. "You cannot leave me now. I am with child!"

Josselin's face almost split itself with a grin. Lifting her up he swung her about with a joyous whoop. "That's wonderful, enchantress! When? Are you certain? Why didn't you tell me before?" He set her down, kissing her nose as he did so.

"I am only just sure," she sniffed. "You won't go, will you?"

"Of course I must go. Bishop Odo is the king's brother, and I am the king's man as well as his friend, Mairin. Certainly I will go, but it is unlikely that I will be gone for long. You have your mother, and you are safe here at Aelfleah. When is my son to be born?"

"*Your son?* It could very well be a daughter, my lord! Our child will be born in February." She gave a small chuckle. "I should give birth at the same time the ewes are lambing." She snuggled against his chest, rubbing her cheek against the fabric of his tunic.

He enclosed her within the circle of his embrace, and his lips brushed against a soft tendril of her hair that had escaped her coif. "If it is a son we shall work to make a daughter. If you give me a daughter, then we will endeavor to make a son the next time."

She thought about his words in the weeks that followed, and she found them comforting. She wanted a large family, and she knew that he did also. They had talked about it often in the dark of many nights while snuggling together within their curtained bed. The part of her that was coolly logical knew that if they were to prosper in this new England then Josselin must be not only loyal, but he must be outstandingly so. It was within the king's power to create a peerage, and if Josselin could earn such an honor by his usefulness and his loyalty, then there would be more for their children.

There would be the castle for their eldest son, and father's title. Aelfleah would go to their second son. The third son could have Landerneau if she could get it back. She had never considered reclaiming her inheritance in Brittany, but the child growing within her had suddenly made her mindful of the importance of a man having possessions. She remembered the king's surprise when she had said she didn't want Landerneau. She knew he thought her foolish. The child now growing beneath her heart made her think differently.

Her father's estate was rightfully hers, and Blanche's daughter had not the legal right to it. It was true her half-sister was as much a victim as she herself was. Of late she had for the first time in her life seriously considered what her half-sister might be like. Putting her mind to it she had seen a sweet-faced child with their father's russet hair. Each time she concentrated upon it she saw the child kneeling in prayer, and once the little girl appeared to her in the garb of a religious. It came to Mairin that the unknown child who was her half-sister wanted to be a nun.

Concerned that she might be overruling her instinct with her personal desires, she asked Dagda to cast the rune stones for her. Each time the answer was the same. The fate of Mairin's half-sister was with the church, not in marriage. Her conscience clear, she resolved to regain her lands in Brittany. She would see her half-sister had a decent dowry so she might enter the convent of her choice, but Landerneau belonged to her! It was her inheritance for her children!

Having settled in her mind the three estates upon her three nonexistent sons, Mairin decided her fourth son would be for the church, as well as one daughter. The other girls would be married off most advantageously due to their father's position, wealth, power, and his place in the king's favor. It was a wonderful daydream with which she entertained herself during the long and lonely nights Josselin was away aiding the king's brother in his efforts to retake Dover Castle from the troublesome Eustace.

The long summer days slipped by pleasantly. At the castle site the surveyors under the guidance of Master Gilleet had marked off the locations of the castle walls and its towers. The digging of the foundation was well under way. The quarrymen had opened up an excellent location where they might quarry stone for the project. The stonecutters were already shaping the large blocks of dark gray rock that were to be used.

The grain was being harvested. The hay had been cut, and was drying on its racks in the fields. The cattle and the sheep in the meadows were fat with good grazing, and in the orchards the trees were bent almost in two with a bumper crop of fruit. Looking upon it all Mairin felt the quiet contrast between this bountiful and beautiful summer, and the year prior when they had all been awaiting the outcome of Harold Godwinson's rash behavior.

Then one day a peddler arrived at Aelfleah, and told them of a rising on the border just over the hills by a thegn named Eadric the Wild. That night in Dagda's company Mairin ascended the hill to the castle site. Together they watched until dark when they could clearly spot the campfires of the rebel forces.

"Their direction should bring them straight to Aelfleah," noted Dagda grimly. "Rebels like that usually destroy everything in their path. Why are they doing this? Who the hell would they put on the throne in place of King William? There is no one else!"

"How long will it take them to reach us?" Mairin asked, sounding calmer than she actually felt. For the first time in memory Aelfleah was in danger. She had married Josselin because the manor needed a lord to protect it. Now that they were at risk, where was he? At Dover protecting the king's rights! It would be up to her to see that Aelfleah was defended.

"Two days, three at the most," he answered. "It depends upon how much they enjoy their work."

"We must harvest everything we can, and hide it, Dagda. If they burn the fields, the manor people, not to mention all the workers we have here for the castle, will go hungry this winter. Damn! If Josselin were here we might fight them off, but he has taken all of his men with him. We are left with nothing but serfs. We might escape the carnage but for this damned castle site! Did I not warn him about that? It's like a beacon drawing our enemies onward!"

"The castle is a good idea, and it is necessary," he said bluntly, and she looked at him, surprised. "Listen to me, my lady Mairin. England's days of innocence are gone. So are the days when this manor lay secreted and unnoticed in our hidden valley. The castle will protect Aelfleah, and few would dare to attack us if it already stood upon these heights." He took her by the arm to steady her. "Come! We have little time in which to prepare for our *guests*."

They stopped at the workman's quarters where Dagda quickly and thoroughly explained to all the assembled men the danger which would soon be upon them. Then he turned to Mairin, giving her the floor, for as the lady of the manor with her husband away, she was the only authority figure they had.

"I want no unnecessary blood spilled," she told them. "Each of you master craftsmen is to gather his men together, and I will see you hidden so that no harm comes to you. When Eadric and his rebels come they will find nothing to threaten them. You will stay hidden until the danger is past. We value the skills that each of you possesses far too much to endanger any of your lives." Then Mairin repeated her speech in French so that the stonemasons might also understand her, and know their position. "I will also need your help tomorrow in the fields," she continued. "If we are to save our harvest in so short a time I will need every available pair of hands. If they destroy the crops, how will I feed you all this winter?" She smiled sweetly at them, and there was not a man within the room who did not silently vow to follow her into hell and back if necessary.

As soon as the faint gray light of morning began to brighten the skies the next day, all the people of Aelfleah streamed from their homes, and went into the fields to harvest the grain that had not already been cut. Most of the workers were city men who knew little about farming, but, their very survival at stake, the castle workmen learned quickly from the serfs who were happy for even inexperienced hands to help them. Both Mairin and Eada worked beside their people encouraging them onward.

Egbert the bailiff saw that the castle, horses, and sheep belonging to the manor were herded into groups, and driven off to more hidden locations within *The Forest*. There had been no serious danger to Aelfleah since her grandfather's time, but Egbert recalled the old man's tales of how the Northmen had once swept inland up the Wye and Severn rivers, where they then anchored their longboats and ravaged the surrounding countryside. So impressed was he by these remembrances that he even managed to find hiding places for the poultry and the doves in the dovecote.

The castle workmen could give Mairin only a day and a half's labor before she sent them to hiding places in the stone quarry and deep within *The Forest*. The young women belonging to the manor who were not yet married were sent off to a nearby convent for safety's sake. Mairin sought to avoid the rape of the women that might easily occur given the temptation of pretty faces.

Shortly after dawn on the third day Eadric the Wild and his men stormed the western hills, firing the barracks and the workshops at the castle site as they came. The manor gates were open to Eadric for Mairin had no intention of even attempting a resistance. Indeed she greeted him at the door to the house, gowned in a soothing blue, her glorious red-gold hair braided, a demure white veil upon her head.

"Given the reputation which precedes you, my lord Eadric, I cannot welcome you to Aelfleah, but neither do I deny you entrance," Mairin said boldly.

Eadric the Wild, a big man with a thick beard and shoulder-length brown hair, looked down from his horse upon the beautiful woman. He felt to remain seated upon the big beast which added to his height would give him an advantage. Mairin's cold words, however, disabused him of any notions of frightening her. He took a moment to appraise her, and staring back at him Mairin thought she had never seen such icy blue eyes.

"You are Mairin of Aelfleah?" he growled at her as he slid from his mount.

"I am."

"What are you building upon the crest of the hill?"

"A castle," she answered him.

"Why?" The cold eyes betrayed no emotion, not even the curiosity his words proclaimed.

"To keep the king's peace," she said.

"Which king?" he snarled.

"There is only one king of England. William."

"The usurper? You build a castle for the usurper?"

"William of Normandy is England's rightfully anointed and crowned king, my lord Eadric."

"The crown belongs to Edgar the Atheling, lady."

"Edgar the Atheling is a child," said Mairin patiently, as if she herself were speaking to a child and not a man. "He could not hold England against invaders. He would be easy prey to those of his own countrymen seeking to rule through him. Besides, our late King Edward chose William of Normandy as his heir. King Edward knew we needed a man of strength."

"So William the bastard claims."

"The pope upheld his claim!" retorted Mairin.

"Bah! A foreigner who knows nothing of England, or of her people!"

"A people who want peace," Mairin snapped back, "but they do not seem to find it when men like you pillage the land!"

"I fight for our freedom, woman!" roared Eadric.

"You fight for what you can personally gain," she replied angrily. "Why else do you rob, and kill, and ravage the countryside? Why have you come here? Aelfleah is a small and isolated manor with little to give."

Though Saxon women were noted for their bluntness of speech, and even encouraged to it by their families, Eadric was taken aback by Mairin's fierce words which touched too close to the truth to satisfy him. She made him very uncomfortable. His reputation as a warrior usually cowed the people with whom he dealt. What was worse was that she spoke before his own men. He would find himself losing his authority if he did not regain control of the situation.

Drawing himself to his full height he thundered at her, "Get into the house, woman, and shut your mouth!"

Mairin smiled mockingly and she swept him an equally taunting curtsy. "Do come into my hall, my lord Eadric. I will give orders that your men be fed, and their horses watered, or would they prefer to pillage themselves?" Then turning she walked back into the house.

"Woman, you try my patience," he muttered following after her, his several lieutenants at his heels.

Eadric the Wild gloried in his terrible reputation. He would have been discomfited to see the wicked grin upon his antagonist's face for he did not frighten Mairin in the least. Indeed she had already decided that he was nothing more than a bully and a blowhard. Like a wounded animal he would be dangerous if and when he was cornered, but she had decided he would be no serious danger to Aelfleah if handled properly. He was a Saxon of the old school, and he had simply not yet come to terms with Harold's defeat. He would continue to fight uselessly until he either accepted the inevitable or was killed. Eadric was a wealthy man, but he was not a man to concern himself with the comforts that life could offer. He lived as the Saxons had lived a hundred years earlier, in a large noisy hall filled with retainers and animals, both of whom scrabbled for bones and other leavings amongst the rushes. He was taken aback by Aelfleah's small neat hall which was divided from its entry by a beautiful carved screen. The rushes upon the polished floors were clean for they were changed weekly. The hall had a pleasant air to it due to the sweet herbs that were scattered amid the rushes. In the large fireplace great logs burned warming the room nicely, and seated by the fire was a handsome woman who arose to greet them.

"This is my mother, the lady Eada, widow of Aldwine Athelsbeorn," said Mairin.

"Lady," said Eadric the Wild, "I am honored to meet the wife of so illustrious a man as Aldwine Athelsbeorn."

"Thank you, my lord," said Eada, and then she returned to her seat.

"Bring wine," Mairin commanded her servants, and waved Eadric to another seat by the fire.

The wine was brought, and passed among the visitors, and then Eadric said, "One of my lieutenants is an old friend of yours, Mairin of Aelfleah. He tells me that you are promised to him."

"I am promised to no one," said Mairin, "and besides I am—" but before she might finish, a bearded blond man came forward.

"Do you not recognize me, Mairin?"

She peered closely at the man, then her face grew dark with anger. *"Eric Longsword!"*

"Aye! I have come back to claim you, Mairin! I have pledged my fealty to Eadric and Edgar the Atheling, and when you are my wife we shall hold Aelfleah for them. I have so sworn it!"

"Indeed," replied Mairin scornfully, "have you, Eric Longsword? Did I not warn you that I would not marry you? That has not changed. Why would I promise myself to a traitor for that is what you are. A traitor who fought with Tostig and Harold Hardraade against England! I would not wed with you if you were the last man on earth!"

"The choice is not yours, Mairin. Aelfleah is strategically placed, and we need it. It is your duty as a loyal Englishwoman to wed with the man who can hold this manor for England's rightful king."

"Which is precisely what I have done, Eric Longsword! I was married the day before Christmas last to Josselin de Combourg, a loyal knight of England's rightful king, William. I am my lord's loving and faithful wife, and I will bear his child next winter," she finished triumphantly, one hand placed over her belly for emphasis. Then her face darkened again with anger, and she said in an icy voice, "How dare you claim a betrothal with me, and how dare you lead these outlaws here to my lands to wreak havoc! Never did my family give you the slightest hope of a marriage between us. Nor did I! I had not thought you a man of such strong imagination, Eric Longsword."

"If you are married then I shall kill your husband, Mairin," he said coolly. "I mean to have you. I have never denied my passion for you. From the first day I saw you in Constantinople I wanted you. My feelings have not changed. You need a strong man who can teach you how to bend to a husband's will. I am that man. William will be driven from England, and the Atheling will rule as he should. You will be *my* wife with *my* babe in your belly. As for the brat you now carry, if it lives it can be given away."

Mairin stared at Eric Longsword shocked, but then she burst out laughing. Turning to Eadric she said, "This man is stark raving mad, my lord. You had best lock him away lest he be a harm to himself, or others dear to you. As for me I shall bear his company for hospitality's sake, but if he comes near me again I will have my retainers fling him from my hall out into the barnyard where such an animal belongs!"

Eadric looked shrewdly at Mairin, and asked, "Where were you married?"

"In London by Odo, the bishop of Bayeux, and in the presence of the king, my mother, William FitzOsbern, William de Warenne, the Count of Eu, Robert de Beaumont, and Hugh de Montfort."

"Where is your husband now, Mairin of Aelfleah? Did he flee at our coming?"

"Nay, my lord. He is with Bishop Odo seeking to retake Dover Castle from the traitorous Picard, Eustace of Boulogne. It was his duty to support the king's brother."

Eadric the Wild nodded his understanding. Then arising he said, "There is nothing for us here. We move on! Order the men to burn the fields and drive off the livestock. We will have something for our trouble!"

Eadric quickly discovered that the manor fields contained nothing but stubble, and that the livestock, even the poultry, had seemingly disappeared. It suddenly occurred to him that although they had burned a large barracks and workshop complex on the castle site, there were no workmen there. Nor were they to be found, nor was there evidence of the manor's livestock, or poultry, or pretty girls. Into his cold eyes crept something akin to admiration, and he chuckled although the sound held no mirth. "It would do absolutely no good to ask, would it?" he said.

"No, my lord, it would not," she answered softly.

"Then I shall not, Mairin of Aelfleah, for you have bested me once too often before my men. Still you shall not escape me entirely unscathed. Burn the village and the church," he ordered.

"What about the manor house, my lord Eadric?" demanded Eric Longsword viciously.

Eadric saw the panic leap into her eyes. It pleased him, but what pleased him more was that she went down upon her knees to him pleading loudly that he spare her home. "I fight for England," he said loudly and loftily. "I do not make war upon helpless women and babes. I will spare your house, Mairin of Aelfleah."

"Oh, thank you, my lord!" she cried, brushing an imaginary tear from her eye. She was tempted to ask him: if he didn't wage war on women and children, why was he burning the manor village? Discretion fortunately overruled her tongue.

He turned from her, but not before she had seen his lips quirk with amusement. She would have been a formidable opponent had she been a man, he thought. She planned her battle well, and knew when to retreat to cover her losses. He felt little satisfaction as he rode from Aelfleah.

Behind him the manor peasants managed to save the church, but for the roof, although the entire village was destroyed. Still as they picked through the rubble of their homes that afternoon there were certain items that were salvageable. Mairin promised them that their homes would be rebuilt as quickly as possible. The castle workmen returned from their hiding places, and were immediately pressed into rebuilding the village. This time the cottages raised would be of stone, but for their thatched roofs, so that should the village ever be fired again it would be easier to rebuild.

Within a month the cottages were done. The new barracks and workshops once more stood upon the hill. As the castle workmen had helped Aelfleah's people to save their harvest, so Aelfleah's people had aided the castle's workmen to rebuild. The manor quickly settled back to its normal routine. The grain brought from its hiding place was threshed, and stored away in dry places to be ground into flour only as needed, for flour did not keep long once ground. The apples in the orchard were ready for harvest, and the cider was being pressed as Josselin de Combourg returned home to his wife and his lands.

Mairin was loath to discuss her defense of Aelfleah, but Eada was not. "Aldwine would have been so proud of her," the older woman bubbled. "She managed to unite everyone. She saved the entire harvest, and all the livestock. Not a woman was raped, nor a man killed, nor any child carried off! 'Tis true we lost the village, my son, but it is already rebuilt, and this time of stone, but for the roofs. No man could have defended Aelfleah and its people any better. As for that cheeky Eric Longsword, she sent him packing once and for all! Why, the nerve of him telling Eadric that he was betrothed to my daughter!"

"*Mother!*" Mairin flushed.

"*Eric Longsword?*" Josselin's attention was suddenly engaged. Mairin's defense of Aelfleah had not surprised him, although her cleverness at getting in the crop and hiding the workmen had astounded him, but Eric Longsword? "Who is Eric Longsword?" he asked.

"A fool!" snapped Mairin.

"His father was a thegn in the north, loyal to Tostig," said Eada. "He served in the Varangian Guard in Byzantium where we first met him. He has always been taken with Mairin, and tried to court her after Basil died, but she would have none of him. He dared to tell Eadric that Mairin was to be his wife, and that he was to gain control of Aelfleah. To such end he swore fealty to Eadric and the Atheling. Mairin corrected him quickly enough, and Eadric realized that Eric Longsword was but bragging to gain influence."

"I will kill him," said Josselin calmly.

"You will stay here and protect us, my lord!" said Mairin sharply. "I am not well with this child I carry, and I can take no more excitement!"

Josselin looked at Eada. "What is it?" he demanded.

Eada shook her head. "She has been staining blood ever since Eadric came. She may lose the child, and I would not be surprised for she labored in the fields to get the harvest in like any common peasant."

"You labored beside me, mother, and in the village too when we aided our people to haul thatch."

"In your condition? Are you mad, Mairin?" he shouted angrily at her.

"How could I not labor with our people, Josselin? It is up to the manor lord or his lady to set the example."

"But you are with child!"

"So were half the women of the village, and none of them is the worse for it," she retorted.

"They are peasants," he protested, "and strong like beasts of burden. You are my wife, and delicate."

She sniffed. "God's will be done," she said. "If the child is not right it is better I lose it now."

He looked at her horrified. "How can you say such a thing?" he demanded.

"Men!" she claimed derisively. "What do you know of babies but that you sire them? I have seen strong, ruddy babies come into this world. I have seen pale and weak ones arrive blue and misshapen to linger a few days or a few years, breaking their mother's heart either way. If the child is not to be healthy, I should rather not bear it, and be weakened by such a birth. Is that so wrong?"

He looked confused. She was once again making logic out of what must surely be wrong. Yet he did understand what she was saying. Still, this was *his* son that they were speaking of, and he wanted that child desperately.

Mairin saw the play of emotions across his face, and reaching out she touched his cheek. "God's will will prevail, my Josselin. If it is his desire that this child be saved then it shall. We shall pray for it, my lord. Together we shall pray for our innocent child."

They prayed with sincerity upon the cool stone floors of the newly roofed church. Less than a week later, Mairin miscarried of their child. A tiny scrap of humanity so small that they could not tell if it had been the much-sought-for son, or a daughter. Mairin, who had been so calmly logical the week before, wept bitter tears in her husband's arms.

"It isn't fair," she kept repeating. "It just isn't fair!"

"There will be other children," he comforted her, feeling equal disappointment. "I am just glad that you are safe, enchantress mine. I can accept the loss of our child, but I could not have accepted the loss of you."

His loving words heartened her. "We will begin at once," she said, "and we will work very hard to gain our goal, my lord."

"Yes, Mairin, we will work very hard," he agreed, a smile upon his face. "We'll start tonight!"

"You most certainly will not!" said Eada. "You will need several weeks' rest to rebuild both your strength and your poor injured body, my daughter. Surely you understand, Josselin."

"I will abide by your wisdom in this matter, mother," he replied.

"Josselin!" Mairin protested.

"Do you want more lost babes, my daughter? That is what will happen if you do not allow yourself time to heal."

Mairin pouted, but Josselin said, "This matter of Eadric the Wild has caused us to fall behind with the castle. I will have to spend the next few weeks personally overseeing the renewal of construction if we are to have the outer walls half-finished by winter. We shall be able to work except on the coldest days."

"And what am I to do while you are busy with your castle?" grumbled Mairin.

"Get well enough to bear our children, and oversee the manor as you have been, enchantress," he said, a twinkle in his eye. "When you are well enough I intend keeping you very busy of the nights until our labors show signs of bearing fruit once again."

Mairin smiled, and lay back against her pillows. She was content now. "My mother," she said, "has raised me to be a dutiful wife, my lord. It shall be as you so desire."

Eada snorted. "Hummmmph," she said, and then they all laughed.

In the weeks to come Josselin involved himself in the serious business of building his castle. Master Gilleet had been highly recommended, and his plan for Aldford, as the castle would be called, was a sound one. The most important concerns for Aldford were that it be able to resist attack, and withstand siege. With this in mind the castle site chosen was perfect, an outcropping of solid rock that overlooked Wales to the west.

The castle was to be constructed so that its northwest walls rose above the sheer cliffs upon which the entire structure was to be placed. It made that side of Aldford virtually impregnable to attack. The outer walls of the castle, called the outer curtain, measured one hundred and fifty feet on each of its four sides. They stood twenty feet in height, and had rounded towers placed at strategic intervals that rose an additional ten feet above the outer walls. Between the outer curtain and the inner curtain, which were the walls of the castle structure itself, was a courtyard called the outer ward.

There was to be but one entry point into Aldford. Along the outer curtain walls that faced down into Aelfleah's valley a stout wooden ramp would be constructed across the moat leading through U-shaped gatehouse towers into the outer ward. A heavy timber grille called a portcullis was set between the towers of the gatehouse. It could be raised or lowered to open or to bar admittance through its passage. The entry to the outer ward could only be reached by a narrow winding road that had been worn over the years into the side of the hill upon whose crest Aldford was being placed. The entire road would be visible from the castle's watchtowers. The road was to be slightly widened, and improved.

The walls of the inner curtain being the walls of the castle itself were seventy-five feet in length on either side. Unlike the walls of the outer curtain which were but eight feet in thickness, the walls of the inner curtain were twelve feet thick. They stood thirty-five feet high with towers that soared to fifty feet. The added height of these walls allowed defenders on the tops of the walls to fire over those men guarding the outer walls. There were walks and staircases along both curtains that connected each section of the structure with the others. A low wall edging the curtains called a battlement would protect anyone walking upon the walls from attack.

The castle building was constructed around a quadrangle called the inner ward which was accessible only through the U-shaped inner gatehouse which was also fitted with its own portcullis. At each corner of the building was a square tower. There was to be a Great Hall in the castle as well as apartments for the lord's family, the bailiff and his family, and the cook and his family. The kitchens would be located next to the Great Hall. There would be barracks for the castle's garrison and stables for the horses. There would be a mews containing the dog kennels and a place for the falcons. The well was to be dug within the inner ward so that it could not be poisoned by an enemy, and there would be a blacksmith's shop as well.

It would take several years to complete Aldford Castle, and Josselin knew that the partially built structure would be quite vulnerable until well after the king had completed his conquest of England. There were yet troublesome and repeated rebellions springing up like small brushfires all over the land. Each one of these insurgencies had to be put down, and the two co-regents were kept busy. Members of the Saxon nobility foolish enough to still believe they might overcome William of Normandy found their estates confiscated, and were forced to flee for their lives.

The king returned from Normandy on December 6th. He immediately laid siege to the city of Exeter. The thegns of Devon had long since given their submission, but Exeter held out for eighteen days, finally agreeing to accept William provided they could retain all their former privileges. Gytha, Harold Godwinson's mother, and her daughter left England. Of Harold's wife, Earl Edwin's sister, and her children by Gryffydd of Wales there was no trace. They seemed to have disappeared from the face of the earth. William then marched through Devon, Somerset, and Cornwall accepting submission from hitherto rebellious thegns.

In the west Eadric the Wild came over the border from Wales to once more harass the English both old and new. This time he steered well clear of Aelfleah concentrating his unfriendly attentions upon Hereford until he was firmly driven off back to his own lair. The eleven-year-old Edgar the Atheling with his mother, Agatha, and his elder sisters, Margaret and Christina, fled north, and sought refuge with King Malcolm of Scotland.

Winter gripped the land with especial ferocity that year. The inhabitants of Aelfleah kept to the indoors huddling about their fires. Little work could be done on Aldford, but on the days that the wind did not howl too bitterly the half-finished walls of the outer curtain were filled carefully with rubble, a mixture of stones and mortar. Provided there were no serious delays the work would go faster in this new year.

Easter fell on the twenty-third of March. Soon after, a royal messenger arrived at Aelfleah. He appeared suddenly upon the crest of the eastern hills one day, and galloping down the narrow road he raced across the icy little river and through the gates of the manor with elaborate flourish.

The workers in the fields stared goggle-eyed. Dismounting his horse he looked disdainfully about him, but his mouth fell open in slack-jawed wonder as Mairin appeared in the entry of the house.

"I . . ." He swallowed hard, then remembering who he was he drew a deep breath. "I come from the king for Josselin de Combourg."

Mairin smiled, and forced back a chuckle. How often in her life had she seen the same silly look upon male faces. "You are welcome to Aelfleah," she said showing far more composure than she actually felt. "My husband is at the castle site, and I have sent for him. Come in, and have refreshment. You have obviously traveled a long way."

The messenger, who was no more than fourteen, stumbled after her to again be surprised as he entered the house. Inside it was every bit as elegant, if not more so than any Norman noble's home in which he had been. His hostess seated him before the fire, for which he was grateful, it being a chilly day. She herself poured him a goblet of wine. Thirstily he gulped at it.

"I am the lady Mairin of Aelfleah," Mairin said.

Quickly the boy put down the goblet flushing as he did so for he had shown appallingly bad manners by not introducing himself before he entered the house. He stood saying, "Your pardon, my lady, I am Robert de Yerville, a page in my lord William's service."

"Then welcome again, Robert de Yerville." Mairin smiled at the boy. "Have you come all the way from Winchester?"

"Yes, my lady."

There was a long silence in which the boy shifted uneasily, and Mairin finally said, "My husband should not be long in coming."

Josselin arrived almost before the words were spoken, much to her relief. "Robert de Yerville! You have grown, lad! Why, you must stand close to six feet," Josselin said by way of greeting.

"Just an inch short of it, my lord," the boy answered, breaking into a grin, and obviously pleased that the lord of Aelfleah had noticed his growth. Then he became serious. "I bring you a message from the king," he said, reaching into his tunic and drawing out the rolled parchment which he handed to the older man.

Josselin broke the seal upon the message, and unrolling it spread it upon the table to read. "The queen is due in England at any minute," he said aloud. "She's to be crowned on Whitsun at Westminster. We're invited, Mairin, Eada too if she wishes to come."

"No thank you," said Eada, having overheard as she entered the hall. "You will tender my regrets to the king, Josselin, but I have no desire to do any more traveling than I have already done! Besides if you are going to the queen's coronation it is bound to be a splendid affair, certainly more so than was the king's. Mairin must have new and beautiful clothing so she will not shame you. We have scarcely over a month before you are due in London. There would be no time to make clothes for us both. I am content to remain at Aelfleah."

"Oh, mother, you must not! When will you ever again be invited to a coronation?" Mairin protested.

"Mairin, my mind is made up. You will not appear this time amid a group of battle-weary men for whom the sight of any female is pleasing. You will be amongst the high and the mighty of King William's court. This time there will be many women. They will all be splendidly dressed and coiffed, and ready to judge all other women. You must not shame us. How you look and behave will help Josselin to gain new honors. You want that, don't you?"

"Why are you always right?" Mairin demanded teasingly.

"Because I am your mother," returned Eada calmly, but her blue eyes were twinkling.

Robert de Yerville stayed with them the night before going toward Worcester to tender the king's invitation to other nobles and their families. William adored his intelligent and strong-willed wife, and he wanted her coronation as Queen of England to be a magnificent spectacle.

"I have worried that we would not be able to use all those wonderful materials we brought from Byzantium before they were ruined," said Eada. "It pleases me that you will be an excellent representative of our people amongst the great of King William's court. Your father would be proud, I know," said Eada.

The two women set to work to create Mairin a wardrobe worthy of the occasion. Josselin had decided they would be in London for several days, and so Eada determined that her daughter would need a full dozen changes of clothing, but Mairin overruled her.

"I do not wish to draw undue attention to us, mother," she said. "As it is, the marvelous fabrics we are using will be envied."

"You are every bit as good as any Norman lady!" huffed Eada. "You were a princess of Byzantium."

"I am no longer, mother. I am but the wife of a simple knight which is just what I prefer to be. If we plan carefully I can interchange the tunics and the skirts which will make it appear as if I have more clothing than I actually do. Besides it will be difficult to transport too great a wardrobe."

Josselin agreed with his wife. It was wise to keep the knowledge of what they possessed to themselves, and not arouse undue curiosity about Aelfleah. It was decided that Mairin would take but five tunic dresses: two, a violet and a pale dove gray each with gold woven into the fabric, would be of brocatelle, a brocade-like fabric with a more highly raised pattern. Two would be made of silk—one of indigo blue with silver embroidery at the neck, sleeve cuffs, and hem, the other a cheerful plain yellow; the last tunic dress was of a turquoise lampas which was a patterned damask-like fabric.

There would be an equal number of skirts. One of cloth of gold. Another of silver. Two taffeta, one black, the other a light blue. The last skirt was of royal-purple damask, a color not usually allowed out of Byzantium where it was reserved only for the emperor and his subjects. Constantine's empress had, however, given Eada a bolt of the stuff as a parting gift.

Watching their frantic activity over the next few weeks Josselin found himself tempted to tease his women. "What of my wardrobe?" he asked. "Is Mairin to be the only one in this family with new clothes? I thought it was usually the male who sported the finer plumage while the little brown wren sat dutifully on her nest."

"What of all those clothes mother and I sewed for you last winter?" she parried. "I have not seen you wear half of them, and there are some beautiful garments amongst them. Besides, no one looks at men."

"The women do," he said seriously.

"Well, they had best not look at you, my lord! I suppose you left behind any number of silly creatures in Normandy who think they can still cast sheep's eyes at you. They will quickly learn otherwise!"

For a brief moment he remembered Blanche de St. Brieuc, and as quickly put her from his mind. Blanche was in Brittany. She was not, nor had she ever been, a part of or had access to the Norman court. He didn't intend upsetting Mairin with old and bitter memories. "Why, enchantress," he said, "there is no one who could take me from your side. I love you."

"Then you shall not be besieged by former amours?" she said, sounding a trifle disappointed.

He shook his head. "No," he said.

"Men never tell," she grumbled.

"It would not be chivalrous to do so, enchantress," he answered her.

"Then there *is* someone!" she pounced, and flung herself at him pummeling his broad chest.

He caught her slender wrists and prevented damage to his person, and laughingly replied, "You threaten me with direst consequences if I admit to previous loves, and are disappointed that I do not." He wrapped her in his embrace, and looking down into her face said, "I love you, Mairin of Aelfleah! As to my life before we met, I admit nothing. I deny nothing. What was is past for me, and you are all that matters."

Her heart pounded wildly at his passionate declaration, and her lips softened as his mouth met hers. The kiss was a deep and an ardent one. His tongue swirled about hers in fiery love play. Both forgot Eada who, with a smile of remembrance, turned away from them and concentrated upon her sewing. Mairin was just barely aware that her husband had lifted her into his arms, and was carrying her up the stairs to their private chamber. Her head fell back upon his shoulder, and she sighed softly with contentment.

Setting her upon her feet he began to undress her and Mairin reciprocated his actions, pulling his clothing from him with unhurried haste. Together they fell to the bed wrapping themselves about each other in their fervor. They kissed and they kissed until Mairin's mouth ached with the sweetness of their love. Her hands reached out to caress his body as he caressed her with lengthy, hungry touches. His back was so long. His buttocks so tight. His chest hard with muscle.

Josselin groaned with pleasure at her touches, and let his lips wander at will. She was so soft. The texture of her skin was like a rose petal. Her breasts seemed to melt into the curve of his palms. Her little belly quivered like the waters of a forest brook as it tumbled over the pebbles in its streambed. He suckled upon the hard nubbins of her nipples making her whimper. Tenderly he sank his teeth into her delicate flesh, and the sound she made was like a plea.

He was a little ashamed that he could not wait. He simply had to have her! She obviously felt the same way for the moment he moved to cover her body with his she parted her legs for him accepting his hard length within her. He used her fiercely, pressing forcefully into her softness and she eagerly welcomed him with equally tempestuous thrusts of her hungry body. Unable to control himself at all he felt his seed explode with a rush pouring from his hard flesh to flood her throbbing womb.

"Yesss," she breathed hotly into his ear. "Oh, yes, my lord and my love!" and she shuddered with the force of their shared passion.

Their bodies were wringing wet, and they lay panting beside each other for he had automatically roled from her so he would not crush her.

"I have never," he finally managed to gasp, "known a woman who had such capacity for love."

"Yet I cannot conceive," she said softly.

Josselin pushed their pillows up against the back of the bed, and half-sitting he pulled her into his arms drawing the coverlet over them. "Sweeting, you lost the child before St. Matthew's Day. You were not able to couple with me before Twelfth Night, and that is barely three and a half months ago. It is not that long. You will conceive before this year's harvest, I am certain. Do not fret yourself. If I am not worried why should you be?"

"If I had not been so foolish we would now have our first son, and I would be so proud to meet the king again. He will wonder why we have no child, and think he has done you a disservice rather than a kindness in seeing us wed."

"Nay, enchantress. Should he ask I will tell him the truth. That while I fulfilled my obligations to him you were left alone to face the wrath of Eadric the Wild. I will tell him of how you saved Aelfleah, and outwitted the rebel. The king will be proud of you, Mairin. He greatly values loyalty and courage."

"I am glad," she said wryly, and encouraged by his loving words, feeling a little less sorry for herself. " 'Tis all I will have to offer this time. I envy the queen her family."

"Do not," he said. "I love my lord William, but his children are an unenviable lot. Young Robert is too much his mother's son. Richard, Agatha, and Adeliza all fancy themselves greatly. Adela and William Rufus are two peas from the same pod. Bad-tempered brats who will only have their own way. There is not one of them can match their father, and therein lies the tragedy."

"You are too harsh in your judgments, I think, my lord. These are but children you speak of, and as they grow they will surely change for the better."

"Nay, Mairin, I am not hard. I am realistic. Remember I grew up at the Norman court. Robert of Normandy is fourteen and his sisters Agatha and Adeliza are thirteen and twelve. They are grown. When Earl Harold came to Normandy several years ago a match was arranged between him and the king's eldest daughter, Agatha. Then Harold killed the Welsh king and forced his widow into marriage, which left poor Agatha jilted and shamed. So the king next arranged a match for the lady Agatha with Herbert, Count of Maine, but he died. Now my lord William has arranged a match for his daughter with Alphonse of Leon, but the girl refuses to go, and swears she will die a virgin. Our Blessed Lady deliver me from children like that!"

"It is obvious," said Mairin, "that the king's children are never disciplined. If they were beaten more often they would be the better for it."

"Did your father beat you?" he demanded.

"Of course not! I did not need it, but my brother, Brand, was forever feeling father's leather strap. Once father wore out three stout birch switches in one beating on Brand. Brand was very strong and equally stubborn."

"Josselin laughed. "Well, I shall indeed beat our children if they need it, but with you for a mother I doubt they will ever feel our wrath, enchantress."

"If I can but conceive," she worried.

"You will, sweeting," he said tenderly, kissing her brow. "Now perhaps we should make another attempt."

She turned her head so she might look up at him, and her mouth curved itself into a sensuous smile. "Whatever you desire, my dear lord, my love. Have I not said mother raised me to be a dutiful and obedient daughter?"

Josselin laughed softly. "Mairin, my dearling, sweet enchantress mine, I have been married to you long enough to know that your dutiful obedience is only for those things that please you."

"Then perhaps, my lord, I should dress and return to my sewing," she said.

"If it pleases you, lady," came the cool answer.

"*Josselin!* If you send me from our bed I shall never forgive you!" she cried.

Pulling her back into his embrace he chuckled, saying, "And if you really believe me, and go, lady, I shall never forgive you."

"Villain!" she retorted, and gave his tawny hair a rough yank.

Then their lips met once more in passion, and after a long sweet while they came together again.

Part Four

The Lady of Aelfleah

England and Scotland, 1068–1070

Chapter 12

"Helas, this dampness will surely kill me!" complained the Duchess Matilda irritably. "A king's house should not be built on the edge of a river's bank." Standing upon a little stool she gazed curiously out of the window at the Thames. It was a placid, muddy river, not at all like the rivers of Normandy, or Flanders where she had been born and raised. Still it seemed to generate more moisture and dankness than any river she had ever known. She had never been so cold in her entire life, she thought. Perhaps it was because the sun did not shine as much here in England as it did in Normandy. Nothing ever had time to dry out. It made her cranky, or perhaps it was the child she was currently carrying that altered her moods these days.

Her children. The duchess sighed. *Robert, her eldest.* So charming, witty, and well-spoken, but a boy who gave away too much, made lavish promises he could not keep, and was far too eager for his father's duchy in Normandy which he was not yet wise enough to govern. God only knew she loved him, but he seemed unable to attain his early promise and that worried her deeply. William had amassed such great holdings, but Robert, his chief heir, showed no signs of being strong enough to retain them.

Richard, her second-born, was too much like Robert, but he lacked ambition. Richard simply found life amusing, and had little hope of much more. Perhaps he worried Matilda most of all, for she believed a boy should not be so bored with life, nor should his direction be so aimless.

Then there was the troublesome Agatha, their eldest daughter. Matilda had left Agatha at home in Normandy to meditate upon her sin of great disobedience to her parent's will. A small smile touched Matilda's lips for a moment. Agatha was every bit as stubborn as her mother had once been, but she would never tell her daughter that. Agatha needed no further encouragement to rebellion.

Of their three sons only the youngest, William Rufus, had accompanied his mother to England. Matilda grimaced. He was her own son, and yet she found him a most appalling child. She had brought him with her in order to allow his four younger sisters a respite from his constant and unmerciful teasing. He gave them no surcease whatsoever, and only one of them was capable of matching his vile disposition, and thereby that one, Adela, at four showed every indication of being as nasty as her male sibling. She already pitied the man Adela would marry, for even beating Adela regularly did not seem to sweeten her temperament. The duchess placed a protective hand over her belly. Pray God and his Blessed Mother that this child was another son. A son like her beloved husband, William.

"Madame."

Matilda turned from the window. "Yes, Biota?" she said to her serving woman.

"You asked that Josselin de Combourg be brought to you when he arrived. He is awaiting your majesty's pleasure even now." Having been with Matilda since infancy, Biota knew Josselin well. He was one of her favorites.

The duchess stepped down from her stool. There was a smile upon her pretty face. "Ask him to come in, Biota," she said. Then she turned to her ladies. "Attention, mes dames! We have a visitor."

Like a small flock of chattering birds the queen-to-be's ladies clustered about her, giggling and preening. They all remembered the handsome Josselin de Combourg, and knew how well he had done here in England. Biota hurried to the door to admit the visitor who entering gave her a hearty kiss on her ruddy cheek, and whispered something that caused the older woman to blush though she chuckled, and smacked at him fondly. Matilda thought she had never seen him looking so well. He was taller than her husband by several inches, and handsomer than William, bless him, had ever been. Another smile spread across her lips. She had had a weak spot for Josselin since he arrived as a gift from William to serve her as a page in the turbulent days before their marriage. She could never forget his kindness to her in those years.

"Josselin de Combourg my dear friend," she greeted him holding out her tiny hands to him.

He took those two little hands, hands no larger than a child's, and kissed them reverently. "My gracious lady Matilda! How happy I am to see you, and to see you blooming with obviously good health. Is it what I suspect?"

Matilda laughed, and nodded. "Yes, Josselin, I am once more with child. This one to be born in the autumn, and pray God it is a son! But tell me of you, my friend. I have not seen a great deal of my lord William since he first came to England, and when we did meet I had so many other things to talk with him about. It is not easy being responsible for my husband's holdings in his absence. I remember him telling me that he had found an estate for you. Is this so?"

"Yes, madame. The king rewarded my service to him with a beautiful little estate in the west near the border with Wales. I am even now raising a small castle there to keep the king's peace. If you can spare me the time, madame, I will be happy to tell you all my adventures since my coming to England."

"Oh, I should so like that, Josselin! William has not had much time for me since I arrived. These English are yet being troublesome. I have traveled most simply, escorted only by Bishop Hugh of Lisieux and my youngest son. I have not even a minstrel to amuse me and wile away the long hours. First, however, I have what I hope will be a surprise for you. I have brought with me amongst my ladies an old friend of yours."

Josselin looked genuinely puzzled, and the women about the queen giggled.

"Come forward, Blanche de St. Brieuc!" the queen cried gaily, and her women playfully pushed Blanche forward with much merriment.

"Josselin, my dearest lord! Are you not surprised?" Blanche stood smiling fatuously at him, her fingers worrying the twisted golden rope of her girdle. She was wearing her favorite blue, and had silver ribbons braided in her golden hair.

For a moment Josselin felt genuinely ill. All he could think about was how he was going to explain Blanche to his wife for Mairin would be furious with him. He had honestly never expected to see Blanche de St. Brieuc again. What in God's name was she doing here? Why had she followed him to England?

Breaching all good manners Blanche threw herself into his startled arms and pressed her mouth to his passionately. "Oh, chéri, I have missed you so!" she sighed gustily.

"Madame, you forget yourself, and where you are!" He quickly thrust her from him. He had to straighten this out immediately for here was his sweet queen looking so pleased as if she had done him a great favor.

"Why, Josselin, are you not pleased to see Blanche? It was my understanding that when you had made your fortune, you and this lady would be united." The queen looked coyly from him to Blanche and back again.

"Madame, I must speak frankly to you though my words will seem less than chivalrous. I cannot imagine how you came to believe that this lady and I had an understanding of any kind. How could I commit myself with honor to any woman when I had not the means of supporting a wife? When I could offer her nothing, not even a respectable name? Madame, you above all people know me better than that!

"I met this lady three years ago when I was at Combourg seeing my parents. I visited in her brother's house at his invitation, but never was any mention made of an alliance between myself and this lady. I am distressed she should have believed such a thing. Her brother will, I know, attest to the veracity of my words."

Matilda was very upset by this unexpected turn of events. To have offended a dear and old friend was bad enough, but to have been taken in by this . . . this adventuress who had played upon the softness of her nature was totally unforgivable. Her blue eyes grew hard. Drawing herself up to her full height, which was but four feet, two inches, she demanded, "Well, madame, what explanation do you have for this situation? Though you have not lied openly to me, neither have you been truthful."

Blanche de St. Brieuc was no fool. She had taken a gamble, but perhaps all was not yet lost. She flung herself at the queen's feet. "Oh, madame," she sobbed quite convincingly, "have mercy upon me! I have been sick with love for Josselin de Combourg ever since we first met! Can you who know him so well blame me? Knowing his honorable character I knew he would not dare to even suggest a match between us until he had made his fortune. After all," she could not resist adding, "I am a de St. Brieuc and, it is true, above him in station, yet I love him! I thought if I could but come to England now that the king has rewarded his loyal services, if he could but see me again, he would finally dare to speak the reciprocal passions I know he holds for me. How else could I get here except traveling amongst your ladies? I realize, dearest madame, that I have been bold and even rash. Both traits of which are unbecoming in a woman of my station, but I could not help myself! I love him! Oh, please, please, say that you will forgive me."

The queen, though a practical woman, was also a romantic one at heart. Blanche's plea had moved her near to tears. "Yes, yes," she said, and bending, aided Blanche de St. Brieuc to her feet. "It is true, ma Blanche, that you have exhibited indelicate behavior for one of your rank, but I understand this wonderfully cruel emotion called love. I know the lengths to which one can be driven when caught within its thrall. I am very angry with you, but nonetheless I will forgive you." She turned to Josselin. "And perhaps Josselin will forgive you also, and rectify the difficulty between you both. What say you, my dear friend Josselin? A man with an estate needs a good wife, eh?" Matilda cocked her head at him, and smiled winningly.

"That, dearest madame, was a part of what I had to tell you," he said. "I already have a wife. We have been married almost two years. She has come to London with me for your coronation, and I would have your leave to present her to you. When the king gave me Aelfleah, he also gave me its heiress to wive. I often fear if he knew the great kindness he had done me he should take it all back. The king gave me not just lands, he gave me someone whom I love better than life itself."

"Ohhhhhh!" Blanche de St. Brieuc collapsed dramatically onto the floor in a swoon.

Matilda waved her little hands impatiently. "Remove her," she said to her women. She had no more sympathy left for Blanche. The woman had shown an inexcusable lack of manners, and had only gotten exactly what she deserved.

The fluttering ladies half-dragged, half-carried Blanche de St. Brieuc from the room, and Biota at a signal from her mistress barred them reentry stationing herself in the anteroom side of the queen's apartments before the door. Matilda settled herself into a high tapestry-backed chair with a footstool, waving Josselin to the matching chair that faced it.

"Now tell me everything, Josselin," she said to him, leaning forward, her elbows on her knees to listen intently as he spoke. Sometimes she smiled at his words, other times bit her lip to prevent her laughter from spilling over. When he spoke of how Mairin had defended Aelfleah, and lost their expected child shortly afterward, Matilda's pale blue eyes filled with sympathetic tears. "Ah, ma pauvre," she said. "Your Mairin is a brave woman. She is just the kind of wife you need here in England. I do not see la Blanche defending her home in such a manner. I do not think this Eadric the Wild would have been impressed by a woman stamping her foot, which is what Blanche surely would have done."

"She is very eager to meet you, my lady Matilda. She envies you your family for like me she is anxious to have children."

"Of course you must bring her to me this very day, my friend! I am extremely anxious to meet your enchantress. What a charming love name that is, Josselin. I have always suspected for all your admiration and emulation of William's character that you were a romantic deep in your soul. Now there is something else you have not told me. I see it in your eyes. Do you wish to make further confession?" Matilda was smiling playfully, but she was anxious to make amends to her old friend for her part in the matter of la Blanche.

Josselin hesitated a moment, and then he said, "It is Blanche de St. Brieuc, madame. I have not told my wife of our acquaintance."

"Surely it was not necessary, Josselin," the queen replied. "Your wife was a widow when you were wed, and certainly not so innocent that she could believe you did not know other women. I will admit it is awkward, but I shall send the creature home immediately after the coronation. Regretfully she cannot go sooner as no one is leaving for Normandy until next week. For all her lack of delicacy she is still a lady. Besides I need the tiresome wretch for the moment. Although I do not really know her, one of my ladies grew too ill to travel at the last moment, and la Blanche had some connection with the Montgomeries, a family who have influence with my husband. I am absolutely mortified to have embarrassed you."

"It is worse than simply not having told Mairin about another woman of my acquaintance, madame. Blanche de St. Brieuc is my wife's stepmother."

Matilda gasped, her eyes widening with shock, and Josselin went on to explain. When he had finished she said quite sensibly, "It is very unlikely that Blanche will recognize your wife, my friend. After all she was but a little child when she last saw her. Your Mairin, however, is bound to recognize Blanche de St. Brieuc. You will have to tell her before she sees la Blanche, else she will never forgive you. Go home and confess to her. Then bring her to see me. I am certain that if I vouch for your good character, Josselin," the queen finished with a smile, "your wife may just forgive you. If she does not, how will you two ever produce that large family you so desperately desire?"

He arose from the chair opposite her, and kneeling he kissed her outstretched hand. "Mille merci, madame. I am most grateful for your aid." Then standing he crossed the room, and departed her presence. Leaving the king's house, he sought his horse in the courtyard and rode back across the noisy city to their little house by the orchard. A servant ran to take his mount and stable it as Josselin entered the building. He found Mairin in the back garden cutting flowering branches for the hall.

She turned to greet him with a smile. "You have seen the queen?"

"Yes," he said kissing her brow, and leading her to a bench by a bed of lavender. "She has asked to meet you. We are to come later today, but first there is something I must tell you, enchantress."

With a teasing tone she said, "Ah, I can guess. You did not answer me fully when I asked you about the women you knew at King William's court in Normandy. One of your old flirts is among the queen's ladies, and now you must confess to me before the lady, jealous that you are now wed, tells me herself." She laughed. "Is that not right, my lord?"

"Yes, and no, enchantress. I met the lady involved at Combourg. Later I visited her brother's home at his request and she was there also. There was never any romance between us although I will admit to our flirting with one another. My landless state, the situation of my birth, made it impossible for me to offer anything to any woman. Even had I been able to I would have offered this woman nothing. She, however, thought otherwise. She somehow learned that I had been given an estate here in England. She went to the Norman court, and when one of the queen's ladies grew too ill to travel with her mistress to the coronation, this lady used the influence of friends to be appointed to the vacant position. She led the queen to believe that we had made informal promises to one another."

"She is very bold, this lady," remarked Mairin. "You have I trust, told her that you already have a wife."

"I told the queen immediately in the lady's presence."

"And who is this lady, Josselin? You have been very careful not to mention her name, but surely you must tell me else I be embarrassed before the queen and her women."

"Enchantress, you must forgive me for not having told you before, but you will understand that I did not wish to pain you. My acquaintance with this lady occurred long before I even knew of your existence. I never expected to see her again, and therefore saw no reason to distress you. The lady in question is Blanche de St. Brieuc."

"*That bitch?*" The words were hissed, but then to his surprise Mairin laughed. "By God she must be desperate to have followed you to England." She turned, and looked at him, her violet eyes carefully searching his face. "You swear on your mother's honor that there was really nothing between you?"

"I swear it, Mairin! There was nothing."

"I believe you, Josselin, but God help you if you have lied to me. I will kill you!"

He believed her. "I love you, enchantress," he said simply.

"And you love Aelfleah," she answered him.

"Yes, I love Aelfleah too, but I am an honorable man, Mairin. I have not lied to you ever."

"You split hairs with me, my lord," she said, "but no matter. I believe you when you say you sought to protect me from painful memories. Have you told the queen my whole history?"

"Yes, and she is furious at Blanche for her deception. She intends to send her back to Normandy, but she cannot do so until next week when others will be returning. Now, my wife, the question is, what do you intend to do?"

Mairin laughed again, but the sound lacked true mirth. "I am seventeen now," she said. "When I left Landerneau I was not quite six. I do not think my stepmother will recognize me despite my hair and my name. She is not that clever for all her evil. I expect she has not thought of me in years, and if she has she has thought me long dead. The only importance I ever held for her was that I stood in her daughter's way regarding the inheritance of Landerneau. Once that was taken care of I can assure you she put me from her mind."

"Then you will forgive her the past, and not make yourself known to her?" he asked.

"I did not say that, Josselin. Nay, I want my revenge on Blanche de St. Brieuc!" She caught his hand, and looking into his eyes she kissed his hand. "Grant me that, my lord, I beg you!"

"What the lady Blanche did was wrong, Mairin, even criminal. But think, enchantress! You did not really suffer by her actions. You were far better off here in England with your foster parents than you would have been at Landerneau with Blanche de St. Brieuc, your guardian. She might have killed you!"

"That," said Mairin, "was her mistake. She should have!"

"What would you do then?" he said.

"Do you remember when we were married," said Mairin, "and the king asked me if I wanted Landerneau returned to me, and I said nay? Well, when I carried our child I began to think on it, Josselin. Aldford and whatever future honors you may gather in your lifetime will go to our eldest son. Our second son should have Aelfleah. Our third must have Landerneau."

"And what of your half-sister? You will destroy her chance for marriage if you take Landerneau. You know it is her dowry. Do you think to hurt Blanche de St. Brieuc by striking out at her child?"

"Did you know my half-sister?" asked Mairin coolly.

"No. I never saw the child, but I do know that Blanche was proud to have managed a match with a younger son of the Montgomerie family."

"The girl does not wish to be wed in the worldly sense," said Mairin. "Of late I have seen her in my mind's eye. I do not understand why after all these years this should be so. She was not even born when I left Landerneau, but somehow I know she has no desire to be married as we are married. My half-sister desires to be a bride of Christ, and I will gladly dower her into a good convent. This other marriage is what her mother wishes, and she is forcing her own daughter from a true vocation, in order to further her own ambitions. It is typical of the bitch, but as she did not have her way with me, neither will she have her way in this matter of her own child. My revenge on Blanche de St. Brieuc is to allow my poor half-sister her wish. Without the girl or Landerneau, what does she really have?"

"How can you be certain what you believe is true?" he demanded of her. "Perhaps what you think you see is only what you desire, Mairin. Beware lest in your desire for revenge you harm an innocent girl."

"I know it is true! I do not see things that are not so! All my life I have listened to the *voice within*. When I act according to its advice I prosper. When I ignore the *voice within* I fail. It has been a long time since I received so clear a vision. The frustration of my life is that I rarely see things regarding the people close to me. If I could I would have warned my father and brother against going to fight the Norwegians! However, what I have seen regarding my half-sister is true, Josselin. Please believe me."

"Then you have surely found a perfect revenge against Blanche de St. Brieuc, Mairin. Because Landerneau was her daughter's, and her family could not afford another dowry, she has never rewed. She lives as a pensioner in her eldest brother's house, and as you might guess, does not get on with her brother or his wife. Her daughter's marriage would have afforded her an escape. She might have gone to live with her daughter and son-in-law, perhaps even found another husband. She has not lost her prettiness, not being old yet. There is always some unimportant knight eager of allying himself to a powerful family like the Montgomeries who would have been willing to take her in marriage without a dowry. She is even young enough to still bear children. Now she will have nothing."

"It is not punishment enough for her cruelty to me or to my father, Josselin! On his deathbed father called out for me, and she would not let him see me. His body was not even cold on his bier when she sent me into slavery. She took not just my estates from me, she took my good name. By declaring me bastard-born she shamed my mother's name and memory! If she had believed she could have killed me and escaped retribution, she would have! I do not think I am overly harsh in taking everything from her and leaving her to live the remainder of her life, which I pray God be a long one, alone!"

"For all your years in gentle England, for your marriage in civilized Byzantium, you are still a pure Celt," he said.

Mairin laughed, and now the sound was light and happy. "My lord, you flatter me!" she said. "I am indeed a Celt, and my anger burns long even if the flame seems not to be there."

"I will remember that, enchantress," he answered her. "I think you are a dangerous woman though you seem nothing more than a great beauty. You are a complex creature. I am not certain that I should not fear you."

"If you are faithful to me, my lord, you need never fear me. I love you, my Josselin!"

He took her into his arms and held her close against his heart. She was not, he knew, being overly cruel in her treatment of her half-sister and her stepmother. Landerneau was indeed hers by right and unless she reclaimed it, her name and that of her mother would never be clean from the stain that Blanche de St. Brieuc had placed upon them. It rather pleased him that she was thinking in terms of three sons. "What if we have a fourth son?" he asked her.

"A family can always use a bishop," she answered him, looking up into his face.

Josselin laughed aloud. "And at least two more in case of illness or accident," he said, and she nodded vigorously. "How many daughters?" he demanded.

"Possibly four," she said. "Three good marriage alliances, and an abbess to go with the bishop."

"You're as ambitious as a reigning queen," he chuckled, slapping his knee with his free hand.

"Make the right alliances over the next several generations, and this family could give England a queen one day," she replied seriously.

"First things first, enchantress," he answered her. "Let us go and see our queen, and you may get your first good look at your stepmother in many years. Since you so like the game of cat and mouse you will enjoy knowing she does not recognize you, although your very existence as my wife is apt to drive her to a frenzy."

"What shall I wear?" Mairin pondered mischievously. "Something elegant, but not too showy. No. Something that will bring out the perfect clarity of my skin, and flatter my hair. The turquoise tunic and the cloth-of-silver skirt! They should be just right."

God have mercy upon poor Blanche de St. Brieuc, thought Josselin to himself. She has no idea how serious an enemy she had made in Mairin all those years ago. My wife is correct when she says that Blanche is not clever. Still what she did was totally unforgivable. For a moment he imagined Mairin as a little girl barely out of babyhood, and suddenly torn from her home. Not even allowed the time to mourn the father she adored. The terrible enormity of Blanche's crime shook him to the core. There was no doubt in his mind that without the faithful Dagda Mairin would have been lost for she had been too young to protect herself.

Nara had come with them to London and with her help Mairin was quickly made ready. The cloth-of-silver skirt was long, and very full, its fabric falling gracefully into trailing folds. Over it was a second skirt of gossamer-sheer silk sarcenet through which the silver glowed in contrast. That was a fashion trick she had learned in Byzantium. The overskirt was the same blue-green of Mairin's tunic, which was made of lampas, a patterned damask-like fabric. The long sleeves of the tunic widened from elbow to wrist, and the garment was girded with a belt of linked round silver disks each one of which had a moonstone in its center. Kneeling Nara slipped each of her mistress's feet into a soft blue-green shoe that buttoned up the front with little pearls. Mairin wore her hair low on the nape of her neck in Anglo-Saxon fashion. Over it she placed a silver embroidered veil with a gold-and-pearl chaplet to hold the veil in place.

"You will have the queen's ladies gnashing their teeth in envy of your garments," said Josselin, smiling. "Norman ladies think themselves vastly superior to everyone else."

"Wait," Mairin said, "I have not yet chosen my jewelry." Studying the box which Nara held open, she finally drew out pear-shaped earrings of pink crystal, and a matching necklace from which hung a beautiful Celtic cross fashioned from Irish red-gold. She also chose two rings, one a large single diamond surrounded by amethysts, and the other an enormous baroque pink pearl. "To wear additional rings would be to appear immodest," she said wryly.

"And how clever of you to have dressed to complement me," he said with a small chuckle. He was wearing a vermilion-and-gold tunic with a matching vermilion mantle. It flattered his tawny dark blond hair.

"Have we not always complemented each other from the first, my lord?" she teased him back.

They rode together to the king's house in Westminster, drawing looks both admiring and curious from the Londoners in the streets along their route. It was unusual to see two such attractive people upon two such magnificent horses.

"Are you nervous?" he asked her as they made their way to the queen's apartments.

"A little," she managed to admit as Biota opened the door. Mairin's eyes quickly took in the women within the room as they entered. She immediately spotted Blanche, and though their eyes met momentarily there was no sign of recognition from the other woman. Then she saw the queen, knowing her instantly from Josselin's careful description.

Matilda of Normandy gave new meaning to the word "petite," for though she stood but fifty inches high, every bit of her was in perfect proportion, and she was very pretty. Her skin was fair and she had lovely rosy cheeks. Her silver-blond hair was braided into a high coronet in an attempt to add to her stature, and her bright blue eyes were lively with interest. It was obvious that she missed little with those eyes.

Mairin walked directly to the queen, and knelt gracefully, her beautiful head bowed in submission.

Matilda nodded with approval at Josselin, and then said in a musical voice, "You may rise, Mairin of Aelfleah."

Mairin stood. "Welcome to England, my lady queen," she said to the seated Matilda.

"Thank you, my child," the queen replied, and then she said to Josselin, "I understand what you meant when you said that my lord William did you a great service, Josselin. Your wife is lovely, and her manners are flawless." She turned her attention back to Mairin. "I understand, my dear, that your first husband was Prince Basil of Byzantium."

The queen's ladies looked interested now. This was obviously someone more than just a simple little Saxon wench. They were quite curious particularly given the drama involving Blanche de St. Brieuc.

"Yes, my lady queen. Prince Basil was my husband until his untimely death. We were wed when my father, Aldwine Athelsbeorn, may God assoil his good soul, was King Edward's trade emissary to Constantinople. Then when King William came to England he saw that I was matched with my beloved lord and husband, Josselin de Combourg."

"It is good to be loved," said the queen, and Mairin realized the truth in Matilda's simple words.

"Oh, yes, madame!" she agreed, and Matilda smiled warmly.

They spoke for several more minutes on unimportant things, and the queen said, "You will both stay and take the evening meal with us." Although worded as an invitation, it was truly a royal command. "Now, Josselin, my friend, go and pay your respects to my lord William. Your sweet wife will remain here with me until it is time to eat."

Mairin felt her heart quicken. She had not thought to be left alone with the queen and her ladies, but Josselin, bending to kiss her upon the cheek, whispered, "Courage, enchantress!" and then he was gone. For the next hour Mairin sat upon a stool by the queen's side, and conversed with Matilda and her ladies. Her flawless, accentless French made her seem very much like them. All the while she could see Blanche de St. Brieuc edging closer to her until finally the two women were right next to each other.

Finding an opening Blanche said, "I knew your husband, Josselin, in Brittany, for we are both Breton-born. We were very *close*."

"You knew each other as children then?" answered Mairin innocently. "Are you also a highborn bastard, lady?"

Blanche's fair white skin grew mottled with color, and her pale blue eyes filled with angry outrage. "I?" she gasped. "*Bastard-born?*"

The queen's other women who did not like this substitute lady giggled behind their hands. Mairin's violet eyes grew wide and questioning. Matilda hid a small smile. Knowing the truth, she knew that Mairin was toying with her enemy.

"Madame! What on earth would make you think I was not trueborn?" Blanche's voice was now squeaky and high-pitched with her indignation.

"Surely no respectable lord would allow his daughter to play with a bastard-child," replied Mairin sweetly. "Since you knew my husband as a child I assumed you must be as he. Gracious, have I made a mistake?"

"You most certainly have, lady! I am Blanche de St. Brieuc. My family is one of the oldest and most respected names in Brittany. My late husband was Ciaran St. Ronan, but as his name was not as good as mine, I took back my family's name when I was widowed. I did not say I knew your husband when I was a child! You misunderstood! I knew Josselin several years ago."

"How nice," said Mairin, pretending that she did not understand the innuendo.

Blanche gritted her teeth. Did not this idiot Saxon girl comprehend what she was trying to tell her? "Your husband and I were *very close,*" she repeated, and then added, "We were *intimate* friends."

The queen's ladies were goggle-eyed for Blanche de St. Brieuc had practically admitted to Josselin de Combourg's beautiful young wife that they had been lovers. Surely she understood that. They looked to Mairin to see what her next move would be.

"*Ohhh,*" said Mairin, not disappointing them. "You mean that you were one of my husband's whores?" Then looking about at the very shocked Norman ladies with their open mouths she continued, "Have I said the wrong thing, my lady Matilda? We Saxon women are taught to be outspoken. I hope I have not offended you."

The queen held back her laughter. This beautiful young vixen was obviously enormously intelligent, and had she been wed with a powerful man would certainly have been someone to be reckoned with. Her innocent bluntness had the queen's ladies totally fooled. Matilda was not so gullible, but she frankly liked the way Josselin's wife played with Blanche de St. Brieuc. It was like a beast of prey playing with its next victim. Blanche was close to destruction but she didn't even know it.

"Gracious St. Anne!" Matilda said, feigning equal innocence. "You are indeed blunt, my lady Mairin. We Norman ladies are more gentle in our speech."

"Since I am wed with one of King William's men," said Mairin sweetly, "I will try to emulate your good example."

The queen nodded, and then rising said, "It is time for dinner, my ladies. Come, let us join the men in the hall. Mairin, you will stay by me until we can find your husband." Then lowering her voice as they walked along she continued, "You could destroy a mounted and armed troop with your seemingly innocent tongue, my lady. I dare not let you from my side until you are safe in Josselin's custody."

The Great Hall of the king's house was a busy place. At one end of it a fireplace large enough to take huge whole logs of oak blazed busily. A highboard had been set up on one side of the room where the king, his queen, his family, and those great nobles who were in his favor sat. The rest of the court, Mairin and Josselin among them, found seats according to the rank above or below the salt at wood trestle tables set up about the room. At each place there were trenchers of fresh bread and silver goblets. There were no implements for the diners carried their own knives and dainty spoons. One's fingers, however, were the preferred method of eating for they worked better than anything else.

William was not stinting of his guests during his queen's coronation week. There was both variety and quantity in the food. Oxen and sheep were roasted whole. There were sides of beef, and venison. Pigs had been cooked to succulence, and were presented with whole apples in their mouths. There was game. Partridge, grouse, and woodcock. There were rabbits, in stew, potted, and in pies with golden crusts. The fowl—several hundred capons, geese, and ducks—were sauced with lemon and ginger. A whole peacock had been cooked, reassembled and refeathered, and was presented at the highboard where it sat in solitary splendor.

A bounty of the sea had not been overlooked. Salmon and trout were available broiled in wine and herbs, or sauced with dill and cream. There were barrels of oysters, and boiled prawns with Dijon mustard sauce, and cod cakes in cream and fennel, and smoked herring.

There were bowls of new lettuce that had been braised in white wine, and tiny young peas as well as bowls of a mixture of several grains that had been cooked to the consistency of cereal. There were wheels of different cheeses. A hard yellow cheddar, a soft Brie from France, and cream cheese. There were wild English strawberries, and early cherries that had been brought from Normandy, and little spun-sugar confections. There was wine for everyone, or beer for those who preferred it.

Mairin stuffed herself with venison, and goose, and the prawns, licking her fingers daintily to get every drop of the sauce. Still hungry, she had taken a slice of beef, and another of roasted pig, managing to obtain an outside piece with its blackened crispy skin which she particularly relished. The peas were delicious, as was the Brie and cherries. Marin finished everything she took, including her trencher of bread. Finally satisfied, she sat back with a smile after washing her greasy fingers in a bowl of warmed water scented with wildflowers that a servant offered her. Around her many others were simply wiping their hands on their clothing.

Looking at Josselin she said, "I hope I haven't disgraced you with my appetite."

"You eat with the attitude of someone who has some serious task to complete."

"I do, my lord. Will you support me?"

"Aye, enchantress. It does not displease me that you seek to regain your Breton holding."

Without another word Mairin arose from her place and walked through the hall to stand silently before the highboard. Many saw her there, but to admit it before she had been noticed and acknowledged by the king would have been a breach of etiquette.

The queen leaning over whispered into her husband's ear, "William, here is Josselin de Combourg's bride. It would please me if you would grant her the boon she requests, my loving lord. She pleases me."

The king's eyes flickered over Mairin, enjoying her beauty quite frankly. Putting down his goblet he said, "You have our attention, Mairin of Aelfleah, and our leave to speak."

Mairin curtsied deeply, her silver skirts blossoming about her.

"Perhaps," she said, "you will remember the day we first met, my lord. My wedding day. On that day you asked me if I did not want my Breton holding returned to me, and in haste I said nay. Though my lord spouse did not chide me for my decision I have thought much about it since. If, my lord William, I changed my mind, would you return those lands to me?"

"The lands are yours by right, my lady," said the king, "but what of the others involved?"

"My half-sister is betrothed, it is true, my lord William. However, I believe she would far rather be a bride of Christ than the bride of man. I would dower her most generously. My quarrel is not with her."

The king leaned across his wife and spoke to a man seated on the other side of her. For several minutes they conversed, and then William spoke again to Mairin. "The boy involved in this match has died just this spring of measles. No new match has been yet arranged for the girl. This is my lord Montgomerie, the head of the family to which the lad belongs and the family who have fostered your half-sister. He tells me that as much as he regrets the loss of those lands, you are correct. The girl would far rather enter a convent and spend her life in prayer serving God. What say you now to that, Mairin of Aelfleah?"

"That I would reclaim my inheritance of Landerneau from the St. Brieuc family who stole it from me when I was but a mere child! I demand the king's justice, my lord William! I am Mairin St. Ronan, the legal and true-born elder daughter of Ciaran St. Ronan, Sieur de Landerneau, and of his first wife, Maire Tir Connell, a princess of Ireland. My stepmother, Blanche de St. Brieuc, falsely accused my mother, may God assoil her innocent soul, of giving birth to me without the sacred bonds of matrimony. She dared not do this while my father lived. Nay! She waited until my father was dead to declare it. In collusion with her uncle, the bishop of St. Brieuc, she then sent me from my rightful place into slavery so she might steal my holdings for her own daughter. Like Judas she took silver in exchange for my life. I was but five years old!"

There were shocked gasps throughout the hall, and at least two women fainted while several others swooned against the men seated next to them. It was no crime to be ambitious for one's child, particularly when one was a second wife, but Blanche de St. Brieuc's ruthlessness in selling her little stepdaughter to a slave merchant was evil at its most shocking. Many looked openly about the Great Hall for a glimpse of this obviously godless creature.

"My lord William knows that good fortune, however, followed me to England," Mairin continued, "and I was rescued by a noble thegn, Aldwine Athelsbeorn, and raised by him and his wife as their own beloved child. When my foster father fell at York with his son, his estates were willed to me. I would not have sought to reclaim my lands in Brittany but that my half-sister does not need them or want them. I do! They are mine by right! Give me the king's justice, my lord William! Return Landerneau to me so that I may pass it on to my heir. So that my father's line will not perish entirely," she concluded.

If Mairin had thrown a bag full of hissing serpents into the center of the room she would not have caused a greater commotion than she now did. She had spoken clearly, and all in the hall had heard her. Blanche de St. Brieuc stood up, and stumbled forward to face her accuser. She peered hard into Mairin's face, and then her blue eyes grew round with belated recognition.

"I should have killed you myself," she hissed plainly for all to hear.

"Yes," said Mairin, and she smiled cruelly. "You should have!"

Blanche turned to the king. "She demands the king's justice! Then so do I, my lord William! She lies! She is bastard-born! The slimy get of some nameless Irish peasant girl who undoubtedly whored to gain a coin or two. Who knows if she is even Ciaran St. Ronan's child! Landerneau belongs to my daughter, Blanchette. Her paternity cannot be in doubt!"

Mairin laughed mockingly, "Ahh, stepmother, you still sing the same tired old song, but this time you have not your loathsome uncle to aid you in your perfidy."

"There is no proof of your alleged parents' marriage," snarled Blanche de St. Brieuc.

"But there is, madame, and there was at that time when you stole my lands from me."

"Then why did you not show it?"

"Because those who wished me well feared you would murder me in order to gain Landerneau for your child," Mairin replied bluntly. "You were, after all, quite willing to tempt and subvert a bishop of the holy church to gain your way. You even admit now that you had murder in your heart!"

"Show me the proof!" Blanche demanded.

"The king has already seen it," came the reply.

"It is a forgery! It is a forgery!" screamed Blanche. "You seek to defraud Blanchette! I will not let you do it!"

The king's hall was agog. Its many inhabitants swung their heads back and forth between the two combatants. Each had spoken clearly. There was no doubt as to the source of the quarrel between the two women. There was a contingent of Breton knights in the hall, and to a man they found themselves outraged with Blanche de St. Brieuc's treatment of Ciaran St. Ronan's daughter. The Sieur de Landerneau had been an honorable man. He would not have attempted to set a bastard daughter over a legitimate heir.

"Silence!" The king's voice roared over the cacophony. The Great Hall grew quiet. "Landerneau is the rightful property of Mairin St. Ronan. I, myself, saw the proof of her claim the day before my own coronation. She possesses the marriage lines of her parents, and my brother, the bishop of Bayeux, has authenticated them. There is no doubt that her parentage is as she has always claimed. She is her father's trueborn daughter, Landerneau's legitimate heiress.

"Despite cruel treatment at the hands of her stepmother the lady Mairin's heart is good. She wishes no harm to the half-sister who was not even born when she was sent from Landerneau. Knowing of Blanchette's true vocation to holy mother church the lady Mairin has offered to dower her half-sister most generously. Blanchette St. Ronan will be taken to my wife's own Abbey of the Holy Trinity, in Caen, where she will be received as a postulant into its order.

"As for you, Blanche de St. Brieuc, you will be returned first to the custody of your eldest brother so that you may make your peace with your family. One month after your return you will be taken to the Cloister of St. Hilary where you will remain for the rest of your natural life. You are not fit for holy orders, but you will spend your last years under the rule of the abbess of St. Hilary's. You will pray and you will fast, and perhaps by the time your life has come to its end you will be cleansed of your sins of greed, pride, cruelty, and hardness of heart. Isolated from the world you will have the time to meditate your own evil, and beg God's forgiveness."

For a long moment after the king finished speaking there was silence in the hall, and then Blanche de St. Brieuc launched herself at Mairin screaming, "I hate you! Your father loved you even more than he loved me! I have always hated you! You cannot do this to me! Not after all these years! I will not let you! You should have been dead years ago, but I will kill you now!" She raised up her arm, and a collective gasp arose from the spectators, for Blanche held in her hand her knife. With a half-growl she attacked Mairin who, totally surprised, could only raise her hands in an effort to defend herself against the other woman.

Mairin had never felt so helpless in her entire life. Backing away from her stepmother, her arms shielding her head, she did not know what to do. All she knew was that she did not want to die. "Ohhh!" she shrieked as Blanche's knife found its mark and slashed its way across her palm. It was then that all of Mairin's survival instincts rose up, and she flailed out with her other arm in an attempt to disarm her antagonist. She hit her mark and to her surprise the knife flew from Blanche's hand. In that moment several of the Breton knights surrounded the raging woman and pulled her away from Mairin just as Josselin reached his wife's side.

Blood poured from her hand. Without thinking about where she was, Mairin pulled up her skirts and tore a piece of soft linen from her camise for a bandage. Wrapping it about her hand to stem the bleeding she swore softly under her breath, and hearing her do so Josselin almost laughed aloud.

"Hellfire! Do you know how difficult if not impossible it is to remove blood from lampas? Damn that woman!" Then as a sudden weakness overcame her she swayed. Her head was beginning to swim. *"Josselin!"*

His arms went about her. "I am here, Mairin. I'm going to carry you."

"No! I will walk from the hall. I don't want the king and his people to think we English are weaklings." Her legs felt wobbly, but even so with his aid they turned to face the highboard.

William could see how pale Mairin was. "Is your wife all right, Joss?" he asked.

"I will be fine, sire," Mairin answered for herself. "The cut is deep, and I have lost more blood than I would have cared to lose, but I will heal."

"You must let me send my own physician to you, my lady Mairin," said Matilda.

"Thank you, my lady queen, but I would decline your kindness. I am a better healer than most, and I prefer to treat myself."

"Then return to your London house, and rest," said William. "We will hope to see you at the queen's coronation in two days' time."

"We will be there," said Mairin in a positive tone. Then she somehow managed to curtsey, and turning took her husband's arm to walk from the hall.

"You are incredible!" Josselin marveled as they gained the courtyard.

"I am going to be very sick," said Mairin as she vomited the contents of her sumptuous dinner onto the paving stones.

"Better?" he asked when her shoulders had finally stopped heaving.

She looked at him with a weak grin. Her hand was hurting like the very devil. "Yes." She nodded, collapsing into a dead faint as the pavement rushed up to meet her.

When she awoke she was lying upon her own bed within their little London house. Someone had removed her clothing but for her torn camise. With a sigh Mairin curled herself into a ball, and slipped back into a deep sleep. She never noticed Nara asleep on the trundle by her side.

Below, Josslin related to Dagda what had happened. The big Irishman's eyes were almost black with his anger. His voice was grim when he said to Josselin, "She will never again hurt my lady! I swear it by blessed St. Padraic, and the Holy Mother herself!"

When the morning came Mairin awoke to find her husband by her side. The dull ache in her wounded hand warned her that her injury could become infected if she did not attend it. Rising, Mairin pulled off her torn camise, and put on a clean one. Over it she drew a plain blue linen skirt, and matching tunic. Slipping her feet into her shoes she hurried downstairs to find Nara attending to the fire.

"Where is Dagda?" she asked.

"He said he had an errand to attend to, my lady," came the reply.

Mairin raised an eyebrow. It was early, and the sun was even now just coming up. "There is a small open-air market a few streets down by the riverbank," she said to her servant. "Go and purchase me several small fresh white onions, a flask of apple vinegar, and a comb of honey. On your way back stop at the baker and get bread." Mairin handed Nara the necessary coins, and the girl hurried out.

A pot of water was heating over the fire, and finding a basin Mairin filled it with hot water, adding a good pinch of dried mint leaves. While it steeped she carefully tore her damaged camise into strips of bandage, and then unwrapping her hand she plunged it into the basin. Patiently she waited for the crust to soak off the wound, and was shortly rewarded with success as her injury began to sting uncomfortably. With an irregular piece of cloth from the camise she began to gently rub at her palm until the water in the basin had turned pale pink, but her wound was clean and freed of the dried blood. She kept her hand in the basin for the slash must remain soft and open until Nara came with the ingredients necessary for the poultice she needed to make.

Dagda returned, and was surprised to see her up and about.

"Where have you been?" she asked him.

"I had business at Westminster," he said quietly.

"My God! What have you done?"

"Something that should have been done years ago, and don't ask, my lady. I've already been to confession to receive my penance." He took her hand from the basin and examined it. "That's a nasty gash you have. Will you treat it yourself?"

"Aye. Nara has gone for some of the things I'll need. What penance were you given?"

"A silver penny donated for the church's poor. Ten aves, and ten paters. More than enough for the soul of a whore though I doubt she even had a soul." He put her hand back into the basin.

"Oh, Dagda! Surely no one has ever loved me the way that you do. You make me feel ashamed."

"Never, my lady Mairin! I am but keeping my promise to your sainted mother. We will not speak on it again now."

Nara returned, bringing with her the requested ingredients, and Mairin instructed her to take one of the onions, peel it, and pound it into a paste. When this was done to her satisfaction she added from her medicinal pouch which was attached to the twisted rope girdle she wore about her waist salt and several leaves of rue which she first crumpled into powder. This mixture was then moistened with a splash of the vinegar and a small section of the honeycomb. What resulted was a thick paste. Removing her injured hand from the water, Mairin spread it over her slashed palm, and then Nara carefully bound the wound with two strips of linen bandage.

"Pot the rest of the ointment," Mairin instructed her serving woman, "and keep it in a cool place."

"Aye, my lady," said the serving woman, and taking the pestle in which Mairin had mixed her poultice she hurried off with it.

"Shall I see if my lord is awake?" Dagda said.

"Aye. I will see to the meal," replied Mairin.

The big man hurried up the stairs while Mairin began cutting up the bread that Nara had brought from the nearby baker. It was still warm. Next she sliced thin slivers of cheddar cheese which she piled upon the bread. She set the bread and cheese upon a grill hung over the flames of the fireplace to toast. Nara brought a small ham to the table, and cut several generous pieces, piling them upon a platter.

"Mind the bread," her mistress instructed her, and set four polished wooden trenchers about the table along with their matching goblets.

"The bread is ready, my lady," said Nara.

Mairin turned back to the fire saying to the serving girl as she did so, "Fetch the pitcher of ale, and hurry! I hear my lord and Dagda coming."

Nara scampered off, and Mairin carefully lifted the toasted bread and cheese onto a wooden platter which she placed upon the table. Upon the sideboard was a bowl of hulled strawberries and she put them next to the platter of ham.

"Good morrow, enchantress," Josselin said slipping his arms about her and kissing the soft hollow on the side of her neck.

She snuggled back against him for a moment enjoying his warmth and his closeness. "Ummm," she murmured as his arms tightened.

"The hand?" he murmured against her skin.

"I will survive," she said dryly. "I dressed it earlier."

"Then I don't have to worry about seeking another wife from amongst the court ladies?" he teased.

"*That,*" she said, "is not amusing, my lord." Then slipping out of his grasp she turned, pouting. "And to think I arose to see to your breakfast myself! Well, sit down, my lord!"

With a chuckle he settled himself at the table's head and motioned to Dagda and Nara to join them. Here in the little London house they could not be bothered with formality for there was no room for it. The table here was T-shaped, and as they began to eat, their men began to drift in from the stables where they slept. Nara had consumed her own meal quickly for it was her responsibility to see that the others were fed. Each man-at-arms was given a trencher of bread filled with a mixture of cooked grains, and a mug of brown ale. The wheel of cheese was placed upon the long end of the T where the men sat. Gratefully they sliced chunks from it with their knives. The lord and lady of Aelfleah were generous to them. Having listened to the tales of other masters while awaiting their own yesterday at Westminster, they realized how fortunate they were.

"I do not want you out in the city today," said Josselin to his wife.

"Nay," she said, "I need to rest. I am yet weak from the blood I lost yesterday. The day is fair, and I would sit out in my orchards which are in full bloom."

They walked together later beneath the hauntingly fragrant pink-and-white apple blossoms in the orchard by the London house. Above them the sky was cloudless and blue. It promised to be perfect weather tomorrow for the queen's coronation. They stood and kissed long slow kisses beneath the curtain of branches.

"When I saw Blanche attack you yesterday I thought I might lose you, enchantress," he said. "For a moment my legs would not move, and I was terrified I could not get to you in time, yet only a few seconds elapsed after she drew her knife before she was taken into custody."

"It felt more like a hundred years," Mairin admitted. "I never expected her to come at me like that. It was plain that she had lost the game."

"I pity the abbess at St. Hilary's who must contend with her," he replied.

"Yes," she said, and nothing more. She did not tell him that Dagda had practically admitted to killing Blanche de St. Brieuc. If Josselin learned of Blanche's death he would not be likely to connect the death with Dagda. She knew what crisis of conscience that deed had cost Dagda for it had been many years since her former warrior had raised his hand against another human being. That he had felt it necessary to do so distressed her. It was better that Josselin not know for she would not want Dagda to suffer for his misguided loyalty to her—or had it been misguided? Perhaps Dagda had known just what he was doing. Perhaps he had been right. Blanche de St. Brieuc had never hesitated to do what she thought necessary even if it meant hurting another.

"What are you thinking of?" Josselin asked her.

"Blanche de St. Brieuc," she said honestly.

"Do not. You frown most fiercely when you do," he said and then spreading his cloak upon the ground he drew her down with him.

"What shall I think of then, my lord?" she said with a little smile.

"Lambing," he whispered, laying her back against his arm. Undoing her girdle he pulled her tunic over her head, and tossing it aside undid the laces of her camise. He slipped his hand between the halves of the soft linen to cup one of her breasts. "Ahhh, sweeting," he murmured as he fondled her, "I want you so very much! I am as randy for you as that billy goat you are forever accusing me of being." His thumb rubbed at her nipple, and he kissed her with mounting passion.

How delightful, she thought, as her head spun with their shared ardor, that each time they made love it was even better than the last. She hoped it would be so forever. His mouth closed over her nipple and tugged upon her flesh, eliciting a corresponding throb from the hidden place between her thighs. She loved the feel of his mouth upon her flesh! Reaching out she threaded her fingers through his tawny hair, and pressed him even closer to her breast.

He slid his free hand beneath her skirts, and up her silky leg. Mairin shifted her body to give him greater access, and her thighs parted. "Ahh, wanton, you are eager," he murmured, his fingers parting her nether lips to tease at her femininity.

"And you, my lord, are not?" she said softly, moving so that she might reach out and slip her hand beneath his long tunic to fondle him. Her hand closed tightly about him as he pushed two fingers into her soft body. Within her grasp she felt him throbbing as his fingers imitated the deed that his manhood craved to do. He was driving her wild by both his actions and with the knowledge that he lusted for her as much as she lusted for him. "Take me!" she whispered fiercely to him. "Take me now!"

With a groan he rolled atop her, pushing her skirts up to her waist, yanking his own tunic up. With one hard thrust he filled her full of himself, and she bit through the cloth of his tunic to score his shoulder with her teeth. Wildly they loved one another, wrapping legs and arms about their thrashing bodies. It was as if they were both possessed by demons. Neither could get enough of the other.

Gritting his teeth he thrust over and over again into his wife's welcoming body. Her nails dug into his fabric-covered shoulders and she made soft little mewling noises while her own body met his eagerly. There was no time or space any longer. There was only the two of them blending into a oneness of such passionate purity that Mairin thought before she lost total control of her senses that they would burst into flame and incinerate themselves entirely.

With a roar that sounded almost victorious, he poured his offering into her waiting womb. Then he sank down upon her half-clad breasts, his breath coming in tearing gasps, and she wept with joy. The sound of her sobbing startled him, but for a long moment he simply could not move. He felt as if his very life's blood had been drained from him.

Sensing his distress she moved to reassure him, patting his head weakly for she herself felt happily exhausted. "It's all right, my lord and my love. It's all right. I am just so happy, for I love you, and I love how we love!"

He managed to roll off her, and propping himself upon one elbow he looked down into her face. "Ahhh, enchantress, you fill my life with such joy. I feel almost guilty for the love we share."

She stopped his mouth with her hand. "No. Love is the blessing that God Almighty has gifted us with, my Josselin. Pity those who do not realize it, and thank our Blessed Lord for opening our eyes to this great knowledge. I have found throughout my life that love is the saving grace. Had not Dagda loved me I should have been lost those many years back. Had not my foster parents loved me I would have had no home. Had not Basil loved me I would not have learned passion. Had not you loved me I would not have become a woman. Death teaches one sorrow, but love teaches one life, for to love is to live. I think that is what God would have us do, my Josselin. He would have us live to love!" Then she drew his head down, and kissed him sweetly.

Her mouth was soft, and faintly reminiscent of strawberries. "I wonder if the church would agree with you, Mairin. You make it all sound so simple."

"That is the secret of life. Simplicity," she laughed. Then she lifted her hips up, and drew her skirts down. "I suggest you do the same, my lord. Should someone come to seek us you would startle them with your bare bottom."

"You were not thinking about propriety a few minutes ago when you lay beneath me clawing me and whimpering. You were quite shameless as you urged me onward. Anyone coming upon us would have been shocked."

"Shocked to hear you bellowing like a bull in stud," she teased him back.

"I did not bellow," he said, sounding offended.

"Yes, you did," she giggled. "You positively roared!"

Breaking off a stem of clover, he tickled her nose. "Did you find it exciting, my lady?"

"Did you?" she countered.

"Aye. I liked playing the bull to your little red heifer," and tossing the clover aside he took her long hair in his hands, and crushed it. "Tonight," he said. "Tonight you will wear nothing but your long hair, and I will love you again until the dawn."

"And then we will not be able to reach Westminster in time," she teased. "We will offend the king and the queen, and how will you explain it, my lord?"

He scrambled to his feet and pulled her up after him. "You are far too logical for a woman," he grumbled, "but dammit I love you!"

"Would you have rather wed with someone like Blanche de St. Brieuc?" she mocked him. At his look of outrage she chuckled. "Well, you liked her well enough to walk in her brother's garden with her. What fools you men can be! The shrew stalked you, and had you not been wed to me when she arrived in England she would have had you, for all your protests. Not knowing her vile character, you would have thought yourself fortunate until too late you realized your mistake."

"But instead," he said, wrapping her in his arms, "I wed myself to an enchantress with a sharp tongue. Now kiss me, you hotheaded spitfire! Both the air and our sparring have made me hungry once again for you."

Mairin's mouth turned itself up in a seductive smile, and she replied in a deceptively sweet and docile voice as she tipped her face up to him, "As my lord commands me, for has my mother not taught me to be a good and dutiful wife?"

"Ahhh, vixen," he murmured against her tempting lips, "I wonder that I should not beat you," and stifling the laughter that bubbled from her throat he kissed her.

Chapter 13

✦

*I*t was unusual that a woman be crowned in her own right, but when William of Normandy had taken his inheritance back from Harold Godwinson, his wife had demanded that she be crowned too. There were those among his own advisers who agreed with Matilda. The strong character of the king could be softened by the mother figure Matilda represented. At first William had resisted the suggestion. England wasn't yet fully conquered. It was not safe for her to come. Wasn't it enough that he was now its king? Matilda thought not. If William was king then she would be legally queen. William loved his wife deeply, and peace within his own house was a necessity. When she would not give up her dream of a coronation he found himself forced to give in to her. Besides, he reasoned with himself, perhaps his advisers were right. Matilda would be good for England.

Whitsunday, May 11th, 1068, dawned clear and warm. The blue sky was cloudless, and the sun shone beneficently upon all of England. It was most obvious that God approved Matilda's coronation as England's queen. Since there was no precedent for the crowning of a Queen of England, the Anglo-Saxon rules that had governed William's coronation seventeen months prior were altered slightly to suit a woman. In addition the Normans brought something of their own to the ceremony. The *Laudes Regiae* which had first been chanted at the coronation of the great French King Charlemagne were now added to the royal ritual of the Anglo-Saxon ceremony.

Although William trusted the populace of London that had so many months ago pledged him their fealty, there was still enough rebellion going on throughout England that he would not expose his wife to unnecessary dangers. The queen's coronation procession was a limited affair which suggested that William considered England totally his and loyal beyond a doubt, but not so long that assassins would have an opportunity to strike. It wound its way from the king's house along the river road into the city for a mile or so, and then back to Westminster Abbey where Matilda would be crowned.

A dozen trumpeters and a dozen drummers in king's colors led the regal parade. The horns sounded sharply in the clear air, the monotonous thrum-thrum of the drums provided marked contrast. Behind the strutting musicians rode a group of mounted knights in full regalia, pendants in the queen's colors floating from the tops of their lances. Their horses were caparisoned in red and gold. They were followed by a choir of a hundred young boys in red gowns with white surplices chanting plainsong. Their young voices drifted upward with sweet clarity filling the air with their praises of the gracious God who had been so kind as to send England Matilda for its queen. Now came those noblemen especially chosen to carry the queen's royal regalia. A black-robed priest waving a censer of fragrant frankincense preceded each man.

The king's youngest brother, Robert, Count of Mortain, carried the queen's newly made crown upon a pillow of royal-purple velvet. William FitzOsbern carried upon his pillow the specially made gold coronation ring with its beautiful corundum ruby. Behind him strutted the six-year-old Prince William Rufus, displaying the queen's dainty golden scepter for all to see upon another velvet pillow. So that none could say the Anglo-Saxons had been overlooked, Earl Edwin of Mercia had been chosen to carry the royal golden orb. His brother, Earl Morkar, was entrusted with the gold-and-ruby coronation bracelets. Neither of these last two looked comfortable in his role. Watching them the king smiled grimly to himself. He trusted neither man despite their vows of loyalty. They were men who lacked vision.

Londoners and visitors alike lined the streets cheering themselves hoarse as the procession passed by. A bevy of beautifully dressed men and women of the court rode by after the queen's regalia, their multicolored garments like so many bright butterflies. Then came Matilda herself upon a snow-white palfrey. Her skirts were of cloth of gold and had been spread over her mount's rump. Her tunic was of indigo blue sprinkled with golden stars. Her waist, somewhat increased in size with her latest pregnancy, was girdled with a belt of gold-washed silver and studded with blue stones. Her silver-blond hair had been parted in the middle and hung in two fat plaits on either side of her head which was smooth on top so the crown might fit without difficulty. A sheer gold veil held by a wreath of white flowers now dressed her head.

The diminutive duchess smiled and waved and won the hearts of all those who saw her. Her reputation for goodness and her godly character preceded her. The English felt safer for her coming. For a brief moment William gained by his wife's good reputation even as his advisers had suggested he would. Surely a man with a wife like Matilda could not be all bad. Of William there was no sign. For the king, not wishing to steal his wife's day, awaited her at the church. The last of the royal parade was brought up by a group of nuns brought from the queen's own Abbey of the Holy Trinity in Caen. As they walked they prayed, their beads slipping swiftly through their fingers.

Back to Edward's magnificent abbey of Westminster the procession went, passing through the main doors and down the main aisle. Within it was cool, and the light coming through the great stained-glass windows warmed the gray stone interior. The voices of the mighty choir, which was made up of men and boys, soared in the heights of the abbey as they chanted ancient Latin plainsong. At the high altar, Eadred, the archbishop of York, waited to do his duty. The coronation involved the hallowing, the investing, and the crowning of the queen.

Squeezed into an aisle space somewhere between the front and the back of Westminster, Mairin and Josselin eagerly answered "Aye" along with the rest of the guests when asked if they did indeed accept Matilda, Duchess of Normandy, as their lawful queen. It was only then that she was administered the oath which was, in effect, a contract between Matilda and her people. The petite duchess's voice was clear and easily heard even in the rear of the abbey.

Now came the consecration of the queen. Matilda knelt, and a young priest removed her wreath and her veil. The archbishop poured a thin stream of sacred oil from an ampulla upon the queen's shining head, thereby anointing her. Next, a flowing cloak of shining cloth-of-gold edged in ermine was attached to the queen's shoulders, and with surprising simplicity Eadred said in a clear, but quiet voice,

"Matilda of Normandy, I crown thee Queen of England, in the name of the Father, and of the Son, and of the Holy Spirit."

Holding aloft the diadem for a moment for all to see, he then placed it upon her head. It was a delicately made crown of pure gold studded with amethysts and diamonds that had been fashioned just for Matilda. The crown, which fit over her entire head, was not a high one, but its openwork design of wheat, grape vines, and lilies was thought to be not only beautiful, but lucky as well.

Anointed and formally crowned, the queen was led down several steps from the altar to a throne that had been set next to an even larger one. It was now that the king joined his wife, sitting first while Archbishop Eadred proclaimed,

"My lord, and my ladies, I give you Matilda, Queen of England!" The archbishop spoke in French. "Monseigneurs, et mes dames, je vous presente la reine, Matilde d'Angleterre!"

A mighty cheer arose from the spectators within the abbey, and when it had finally died Matilda sat to receive the homage of her husband's subjects. Only the most important and major noblemen knelt before the queen, for if everyone had come forward, it would have taken all day.

The king and queen then led a procession upon foot across the green back to the king's house where they would be hosting a huge banquet. Pavilions had been set up out-of-doors, for the weather was simply too lovely to resist. Great pits had been dug, and oxen, sheep, pigs, and roe deer were being roasted whole over the open fires. The turnspits with their reddened faces carefully watched the meat, turning it slowly with measured cadence. Long trestles had been set out for the guests, the royal highboard with its back to the abbey. Great tuns of wine and beer were rolled out, and soon the day turned from the religious solemnity of the crowning to merriment and ribaldry. The servants hurried back and forth from the kitchens holding aloft platters of sauced and dressed fowl, broiled game birds such as lark, sparrow, partridge, grouse, quail, and woodcock, rabbits stuffed with pigeons stuffed with grains and dried fruit, platters of whole sea bass, river trout, and salmon. There were wheels of cheese, bowls of peas, cabbage, tiny beets, and breads of every kind. There were oranges from Spain, and candied violets from Provence, and Norman cherries and English strawberries.

Minstrels arrived to stroll amongst the guests singing the tales of past heroes and deeds. There was one in particular who caught William's fancy by making a new song that glorified the noble king and the love he had for the beautiful and gracious Matilda, by whose presence England was now made fairer. The king rewarded the clever minstrel with a gold ring from his little finger. There were several troupes of jongleurs and acrobats who entertained the guests by singing, playing upon the lute, harp, rebec, hurdy-gurdy, and cymbals, doing juggler's tricks, acrobatic stunts, and imitating all kinds of animals. As the day wore on and the guests grew merrier, some even tried to join the entertainers.

At one point during the banquet, a knight, Sir Marmion of Fortenays, dressed in full battle gear, rode forward upon his horse. Three times he called out a challenge to those assembled.

"If any person denies that our most gracious Sovereign William, and his fair spouse Matilda are lawfully king and queen of England, he is a false-hearted traitor and a liar. As royal champion, I do hereby challenge him to single combat."

The challenge, of course, was accepted by no one.

Since Josselin and Mairin were not of the court, they departed to their house early, not wishing to do so in the dark. Matilda's coronation was something that they would tell their grandchildren about, but now they were anxious to take their leave so they might begin their journey to Aelfleah tomorrow. First it was necessary to pay their respects to the king and the queen. Making their way up to the highboard, they waited politely until they were noticed.

"Speak, Joss!" The king was well fed, and feeling kindly disposed toward all.

"We must go, my lord, but before we do we would thank you for your hospitality."

"The lady Mairin's hand?" the queen graciously inquired. "Is it all right?"

"There is no infection, my lady," replied Mairin, "and in time I will be healed."

"I will feel safer for my wife when Blanche de St. Brieuc is once more across the water," said Josselin. "I did not realize how dangerous a woman she was."

There was a pointed silence, and then the king said, "Blanche de St. Brieuc is dead, Joss. I thought you surely knew it."

"*Dead!*" Josselin de Combourg looked genuinely surprised.

"Dead?" said Mairin, pretending to also be surprised, and feeling a little guilty about deceiving her husband.

"Yes," said William. "After her attack upon your lady I gave orders that she be confined in a small storage room in the attics of The King's House. She was put there with a pitcher of water and a loaf of bread. We intended that she be kept there until she could be returned to Normandy. The door was bolted from the outside, but no guard was placed upon it, for who would want to help her escape? Late yesterday afternoon a servant went to bring her another loaf and a pitcher. He unbolted the door, and entered the room to find Blanche de St. Brieuc upon the floor. She was quite dead. Her neck had been broken. We have questioned every-one in The King's House, but no one saw anything unusual. Nor did they see any strangers, or even hear something that might tell us who did this deed."

"It was as if," said Matilda, "the devil had come for his own," and she crossed herself devoutly.

"I do not remember her as being a woman who easily made friends," said Mairin slowly. "Perhaps among your great train she had a serious enemy. She came to England intending to entrap my husband into a mar-riage. When that path was closed to her she may have foolishly turned onto another and more dangerous course. She was not a woman to be de-terred from her chosen goal. She was my enemy, but may God have mercy upon her soul."

"Yes," said the queen. "May God forgive her her sins."

"Please, madame," Mairin said, "do not tell my poor half-sister of her mother's violent end. I am certain that she loved the lady Blanche, and whatever my stepmother's faults, I believe that she loved her child."

"She will eventually have to learn of her mother's cruelty, my lady Mairin," said William. "Otherwise she will wonder at the loss of Lan-derneau. There is no way we can explain it but with the truth."

Mairin looked genuinely distressed. "I have never met her, of course, but I *know* that Blanchette is nothing like her mother. It would be like trying to compare night and day, fire and water. She is a gentle soul. I fear you will break her heart."

"I will tell her myself," said the queen. "She is still with the Mont-gomerie family, and will remain with them for the time being. With her mother's death she becomes a royal ward. No one can decide her future but the king, and my lord William had decided to allow her to enter the novitiate of Holy Trinity at Caen. When I return to Normandy I will have your half-sister sent to me. She will stay with me until next year when our own daughter Cecily also enters the novitiate at Holy Trinity. The two girls will go together."

Mairin knelt and kissed the queen's hand gratefully. "Merci, my queen! What you have offered to do is far more than I could have ever hoped."

"Mayhap," said Matilda, "you would like to write to your half-sister so that she may be assured that you bear her no ill will. If you can get a let-ter to me before you leave tomorrow, I will see it delivered to Blanchette St. Ronan."

Mairin nodded, and arose to her feet once more to curtsy to both the king and the queen.

The royal couple smiled at them, and William said, "Go with God, and, Josselin, you will keep me informed of the progress of Aldford. Keep your piece of the border safe for me."

"I will, my liege," came the reply, and then with a bow Josselin de Combourg withdrew from the royal presence, taking his wife with him.

On the following morning they departed for Aelfleah, arriving to find the walls of Aldford Castle almost twice the height they had been when they had left. The good weather and the lengthening days combined to allow the workers longer hours at their task. The well, within the safety of the inner ward, had already been dug and walled about. Scaffolding was already in place with plank ramps up which heavy material could be either dragged or pulled or carried.

As the walls of the outer curtain rose, their battlements were constructed. The higher sections of the battlements were called merlons, and had arrow loops within them. The merlons were topped with sharp stone spikes. It was obvious that by summer's end the walls of the outer curtain would be finished, and its towers begun, provided that the weather held. Once that was done it would be difficult to halt construction of Aldford.

Several weeks after Matilda's coronation, word began to filter into Aelfleah's valley of rebellion and revolt. Harold Godwinson's three sons by Edyth Swansneck sailed from Ireland, where they had been exiled, to raid the countryside of the Bristol Channel, and part of the West Country. Fortunately Aelfleah was too remote to be bothered with, but that was not so when Earl Edwin and his younger brother, Earl Morkar, raised a revolt with their Welsh allies.

During those tense weeks of midsummer, no one slept easy. Mairin feared that Edwin and his forces would attempt to take Aelfleah. That would mean that Josselin would fight, and he might be killed. Now that she was certain she was with child again, her concern for her child's father became almost an obsession. When they learned in late summer that Gospatric, newly appointed by King William to govern Northumbria, had revolted and declared for Edgar the Atheling, Mairin was almost hysterical.

"How can the king hold England with all these rebellions?" she fretted.

"I have never known William of Normandy to release his hold on anything he considers his own," Josselin tried to reassure her.

"Edgar the Atheling has sought refuge with his mother and sisters in Scotland. The Scots are raiding!"

Josselin laughed. "It was my understanding that the Scots and the Northumbrians are always raiding each other's holdings. There is rarely peace in that part of England. The Atheling is still too young to seriously challenge King William. Much is done in his name that I suspect he would rather not be done. I think he fled to Scotland in possible preparation for a return to Hungary where he was born, and where he will be safe from all of this. William would have eventually had to either lock him up or kill him. He and his family know this." He put his arms about her, and gently patted her belly which did not yet show her condition. "Do not fret, my love. Rest easy, and care for our child."

"Eadric the Wild is on the march again," she challenged him.

"Do you seriously believe that Eadric would return to Aelfleah after the way you treated him the last time? From what I hear, the man is no fool. Besides, he knows there is nothing here of any real value."

"There is Aldford," she replied.

"Which would take too much of Eadric's time to tear down now, and not being finished yet, is not worth having. A castle, Mairin, is only valuable when it is habitable, and can be used for defense against one's enemies. Aldford is neither. There are easier pickings for your old friend Eadric the Wild than Aelfleah. He knows I am here now, and that I will defend this holding."

The three major revolts of that summer of 1068 each died a stillborn death. The late Harold Godwinson's three strapping sons with their Irish, Danish, and English adherents could simply not consolidate a serious landing on English soil. They caused some damage, and were generally troublesome, but in the end they departed, never to return again.

In the north Gospatric found himself with no real army with which to defy the king he had so rashly challenged. It seemed that those nobles who had so firmly agreed with him while they were all in their cups could not be distracted from their personal feuds and factional fighting to come to his aid against William. Choosing the lesser evil, Gospatric surrendered to King Malcolm of Scotland, and went into exile with the young Atheling.

William then turned his eye, and his armies, to Earls Edwin and Morkar. Both had sworn their loyalty to him. He had even honored them by having them take part in his wife's coronation. They repaid his kindness by rebelling against him. Worst of all, they had broken their sworn oath before God to uphold him and his rights as their king. For William this was the greater of their two sins. His superior forces swept down on them. The Mercians and the Welsh fled, panicked before William's armies. The last of the rebellions for that year was broken.

The king ordered that castles be raised at Leicester, Warwick, and Nottingham. One of the king's loyalists, Robert de Meulan, was created Earl of Leicestershire, and made overlord of a huge portion of Earl Edwin's Mercian lands. Josselin felt safer for his new neighbor. York had surrendered without a battle on Gospatric's desertion, and one of the queen's cousins, Robert de Commines, was made the new Earl of Northumbria. As the year 1068 drew to a close, England, south of the Humber, appeared to be appeased and content with the king.

William, heading for Gloucester with a party of his knights, stopped unexpectedly at Aelfleah to shelter for a night. There were close to forty men in the king's party, and although Mairin knew she could house them somehow she wondered how she was going to feed them on such short notice. They had arrived shortly after midday, which she hoped would allow her time to arrange for an evening meal.

She ordered that a young steer be slain, and at least three dozen chickens. Egbert the bailiff sent several young men into *The Forest* and the successful hunters returned in short order with a young buck, and a number of rabbits which were quickly skinned, boned, and pied. The beef and the deer were roasted slowly over open fires. The chickens, at least six to a spit, were stuffed with grain and dried apples to be roasted in the kitchens. There would be cold mutton in ample supply and plenty of trout from the river. Dandelion greens were steamed in white wine, and there were pickled whole beets. The men at the castle site would be somewhat short of bread due to the emergency, but when Dagda explained to each master craftsman who in turn explained to his own men, they understood. Mairin sent several barrels of cider to the workmen to express their thanks. Large wheels of cheese were ready to be placed upon the tables along with the bowls of grapes, pears, and apples.

Convinced that all was in readiness, Mairin smiled victoriously at Eada. "Well, mother?"

"I taught you well, my daughter," said Eada returning the smile. "I have never entertained a King of England, but you have naught to be ashamed of, for I doubt any chatelaine in any fine castle could have prepared a better meal on such short notice. I am proud of you!"

"I, too," said Josselin, coming in and looking about Aelfleah's hall.

The fire burned brightly and warmed the room pleasantly. The well-polished trestles with their wooden cups at each place and the trenchers of fresh bread were inviting. Along the sides of the room, barrels of wine, ale, and cider were in readiness.

"Mother and I will eat in the solar," said Mairin. "This is an evening for the gentlemen."

The king had gone with Josselin to inspect the castle site, and he was pleased with what he found. The outer curtain was close to being finished, for they had had uncommonly good weather since the spring, and it was yet mild enough in this early December for the workmen to continue. The inner curtain walls were already being raised. When bad weather came they would be able to work inside each gatehouse, finishing it.

"You'll have Aldford finished by a year from this spring," said William, his tone approving.

"If I get another spring, summer, and autumn like this year's we will, my lord. If not, it may not be for another two years. I've a good engineer in Master Gilleet, a good bailiff in Dagda, and uncommonly good workmen."

"You have decided to make your wife's servant bailiff of Aldford, Joss?"

"Aye, my lord. He was born a freedman, and was once a feared warrior. His history is a long and a fascinating one. What is important to me, however, is his total loyalty, his integrity, and the fact that he is enormously well liked here. The manor bailiff has never been away from Aelfleah, and is not sophisticated enough to run Aldford. Egbert did not expect to have charge over the castle. He is a man lacking in ambition. He far prefers a world that is basically an unchanging one."

"Has Dagda sworn his fealty to you?" the king inquired.

"Aye! If I am not here he will hold Aldford for you to the last drop of blood."

"You have done well for me, Josselin de Combourg, Baron Aldford, a rank that will be passed down to your sons and your sons' sons until that time, may it never come, when there are no longer any de Combourgs. The papers will eventually come from court to confirm this, but I shall announce it at supper tonight. Your wife should be pleased. She carries the child well. Pray God it is the next Baron Aldford she houses within her belly."

"Amen!" said Josselin fervently.

It was not, however, a son that Mairin birthed on February 2nd. It was a healthy daughter. Mairin had insisted upon lighting her Imbolc fire at a spot near the castle site. Josselin had insisted upon accompanying her and Dagda, for the path was steep, and his wife was huge with their child. He did not approve of her loyalty to the old Celtic way, and she knew it. She also knew he would not forbid her.

"Look!" She pointed with a graceful finger toward the valleys of Wales below them. "Did I not tell you, my lord? Dagda and I are not alone."

As her own fire had been lit, pinpoints of light had appeared in the dales of Cymru beneath them. Mairin threw back her head and laughed joyously as the flames leapt skyward into the indigo night. She felt happy, for her world was a good place. Once more she had kept faith with her heritage, and made strong again the fragile link with her long-dead and barely remembered natural parents. Then the dull ache that had nagged her back all day grew into a sudden pain of such intensity that she cried out.

"My lord!" she gasped. "You must help me back to the house, for our child wishes to be born."

"Can you walk?" he asked nervously.

"Aye." She nodded, a small, tight smile on her face. "Dagda, tend the flame until the proper moment."

" 'Tis done, my lady," he said quietly. "I will say my own prayers."

Slowly, Mairin and Josselin made their way back down the precipitous path. Once they had to stop. Mairin took her husband's hands and squeezed them fiercely, panting, great beads of sweat popping out all over her forehead. Then as the pain subsided she moved on to gain the house before the next tearing wrench came. To everyone's relief, however, Mairin had a quick and easy labor. Maude Eada Marie de Combourg was born shortly after midnight, slipping into the world with a sputtering howl that grew in volume until the entire manor house had been made aware of her arrival.

If her parents were initially thwarted by her sex, their disappointment was quickly overcome with the knowledge that they had easily produced a wonderfully healthy and beautiful child. There would be other children. Eada was immediately thrilled by her granddaughter, and the fact that the child would bear her name among others. "Maude" was an English version of "Matilda," and "Marie" was for both the saint and for Mairin's natural mother, Maire. Had the baby been the desired son, he would have been called William.

Mairin cradled her finally silent but sleepless daughter who, now swaddled, stared up at her mother with strangely adult eyes. Mairin smiled down at the baby. "She looks like you, Josselin. See! She has your tawny hair, and although her eyes be baby blue now, I would not wonder if they turned the green-gold of yours. And here is your nose in miniature!"

He grinned, and it was as if he was entirely responsible for Maude's arrival. "She does look like me, doesn't she?" he said, pleased.

Eada's eyes met those of her daughter and the two women smiled.

"It is good to have a baby in the house," said Dagda in a mellow voice, and he touched Maude's satiny cheek with his big finger.

"Oh, no!" said Josselin. "You are bailiff of Aldford now, and I need you! Your days of child-rearing are over, Dagda, my friend."

"I will nonetheless keep an eye on the lady Maude as I did with her grandmother and her mother," said the big man. "I will not neglect my duties as your bailiff, my lord. You may always count on me."

Maude de Combourg was baptized the next day in Aelfleah church, her grandmother and Dagda taking their vows as her godparents. Mairin felt well enough to sit at the table in the solar, while her child slept, and write to Josselin's parents announcing Maude's birth. She had only written them once before, and then in Josselin's name, telling them of his success in England, and their marriage. Now she wrote them in her own right, sharing their happiness over little Maude's arrival, and informing them that the king had personally raised their son from a mere knight to the rank of baron. They had not written back the first time, and she had not expected them to, but she could not help but wonder if they were proud of their elder son who had made his own way in the world despite the accident of his birth.

Then winter came to an end, and with the longer days of spring, work once again began upon the castle in earnest. Mairin was now glad of it. There were rumors heard, even in remote Aelfleah, that Sweyn Estrithson, the king of the Danes, was planning an attack upon England.

"Will it never end?" demanded Mairin irritably of her husband. "Why must men constantly war with one another?"

"I cannot answer such a question, but I know there will be no easy peace for England. Not until King William has beaten them all in battle, I am afraid," admitted Josselin. "England has always been a plum ripe for the picking, and many have enjoyed its fruits. The Normans must prove they are strong enough to hold England, and until all the English agree to honestly support the king, we are vulnerable. The north is still restless and uncertain. I do not think it is over yet, but here in Aelfleah we are safe, and we will await the outcome of whatever is to happen."

Now in the spring of the year 1069 the people of Aelfleah learned that in late January past, just before the birth of Maude, a revolt had broken out again in the north. Robert de Commines and his force of knights were trapped and massacred in Durham. The king had returned north in March to defeat the rebels who, at that point, were besieging York. Successful, he had departed south to hold his Easter court at Winchester, leaving William FitzOsbern to hold the north.

Summer came, and with it the anticipated invasion by the Danes. A fleet of two hundred and forty ships under the command of King Sweyn's two sons, Harold and Cnut, and his brother, Jarl Osbiorn, arrived first off Kent. Their move up the east coast of England to the mouth of the Humber was a signal for a general uprising in Yorkshire. Young Edgar the Atheling was now fourteen, and filled to overflowing with enthusiasm, ambition, and high spirits. He had been dissuaded from returning to Hungary, and with his fellow English exiles Earl Waltheof and Gospatric had joined with the Danes. Ten thousand strong they marched upon the city of York, which easily fell to them on September 20th.

The Danes then fortified Axholme Island, and dispersed themselves over north Lincolnshire where they were welcomed by the peasant population who wanted no further trouble. The northern rising encouraged other risings of a minor nature in Dorset, Somerset, south Cheshire, and Staffordshire. By now the king had had more than enough. How could he build a strong England when the land and its people were constantly being beset from both within and without? England had too long been a battleground for those wishing to play at war. The bulk of the country had settled down. The bad example of the north could eventually cause serious problems throughout the entire land.

William was a decent man. He considered himself a good Christian, but these were hard times. Even the church agreed with him that an example must be made of those who would defy the king's authority. They did not, however, anticipate the harsh cruelty of what was to come.

The king marched north once more, moving toward Axholme. With his coming, the Danish forces eased themselves back over the Humber to York. William's younger brother, the Count of Mortain, and his friend the Count of Eu were left in charge of that part of the expedition. A new rebellion had arisen in the west led by Eadric the Wild and his Welsh allies.

It was Josselin de Combourg who had sent the king word of this latest difficulty, and it was Josselin, with his small but well-trained troop of soldiers, who had held Eadric at bay just long enough for the king to get there. The Welsh princes disappeared magically back into the hills from whence they had come. Eadric was defeated, but once more escaped the Normans. Josselin returned to Aelfleah to personally tell his wife he would be rejoining the king in his battle to subdue the north once and for all.

"The king needs as great a show of force as he can muster," Josselin explained to his wife.

"Then go," she said, "but promise me you will be careful. We have a family now."

He had never felt more pride for anyone than he felt for her as he departed their home. She had offered him a stirrup cup, and then sent him forth with dignity, standing proudly before the door of their house. He did not know that when he had passed from her sight she had gone quietly to their chamber to weep silently alone. She feared for him. She would not fret him, however, with those fears. In that moment of her darkest hour, Mairin knew she had at last left her childhood far behind her.

Josselin and his men rode to meet the king at Nottingham, but by the time they had reached it, William, learning that the Danes planned to attempt a reoccupation of York, had gone north again. Josselin followed, easily finding his way, for the king in his anger and impatience left a swath of devastation of such enormity that the north would never really recover. No distinction was made between rebel and loyalist. The land was scorched, and every living male the king's men could find, animal or man, was put to the sword.

Granaries, farms, manors, castles, churches, monasteries, and convents were all burnt to the ground. The air was heavy with smoke and the smell of rotting flesh. Nothing was left that could possibly support life. The king's vengeance was a terrible thing, but there would be no more rebellions in the north because there was no one left in the north. The innocent had suffered along with the guilty, and even the church, which had encouraged William to make an example, was horrified by his actions.

They reached York in mid-December, and the king decided to hold his Christmas court in the burnt city. Messengers were dispatched summoning the nobility to York. At the king's command, Josselin sent for Mairin to join them. It was, he wrote, a royal command. She could not refuse.

"But I can't go!" Mairin wailed. "Maude is far too young to travel."

"Leave her," said Eada. "Of course you cannot take her. She is far better off here at home."

"But who will feed her, mother? She is only ten months old, and still nursing."

"There are plenty of women in the village with nursing babies and milk to spare. The miller's wife! She has breasts like jugs, and is forever complaining her son doesn't drain her. It is time you stopped nursing Maude. You must go to your husband. I will have Enid move in here this very day with her son. Weorth could use a respite from her chatter. Make yourself a potion to dry your milk, and bind your breasts, Mairin. By the time you reach York you will be fit for Josselin, and I do not think he will be unhappy that you are so," Eada finished with a broad smile.

He had sent a small troop of heavily armed men to escort his wife, but they could not screen her from the horrors she saw as they rode. Mairin was appalled at the wretchedness and the wholesale homicide that had taken place in the king's name. Her purse was empty by the time they were halfway to York, for she could not refuse the shoeless women with their haunted eyes, and their clinging, weeping daughters. She went hungry most nights, and shamed her men into sharing their own rations with the homeless, wandering refugees. The worst cases she sent on to Aelfleah to Eada for refuge.

She reached York on December 23rd, and was led by her men to a small anonymous tent set among many in the burnt-out city. Within was a small brazier that gave off a feeble warmth. She had brought with her fresh clothing for her husband and bedding for them to share. Stakes were driven into the dirt floor of the shelter, and two large cured and tanned hides that had been sewn together were stretched and fastened between them. Atop the hides she made a bed of furs. She set two additional braziers on either side of their bed and placed kindling and hot coals from the other braziers in each. Shortly the tent began to feel a bit more habitable.

It was not long before Josselin had come, and he had swept her up into his arms inhaling the sweetness of her. "I have missed you so," he said simply. "I find I do not like being separated from someone I love." Releasing her he looked about, and then, his eyes lighting upon the newly made camp bed, he smiled. "What luxury, enchantress! I have slept on the ground wrapped in my cloak these past weeks. You have no idea how I have longed for our bed at Aelfleah."

Mairin chuckled. "You have grown soft with the good living of our home, my lord. This expedition has been good for you, I'll vow." Then her eyes grew sad. "God's mercy, Josselin! Never had I seen such terrible suffering and devastation as I have seen these last few days. It is horrible! Was it necessary? *Really necessary?*"

For a moment he turned his eyes from her, and then looking directly at her he said, "It was necessary. The peasants welcomed our enemies. Their lords forsook their oaths to uphold the king. How many times in the last three years has William been forced north to put down their treasons? The king is no saint, Mairin. He is a man, and he has his limits. Even when they massacred his wife's kin, Robert de Commines, last January, he forgave them. This he could not. He has destroyed Northumbria and York and wasted their lands. They will trouble him no more."

"When can you come home?" she asked, realizing that his part in the king's revenge must be painful, and that the subject was now closed.

"After he holds his Christmas court, we are both free to return to Aelfleah."

"The king makes a strong point holding his Christmas court in York," Mairin noted.

"Aye, but it is a point well taken," replied Josselin. "It is rumored that Earls Waltheof and Gospatric will submit and be pardoned after Twelfth Night."

"That is outrageous!" cried Mairin. " 'Tis their fault all of this happened. They broke their sacred oaths to the king, and encouraged that beardless boy, Edgar the Atheling, and his Scots allies. Now Waltheof and Gospatric will be pardoned? What of the Atheling, Earls Edwin and Morkar?"

"Those three fled back to Scotland," said Josselin.

"I am surprised King Malcolm puts up with such guests," Mairin muttered.

"Edgar the Atheling's elder sister, Margaret, married the Scots king this autumn past. They are now kin, and he is forced to put up with the lad."

"Will the Scots king support Edgar the Atheling?"

"Not seriously," said Josselin. "Malcolm is too concerned with his own country. Remember, he has only recently overthrown his uncle, Mac-Beth, to regain a throne that was rightfully his. He spent his youth in exile at King Edward's court, and his only brother was raised in Ireland. He has too much to do in his own country to be bothered with a half-grown brother-in-law's problems. It is for his wife's sake, I suspect, he got involved this time. He is newly wed to Margaret and, rumor would have it, totally infatuated with his bride."

"Why are we speaking on politics?" she suddenly asked him.

They had been standing facing one another as they spoke. Now he put his arms back around her, and drew her into his embrace.

"Because you started it, my beautiful enchantress. I have been separated from you for almost two months, Mairin. There are things I would far rather do with you than stand here in speech." He kissed the tip of her nose, his generous mouth quirking with amusement at the smoky look that sprang into her eyes.

"Indeed, my lord," she said softly, and strained closer to him. She could feel the muscled hardness of his thighs through his tunic. Her hands slid up his chest and she wrapped her arms about his neck. The tip of her tongue raced across her upper lip. Teasingly her fingers played with the muscled back of his neck, and she pressed the lower half of her torso suggestively against his body.

A slow smile lit his eyes. "Lady," he said, "you display a behavior most wanton."

"You do not find the bed I brought tempting, my lord? Shall I have it dismantled, and we will sleep separately upon the cold ground?"

"If you do not stop rubbing yourself against me in that shameless way, my enchantress, it will not matter. I am so hot for you right now that I could tumble you anywhere! That delicious-looking bed of furs you have arranged, or even upon the hard ground! Alas, we cannot. Not now at least. When the king heard you had arrived he requested that we join him in his tent for supper. He attempts to make it as normal a Christmas court as one can hold in the burnt-out ruin of a city." Then he laughed, for she made no attempt whatsoever to hide her obvious disappointment. "Sweeting, the nights are longest now. We shall lose little by waiting."

"It will sharpen our appetite for one another," she answered him. "That was what Basil used to say to me. Oh, very well, my lord, there is no help for us now. Can your squire get me some water with which to wash off the dust of my travels? I cannot appear before the king looking like this." Removing herself from his arms, she began to unbind her long hair.

He called for his squire, Loial, who immediately brought water, and having greeted his lady politely, discreetly departed. Josselin sat upon the edge of the camp bed and watched his wife comb out her long red-gold hair. Erotic images arose unbidden within his mind's eye. He pictured Mairin nude, her milk-white skin gleaming in the firelight, her wonderful hair swirling about her body. A small groan escaped him, and she looked up from her task.

"My lord?"

He shook his head. "It is nothing, enchantress." A neat lie, he thought. He wanted her. He wanted her here and now. Damn the king who had called for a Christmas court to be held in York. Had he not, I might be home in my own bed with my beautiful wife!

Mairin rebraided her hair up neatly, and then washed her hands and face in the icy water Loial had brought. She shook out her dark green skirts, and smoothed the matching tunic, retying the gold rope girdle about her slender waist. Rummaging amongst her scant luggage she drew out a sheer gold veil and a small twisted gold chaplet studded with tiny freshwater pearls, and placed them upon her head. Picking up her fur-lined cloak she said, "I am ready now, my lord."

His glazed eyes refocused themselves, and seeing her fully dressed, he sighed. "So you are, Mairin," he said sadly, and rising, took her hand.

"What were you thinking of?" she asked him as they hurried through the encampment to the king's dining tent.

"Of how sweet it is to make love to you," he said. "Of how I wish we were home at Aelfleah, free of royal commands so I might feast upon your flesh in the privacy of our own chamber, and not upon tough and ill-cooked venison within the king's tent."

"Oh, Josselin," she answered him, "your thoughts but echo my own!"

He stopped then, and there in the middle of the encampment, heedless of what went on about him, he kissed her tenderly. "Tomorrow we will be wed three years, enchantress, and on St. Stephen's Day, I vow we will depart for Aelfleah!"

They were welcomed into the king's makeshift hall, a large tent, and joined with the other ladies and gentlemen who had journeyed from all over England to help the king celebrate Christmas. It was as festive and merry an evening as any might have been, but they were nonetheless glad when they were able to leave the hall to return to their own small shelter.

Loial was nowhere to be found, but the three braziers were burning brightly, and the tent was warm. A flask and two wooden goblets had been placed upon the single stool they possessed. They both smiled, thinking that Loial was a romantic young man. Quickly they pulled their clothing off, and standing in the dim, flickering light cast by the braziers, they caressed each other's bodies. Then hand in hand they walked to their bed and slipped beneath the furs to cuddle.

"What of Maude?" he asked her, caressing her breasts, and noting they were once more firm, the berry-brown nipples thrusting.

"Enid, the miller's wife, will nurse her from now on," Mairin replied, reaching out to fondle a familiar masculine buttock. "Do you mind?"

"No," he mumbled from the valley between her breasts as his two hands gently crushed the flesh of those breasts. His tongue stroked back and forth along that deep dale. He was mounted upon her, his thighs imprisoning her. He sat back now to play with those twin temptations, and she reached out to cup and fondle his sex.

"I love your manhood," she said softly as she caressed him. "When it is little and at rest it has the sweetness of a child, but I love it best when you grow long and thick and hard for me, my Josselin. I love it when you fill me full of yourself, and that great beast throbs its message of love within me."

"Do you want me to fuck you now?" he demanded.

"Yes! Oh, please, yes!"

"You are impatient, enchantress," he said, tweaking her nipples teasingly. "Passion, like good wine, should be savored."

"One can always savor the second cup, my lord," she answered, teasing a pearl of fluid to the tip of his manhood, "but when one is dying of thirst, one should drink!"

"Oh, you tempting bitch!" he groaned, entangling his big hands within her thick hair to cup her head, and raise her up so he might kiss her. Their mouths fused bruisingly together, and he felt her guiding him into her body at the same moment that she slipped him her tongue. For a moment he was shocked by the incredible sensation of total bliss that engulfed him. Then slowly regaining his control, he began to move rhythmically upon her.

Mairin shuddered with pure pleasure as she guided the hot length of him within her, and felt him filling her. It was incredible that after all this time their passion for each other only deepened and grew. At the moment he had entered her she had pushed her tongue within the cavity of his mouth, and she had felt a tremor go through him. It always thrilled her that she could make him as weak with excitement as he made her. Pulling her mouth away from his she turned her head, and with her teeth worried at his earlobe. The pointed end of her tongue swept about the shell of his ear, and she blew gently. "Fuck me, dearling," she whispered frantically at him. "Oh, fuck me!"

He needed to master her this night. The blood lust was still hot in his body, and he had a need to dominate. Sitting back upon his heels, still buried within her, he yanked her arms up and pinioned them along the side of her head. Leaning forward slightly, he thrust fiercely into her, and then drew himself almost completely out of her body, only to drive forward once more. Her whimpering, mewling cries urged him to greater passion.

With each thrust of his pelvis a shower of stars exploded within her brain. His ferocity frightened her somewhat, and she half-struggled against him. With a low growl of hunger he forced her to his will, finding her mouth again, and kissing her with such ardor that she almost fainted. It had never been quite like this. There had always been passion and tenderness between them. This was wildness, a wildness that brought sudden, intense pleasure and elation.

Then her fear was gone, and she pushed up to meet his downward thrust. His fierceness had unleashed an equal fierceness within her. She desired him so very much. She had longed for him all the long nights of their separation, wanted him with a burning hunger she had never before experienced in her life. Her nails raked down the smooth expanse of his back, and he groaned.

"Ahh, enchantress, how I have missed you! How I have hungered for you!"

Together they thrashed back and forth upon the bed, and the lush furs she had brought to keep them warm went flying in the fray. The low camp bed shook with the force of their lovemaking. Then suddenly they gained the crest of the wave together, and he discharged his living tribute into her garden of delight, collapsing upon her breasts with a low moan. Her arms went slowly about him in an instinctive movement. Together they lay panting, their bodies covered with a fine mist, sudden exhaustion claiming them before they might even pull the furs back over them.

They slept, but shortly Mairin awoke to find the braziers burning low. The air was chilly, and forcing herself up she winced at the cold, hard earth beneath her feet as she moved about the tent collecting the furs and placing them back upon the bed. When she had completed her task she was surprised to find Josselin awake, and pouring them some wine. They snuggled beneath the furs, sipping at the heady red wine.

"It is past the midnight hour," he said softly, "and it is now three years we have been wed."

"I hope in this year we may have peace in England," said Mairin, "so that the child I will conceive may rest easy."

"I love you," he said.

"I love you. You are my lord, and my life now, Josselin de Combourg. May our marriage last three times, three times, three times three years!"

"Is that not forever?" he teased her.

"Aye, my lord! It is forever!"

"Ahh, enchantress," he said, replacing the cup upon the stool, and taking hers to set by it, "I think the time has come to savor our passion since we have already drunk deeply from its well." Then enfolding her in his embrace, he made her drunk with his kisses.

Chapter 14

❦

Christmas Day dawned grey and cold. There was a threat of snow in the air. At midnight the bells in the burnt-out churches in and about York had begun to toll in an old tradition which warned to the Prince of Darkness that Christ had triumphed by his very birth. They had celebrated the first Mass of Christmas in the same large tent that hosted the evening's meal. A makeshift altar had been raised at one end of the room, and the candles flickered eerily. The tent was packed full, for few had dared to ignore the king's summons to York. It might be an odd Christmas court, but William's point was well taken.

Kneeling upon the hard cold ground, Mairin suddenly felt as if someone was watching her. Careful not to raise her head she surreptitiously glanced around her, but everyone else was silently shivering and bowed in prayer. Still she could not shake the feeling of being spied upon. When the service had concluded she quickly looked about, which she had not been able to do previously. In the rear of the tent, making a hasty exit, she thought she saw a man who resembled Eric Longsword, but surely that could not be. She shivered.

"Are you cold, sweeting?" Josselin asked solicitously of her.

"Josselin, I thought I just saw Eric Longsword in the rear of the church. What would he be doing here? The last time we saw him he was one of Eadric the Wild's lieutenants."

"But you said he had sworn fealty to the Atheling, Mairin. He must be in Scotland with him."

"Then why is he here? If he were with Edgar the Atheling he would be in Edinburgh or wherever the Scots' king celebrates the feast of Christmas."

"Are you certain it was Eric Longsword, Mairin? Mayhap it was someone who reminded you of him."

300

"No," she said slowly. "I am sure it is Eric Longsword. I felt as if someone were staring at me the entire Mass. The back of my neck kept prickling. When I turned about, there he was. I only saw him for a minute, but he was here."

"Perhaps he is with Gospatric or Waltheof, sweeting. If he is one of their men now it isn't suspicious that he be here. Many of their people are beginning to drift into York preparatory to the pardon of their masters. Your mother has said that Eric Longsword had a passion for you. You cannot blame him for looking, Mairin. I should not like to lose you, and if I ever did, you would be hard to forget."

"I am glad that we are going home tomorrow," she said. "York is a grim place now."

"My lord de Combourg?" A royal page stood by Josselin's side.

"Yes, lad? What is it?"

"The king would speak with you, my lord. I am to take you to him."

"I must escort my lady to our tent first, lad," said Josselin. "You will be safe there, Mairin. Loial will stay with you."

She nodded. She wasn't about to argue with him. She had no desire for another run-in with her rejected would-be suitor. When they reached their little shelter, Josselin kissed her. "Do not be long, my lord," she said softly.

He touched her face gently, and smiled into her eyes. "I will give the king short shrift, enchantress." Then he turned to his squire. "Stay with your lady, and protect her as you would protect me, Loial."

"Yes, my lord!" Loial was sixteen, and very serious. A second son, the child of a cousin of Josselin's father, the Comte de Combourg had sent Loial to his eldest son on the eve of his departure for England. Raoul de Rohan had known that Josselin would make his fortune in England, and his cousin's son needed training as a squire before he could be a knight. For younger sons there was only the church or knighthood. The boy worshiped his master, but he silently adored Mairin. This opportunity to prove his manhood in her eyes was a precious gift.

Mairin didn't need to be told of the young squire's devoted admiration for her. It was terribly obvious, for Loial was still too young to know how to mask his feelings from a woman. "It is cold, Loial. Would you like to join me within the tent?" she invited him.

Loial flushed, and swallowed hard, his Adam's apple bobbing almost painfully in his throat. "Thank you, my lady, but I had best remain on guard outside."

"Aye, perhaps that would be better," she agreed, "but if it grows too bitter, or if it begins to snow, you are welcome to come within. You will be no use to my lord with a chill and a fever.' "

"Thank you, my lady." He drew the flap of the narrow entry back so she might go inside. As the flap fell shut and she attempted to adjust her eyes to the dimness, a powerful arm was unexpectedly clasped about her throat.

"If you struggle I will break your beautiful neck. That would be a great tragedy, Mairin Aldwinesdotter," a soft voice hissed in her ear.

Mairin forced herself to relax. She was actually terrified, but she knew if she lost control over her emotions, he would have the upper hand.

"That is better, my pet. Now I am going to release my hold about your neck, but if you cry out, or in any way try to alert that beardless youth who so zealously guards you, I will kill him. Do you quite understand me?" His other hand smoothed over her breasts in a lingering caress.

"Aye," she managed to rasp, pushing his hand away.

He reluctantly loosened his grip on her, and she whirled about to face him.

"I knew it was *you*, Eric Longsword! I saw you at the back of the church, and I told my husband."

"Who probably does not believe you, but to soothe your female nature, has given orders to his unfledged squire to guard you. Do you really think that boy could overcome me in battle?"

"What do you want?" she demanded of him.

"*You!* You belong to me, and I have come for you!" There was an unpleasant glitter in his blue eyes.

"My husband will kill you," she said quietly.

"He won't know what has happened to you, Mairin Aldwinesdotter, but come! We are wasting valuable time." He reached for her again, but she recoiled from him.

"I have no intention of going anywhere with you, Eric Longsword! Are you totally mad?"

It was the last thing she remembered. His fist shot out, catching her on the jaw, and then the darkness rushed upward to claim her. He caught her neatly with one strong arm before she might fall and arouse the young squire guarding the entry. Slinging the unconscious woman over his shoulder, Eric Longsword drew back the flap he had previously cut in the rear of the tent, and departed. She did not know how long she was unconscious, but when she gradually began to become aware of herself and her surroundings once again, her first thought was that it was cold. And wet. She shook her head to part the cobwebs. She was in the most uncomfortable position. She struggled to raise herself, but a hand pressed into the small of her back pushing her back down. She was slung head-down across a horse's back.

"Lie still!" he growled at her.

"Let me up!" she demanded. "Where are we?"

"We cannot stop now," came his reply.

"If you do not, I shall vomit!" she threatened.

Reluctantly he drew his horse to a halt, and sliding from his saddle, pulled her from the animal's back. On her feet again she swayed dizzily as the blood rushed from her head, her eyes widening in shock as he took a dog collar from his pack. Fastening it about her neck, he attached a long leather lead to a small metal ring set into the collar. Then remounting he reached down, and pulled her up before him on the horse. He took up his reins in one hand, firmly wrapping the leather lead about his other hand.

"Where are we?" she repeated as they once more got under way.

"Outside of York," he answered.

"Where are we going?" she persisted.

"Scotland," he said tersely.

"Josselin will kill you," she said again, "and I will help him! How dare you steal me away? You are a beast of the worst sort, Eric Longsword!"

"Be quiet, Mairin Aldwinsdotter!" he told her, and yanked upon her lead for emphasis.

She choked as the collar momentarily tightened. "My head is getting wet," she said, refusing to be cowed by him. "Let me at least pull my hood up, or would you have me catch a chill and die?"

"Very well." He grudgingly adjusted the angle of the dog collar and its lead. Then he allowed her to pull up the fur-lined hood of her cloak. "Now be silent," he ordered, "or I will gag you."

The day was gloomy. A light snow was beginning to fall. Steadily they plodded onward through the gray, and Eric Longsword seemed to know exactly where he was going. Mairin tried to identify any kind of landmark. She considered tearing small bits of the cloth hem from the inside of her cloak so she might leave a trail for Josselin to follow, but the snow would soon cover it. The silence unnerved her.

"How did you get me to your horse?" she asked him.

"I slit the back of the tent," he said quietly. "I had my mount waiting there."

"Josselin will follow us," she said angrily.

"First he must determine in which direction I have taken you. Only then can he follow, and the snow will have covered our trail long since. If he decides we have gone north, where north? You have seen the last of Josselin de Combourg, Mairin. Now you belong to me."

He is mad, she thought. I must escape him, but how? Up ahead she could see the huddled figures of several other horsemen, and she prayed they would be King William's men. The king's men would help her. The waiting men, however, were Scots.

"Ye took yer time in getting here," grumbled the obvious leader. Then he smiled, showing a mouthful of rotting, blackened teeth. "I see ye brought us a wench. Yer a thoughtful fellow, Eric Longsword."

"The woman is mine, Fergus. She's my wife taken from me by the Normans several years ago. I've just retrieved her, that's all."

"He's a liar! I'm—arrgh," she choked as he fiercely jerked her lead, and the collar tightened once more.

Fergus' eyes narrowed. "What's this? The wench doesn't seem particularly willing for someone ye claim is yer wife, Eric Longsword."

"Her silly head has been turned by Norman luxuries, and she was loath to leave King William's court," Eric replied. "Nonetheless, she is mine. She will soon remember her place, even if I have to beat her black and blue to jog her faulty memory. Let's ride, Fergus! We're still too close to York for safety's sake."

"Aye," the Scot agreed. "I'll not feel safe until we're cozy within the Cheviots."

They rode for the rest of the day, and with each hour they rode, the storm grew worse. Finally spotting a farm, they approached it and found an abandoned stone cottage which was fairly large and incorporated its stables. The roof on the building was sound, however, and there was fuel for the fireplace stacked neatly, though from the looks of it, the farmhouse had not been lived in for several years. Cracking the ice on the well they drew up several buckets of water, and saw the horses stabled amid the moldy hay.

To her surprise, Mairin discovered three women riding with the Scots. They looked at her with hostile eyes, but one of them was brave enough to finger her heavy wool cloak admiringly. Supper consisted of dried beef strips, oatcakes, and water. Mairin ate automatically. She knew she must keep up her strength if she was to escape. Wrapped in her warm cloak she huddled by the fire chewing slowly upon the tough beef. The Scots left her to herself, even the women now, and after a while flasks came out, and were passed about. Outside they could hear the howl of the rising storm, and small puffs of snow slipped through the cracks in the stone cottage to puddle upon the floor in the new warmth of the room.

Two of the men slipped off with two of the women. The men returned after a while, their places taken by two others. Whatever was in the flasks seemed to be loosening the tongues of the taciturn Scots.

"So yer wife has spent the last few years spreading her legs for the Normans," said one of the men. "I don't know why ye want her back. I'd have left the whore where she was."

Eric took a long swig from his own flask. "She's not to blame. They came to Aelfleah, our home, while I was away. Don't think, however, that I don't mean to punish her nonetheless. I intend giving her a good beating tonight followed by a thorough fucking. She always liked my fucking. She'll jog her hips which will jog her memory, and then all will be well between us again."

They didn't see her get up from her place, but suddenly Mairin was amongst them. "You whoreson!" she shrieked. "You are not my husband and I'll kill you before I'll allow you to lay a hand upon me!"

Eric Longsword's hand made contact with the side of Mairin's head before her words had died in the air. He followed the first blow with a second one, and the Scots grinned at one another. The man surely knew how to handle his woman.

"Will ye be needing any help?" said Fergus hopefully.

"Nay," came the reply, and taking the hanging lead up, Eric dragged the surprised Mairin from the cottage's main room through the door into the stables. "I'll attend my wife now lest her screaming disturb your rest," he said to his companions. They grunted approval of his actions.

Pulling his reluctant victim along, he slammed the stable door behind him. From someplace within his tunic another length of leather was brought. "Put your arms about that roof post," he snarled, wrapping the leather about her wrists when she complied. She had not dared to refuse him, for she had already learned that each defiance of his will caused him to jerk upon her collar, which choked her. He didn't know his own strength, and she feared he would break her neck. The collar about her throat reminded her of that time so long ago when Blanche had sold her to a slave dealer, and he, too, had collared her like an animal. Then, however, she had Dagda to protect her. How she wished him here now.

Eric Longsword unfastened her heavy woolen cloak and tossed it aside. Carefully he lifted her tunic and pushed it up over her shoulders and head. Loosening her skirts, he let them fall to the ground. He might have ripped her camise, but, thoughtfully, he pushed it up over her head too with the back of her tunic top. She could hear his breath coming in slow rasps as he gazed at her naked back, legs, and buttocks. She stiffened when he smoothed his rough hand down the expanse of her skin and cupped her buttock.

"It is very important," he said in a calm and logical voice, "that you understand I am your lord. I will not be spoken to again as you spoke to me earlier. Now, Mairin Aldwinesdotter, I want you to say to me, 'Eric Longsword is my lord, and my husband.' "

"You are totally mad!" she burst out furiously. "How can you do this, Eric Longsword? You claim to love me, yet you would steal me from my rightful husband, and my child."

"You have a child?"

"A little girl, Maude. She is almost eleven months old."

"I will give you sons," he said matter-of-factly.

"No!"

"Yes!" he said. Then he unfastened the leather lead from her collar. "You are too bold for a woman, Mairin Aldwinesdotter. You do not know your place. A woman should not speak unless she is spoken to, and then she should speak but briefly and with modesty. My father, may God assoil his soul, taught me this. Women, he said, must be taken care of and cherished, for they have not the native intelligence of a man. God, my father told me, created women for several reasons. For man's pleasure, to bear and nurture new life, and to care for a man's home, all his needs, and those of his children. It is all a woman is good for, but you do not seem to understand that, for all that is said about your intelligence.

"When we returned to England, you shamed me before my friends and fellow guardsmen by your coldness to my suit. Still I pursued you and offered you marriage. Your brother, Brand, mocked me, Mairin Aldwinesdotter, and said your father would not squander such a rare and valuable daughter on the heir to but five hides of land. He said your family could get the heir to five hundred hides of land for you.

"I returned home, and then our Earl Tostig was overthrown in a plot that we all knew to be instigated by his brother, Earl Harold. My parents were slain in their own hall, and I but barely escaped with my life to join Earl Tostig. Our lands were taken from us. I did not wish to live away from my country, and so when I learned that Harold Hardraade planned an invasion I joined with him."

For a moment he ceased his speech, and once again he ran his big hands down the length of her naked back and buttocks. Mairin sank her teeth into her lower lip to keep from screaming aloud as he fondled her flesh slowly.

"I knew your father and brother would be with Earl Edwin and his men," Eric finally continued. "I knew Earl Edwin would come to the aid of his puling brother, Earl Morkar. I sought for your kin upon the battlefield, Mairin Aldwinesdotter. I saw your father, and I tell you he was more than worthy of his name. He was a great warrior, and even I, younger and swifter, could not have beaten him. So I thrust my sword into his back, and he fell to the ground mortally wounded. It was then your brash brother appeared, and fool as he was, was more concerned for his father than what was going on about him. He knelt at your father's side, and I was able to fell him in a single blow, but before I might finish your father off, that giant servant of yours appeared in the mist. I was forced to flee, for I could not have hoped to overcome him. Also, if my helmet had come off in a fray, I would have been recognized.

"I came to claim you with Eadric, but again you shamed me and mocked my suit. You avowed a marriage with some accurst Norman! With your father and brother gone, I had intended having both you and Aelfleah. You should have been mine with them dead! You should have been mine, but now you are, for I have taken you from the Norman. Let him have Aelfleah. It is all the Normans want. Land! He will quickly make a new life."

"I am another man's wife," said Mairin desperately. She was numb with the knowledge that Eric Longsword had been the murderer of her father and brother. For the first time in her life she wished she were a man so she might take up a sword and kill him! She had disliked him before. He had made her uncomfortable, but now she hated him with a deep and burning hatred. She didn't know how she was going to escape him, but she would, and then she would avenge the death of Aldwine Athelsbeorn and Brand.

"You are my wife," he told her. "You should have been all along. I am only righting that wrong. We need no holy man mumbling words over us."

"You *really* are mad," said Mairin quietly.

"You need to be taught proper obedience," was his cold reply. He flicked the leather strap by her ear, and instinctively Mairin winced. Eric smiled. "I'm going to beat you," he told her, "and when I am through I intend fucking you. The sooner you learn that I am your master, the sooner we may begin to find happiness."

"You killed my father and my brother," she shrieked, frustrated, at him. "I hate you! I will always hate you!" And I hate that damned calm voice of yours too, she thought.

He aimed the thin length of leather at her back, and was quite satisfied when she cried out. He followed the first blow with several others until her smooth skin was crisscrossed with pale red weals. Still he was not satisfied. After her first soft cry, more of distress than pain, she had clamped her lips shut and refused to make any sound. Angrily he looked about the barn. Nearby was a bale of hay. Kicking it with his foot he found it was solid, and untying her hands so he might free her from the post, he forced her facedown upon the bale, his fingers tightly grasping the dog collar to keep her under control despite her struggles. Then he retied her hands, looping the leather about her slim wrists, cruelly yanking her arms forward over her head.

Content that his prey was again helpless, he doubled the leather strap, and without ceremony brought it down across her naked buttocks. Mairin yelped and squirmed in an effort to escape him, but with a grin of satisfaction he clamped a hand on the back of her neck and began to rain a series of hard blows upon her posterior.

She had never been beaten in her entire life, for Aldwine and Eada had been gentle parents. She knew that being whipped, and sometimes severely, was commonplace behavior amongst parents and children, husbands and wives, but even Josselin had treated her with kindness. She wanted to defy Eric Longsword, but she could not under these conditions. As her stomach was weak for strong wine, so her body could not bear the brutal punishment that he was now administering to her. She could not prevent herself from screaming, from begging him to cease his torture.

"Please," she shrieked, "in the name of the Blessed Mother! Stop! Stop!"

"Not until you admit that I am your lord! That you belong to me, and to no other man!" he ground out through gritted teeth.

"I cannot, I cannot," she sobbed, the tears pouring down her face.

"You can, and you will!" he shouted at her, and redoubled his efforts, laying blow after blow upon her already red bottom.

She felt as if she were on fire, and made a desperate effort to struggle away from him. She had to escape the pain he was inflicting upon her.

Then it came to her that whatever she might say to him would not change the truth, whatever he might wish to believe. She was Josselin's wife no matter what Eric Longsword thought, and as that thought penetrated her brain, so did her intense desire to survive this experience, to escape him and return to her family.

"You are my lord, Eric!" she screamed at him. "You are my lord!"

"Wh-what?" For a moment he seemed confused. "What do you say, Mairin Aldwinesdotter?"

"I yield to you," she said. "You are my lord." Her backside was aching, and she was shaking inside. Let him believe me, dear God, she silently prayed.

"Yes, I am your lord, and it has taken you long enough to accept it, Mairin Aldwinesdotter." Rolling her over he lifted her off the bale and carried her to a pile of straw in an empty horse stall. "Now we will consummate our union," he said, laying her down and fumbling with his clothing as he lay atop her.

He was going to rape her! My God, what had she done in admitting that he was her lord? She had given him virtual permission to attack her! "Please," she pleaded with him, "don't do this thing, Eric Longsword!"

His body lay atop her, pressing her down into the hay. His cold blue eyes stared into her face. "Have you lied to me then, Mairin? Either you accept me as your lord, or you do not. Did you lie to stop the beating?"

"No! No!" His look terrified her. "It is just that I do not feel I know you. It is all so sudden." Her teeth worried her lower lip.

"If you really accept me as your lord then you must accept this. Most are wed without a long acquaintance." He pushed himself off her and stood up. "I want to see you naked," he said, and pulled her to her feet to undo her bonds.

Mairin rubbed her freed wrists for a moment. There was no way she knew to escape him short of death, and she wasn't that brave. A tear slid down her cheek. How could she ever face her husband again after this animal had soiled her and spoilt her for Josselin? His fingers hooked themselves into her collar.

"Remove your garments," he said, and Mairin, having no other choice, did. When she stood nude before him he stared for several moments at her, and then releasing his grip upon her, spread her cloak upon the straw, pushing her down upon it. He stood above her, his legs spread, licking his dry lips like a diner contemplating a good meal. Then without warning, he fell upon her like a madman.

Mairin couldn't help herself. She fought him wildly, but he did not seem to mind. Indeed her struggles seemed to serve as a spur to his ardor. His big hands were everywhere upon her body, squeezing and pinching and fondling. He smothered her with his wet kisses, jamming his tongue into her mouth with a ferocity that left her gagging with disgust, but he didn't seem to notice. Now his lips fastened themselves upon her nipples, and he suckled upon her with strange grunting noises, and when she tried to push him away, his teeth punished her, and she screamed with genuine pain.

His passion was a frenzied one, and now he began to moan and mutter at her. " 'Tis time, Mairin! 'Tis time for me to fuck you!" He pulled her into the curve of his arm to contain her struggles, looking down into her face as his hand fumbled between her thighs. "You'll like my fucking, Mairin! All the little girls liked my fucking!"

She felt his fingers invading her body, eager and thrusting.

"I'm called Eric Longsword for two reasons," he whispered lewdly at her. His breath was foul. "Do you know why, Mairin? Can you guess why?" His fingers were working fiercely within her. "Ahhhh, sweetheart, that's so good! How long I have waited to put myself into your sweet body!" The fingers moved back and forth, back and forth. "Tell me you like my fucking, Mairin!"

She was horrified. Only his fingers had violated her. Was this some terrible joke? Was he only waiting to complete his rape of her? Then suddenly Eric Longsword stiffened, and throwing back his head, howled a Viking war cry before collapsing next to her. His hand fell away from her body, and Mairin was absolutely stunned. She didn't know what to think. What to do. Then hearing a small snore, she turned her head cautiously to discover Eric Longsword had fallen asleep beside her even as Josselin might have done after a bout of love.

She could not believe what had just happened. Was this to be all he was going to do to her? He had behaved exactly like a man who had made love to a woman, and yet he had not really coupled with her. She knew she should be grateful to have escaped him, but she was frightened too. Had he been drunk from the liquid he had earlier imbibed? When he awoke, would he remember what had happened and right the mistake upon his part? Mairin was totally confused.

She lay upon her woolen cloak, her injured posterior alternately burning and itching, and stared up into the rafters of the barn. There was no doubt in her mind now that she was in the possession of a madman. If he was a sound sleeper she might obtain the opportunity to slit his throat, for the small feminine purse hanging from her girdle contained a little knife. If she killed him, however, how could she escape, and which way would she go? Outside their shelter a storm was howling and roaring. She had absolutely no real idea of where they were. Common sense told her that she had to stay with him until the storm stopped, and until they reached some sort of civilization.

She wondered again about what had passed between them tonight. Had he really believed that he was coupling with her, or had it been some macabre joke on his part? Would he go further the next time? She had been absolutely terrified and ashamed by the thought that another man could use her as only Josselin had the right to do. The very thought of making love with her captor repelled her. If he meant to attack her further, how was she to hold him off? It was this thought that warred with her more practical side.

Mairin shivered, and coming back to her senses, realized she was freezing in the drafty barn. She sat up, and turning, looked at Eric Longsword. His mouth was open, and from it emitted a series of loud snores. It was obvious that he was sleeping deeply. Mairin cautiously arose to her feet, and reached for her camise, which she quickly slipped on. Next she stepped into her skirts, and pulling them up, fastened the buttons with trembling fingers. Her tunic top slid silently over her head, and picking up her girdle she fastened it loosely about her waist. She could already feel the warmth seeping back into her veins. Burrowing back into the hay of the horse's stall, she drew the piece of the cloak he was not lying on over her.

Sleep would not come. Mairin was much too anxious. Where were they going? Scotland was every bit as big a country as England. She had to gain more information from her captor, and that would mean playing his game. He wanted a docile lump of a female, and she would be one for him as long as it suited her purpose. He had no blood ties to Scotland, and therefore, he had sworn an allegiance to someone with power. He would be returning to his overlord, and it was that overlord to whom Mairin would appeal. But how long? How long until they reached that power? How many nights must she bear his advances? Would those advances eventually become the final intimacy? Dear God! she thought. This is a nightmare, and I pray the Blessed Mother that I live long enough to awaken from it.

They awoke to a clear day. The sky was bright blue, and a cold yellow sun shone down upon the snowy landscape. Mairin, her violet eyes lowered modestly, followed Eric Longsword back into the main room of the cottage. Seeing the purplish bruise upon her cheekbone, and her now quiet demeanor, the other men in the cottage grinned apishly at one another, and then at Eric with obvious approval.

"Did she yell louder when ye beat her, or when ye stuck it to her?" demanded the loutish Fergus.

"What do you think?" said Eric with a grin. He slid an arm about Mairin, and openly fondled a breast.

Mairin flushed, but remained silent and still.

"She'll be my tamed little bitch now, won't ye, lovey?"

"Aye, my lord." The words were half-whispered.

"Sorcha's made a wee bit of oat stirabout. Help yerselves, but quickly. We must be off soon."

Mairin managed to discreetly detach herself from Eric Longsword's grasp, and going to the fireplace where the three Scotswomen huddled, she saw a single remaining trencherloaf. She looked for permission from the women, and the eldest of them nodded at her.

"Take it, lass," she said in an almost friendly tone. " 'Tis the last of the bread we carried from York. 'Twill be the oatcakes and dried beef from now on until we reach Edinburgh."

"Thank you." Mairin sliced the loaf in half with the knife the woman proffered. Better not to let them know she possessed a weapon of her own. Scooping out part of one half of the trencher she filled it with the thick cereal, and gave it to Eric. He took it from her without a word, and began to spoon the oat porridge into his mouth with his fingers. Mairin turned back to the fireplace, and put a little of the mixture into her own half of the trencherloaf and began to eat quickly. She knew enough to know that this was no courtly society, and that when Eric was finished eating she had best be finished too.

Edinburgh! So they were headed for Edinburgh, Scotland's chief city. She couldn't be certain, but she would wager that Eric Longsword had pledged his loyalty to King Malcolm. That would mean he would be taking her to court, provided she remained the docile female he believed a woman should be. She knew men enough now to know that he would want to show off her beauty to other men. To be envied, and to be congratulated upon his good fortune in having such a beautiful woman for his own.

"How far is Edinburgh?" she softly asked the woman who had spoken to her. Her voice was guileless. Her expression bland.

"At this time of year? Five to seven days," came the reply. "We'll be making our own path, ye see, with the roads snowed over like they are. If the roads was clear 'twould be no more than three days." The woman reached out and touched the bruise upon Mairin's cheekbone. She winced. "He wasna gentle," the woman said, "but ye'll heal before we reach the city."

The men had finished with their meal, and realizing that she would see little, if any, food before nightfall, Mairin hurried to cram the rest of the cereal and bread into her mouth, washing it down with water from a cup her talkative companion was kind enough to offer her. The horses were saddled, and they began their journey north once more. As yesterday, Mairin rode before Eric Longsword upon his large horse. Today, however, he did not hold the leather lead to prevent her escape. Instead he slipped his hand around her to clamp it tightly about her breast, and as they rode he kneaded her flesh with such regularity that she thought she would go mad. She could already feel the black-and-blue marks he was impressing into her skin.

They rode the entire day, stopping only once to relieve themselves in the bushes along their route. That night they sheltered in a barn, and because there was no privacy, he did not attempt to use her, although she heard the sounds of coupling from the others in the dark of the otherwise silent barn. It was that way for the next few days. Oatcakes, dried beef, and water at dawn and nightfall. A long day in the saddle with Eric crushing her breasts as they went. Cold and dark nights in either a barn or, as one night, in an empty sheep fold.

Mairin was becoming exhausted. Never had she been faced with such hardship, but she was determined to survive, if for no other reason than to have her revenge upon the murderer of her father and Brand. Despite his unwelcome attentions, and the occasional lewd words he whispered in her ear as they rode, she managed to maintain an element of calm. Fear, she realized, was her greatest enemy. Fear could destroy her, leaving her helpless to this madman.

The night before they reached Edinburgh, they were finally able to shelter at an inn. It was a poor place which offered them little privacy, but strangely a decent meal. They sat at a common table, and the serving girl slapped trenchers of a rather tasty concoction of lamb chunks and vegetables before them. Mairin ate hungrily, finishing her meal down to the last crumb of bread, thirstily drinking the bitter ale which, for some reason, tasted delicious to her. Color and warmth began to seep back into her face, and Fergus, looking closely at her for the first time, realized that here was an incredibly beautiful woman.

His beady dark eyes narrowed. "We've shared our women wi' ye, Eric Longsword. Are ye sure ye'll nae give us a taste of this sweet cunt of yers?"

"Mairin is my wife," Eric said coldly. "You cannot compare her to these trulls of yours."

"Come on, man, what difference can a few more cocks up her hole make to her? Hasn't she whored for the Normans? Did ye ask her how many times they stuffed her, and how many of them she entertained?"

"She was but one man's mistress," Eric replied icily, "and he used her gently. I can forgive her that, and return her to my side as my wife. I will not have her abused by the likes of you. Fuck your own women. I have no intention of sharing my wife with you." He arose, pulling Mairin up behind him, and shouting to the innkeeper, tossed him a coin. "See that my friends have all the whiskey they want," he said, and stamped off dragging Mairin with him.

Eric had managed to secure them a tiny private chamber with a good-sized pallet. Mairin, silent until they reached it, said as he closed the door, "What is your will, my lord?" Please, God, she prayed, don't let him hurt me again.

Eric checked the door, and finding it had a heavy metal bolt upon it, threw the bolt, saying as he did, "I haven't seen you naked since the first night. Take your clothes off for me, but do it slowly this time."

With shaking fingers Mairin undid her garments, removed them, and carefully laid them aside. When she was finally nude she pirouetted at his command, and then lay down next to him. What followed was almost a replica of their previous night, and afterward when he slept once more Mairin was vastly relieved, and said prayers of grateful thanks. She did not know why he was behaving as he did, but she was enormously glad to have once again escaped being really raped.

When morning came he said to her, "You did not struggle against me last night. Is it that you are coming to enjoy my loving?"

"Is a woman supposed to enjoy lovemaking, my lord?" she fenced with him. "The church teaches us that what we do together is simply for the purpose of begetting children. I try to be a good daughter of the church."

"You are a cold woman, Mairin, and I would not have believed it," he grumbled.

"If I do not please you, my lord, then let me return to my hus . . ." She caught herself in time. ". . . home. My mother is all alone."

He smiled slowly, but his eyes remained like pieces of cold blue lapis stone, hard and unfeeling. "In time," he told her, "I will have you burning inside like hot coals for my glance. It has been hard for us upon the road, but tomorrow we will enter Edinburgh, and I have a small house there where we will live for the time being until I have earned lands from the king. At least there we will have our privacy, and I will fuck you regularly each night. You have obviously not been fucked enough, for if you had, you would like it better. In a few weeks I will have you clawing and yelling with passion every time I get you on your back. There will come a time when you will not be able to get enough of my loving. I know how to keep a woman happy."

"Yes, my lord," she answered him coolly, but her mind had pounced upon the information that he was now a liegeman of King Malcolm. If she could just get him to take her to the Scots court. If she could get to the king and queen and tell them her tale, surely they would help her. She knew that Josselin would come to her rescue if he only knew where she was, but how could he know under the circumstances? She had to find some way of telling him, and the king and queen seemed to her to be her only path.

Mairin had learned from Eric as they had traveled from England that their companions were freedmen, Scots who hired out their allegiance for a price. They had gone to York at the behest of the king, with Eric Longsword as their captain, to gather information as to the true strength of King William's armies, and the real mood of the English people. The border country on both sides of the Cheviot Hills was always in dispute between England and Scotland. The raiding that went on back and forth was not unusual, but King Malcolm wanted to know if his young brother-in-law really had a serious chance of regaining the throne of England before he committed any more of his time or his gold to such a project.

Malcolm of Scotland was in love with his wife, the Atheling's elder sister, Margaret. If Scotland's aid could make the difference between the boy regaining his throne or not, he was willing to help Edgar for the love he bore his wife. If, however, as he suspected, there was no real chance of Edgar ruling England, he wanted to know that also. His Meg was not stupid, and she wouldn't want him wasting lives and gold that were Scotland's. Not now. Now that she was expecting their first child.

Eric Longsword and his companions traveled the remaining distance into Edinburgh by early afternoon. It was there that he and Mairin left Fergus and his friends, who hurried off to a nearby tavern with their women.

"Will I get to see the king and his queen?" asked Mairin of her captor. Her request sounded very young and ingenuous to his ears.

"I don't know if I want to share you with other people right now," he pondered.

"You do not love me at all!" Her tone sounded injured, and she pouted at him adorably.

"Mairin, I do love you!" he protested. "I would do anything to make you happy."

"Then take me to see the king and queen," Mairin responded. "A woman can be a great help to a man who is seeking to advance himself, especially a beautiful woman like me." She gave him a flirtatious little smile.

"How is that so?" he asked her. He sounded suspicious.

"Silly," she said to him, then she giggled. "If these Scots see what a beautiful wife you have they will think you must be very worthy of their consideration. After all, you would not have a beautiful wife if you weren't worthy, now would you?"

He thought a moment, and decided that she might be right. "Perhaps you are correct," he said grudgingly. "Still I am loath to have other men admiring your beauty. We have had so little time together."

"I cannot be happy with you, Eric, unless I am allowed to go to court," she told him, and then her voice grew wheedling. "If you take me to court to see the king and queen, I will show you some of the lovemaking tricks I learned from Prince Basil in Byzantium."

"I am surprised that that half-man could even get it up for you." Eric sneered.

Mairin gave another simple giggle. "Ohh, you would be surprised what Basil could do," she implied suggestively, turning her head to look guilelessly up at him. Slowly her tongue licked back and forth over her upper lip.

Eric felt his heartbeat accelerate. He had heard that there were secret erotic arts known only to a few in Byzantium. Someone such as he would have never had access to such things. Mairin was telling him that she was acquainted with these arts, that she would practice them upon him, share her knowledge with him, and all he had to do was show her off to the Scots court. God only knew it was a simple woman's request. Of course she wanted to see the Scots king and his consort. It was just the kind of thing a female would desire, and she offered him so much in return, adorable little fool that she was. "Well," he said, "perhaps in a few days

when you have rested I could take you to meet the king, for I must go myself to render my report. We've traveled very hard, Mairin. You look exhausted. We could use hot food and a good night's rest in a decent bed."

"And a bath!" she said.

They had been riding through the city as they spoke, and now he
stopped before a small house on a respectable street. "This is where we
will live," he said.

The house was built of stone, as were most houses in the north. It was
not very big, but it had two stories and the roof seemed sound. Walking
about the main floor of the building she found there was a little garden in
the rear that had its own well, a veritable luxury. At least she wouldn't
have to walk to the public fountain for water. The house, however, was
filthy. It was obvious that its previous tenant had not been much of a
housekeeper.

Taking charge, she imperiously set Eric to hauling water from the well,
which she boiled in a large black iron caldron hung over the hot coals of
the fireplace. He first had to sweep a nest of mice from the cold hearth
before he might even lay the fire. They scampered off noisily, but Mairin
ignored them. Time enough to get a cat, and besides, once she got to
court she would escape Eric Longsword and his musty house.

Having found a broom in good repair, Mairin vigorously swept the
larger of the two rooms upon the main floor of the house. The smaller
room was obviously a pantry of sorts. The dust removed from the floors,
and the cobwebs from the corners, she scrubbed down the oak trestle with
the hot water using a half-bristled brush she had found in the other room.
Next came the benches.

"I didn't bring you to Scotland to be a servant," he complained to her.
"I will get you a serving wench tomorrow."

"If you think I am spending a night in this place without cleaning it,
you are mistaken, Eric Longsword! I know your mother did not keep a
dirty hall. If there is not an oak tub in this place, then I implore you to
go to the barrelmaker and bring me back one. I must have a bath
tonight." She smiled at him. "You may watch me bathe if you like," she
tempted.

With a grin he left her, saying as he went, "I will stop at the bakehouse
and bring us supper too. We can visit the market tomorrow, but tonight
we must eat."

In his absence, Mairin hurried upstairs to the second floor of the house
to find but one loftlike room with a large bed within it. Opening the

wooden shutters on the single window, she let the cold January air into the room while she beat the hangings of the bed free of dust and cobwebs. In the trunk at the bed's foot, she found well-worn but clean sheets, the faint odor of lavender clinging to them as evidence of some past owner. Mairin yanked the dusty fur coverlet from the bed, and shook it out of the window, leaving it to air until she remade the bed with the clean linen. The coverlet restored to its place, she closed the shutters and barred them. The room was now freezing, but it was clean and smelt fresh.

Downstairs once more she added more fuel to the fire, and closing the door into the back garden, sat down to rest from her labors. How soon would Eric take her to court? How long before she might escape him and his hateful attentions? At least he was fooled by her attitude. He seemed to like the childish silliness she affected in her effort to disarm him. Despite the gravity of her situation, she found it amusing that knowing her so little he had still desired her. Of course it was her beauty that had attracted him. Her curst beauty! Her beauty which had been responsible for all the real unhappiness she had ever suffered in her life.

Eric returned triumphant, bringing with him an oaken tub which was carried by the cooper's two apprentices. "Where do you want it?" he demanded of her.

"Here," she said. "On this side of the fireplace."

The oaken tub was placed according to her directions, and the two young men departed.

"It's not very large, I know," he said, "but the cooper's wife said it was large enough."

"It is," she answered. "Since we have no servants you will have to put it in the pantry after I have bathed. You must bathe too, Eric Longsword. You stink worse than a dung cart!"

"Very well," he agreed with her, "but first I have brought our dinner from the bakeshop. There was no selection. I hope you like rabbit, and here is bread, and I know you like apples." He placed his purchases upon the newly cleaned table. "Let us eat," he said, sitting himself down at the trestle. He tore the roasted rabbit in two, and shoved the smaller half in her direction.

No wonder the table was so filthy, she thought. She reached for the loaf, and broke off a piece for herself. They spoke not at all as they went about the business of eating their meal. Mairin was careful to lick all the grease from her fingers, using a piece of bread for a final cleanup. She did not want to get her only skirt and tunic dirty. Part of proving to King

Malcolm and his wife who she was would be her appearance. She couldn't look slovenly. She must be every inch the lady of Aelfleah.

"Shall I fill the tub with hot water for you?" he asked her when they had finished the meal and she was storing the leftovers in the pantry.

"Please," she answered.

He emptied the large open kettle of boiling water into the oaken tub, and then added several buckets of cold water from the well so that the temperature of the bath was comfortable. Having rescrubbed the table clean, Mairin began to undress before the fire. There was no need for false modesty on her part as he had already seen her naked on several occasions. Stepping into the tub, she sat down to enjoy a soak. There was no soap with which she might wash, but a rough cloth was enough to scrub away the grime of her travels once the warm water had loosened the dirt. It was not a bath over which she wished to linger, and so when she was done she stepped quickly from the still-warm water, shaking herself like a puppy as she did to remove the excess water.

"Let me," he said, coming forward with a small piece of clean cloth with which he proceeded to rub her dry. When he had finished he said, "Take your garments, and get into bed, Mairin. I will bathe and join you shortly."

She didn't argue with him. It was much too cold away from the fire. She had hoped to launder her camise in the bathwater, but that could be done in the morning. She doubted they would go to court tomorrow. Gaining the bedchamber, she carefully laid her skirts and tunic over the linen trunk, and climbed between the icy sheets. When he followed her several minutes later, he was wearing his tunic. It is strange, she thought as he joined her. He seems to enjoy seeing me naked, Mairin thought, but I have never seen him naked. Then she counted her blessings, for she knew she didn't want to see him unclothed.

Reaching out, he pulled her into his arms. "It is cold," he said. "Let us warm each other."

As she was clasped tightly in his embrace, Mairin's heart hammered with her fear. She was still not convinced he didn't intend to rape her, and tonight would certainly tell the tale. His actions upon their journey might have simply stemmed from a fastidiousness. He could be a man who simply liked his comforts. She almost cried out, catching herself in time, as he began to fondle her breasts.

For several long minutes he contented himself with squeezing, pressing, and cupping her flesh. Noisily he sucked upon her nipples as he had on the other nights in which he had abused her. Tonight, however, he seemed in no great rush, as he had on the other nights, to cease in his sport. Slowly his tongue encircled each nipple in its turn. Mairin shifted uncomfortably. In the past he had been in haste to have her in his own strange fashion. It was not so tonight. He took a nipple between his thumb and two fingers, and pulling the flesh out, pinched it hard.

She whimpered.

Eric smiled softly. "You liked that, didn't you?" He took the other nipple, and pinched it, his smile widening when she protested his action. "Pain," he said, "can be pleasurable, my pet." He swung himself over her body, straddling her with his thighs, the fingers of one hand digging into her head as he grasped her harshly by her long, thick hair. "You did not answer me, Mairin. You like it when I hurt you a little, don't you?"

"No!" she whispered.

Yanking her up by her head, he slapped her cruelly several times. "Liar!" he said. "I've known women like you before. Cold little bitches who need their bottoms warmed before they can enjoy a man. Before I took you that first night I whipped you, and you were hot for me afterward. The last time you lay like a sodden lump beneath me, and I realized what your problem was."

"That is not so!" she protested.

"Then perhaps there is something else you need to excite your fires. Something forbidden, but infinitely delicious." Releasing his hold upon her hair, he pushed her back, and sliding himself down her body, pulled her legs apart with strong fingers to plunge his head between her thighs. She felt his lips fasten about her flesh there, and she shrieked a protest, struggling wildly to evade him.

Raising his head a moment he glowered threateningly at her. "Do not fight me, Mairin," he warned, "or I will beat you again, and still have my way with you in the end." Then lowering his head again, he feasted upon her shrinking flesh.

Mairin shivered violently. The bruise upon her cheekbone was only just disappearing. If he beat her she would not be able to go to court and make good her escape from this madman. It was better to allow him to have his way, wasn't it? It was better to allow him his way, she kept repeating to herself as his hateful mouth fastened upon her, and his probing tongue began to lick at her, and despite her aversion to him, she could feel her body beginning to weaken, beginning to warm and respond to this horror.

No, she silently told herself. *I feel nothing. I feel nothing.* Heat was beginning to seep into her veins, followed by a delicious languor. Mairin was shocked by her reaction. How could her body be responding to this man who was violating her? She despised him. She lived for the moment she might escape him and for her revenge. Yet her hips would not stay still, and to her immense horror, she could feel her crisis approaching. *No! No! No!* she screamed silently, and then with a vocal sob of submission, she slid over the brink.

She did not linger long within passion's embrace, for her guilt was overwhelming. Desperately she clawed her way back from the soft and warm darkness to find her captor grinning over her, and it was all she could do in that moment to keep her hatred of him from spilling over, and clawing his eyes out.

"So," he gloated, "that is what you need to fan the flames of your desire!" Then his fingers were once more pushing into her, and he was muttering vile obscenities into her ear as he thrust those hateful fingers over and over again within her helpless body.

Afterward, however, he did not sleep immediately as he had the other nights, and she was forced to bear his attentions twice more before he was satisfied. She was nervously exhausted by the time he finally slept, and as his loud snores ripped the fabric of silence, she allowed herself the luxury of tears. Tears which she had not shed since her capture by this maniac.

She wanted Josselin. She wanted to be home at Aelfleah with little Maude and Eada and Dagda. *Dagda!* If Dagda had been with her, Eric Longsword would have never gotten away with this abduction. He had wanted to come, not liking the idea of her traveling without him, but she had refused her permission. She was a grown woman now, she had told him. He was bailiff of Aldford, and must remain with the half-built castle. It was his duty, she had told him grandly. Now she wished she had not. Tears still wet upon her cheeks, she finally fell into troubled sleep.

Eric Longsword informed his captive on the following morning that they would be going to the Scots court the next day. Then he left her alone in the house without a word as to where he was going, or when he would be back. He seemed to assume that she would not attempt to escape, and he was correct in that assumption. Not that Mairin did not consider the possibility, but she realized a woman alone was prey to both two-legged and four-legged animals of which there were many between Edinburgh and Aelfleah. She had no money, and she had no horse. She was better off taking her chances at the Scots court.

While he was gone, she took the opportunity to wash her camise, placing it before the fire to dry. When it was once more wearable she put it on, and set to work sponging stains and brushing the dirt from her indigo-blue skirts which were made from fine-spun Aelfleah wool, and the slightly lighter blue brocatelle tunic she had been wearing when he had kidnapped her. She looked critically at the garments. They were well made, and of the best fabric, and she was grateful that her girdle was an elegant twisted golden rope, and that her earrings were fat, showy pearls and deep red garnets. It had been Christmas Day, and she had dressed in the best of the little clothing she had brought with her to York.

Her hair needed to be washed, and she lugged water from the well in the garden to heat over the fire. When it was ready, she scented it with two cloves which she removed from her pomander and crushed. The pomander ball, a Spanish orange stuck round with precious cloves, was another indication of her social status, and would hopefully help to convince the Scots that her story was a true one. Josselin had given it to her the day before Christmas to commemorate their three years of marriage. She had no idea of where he could have found such a rare and valuable item within the ruined city, but she had been delighted by the gift which hung from her girdle. Toweling her long, wet hair to help it dry, she sniffed its elusive scent and smiled. It made her feel that all was not lost. That she would be rescued.

The rest of the day passed uneventfully. Eric returned in late afternoon with no explanation as to where he had been. He again brought them supper, and after eating they went to bed, but strangely he did not seem interested in her and slept almost at once. With a soft sigh of relief, Mairin rolled onto her side, and slept herself until dawn. In the morning, she was well-rested for the first time since her capture. She could eat little, for her excitement was too great, a fact which seemed to amuse Eric as he wolfed down the remainder of the past evening's meal.

Mairin took hot water from the kettle and washed her face, neck, and hands. Carefully she dressed herself, taking time to braid her long, beautiful red-gold hair into plaits which she looped gracefully and fastened with golden pins above her ears. She had her gold gauze veil and the little gold-and-pearl chaplet, for she had been wearing them when Josselin had left her. Hopefully, she looked every inch the lady she was, and could convince the Scots of her plight.

Eric Longsword seemed pleased by her appearance. "You are the most beautiful woman in the world," he said. "I will kill anyone who dares to even look at you."

"Thank you for the compliment, my lord, but it will not do your case any good if you appear quarrelsome before these Scots. After all, we are strangers in this land. You need have no fears, for I would never stray from your side. There is none to compare with you, my lord."

He grinned at her, obviously quite pleased by her words. "How envied I will be," he said pridefully. "Every man who sees you will want you, but you are mine."

"Of course, my lord," Mairin replied smoothly. "There can be no other for me but you."

He pulled her suddenly into his arms, and kissed her noisily. "What a woman you are!" he said.

She smiled up at him. "You have only just begun to know, my lord," she said sweetly.

Chapter 15

Since the sixth century there had been some building representing authority upon the great Edinburgh rock. In the beginning it had been a fortified place, a place to defend, but now there was only a small castle upon the rock that served as the king's house when he was in Edinburgh. It was here that Eric Longsword brought Mairin, who was trembling with excitement at the thought of escaping her captor. She had heard while in York of the marriage that had taken place in late summer between the widowed Scots king, Malcolm Ceann Mor, and Edgar the Atheling's eldest sister, Margaret.

The Anglo-Saxon heir and his family had taken refuge with the Scots, and from the moment Malcolm had seen Margaret, he was like a man possessed. He wanted the serene beauty for his wife as he never wanted any woman. Widowed several years, he certainly did not lack for women companions. His first wife, Ingeborg, had been the Earl of Orkney's daughter, and they had had three sons, only one of whom was living: Duncan, the eldest. Flaxen-haired Ingeborg had been loyal throughout all the years of turmoil only to die as he finally attained his complete victory. She had been a good woman, and he had been genuinely fond of her.

At the age of thirty-eight, however, love had found Malcolm Ceann Mor for the first and only time in his life. Margaret of England had entered his world, and he knew immediately that he could never really be happy until he had made her his wife. Beautiful Margaret, with her heavy dark red braids and her gray-blue eyes, was past twenty, and having not yet found a husband, had concluded that God wanted her for himself. She had full intention of returning to her mother's native Hungary where she had spent the first half of her life, and entering a convent with her younger sister, Christina.

When her royal host pursued her with the kind of passion she had hitherto only heard sung about in epic poems, she was frightened, angry, indignant, intrigued, and flattered by turns. She was related on her mother's side to Henry, the Holy Roman Emperor, but her father was a poor exile. No matter he was a legitimate heir to the English throne, he was an exile. No one had ever made a fuss over Margaret, and once Edgar was finally born, she and Christina faded even more into the background of their world. Everything was for Edgar, and even more so after their father's death when Edgar became the Atheling.

But Malcolm Ceann Mor would not be denied. He wanted the lovely Margaret for his bride, and neither her protests of a religious calling nor her brother's reluctance to override his sister's desire would stand in his way. Margaret's mother was a shrewd woman. When she saw which way the wind was blowing, she sat herself down and considered all the possibilities. She didn't really believe for one moment that her eldest child had a true religious vocation, although she could not deny that Margaret was deeply devout. A husband, Agatha of Hungary decided, was just what her child needed. Although the large, bluff man who demanded Margaret for his wife was not the match she had envisioned for her daughter, he was not unsuitable either.

He was a king, and if he was not a prestigious one, neither was he a poor one. He had but one living heir whose two brothers had died in their youth. Margaret was young enough yet to bear a husband several children. If the king's only heir managed to get himself killed in one of those border skirmishes the Scots seemed to be always having with the English, then Margaret could easily be not only a Queen of Scotland, but the mother of a King of Scotland. Agatha smiled to herself. It was much better than languishing in a convent the rest of her days. There was also the advantage for Christina in having a reigning queen for a sister. A good match might also now be provided for her second, and equally dowerless, daughter. If Edgar was not going to be King of England, and as much as she wished it, she knew in her heart it would never come to pass, then it was not a bad thing to have a daughter who was a queen.

Agatha set about to win her eldest child over to the king's suit. Did Margaret ever stop to consider that they had been led here to Scotland for a purpose? Here was King Malcolm, a good man and a widower with but one living child and in desperate need of a wife. True, Scotland was still very much a tribal society, but they were a Christian country. Their church, Agatha noted to her daughter, was not the most orthodox of

Catholic churches, having many Celtic influences. Perhaps Margaret had been led here to be the king's wife *and* to reform the Scots church. To bring it into conformity with the Holy Mother Church before it cut itself off from Rome as did the rebellious church in Byzantium.

Margaret pondered her mother's words, and glanced across the hall at Malcolm Ceann Mor. He stood well over six feet in height. He had to be at least a foot taller than she was. He was a big man with massive shoulders and a large head of black hair. She would make him shave that bushy beard of his when they were wed. She did like his smoky gray eyes, however, and the little laugh lines at the corners of those eyes. Perhaps . . . just perhaps, she considered thoughtfully.

Malcolm Ceann Mor adored Margaret of England. He would have slain dragons for her, Agatha realized too late, the marriage contracts being already signed. He had been generous though. Margaret would have her own income, free of anyone else's interference. She would be crowned Queen of Scotland, and have whatever she might desire within reason. Christina would be provided for with a suitable husband, and Agatha would be given her own estates so she might retire in peace. As for Edgar, here the king grew canny. He could help his brother-in-law just so much, Malcolm told Agatha, but Edgar would always have a home and a welcome in Scotland. With that, Agatha was forced to content herself, for to ruin Margaret and Christina's chances for happiness chasing a will-o'-the-wisp for Edgar was foolish, and Agatha was not a foolish woman.

The wedding had been celebrated in late summer of 1069, and now in January of 1070, Margaret of Scotland already bloomed with the visible evidence of her husband's love. Their first child would be born in late spring. Most men attaining their deepest and dearest desire would have long since grown bored, but not so Malcolm Ceann Mor. With each day that passed, he grew more and more enamored of his young wife. There was nothing, the gossips declared, that he would not do for his Meg. Mairin counted upon that factor, for she had no intention of appealing her plight to the king. It was the queen upon whose mercy she intended throwing herself.

The young queen had brought the sophistication of the Hungarian court to her new home. The Great Hall of the king's house was clean, warm, and cheerful. It was a large rectangular room with gray stone walls and carved oak beams that held the soaring ceiling. At the far end of the room was a single window, arch-shaped, that had real glass in it. On either side of the room were blazing fireplaces, each large enough to take several whole logs. Into their chimney fronts was carved the king's coat of arms. The wooden floors had fresh rushes upon them, and the monotony of the otherwise gray room was relieved by the brightly colored banners that were hung from the walls upon gilded pikes. Among those banners was one that Malcolm Ceann Mor had captured from his uncle, MacBeth, when he had taken back his crown.

Eric Longsword paraded Mairin about amongst the half-savage lords of the Scots court. Her cheeks grew bright pink on more than one occasion as the openly admiring glances of these men touched her. Her captor was enjoying himself hugely, blatantly displaying her beauty and loudly proclaiming to any who would listen his sexual prowess with her. They moved at a snail's pace through the hall, Mairin keeping her eyes modestly lowered all the while, for she was greatly embarrassed by Eric's loud and constant bragging. Finally they reached the royal dais where the king and queen sat.

"So, Eric Longsword, this is your long-lost wife," said Malcolm Ceann Mor.

"Yes, my liege. I promised her I would bring her to court, for she vowed she could not be happy with me again unless she came."

"What is her name?"

"Mairin of Aelfleah, my liege."

"Look at me, Mairin of Aelfleah," the king commanded her. "I would see your face."

Mairin raised her eyes to him. His mouth, she thought, was like Josselin's. It was a large and sensuous mouth. Her heart hammered wildly, and she almost cried out her plight to him, but with a supreme effort of will, she restrained herself. She must wait to meet the queen.

"You are very beautiful, Mairin of Aelfleah, as Eric Longsword has told us," the king said in a kindly tone. "Your husband is a fortunate man." He looked back to Eric. "You may present your wife to the queen now."

"My gracious lady," said Eric, politely bowing to Margaret, "I would present to you my lady wife, Mairin of Aelfleah."

The young queen smiled graciously at Mairin. "You are welcome to Scotland, my lady."

To the queen's surprise Mairin knelt, and catching the queen's gown, kissed the hem of the garment and said, "Madame, I beg of you to help me!"

Margaret looked startled at this sudden turn of events, and the king said, "What is this? What is it you want, lady?"

Mairin felt Eric Longsword's fingers digging cruelly into her shoulders. "My wife is not well, my lord," he said, trying to drag her to her feet. "Her captivity amongst the Normans has weakened her mind. I can never be certain when these terrible spells are going to come upon her."

"My lady queen," persisted Mairin, refusing to allow him to move her, "in the name of the Blessed Holy Mother Mary, I beg you to hear me out. I am not mad!" She raised her eyes to the queen, silently pleading with her, and Margaret, who knew fear when she saw it, said,

"Take your hands from your wife, Eric Longsword. I believe her when she says she is not mad. I would hear what she would say to me." The queen then turned to the king. "This woman is afraid, my lord, and comes to me for aid. I would know why."

The king nodded his agreement. There was nothing he would deny his Meg. "Speak, Mairin of Aelfleah, but bear in mind the delicate condition of the queen as you do so."

"My lord king," said Mairin, "I would not hurt your lady. I know the joys of motherhood. I have a little daughter, Maude, who will be a year old in another few weeks." She then turned to the queen. "My lady, I beg you to help me for the sake of my child. Eric Longsword is not my husband. I am the wife of Josselin de Combourg, the lord of Aelfleah. Eric Longsword kidnapped me from York on Christmas Day where I had gone to join my husband for King William's Christmas court." Unbidden tears slipped down her cheeks. "I want to go home to my husband, and our child. Please help me, my lady! I beg of you!"

Before the queen might reply, Eric Longsword said, "She is mad, my liege. The coming of the Normans caused her to miscarry our child, and she has never accepted it. Let me take her back to our house." He put his hands once more upon Mairin's shoulders.

"He lies!" Mairin said furiously, shaking him off. "I am the daughter of Aldwine Athelsbeorn and his wife, Eada. I am the wife of Josselin de Combourg, the lord of Aelfleah. This man sought my hand in marriage before the coming of King William, but my father would not give me to the heir to but five hides of land! Eric Longsword has admitted to me that he sought my father and brother out at the battle of Fulford, and slew them both. Would I wed with the murderer of my father and brother?"

"What proof can you offer, Mairin of Aelfleah, that what you say is true?" asked the queen.

"I was wed to my lord husband, Josselin de Combourg, the day before the feast of Christmas in the year 1066. We were wed in the presence of

King William, the ceremony performed by his brother, Bishop Odo. You have but to send a messenger to England to the king. Josselin must be frantic. He will not know where to look for me! If you could but send a messenger to Aelfleah too. My mother will be so worried. She could also confirm the truth of my words."

"It is deep winter," said the king. "It would be hard to get a messenger through now, particularly after this last storm."

"Do not let this man take me back!" begged Mairin. "Do not force me into an adulterous state, and imperil my immortal soul, my lord king! If not for my sake, then think of my little daughter who weeps for her mother! I would be a servant in your house before I would go with Eric Longsword again, or slay me now, my lord, but do not force me back with this man!" Mairin bowed her head in submission as if a prisoner awaiting the axman's blow.

"She shall not return to him," said the queen firmly.

"Margaret, Eric Longsword is my liegeman," said the king.

"Malcolm, I will not allow this poor girl to be further abused. Until the truth of her words can be proved or disproved, she will remain with me."

"Very well, Meg," the king said quietly. "It will be just as you wish it." He looked at Eric Longsword. "Mairin of Aelfleah will remain with the queen until this matter can be straightened out."

Eric Longsword glared at the back of Mairin's head, but she didn't see him. Her whole body was awash with relief, and for the moment she was incapable of even rising. "Thank you, my lady," she said gratefully to the queen, and looking down into the incredibly beautiful face, Margaret knew with unwavering instinct that Mairin was telling the truth. At a nod from the queen, the laird of Glenkirk came forward to help Mairin to her feet.

"Take the lady Mairin to my apartments," she instructed the laird, and then looking to the abbess of St. Hilda's asked, "Will you accompany them also, my lady abbess?"

The abbess, an elderly woman with a worn and kindly face, nodded her assent, and moved to Mairin's side. The trio turned to exit the hall, to be momentarily blocked by Eric Longsword. Automatically the laird's hand went to his dagger, and the abbess set herself protectively near Mairin.

"You will regret your actions, Mairin of Aelfleah," Eric said venomously. "You are mine, and you always will be!"

"No," Mairin said quietly, "it is you who will regret your actions. Josselin will kill you for what you have done."

He stepped aside then, and they moved past him leaving the Great Hall of the king's house to find their way to the queen's abode.

"Puir child," sympathized the abbess. "What a terrible experience ye hae had. Ye were wise to ask the queen's aid. Never has there been such a good woman as our Queen Margaret."

"Bride stealing is one thing," said the laird of Glenkirk, "but stealing another man's wife is a foul deed. Yer husband will hae to kill him if he has any honor at all."

"I wish I could kill him!" said Mairin fiercely, and the young laird grinned at her.

"Child, child," admonished the gentle abbess, "ye must na say such a thing. Dinna put yer precious soul in danger of hellfire over the likes of a man like that."

They reached the queen's apartments, and seeing them safe inside, the laird of Glenkirk took his leave of them. The abbess explained to the queen's serving women that Mairin was to be the queen's guest, and then she motioned Mairin to sit with her by the fire while they awaited Margaret's coming. The young queen did not keep them waiting long, arriving with her mother and sister several minutes later.

"Eric Longsword attempted to cajole my lord, the king, into returning you to his custody," the queen said with a chuckle. "He but succeeded in annoying Malcolm. You will be quite safe with me, my lady Mairin. Now tell me just how you came to be in this man's clutches." The queen settled herself into a chair by the fire facing Mairin, instructing her and the abbess to reseat themselves. The queen's mother sat by her eldest daughter while her younger daughter sat down upon a stool by her mother, resting her head upon her parent's knee.

"My husband and I live on the manor of Aelfleah which is close by the Welsh border near Hereford and Worcester. My husband came from Normandy with the king, and being his liegeman, went with him to subdue the recent rebellions in the north." Here Mairin stopped, and blushed. She felt somewhat uncomfortable speaking before Edgar the Atheling's mother, but Agatha, realizing her plight, waved her hands and said,

"Do not be embarrassed, my lady Mairin. I have faced the fact, if others haven't, that Edgar will never be King of England. I dislike all this killing in his name. Go on with your story."

"The king ordered that his Christmas court be held at York," Mairin said. "My lord sent for me to come and join him, and I did." For a moment her eyes were sad with the memory of her trip from Aelfleah. "The devastation was too terrible to behold," she said simply.

"A king must be strong," said Agatha approvingly.

"I reached York safely," Mairin continued. "We celebrated the third year of our marriage together, and Josselin gave me this." She held up the pomander, which was admired by the other women. "On Christmas morning we attended Mass, and all through the service I felt as if someone were staring at me, but from my vantage point I could see no one, and I dared not turn. Finally when the Mass had been concluded I did turn about, and I thought I saw Eric Longsword, but then he was gone. I told Josselin, and he said that perhaps Eric had sworn fealty to Gospatric or Waltheof, for their men were beginning to reenter the city prior to their master's submission to King William.

"A royal page came then, and told my lord that the king wished to speak with him. We were leaving early the next day, and the king was busy. Josselin escorted me to our tent, and left his squire, Loial, to look after me. The boy admires me, and I told him he might join me inside if it became too cold. I entered the tent, and it was there that Eric Longsword accosted me, putting an arm about my throat, and threatening to kill poor Loial if I cried out. He said he was taking me with him to Scotland, that I should be his by right. When I said I would not go with him, he hit me in the jaw rendering me quite unconscious. When I awoke we were far from York."

"How absolutely terrifying!" said the queen's sister, Christina.

"It was very terrifying," Mairin admitted, "and the thought that my lord husband would have no idea of where I was, was even more frightening."

The queen glanced about at her serving women, all of whom had been listening, and were now goggle-eyed by Mairin's tale. "Leave us, all of you," she said in a no-nonsense tone of voice, and the women reluctantly departed. "There is no need for any more gossip than this incident will engender naturally," she said.

"Thank you, my lady," replied Mairin. "I am so shamed by all of this."

"How did you first meet Eric Longsword?" asked Margaret.

"My father, Aldwine Athelsbeorn, was sent by King Edward to the emperor, Constantine Ducas, in Byzantium. It was my father's duty to negotiate a trade agreement between the two countries. My mother and I went with him, leaving my brother, Brand, at Aelfleah. We were in Constantinople over two years, during which time I was wed to Prince Basil Ducas, the emperor's cousin."

"You are a princess of Byzantium?" Christina was now very impressed.

"I was once," said Mairin, "but Basil died unexpectedly in the first year of our marriage so I returned with my mother to England. Eric Longsword was a member of the emperor's Varangian Guard which is made up of Anglo-Saxons and Norsemen. He escorted our party home to England as he and his troop were due for leave. I was in mourning for my first husband then, and yet he dared to approach me. I rebuffed him. Later he suggested to my brother, Brand, that he would be a good match for me, but Brand laughed and told him no.

"He thought that if I were alone and helpless I should turn to him, so he killed my father and brother in the battle with Harold Hardraade. Then King William overcame Earl Harold, and not realizing that I was legally my father's heiress . . ." here Mairin smiled. "He did not know that my father had a daughter. So not being aware of my existence, King William sent Josselin de Combourg to be Aelfleah's new lord, but the manor was my legacy, and the only dowry I could bring a husband. Josselin and I were at immediate loggerheads. He claimed Aelfleah by right of conquest, I by inheritance. What was worse, the king had charged him to build a castle to help keep the peace. Aelfleah is very isolated, and the main reason for our prosperity over the years has been that we have escaped marauders because no one knew we were there. Josselin wanted to build his castle upon the boundary of our western hills, but I did not want him to do so."

"But how did you come to be wed?" burst out Christina.

Mairin laughed. "Josselin and I decided that marriage between us was the only solution to settle Aelfleah's ownership. We went to London with my mother for King William's coronation, and the king agreed with us. He ordered us married in his presence, and that of his closest friends, and by his brother, Bishop Odo. It was not quite the wedding I envisioned," she admitted.

"Do you love each other?" the curious Christina persisted.

Mairin's face softened and her eyes grew dreamy. "Oh, yes, I love him very much," she said.

"I think that is the most romantic story I have ever heard," young Christina sighed.

"When did you see Eric Longsword again?" asked the queen.

"Several months after our marriage, Josselin went to aid Bishop Odo at Dover. While he was gone Eric Longsword led Eadric the Wild to Aelfleah. He had told Eadric that I was his betrothed wife, and that we would hold Aelfleah for Eadric." Mairin had wisely amended her story so as not to offend Edgar the Atheling's family who were sheltering her. "I was expecting our first child at the time," Mairin continued. "I lost that baby shortly after Eadric and his raiders left us." She then went on to explain how, knowing that Eadric and his men would be coming to Aelfleah, she had helped and led her people so that the manor's harvest was saved instead of being burnt. She explained to the listening women how they had hidden the livestock to prevent their being driven off, and hidden the castle workers and master craftsmen, and sent the young girls to a nearby convent for safekeeping. "The last time I saw Eric Longsword before he kidnapped me from York was as he rode off with Eadric the Wild," Mairin finished. "I know he probably felt very much a fool, having been publicly proved a liar. I never expected, however, that I should ever see him again."

"Did he ravish you?" Christina's blue eyes were wide with curiosity.

"*Christina!*" Both her mother and her sister spoke simultaneously. Their tones were equally shocked.

"Nay," said Mairin, "it is all right. That is the strangest thing of all. He did not, but he believes he did." Mairin turned to the lady Agatha. "Lady, this is not a tale for an innocent girl."

The queen's mother nodded, and said to her younger daughter, "You will go to your chamber, Christina, and meditate upon the sin of excessive curiosity and a thoughtless, too-quick tongue." Agatha's tone was a severe one, and her demeanor was unsmiling.

"Yes mother," said the chastened Christina, rising from her place, and then she turned to Mairin. "If I have offended you, my lady, I beg your pardon."

"You have not offended me," said Mairin and she smiled at Christina. The girl could not be more than a year younger than she was, but as a married woman with a child she felt so much older.

With a curtsy to her elder sister, her mother, the abbess, and Mairin, Christina left the room.

"Continue on with your tale," said the queen. "You say that Eric Longsword did not ravish you although he believes that he has? I do not understand at all."

"My lady queen, imagine for a moment that you are in my position. You have been stolen from your husband by a rejected suitor. That first night you are together sheltering from a blizzard in an old barn. He beats you, and you know, because he has threatened it, that he will next ravish you."

Mairin's three listeners shuddered openly.

"When he had finished beating me, he made me disrobe, and he threw me down upon the straw, flinging himself upon me."

"Ohhh!" The elderly abbess's eyes were round.

Mairin quickly explained to them how Eric had fondled and kissed her, attacking her not with his manhood, but with his fingers. "He actually seems to believe that each time he does this thing he is coupling with me. It is so strange, but you have no idea how relieved I was each time he forced me to his bed that he did not actually rape me. How could I have faced my husband under such circumstances?"

"He never really once . . ." began Agatha, and then she flushed.

"Nay, lady. Not once, though he believes he has. I would swear it on the Holy Cross!"

"Who is your patron saint?" asked the queen.

"The Blessed Mother," said Mairin. "My name day is hers, August 15th."

"It is obvious," said the queen, "that our Blessed Mother was watching over you, Mairin of Aelfleah. Your escape is nothing short of a miracle. I have believed you from the first, and hearing your full tale, know for certain it is my duty to shelter you from this wicked man. I will see that my husband, the king, sends to England so that your Josselin may come for you, and you may be reunited."

Mairin burst into tears of relief, and slipping from her chair to her knees before the queen, took Margaret's hand and kissed it. "How can I thank you, my gracious lady?" she said.

"Stay by my side until my child has been born," said the young queen. "Your husband will not be able to reach you until the spring, and my child is due then. The ladies of my court are good and kindly women, but they lack education and refinement. I miss these things, for I had them in Hungary, and I had them at King Edward's court when we first came to England. You are close to me in age, you have traveled, and you are obviously educated. Do you read?"

"Yes, my lady, I do."

The queen motioned Mairin back to her chair, and said, "Then we shall read together, and discuss what we have read. It will keep me content in these last months of my confinement." Margaret smiled at her, and Mairin knew she was finally safe.

She was not loath to becoming a member of Malcolm Ceann Mor's court in return for her safety. The king took an interest in everything that was of concern to the queen, and so Mairin found herself under his strong protection as well. Malcolm Ceann Mor had not survived the civil war of his childhood, his flight to England as a boy of ten, all the years in between, and finally his successful struggle to regain his rightful throne by being stupid. Recognizing in Eric Longsword a man who would not be deterred, he arranged that Mairin sleep in a small chamber within his wife's apartments.

"Attempt to regain custody of the woman before Josselin de Combourg's arrival, Eric Longsword, and you forfeit my friendship," he warned. "I will hunt you down. You will have no place else to hide."

Mairin settled into her life as the queen's companion. She was relieved to be safe again, but she missed Aelfleah and her family, but her mother, she knew, would keep Maude safe. Her greatest concern was Josselin. It was going to be very hard for him to accept what had happened. He was such a proud man, but then their love for one another would sustain them. She knew it!

January passed, and on the eve of Imbolc she was amazed to find that the Celtic fires were lit all over Scotland. Indeed, the court made quite a festival of the occasion although the queen did not approve.

"It is not Christian," she said.

"There is no harm in it," said Mairin softly. "It is an old folk custom, and we do it at Aelfleah. Over the hills of Wales the Cymri dot the entire countryside with their fires. It is part of our heritage. 'Tis but an excuse to ease the long dull days and nights of winter. Do not forget, my lady queen, that the penitential season of Lent will soon be upon us."

Halfway through February, Mairin found herself growing ill in the morning, and beef, her favorite meat, became repugnant to her. Having faced such a condition twice before, she realized that she was once more with child. A child conceived during that passion-filled night in York with Josselin. *Their son!* This was their son! She just knew it! Protectively she placed her hands over her flat belly.

"I am with child," she told Margaret. They had become friends now, even sharing secrets about their husbands.

The queen was delighted. "How fortunate you are that you did not miscarry of him while you were in that awful man's clutches." The queen did not even consider the possibility that Mairin might have lied to her about Eric Longsword, and that the child was his.

Mairin nodded. "He was so newly conceived too," she said. "Aye, my lady, I am lucky, but if you believe the Blessed Mother protected me from

Eric Longsword, then she also protected my son. I know it is a son! William de Combourg. That is what we plan on naming him. Before Maude was born we decided that a son would be William, a daughter Maude. What will you call your son?"

"Edward," said Margaret, "after King Edward who was so kind to us when we were children at his court."

Mairin made no attempt to conceal her condition. Indeed, she was proud to be once more with child, for she and Josselin desired a large family. The hardest thing was not being able to tell him, and not being able to share her news with Eada. She said a silent prayer of thanks for her mother. Because of Eada she knew that her daughter would be well taken care of and safe.

The laird of Glenkirk had taken it upon himself to squire her about. His name was Angus Leslie, and she was very grateful for his company within the Great Hall of the king's house, for Eric Longsword had not been forbidden the court. A day did not pass that she did not see him glowering at her from someplace within the hall. Until Josselin came and proved her truthful, she was forced to bear his presence.

Angus Leslie did not like Eric. "The man has the look of a coward to me," he said to Mairin one afternoon as they strolled out-of-doors in Margaret's little garden. There was still snow upon the ground, and the skies were threatening more before the day was out.

"He is a coward," said Mairin. "He told me that he struck my father from behind because he knew he could not hope to defeat such a skilled warrior as Aldwine Athelsbeorn. I believe Eric Longsword to be mad, Angus. Perhaps that is why he frightens me so."

"I'll give the man one thing," said the laird.

"What?" she asked him.

"He's got good judgment when it comes to women," he told her with a shy grin.

Mairin's violet eyes twinkled with delight. The laird of Glenkirk wasn't a handsome man. He was very tall and lanky, and his nose was just a trifle too big for his face, although it was certainly in correct proportion with his wide mouth. His hair was the russet brown of an oak leaf, and his deep blue eyes were warm. "Why, Angus," she teased him, "are you complimenting me?"

The laird came as close to blushing as a grown man could, and he said, "Damn, my lady Mairin, dinna be like the little flirts that people this court. Ye know yer a beautiful woman, and I am a blunt man. The truth of the matter is that I envy yer husband. I've nae had time for a wife, though my relatives tell me 'tis my duty to wed. I frankly admit I wouldna mind if ye were my lass, and the bairn in yer belly were my son. So until yer husband comes to claim ye, I'll look after ye as if ye were mine, and not another's."

She put her hand upon his sleeve, and Angus Leslie looked down on her from his great height. "Angus Leslie, 'tis the nicest thing anyone has said to me in months. I'm proud you are my friend. Now I shall tell you a secret. There is a young lady of this court who would give her life for just a kind word from you. Are you interested in knowing who she is?"

"Aye," he said slowly, looking both curious and puzzled at the same time. Together they reentered the warm Great Hall.

" 'Tis the lady Christina who admires you."

"The queen's sister?" He had lowered his voice. "Surely yer mistaken. I could not aspire to the queen's sister."

"She will hear no talk of marriage for her, although I will wager if the right man were mentioned, she would change her tune. The queen would have her wed happily."

The laird of Glenkirk looked thoughtful, and he glanced across the room to where the flaxen-haired Christina sat demurely sewing by her sister's side. "She's a bonnie lass," he noted almost to himself, and Mairin smiled.

"Go and speak to her," she encouraged him.

"What would I say?" He looked so panic-stricken that Mairin almost laughed aloud.

"Go and tell her that I would like her to join us in a goblet of mulled cider, Angus. Then escort her across the room to me."

"I couldna do it! She would think me bold," he protested.

"A woman occasionally likes her man to be bold, Angus," she told him. It was time this big Highland chief did some serious courting, and not of other men's wives, Mairin thought. He was ripe for plucking, and she knew for a fact that young Christina was quite taken with Angus Leslie. "Go on!" she encouraged him with a little push. "You would rush into a battle quick enough, Angus Leslie. Well, think of courting as a battle. You want to win the battle, do you not? Leslie men are surely not faint of heart."

Squaring his shoulders the laird walked across the room without so much as a backward glance. Mairin smiled, watching him bow and greet the queen and her sister. She was quite enjoying playing matchmaker. Then a voice hissed meanly in her ear.

"What will Josselin de Combourg think when he comes to find ye with my babe in your belly?" Eric Longsword was by her side smiling nastily.

She looked scathingly at him. "The child I carry is my husband's, conceived just before Christmas. The child could not possibly be yours, and you know it."

"I fucked you enough," he snarled.

"Not with anything that could produce life," she snapped back at him, "and you know it!"

"Bitch! The child is mine, and I shall swear it to your husband."

"If you do then you will be lying, Eric Longsword, and God will strike you down for the lie. The child is Josselin de Combourg's, and no amount of wishing upon your part will make it otherwise. You know it to be so." Then Mairin turned from him and walked across the hall to join the queen. Angus Leslie had already forgotten about her, and was talking quietly to Christina, whose face was animated and whose cheeks were a pretty shade of pink.

"What did *that* man want with you?" the queen asked. She always referred to Eric as *that* man now.

"He says my child is his, and that he will tell Josselin so," replied Mairin. "It is not so, my lady Margaret! I have not lied. There is no way in which Eric Longsword could have possibly conceived that child on me. It will be hard enough for Josselin to accept the fact that I was in that madman's company for several weeks, but if Eric raises doubts in my husband's mind about our child, what will I do?"

"Our Blessed Mother has protected you so far, Mairin. She will continue to do so," said the queen, "and I will pray for you that all goes well." She looked to her sister, and then back at Mairin. "Have you been matchmaking?"

"Have you not seen how your sister's eyes follow the laird whenever he is about?" Mairin answered. "I have come to know Angus well since my arrival here in Edinburgh. I believe him to be a good man, my lady."

"She could have a great lord," said Margaret thoughtfully.

"She does not seem to want one," replied Mairin.

"I want her to be happy," said the queen. "She does not remember Hungary as I do, and as you can see, she has our father's Anglo-Saxon coloring and look. Had I not wed with my lord, the king, I doubt there would be any chance of marriage for her."

"Angus Leslie would take her to wive in naught but her shift," said Mairin. "He doesn't know it yet, but he is a man about to fall in love."

Margaret smiled at her friend. "You like him!"

"Aye, I do. Christina has been in love with him for some time now, my lady. Look at them together. They look right, and from the dazed look upon Angus' face, I believe he has already succumbed to your sister's charms. He is practically in love, and he is ready to take a wife. Christina would be happy with him."

"We will see," said the queen with another smile. "Let us see how their courting goes, and then I will speak to my lord, the king."

The spring came, and toward the end of May the queen was brought to bed of a fine son who was baptized Edward on the very day of his birth. It was on that same day that Josselin de Combourg arrived in Edinburgh to reclaim his stolen wife. He had gone almost mad when he had returned to his tent that Christmas Day to find Loial dutifully and unknowingly standing guard over his empty dwelling. The young squire had wept with shame when Mairin's loss was discovered. The slit rear of his quarters told Josselin how the kidnapper had entered and removed his wife. The snow, only just beginning to fall then, had not yet obliterated the place where Eric Longsword's horse had been tethered and waiting.

Eric Longsword. He knew without a doubt his wife's kidnapper. Had Mairin not seen the man behind them in church that morning? He went at once to the king and explained his plight. William was sympathetic, and over a dozen knights volunteered to help Josselin seek his wife. They divided themselves into several search parties, and each went off in a different direction, for Josselin really had no idea of where to look. By now the snow was falling heavily, and so the searchers were forced to return to York by nightfall. No trace of Mairin or her captor had been found. After the storm had subsided they had searched again, but in the desolated, and now devastated, countryside surrounding York, few people could be found alive, and those who were found were not overly willing to cooperate with Norman knights. Pressed, they admitted to having seen nothing, and certainly no one of Mairin's description.

Josselin had returned to Aelfleah, for he thought that perhaps Eric Longsword was still affiliated with Eadric the Wild. He would go home first, and then into Wales to seek Eadric. Eada was horrified to learn of her daughter's kidnapping.

"How could you leave York?" she demanded of Josselin.

"There was no trace of her there," he said. "I have to start looking somewhere, and Eadric the Wild seems like the logical place to begin."

"Perhaps," Eada mused, "but I suspect Eric Longsword is long gone from Eadric's service, for Eadric was not overly pleased to find that he had lied to him about his position with Mairin and Aelfleah."

"If she is not there, I do not know where to go," said Josselin.

"Ask Eadric," replied his mother-in-law. "He may know something, and I think he may be getting ready to swear his fealty to King William."

"Why do you think that?" Josselin asked her.

"His rebellions have come to naught, and the lesson of Northumbria cannot have gone unnoticed by Eadric. His allies have melted away. He must either swear fealty to William, or face the same fate as Earl Edwin. Offer him friendship in the king's name as well as your own. It will salve his pride, which is great, and give him the opening he seeks to come to the king with his honor intact."

Josselin smiled at Eada, and then he gave her a hug. "How did you get so wise, mother?"

"By living so long," she answered him with a smile. "Now go and find my daughter, and bring her safely back home."

He had taken Eada's advice and gone with a small nonthreatening force to the stronghold of Eadric the Wild. He had been received with cautious hospitality at first, but that hospitality had become openly friendly and cooperative when he had extended his hand in friendship. Eada had been correct. Eadric the Wild was anxious to make his peace with William. Josselin assured him he could arrange to have his neighbor—for were they not good neighbors now?—received with honor and friendship by King William. The purpose of his visit, however, was a sad one. Eric Longsword had come to York in December where he and his wife, Mairin of Aelfleah, had been called to the king's Christmas court, and Eric had stolen the lady Mairin away. Did Eadric know perchance where Eric Longsword might be?

Eadric was horrified by Josselin de Combourg's news, but then he said, "I cannot help you, my friend, for I have not heard from that cowardly bastard since I sent him from my service. Do not fear, however, for your wife is a brave woman. If she does not escape him, she will find a way to send you word as to where they are. I do not believe he would dare to come back to me, for I do not take kindly to men who lie to me. I think the fellow is mad. With Tostig dead, Eric might have gone north with Edgar the Atheling's people to Scotland. Have you looked there?"

Josselin had returned to Aelfleah dispirited, but Eada had agreed with Eadric's analysis of the situation. The winter was severe, however, and Josselin would have to wait until spring before he might venture north again. In his first and immediate concern to retrieve his wife, Josselin had not considered the fact that Eric Longsword was Mairin's rejected erstwhile suitor. As the winter wore on, that nagging thought crept into his mind, and he could not exorcise it. He knew that Mairin would not willingly accept Eric as her lover, but how could his wife hope to overcome a determined man's strength? He knew with certainty that Eric had forced his wife, and try as he might, he was unable to accept the fact despite Mairin's innocence in the matter.

Still he owed it to her to find her, and bring her home to Aelfleah. Until he did, this terrible matter, not of their own making, could not be resolved, and it must be if they were to go on with their lives. First though, Eric Longsword must die, for he had besmirched the honor of Josselin de Combourg by kidnapping and violating his wife. Josselin found that as images of his beautiful wife struggling within the embrace of the other man grew, so did his thought of Eric Longsword struggling in his death throes at the end of Josselin's lance grow as well.

Dagda sensed the violence within his lord, and said, "You cannot hold her responsible."

Josselin turned agonized eyes to the big man. "I do not. Not really."

"Yes you do, my lord, and if she knows it you will kill her love for you. She will never forgive you. Her greatest weakness is that she has a long memory for an offense."

"God have mercy on me, Dagda! How can I put these terrible thoughts that plague me from my mind? Eric Longsword has used my wife in a way that is my right alone. I forgive her, but how can I forget it?"

"You *must*, my lord. Perhaps if you thought more like your Celtic ancestors you would understand. Our bodies are but shells to house our souls as we go through our lives. As we end each life we live, we shed those shells as a snake sheds its skin. It is not the body's shell that is important, it is the soul. A hundred men might possess my lady Mairin's body, but none would touch either her heart or her soul, for they are yours alone. Will you allow your pride to destroy your love, my lord? Think on it."

He did as he rode north with the messenger who had arrived at Aelfleah in mid-May to bid him come to King Malcolm's court in Edinburgh, where he might find his lost wife. Dagda had insisted upon coming with them, and Josselin had not dared to forbid him, for there was something about Dagda's strength that he felt he needed, and he was ashamed of his own weakness, for in his heart he knew he loved her yet, and always would. They arrived in Edinburgh to learn that the queen had just that morning given birth to a lusty son.

Along their way Josselin had learned that his wife had come to the Scots court in early January, and upon being presented to the queen, she had thrown herself upon Margaret's mercy. Her tale had caused quite a stir amongst the court, and Queen Margaret had taken the lady Mairin into her household under her protection, much to the anger and chagrin of Eric Longsword, who claimed she was his wife. That news in itself offered a certain relief to Josselin. Mairin had been in her captor's custody a relatively short time. Considering their flight, and the severe winter weather through which they had traveled, perhaps she had escaped ravishment by her captor.

As Mairin ran toward him, her beautiful face alight with joy, his hopes plummeted, for she was obviously with child. He almost groaned aloud. His beautiful and exquisite enchantress violated by a man little better than a savage beast, but for her sake he would accept her bastard even as his father had accepted him. It was ironic that he be faced with such a situation, but still it could not be easy for her either, he realized. She was forced to carry and bear the fruit of her shame.

"Josselin, my love!"

He opened his arms to her, enfolding her within his embrace. He felt tears pricking at his eyelids unbidden, and he buried his face for a moment in her neck to hide them. "Sweet Jesu, enchantress," he said, "I feared I should never see you again!"

"I am with child," she said, and her voice was happy. "It is a son this time, Josselin. Our son, William, who will be born by Michaelmas at the latest! It was a blessing that I did not lose him before we reached Edinburgh."

"*Our son?*" His voice sounded stupid in his own ears.

She pulled from his embrace, and stared him in the face. "Aye, my lord. Our son," she repeated, and now her tone was sharp.

They had met within the courtyard of the king's house, and as they entered the Great Hall so that Mairin might bring her husband to the king, Eric Longsword was suddenly before them, and he grinned sneeringly.

"What think you of your fine wife, my lord de Combourg, and of the son I've put into her belly?"

With a savage roar Josselin leapt forward, reaching out as he did so to grasp his antagonist about the neck. Before his fingers might close about his enemy's throat, however, two men put themselves between the warring parties.

"My lord, no!" he heard Dagda say.

Slowly the red mist that had risen up before his eyes subsided, and although his anger was as hot as it had been moments before, at least his reason had returned. As his eyes focused he saw Eric Longsword being held at swordpoint by a tall, lanky man with a large nose dressed in a knee-length dark wool tunic, a blue-and-green length of cloth with narrow bands of red and white thrown across his shoulder, and held by a silver-and-enamel pin.

"Angus Leslie, laird of Glenkirk," drawled the man with a smile that went all the way to his eyes. "Dinna gie our *friend* here an easy death, my lord. We've been waitin' for ye to get here so we might watch ye destroy the turd at yer leisure."

Josselin felt the laugh bubble up, and he opened his mouth to release it. "On reflection, Angus Leslie, I believe I shall enjoy slowly slicing this wife-stealing rogue to ribbons."

"Verra guid, man, for the king's planned to make a festival of it."

"Let him go," said Josselin. "I'll not kill him yet."

Angus Leslie lowered his sword, and sheathed it.

Eric rubbed the spot on his neck where the weapon had pricked his skin, and then looking at Josselin he said softly, "Ye've not answered me, my lord de Combourg. What think you of the babe with which I've filled Mairin?"

"Liar!" Mairin spat at him, and her eyes were blazing with anger. "I will not deny ye kissed me, and ye fondled me, but never once did ye do that which would put a child in my belly. The child is my husband's child, conceived in York before you stole me away. I would swear it on the True Cross!"

Those within the Great Hall of the king's house turned as the voices rose, and listened avidly at the exchange going on between the two men and the woman. Most believed Mairin, for Margaret believed her, but there were those doubting Thomases amongst the members of the court who, believing that Eric Longsword had raped his captive, thought that surely the child Mairin carried must be his, and that she lied to her husband to protect that baby.

"Mairin, this is neither the time nor the place to discuss this," Josselin told his wife.

"I disagree, my lord," came her answer. "Either you believe me, or you believe Eric Longsword."

"I believe that you believe what you say, enchantress. I know you would not deliberately lie to me."

"This child is your own true child, my lord. If you will not accept it then you no longer accept me, for without trust between us, we have no real marriage." Before he might answer her, Mairin turned and left the hall.

Eric laughed. "The child is mine," he said, "for I fucked her first the same day I took her back from you. You may kill me, Josselin de Combourg, but it is my son who will inherit Aelfleah. Even if he does not look like me, you will know he is mine, and if you do not want to lose her, you must accept my bastard for her sake." He laughed again, and it was an eerie and high-pitched sound that came forth from him. "I do not care if you kill me, for without Mairin I have nothing for which to live, but I shall not really die, shall I? I will live to haunt you in my son.

"Shall I tell you how your wife writhed and moaned beneath my cock? How she begged me not to stop? How she begged for more, and how her sharp claws spurred me onward to satisfy her as you have obviously never satisfied her? She is a glorious fuck with that white skin and that flame-red hair of hers. I cannot remember ever having enjoyed a woman more. Shall I tell you what she said to me after I first took her?"

Dagda's big fist shot out, and Eric Longsword crumbled into a heap at Josselin's feet. Josselin did not think he could move, and even Angus Leslie was stunned by the viciousness of Eric Longsword's words.

Finally, after what seemed like a very long time, the laird of Glenkirk said, "The man is totally mad, ye know. His words are cruel, but ye must nae believe him."

"Would you if Mairin were your wife?" asked Josselin.

"If Mairin were my wife, I would trust the lass if she told me nay. Yer a lucky man, my lord de Combourg."

"We are speaking about my wife, and the possibility that she carries a son. Is he my heir? Or is he not?" Josselin said stiffly.

Angus Leslie nodded slowly. "Aye, 'tis hard," he said, "but ye'll have to make peace wi' yerself for her sake, and there is always the chance 'twill be a lass."

"Are you enamored of my wife, Angus Leslie?"

The laird grinned his quick grin. "I might have been, but that she would nae let me be. Instead she turned my mind and heart to the bonniest maiden I could have ever dared to aspire to, the queen's younger sister. We are to be wed, and I hope both ye and Mairin will be here still to share in our happiness."

It was Angus Leslie who then brought Josselin de Combourg to meet

Malcolm Ceann Mor. The king welcomed his guest, and having seen the parchment upon which the marriage between Josselin de Combourg and Mairin of Aelfleah was recorded with the seals of both King William and Odo, the bishop of Bayeux, the Scots king ruled that Mairin of Aelfleah be returned to her lawful husband.

"What would ye do about Eric Longsword, my lord?" he asked Josselin.

"I would meet him in armed combat," was the reply.

"Death to the loser?"

"Aye, my lord king. No quarter to be given."

"I understand that yer honor must be served, my lord de Combourg, but what if ye should lose? Yer wife would be helpless to the villain, and yer children fatherless. I am willing to see this man, who by law is my liegeman, punished for what he has done."

Josselin shook his head. "The right is mine, my lord king. I cannot rest until I have revenged myself and my innocent wife upon this man. I will not lose the battle. God is on my side."

The king nodded, understanding Josselin's viewpoint. Had he been in this knight's boots, he would have wanted it the same way. "I will see Eric Longsword is imprisoned until the day ye meet him upon the field of honor, my lord de Combourg. That day, however, must be postponed for the time being. Today I have become the father of a fine son, and I will allow nothing to mar the celebrations surrounding my son's birth. Shortly my wife's sister will be wed, and nothing must spoil her happy time either. After Christina's wedding we will arrange the tourney in which ye may avenge yer family's honor upon the field of battle with Eric Longsword. Are ye content to wait until then, my lord de Combourg?"

Josselin nodded.

"Good!" said Malcolm Ceann Mor. "Then until that time, ye and yer beautiful wife will be my guests. Welcome to Scotland, my lord de Combourg! Welcome to Scotland!"

Chapter 16

Two small private rooms had been found to shelter the newly reunited couple within the king's house on Edinburgh Rock. It was here that Angus Leslie led Josselin after his interview with the king. For a long minute after his guide had left him, Josselin stood outside of the unadorned wooden door. Then suddenly, before he might regret his actions, Josselin put his hand to the handle of the door, and turning it, walked into the room to find it empty.

Surprised, he looked about him. It was an inside chamber in which he found himself, and there were but three pieces of furniture within it. A small rectangular oak table, and two straight-backed chairs. He moved across the little room, opening the door on its far wall to enter into a second chamber which had a window, a corner fireplace, and a large bed which took up most of the chamber. It was here he found his wife standing by the open window gazing out over the city below.

"We must remain here in Edinburgh for the present," he said awkwardly by way of greeting.

"Why?" she demanded, her back still to him. "I want to go home to Aelfleah before it is impossible for me to travel. I miss my mother, and Maude has not seen me in almost half a year."

"Eric Longsword must be punished for what he has done, and I must be the instrument of that punishment."

"Cannot King Malcolm see to it?" Her voice lacked warmth.

"He could if I would let him, which I will not. Eric Longsword has compromised my honor, and it is my right to meet him in a trial by combat."

"What about my honor?" she demanded.

"It is our honor I fight for, Mairin."

"Nay I think not, my lord. You will fight with Eric Longsword and you

346

will kill him, but not for the love you bear me or because you are outraged by the abuse that man has done me. You will fight with him, and you will kill him because you believe he has raped me and put his child in my womb. A child whom you must acknowledge. A son who will be your heir. You do not fight for me, Josselin. You fight for your own sense of outrage, but I tell you now, once and for all, that you are wrong." It was then that she turned to face him, and he saw an anger in her eyes that she sought desperately to keep under control.

Anger? Why should she feel anger toward him? Was he not the injured party? "This is the second time that you have sworn to me the child you carry is not the child of Eric Longsword, Mairin. I love you, enchantress, and I want to believe you, but how can I?" he asked her and his tone was desperate.

"Why do you accept his word over mine, Josselin? Is it because he is a man, and therefore more trustworthy? I am your wife, and when have I ever lied to you? Eric Longsword beat me, and he used me with his hands, and his mouth, but I do not believe he is capable of having a woman in the normal sense. He did not rape me. I shall be even more direct, my lord. He did not once penetrate my body with his cock, nor did he ever loose his seed into me. I can be no clearer than that, Josselin. The child that's growing within my womb was conceived by us in York. If that child is as I believe, a son, and you refuse to accept him, I shall appeal to both the church and to the king. I will say nothing more upon the matter, nor will I ever defend myself to you again."

He was stunned by her coldness, and he could see how very angry she was at him. His first instinct was to be angry back, but some tiny sane voice within him warned him that if he were it would be the end between them. He did not want that, and he believed that she did not want it either. In his mind he could hear Dagda cautioning him. It suddenly occurred to him that though they had been separated for five months, not once in all that time had he been under threat of death or any other serious danger. She had, and her fears had not only been for herself, but for her unborn child as well. One of them had to be the first to yield in this terrible situation, and he could see it was not going to be Mairin. He was capable of being just as stubborn, but if he were, then the breach between them would only widen. Josselin realized, if he wanted his wife back, that he would have to be the one to make the first move. It was he who would have to swallow his pride, for hers was every bit as large as his, and she had been driven to the breaking point by now.

"Help me, Mairin," he said softly to her. "It is hard for me also."

"I cannot make you believe me, Josselin," she answered him, but her voice was a tiny bit less rigid.

"I do not understand how you could have escaped ravishment by him."

"At first," she explained, "I was terrified. He made it quite plain what he intended doing. As we rode through the storm that first day, he guided his horse with one hand, while fondling my breasts with the other. I was so ashamed, and yet I did not want to die. I wanted to live to get home to Aelfleah to you and little Maude. I thought surely you would find me before nightfall, but you never came."

"I did not know where to look," he said, "and the snow covered your tracks, though I would not have known whose tracks they were even if I had found them."

She nodded. "I know that now, but then I had such hope and faith in you, my lord." Quietly Mairin went on to tell him of her trek through the winter weather with her captor. Of how they had met with the others, and sheltered that first night at the abandoned farm. Of how she had learned then that they were heading for Scotland. As she told him her tale, he felt himself torn, for she had been correct when she had said he had no right to doubt her. Yet within him was that element of doubt that tortured him unbearably, particularly in light of Eric Longsword's brutal words. She seemed to be hiding nothing from him, for she was most graphic in the telling of her plight, but she still insisted that Eric Longsword had not raped her.

When she finally finished with her narrative, she looked with questioning eyes upon him, and he knew what he must do if he was to retain the love and respect of his beloved enchantress. "I believe you, Mairin," he said. "I truly do!"

"And you accept the child that I carry as your own true child?" she demanded further of his patience.

"Aye," he said without hesitation, and to his great surprise she burst into tears, and threw herself into his startled embrace. Instinctively, his arms closed about her, and feeling her familiar warmth against him, the softness of her glorious hair against his cheek once more, he felt all his serious doubts temporarily melt away. "Ahh, enchantress, you must not weep. We are together again, and I will never allow you to be parted from me again," he vowed lavishly, and then he stroked her head in an effort to comfort her.

"I was so afraid," she whispered, "but I was more afraid of showing him my fear, for I knew if I did, I should be lost, Josselin. I did not want to be lost from you forever."

It was those half-sobbed words that made him realize how very brave she really had been. "If you should desire it, I will send you home now while you can still travel in relative comfort. The child should be born at Aelfleah."

She shook her head in the negative. "Nay. It matters not where our son is born, any more than it matters where he was conceived. I want to be avenged upon Eric Longsword also. I want to see you kill him. I would kill him myself if I could!"

"King Malcolm will not arrange the trial by combat until after the celebrations for Prince Edward's birth and the celebration of his sister-in-law's marriage are completed. It is almost June. The child you have said is due by Michaelmas. It may be August before this matter can be concluded."

"All the more reason for me to stay, my lord. Have we not been separated enough these last months?"

"At least Eric Longsword will not bother us further," he told her. "The king has ordered him imprisoned until we meet in combat."

"Why now?" she asked. "He has been free to slander me with his words and his lies since we arrived here."

"He claimed marriage with you, Mairin, and a husband's rights. You denied it, causing doubt. The matter is now settled, for I brought with me the proof of our lawful union. That is why the king has ordered the villain caged."

"Good!" she said in such a positive tone that he could not help but laugh.

"I almost feel sorry for the man," he said.

"That is because you have me back," she noted smugly, and he laughed again.

"Aye," he answered her, and felt, much to his own surprise, a sudden stirring in the region of his loins. "I have you back, enchantress mine. Now what shall I do with you?" There was no doubt in his mind of his need to possess her, to reaffirm the marriage bond between them.

She smiled at him seductively. Much more seductively, it seemed to him, than he remembered. "You have traveled far, my lord," she said. "Undoubtedly you are greatly in need of both a hot bath and a warm bed. I shall see to both immediately," and she did.

With quiet efficiency, she went about the business of ordering the king's servants to bring a large oak tub for the king's guest. A line of sturdy serving men hurried to and fro from the antechamber of the tiny apartment, bringing buckets of water, enough to fill the tub, and a serving wench came from the queen bearing a small cake of soap with which to bathe Josselin. When they had all gone, and Josselin had stripped off his clothing to settle himself comfortably in the tub, Mairin came in nothing but her camise to wash him as was her wifely duty.

Kneeling over the tub she took up the soap, and dipping it first in the hot water, smoothed it slowly in a circular motion over his broad chest. Neither of them spoke. Her hands moved up over his shoulders and his neck, washing first, rinsing afterward. Then she turned her attentions to his long back, her gentle hands sweeping up the length of it, rubbing, rubbing, the soap feeling like silk against his masculine skin. She swept down to the very base of his spine, causing him to shift as she transferred her busy hands to his buttocks.

Her own skin was flushed rosy by the steam that swirled up from the water, and the dampness had fused the fabric of her camise to her breasts. Her nipples were very prominent, and his male organ, titillated by their sight, now thrust up through the water of the bath. A small smile played about the corners of her mouth, but she remained silent as she slipped the soap over the muscles of his hard belly, moving down to cup his pouch as she made a play at washing it.

"You will not forget my feet?" he said through gritted teeth.

"Nay, my lord, I will wash your feet," she said, and thrusting both hands into the tub, manipulated the soap over first one of his legs, beginning with the thigh, and working down his calf to his feet where she pushed a finger slowly and suggestively through each of the separations between his toes, and then she did his other leg.

He was prepared to leap from the tub, but before he might, she was roughly washing his thick and tawny hair with almost gleeful vigor, scrubbing at his scalp with a vengeance that caused him to yelp with protest. "Lady, have mercy! That is my poor head you are attacking!"

"I am aware of all your body parts, my lord, including this rude fellow"— she gave his pulsing manhood a teasing squeeze—"who so boldly stares at me!" Then she dumped a bucket of clean warm water that stood by the side of the tub over his head, following it with a second bucket, this time of cold water. "There," she said, satisfied, "you are fit for human company once again, Josselin de Combourg!" and Mairin stepped back from the tub.

With a grin he stood, shaking the excess water from his long body, taking the rough cloth she handed him to dry off his head and his skin. The anteroom was chilly, but when he again reentered the bedchamber, he found she had closed the wooden shutters upon the single window that lit the room, and a small fire burned within the tiny corner fireplace. For a moment he did not see her, and then as his eyes became accustomed to the gloom, he found her comfortably settled upon the big bed, nude.

"Now, my lord, having done my wifely duty by seeing to your cleanliness, I will now attend to your other needs if you would have me do so."

He let his eyes travel over her in leisurely fashion. The child to be born in a few months' time had already rounded her belly pleasantly. For some reason she looked lusher to his eye than he could seem to remember her. She was infinitely tempting, and even the faint doubt niggling deep within his mind could not deter his desire for her.

Leaning upon an elbow, Mairin looked up at him. The bucket of cold water that she had dumped over him had certainly not dampened his desire for her. His manhood thrust straight out from his body. Her violet eyes twinkled as she fastened her gaze upon it, and then looked up to meet his smoldering glance. "Not even some willing serf wench, my lord?" she teased him.

"Nay, enchantress," he said softly, and lowered himself to the bed beside her. Their lips met in a tender kiss, and then another and another. Gently he pressed her back into the bed, kissing soft kisses upon her cheekbones, her eyelids, along the side of her face to the shadowed hollow beneath her earlobe which he then nibbled.

Mairin felt herself relaxing for the first time in months. It was as if they had never been parted, and she sighed with pleasured contentment. Reaching up she stroked the back of his neck with her hand.

"There is no one for me but you, enchantress," he whispered in her ear. His lips traveled along the line of her shoulder, and then moved on to her beautiful breasts which in her pregnancy were extremely sensitive. He kissed their rigid little nipples, and then he began to lick each one in its turn. His tongue seemed almost hard, and as it lapped at her tender flesh, his hands caressed her body, kneading at a breast, smoothing over her torso. He turned her against him so that her bottom pressed against his manhood, and for several long sweet minutes he simply fondled her breasts. Then he gently enclosed her belly within his two hands and, to his surprise, he felt the faint, fluttering movement of the child.

"He kicks hard for someone so small," Josselin said softly.

"He will need to be strong, my love," she answered him, and turned herself so that they faced one another.

"I would have you," he said to her, "but only if you do not think it would hurt the child."

"We did not hurt Maude. Indeed, I believe our innocent desire for one another is good for the child." She opened her thighs to him, and he slid between them, easing one of her legs under him and the other over him.

Reaching down, Josselin touched her with his fingers and found that she was moist and ready for him. Tenderly he penetrated her, and the look of joy upon her face as his pulsing manhood filled her brought him almost to tears. Her violet eyes seemed to fill her pale face, and when he saw the glistening silver beads of her own tears upon that fair face, he knew that she felt as deeply as did he. Together they loved one another with gentle passion until they were transported together by ecstasy into that enraptured world known only to lovers.

Afterward as she lay sleeping, sated and content with his lovemaking, Josselin gazed down upon his slumbering wife, and asked himself how he could possibly doubt her. If she said the child was his, it was his—and yet the tiniest shred of doubt niggled at him. He, himself, had been born a bastard, but there had been no doubt as to who his parents were. His mother had been above reproach in her morals. She had never known another man but his father. He had to forget. He had to swallow his doubts, for if he did not, he would lose his wife, and Mairin, he realized, meant more to him than anyone, or anything else in the world.

The Scots court lacked the sophistication and the elegance of King William's court, but it had a rough charm that Josselin found himself enjoying. The influence of young Queen Margaret was beginning to be felt, however, and the wives and daughters of the nobility found they liked the delicacy, the good manners, and the charm the queen had brought with her. Away from the king's house, though, the men behaved as they had always behaved. Josselin found himself hunting for stag and game birds, and fishing for salmon and trout with Angus Leslie and his friends throughout most of the summer.

He returned each evening relaxed and content, and Mairin would bathe him as she had that first day. Their evenings were spent within the Great Hall eating and socializing with their new friends, listening to the pipers who played wild and haunting tunes upon their instruments that could set a strong man to weeping, and watching the men dancing dances so old that their real meanings had been lost somewhere in the mists of time.

The king had a bard, an old man who stood six feet, six inches in height, had a mane of snow white hair, and a voice as clear and pure as mountain air. His name was Seosaidh mac Caimbeul, and when he sang his stories of days past, battles won, and loves lost, there was a silence in the Great Hall so deep that a man might drown within it.

The king's infant son, Edward, thrived at his mother's breast, and the court rejoiced with Malcolm Ceann Mor and his wife. Margaret's labor had been relatively easy and trouble-free, and she was anxious to have more children. Her friendship for Mairin had not abated and, as Mairin had been by her side, so she promised would she be by Mairin's side when her time came. Both Mairin and Josselin had acknowledged the fact that their child would be born in Edinburgh, for the wedding of the queen's sister would not be celebrated until close to the end of August.

Angus Leslie had thanked Mairin over and over again for giving him the courage to approach Christina. As Mairin had predicted, he had quickly become a man in love, and having the love so eagerly returned by the flaxen-haired princess had been almost more happiness than he could bear. Seeing them together made Mairin happy, a happiness that was increased by her own joy at having been reunited with her husband.

The royal wedding was a happy occasion for the Scots court. The late summer weather was perfect—clear and warm—rather than misty and dank.

" 'Twill be guid grouse hunting soon," remarked Angus during the feasting that accompanied his marriage celebration. "Will ye come to Glenkirk, Joss?"

"I would like to, Angus, but the child is due shortly, and then as soon as Mairin feels we can travel, we must return to England. I should be there now overseeing the castle I am building, and Mairin is anxious about Maude. The child will probably not remember her. Only one thing has kept us here, and now that your wedding has been celebrated, the king will set a date for the trial by combat of Eric Longsword."

"He's been allowed to practice under guard, ye know," said Angus.

"I know. I asked the king to allow him that privilege. I will not fight with a man who has been kept inactive in a dark cell for several months. It would not be honorable."

"Is it honorable, my lord de Combourg, to keep a bridegroom from his bride?" The princess Christina had come up beside them to slip her hand onto her husband's arm. She was a very pretty girl, and particularly radiant this day in cloth-of-gold gown, pearls braided into her flaxen hair.

Angus Leslie brushed her forehead with a kiss. "I promise never to ig-nore ye again, lassie," he said lovingly.

Josselin smiled and, unnoticed, slipped away from the bridal couple to seek his wife. He found her sitting quietly with the queen. There was a lu-minescent quality about Mairin these days that seemed to grow even as her belly grew with the child. She seemed more content than she had in months. Reaching her, he bent and kissed the top of her red-gold head. "Your matchmaking is to be commended, lady. I have never seen a hap-pier couple."

"But for ourselves," she answered him pertly, looking up at him with a smile.

"God works his will in varied ways, does he not?" said the queen. "I wonder, if Mairin had not pointed it out to us, whether we would have seen Christina's love for Angus Leslie. Like me, she might have gone on believing she was destined for the church, and that isn't the case at all."

"Seeing little Edward so robust and filled with life," replied Mairin, "I know it was God's will that you wed with the king."

"What is this about the king?" demanded Malcolm Ceann Mor, com-ing up to join their little group.

"We were discussing the will of God, and how that will has brought us all great happiness because we listened and obeyed our Lord," answered the queen.

"Think ye that I am God's instrument, lady?" teased the king. "I will admit to having a goodly instrument, but I never considered that it was doing God's will. Perhaps I have been wrong."

"My lord!" The queen blushed rosy, but she nonetheless scolded her husband, "Beware of sacrilege lest God punish you for such heedless words in a manner you might not like."

"Heaven forfend," chuckled the king. Then he grew serious, and he turned to Josselin. "This matter between Eric Longsword and yourself. Ye are determined to trial by combat?"

"Aye, my lord."

"So be it then, Josselin de Combourg. You will meet yer enemy on the first day of September. Are ye agreed?"

"Aye," came the short reply. "The sooner the better, for we must get home to Aelfleah."

"If you fight upon the first and sustain no serious injuries, my lord, we might depart for home several days afterwards," said Mairin.

"What of the child? Would it be safe? I thought you meant to stay here until its birth."

"The child is due toward the end of the month. If we traveled slowly and carefully, I think we could reach Aelfleah in time. I think I should rather take that chance, Josselin, and be home for the birth."

"Let us wait and see, Mairin," he answered her. "I don't want to endanger you in any way."

It warmed her heart that he was so careful and considerate of her welfare and that of the child. The danger was minimal. It was his life that concerned her. This combat in which he would engage to assuage his honor could not be a mounted combat, for Eric Longsword had not been trained in such warfare. Mounted combat was something the Normans had brought to England. Therefore, the two men would fight a hand-to-hand combat on foot using swords. Only death would end the battle.

"I do not want you watching our combat," Josselin told his wife the night before the trial.

"What kind of a woman do you think I am that I would not stand proud while you slay our enemy?" she demanded of him.

"You are near to term with the child. You have never seen a trial by combat, have you?"

She shook her head. "Nay."

"It is a fight to the death, Mairin. Our weapons will not be blunted to prevent serious injury. Both Eric Longsword and I will enter the arena knowing full well that only one of us is to come out alive, and even if, God forbid, I do not survive, Eric's death is already a certainty, for King Malcolm will have him executed."

"Then why even bother to fight him, Josselin?"

"We have been over this before, Mairin. Our honor must be avenged. As for Eric, he will seek to kill me because he feels if he cannot have you then I should not either."

She shuddered, then said, "Men are fools, I think, but then as the queen would undoubtedly say, God has given us women no other choice."

Josselin laughed and put his arms about her. "Do not fret, enchantress. God is on my side in this matter. I will triumph over Eric Longsword."

She pulled away from him irritably. "I will see that your squire, Loial, has all your equipment in good order," and she moved away from him.

"She is afraid," said Dagda, who had been standing near them, and had heard everything.

"I wish she would not watch tomorrow."

"I regret you cannot stop her, my lord, but if you cannot, then you must put her out of your mind and concentrate upon the business of killing Eric Longsword. Do not allow your fears for Mairin to take over your mind or you will not be able to keep control of yourself. You could lose your life."

Josselin nodded. "I know," he said, "but I will not lose, Dagda. Even if he kills me, I will kill him first."

"Do not speak of dying, my lord. It is bad luck. Tomorrow you will meet Eric Longsword upon the field of combat, and you will slay him as quickly and as cleanly as you can."

Mairin could not sleep that night. Restlessly she paced the small antechamber, and finally unable to be contained by those four walls, she picked up her cloak and hurried to the chapel. Kneeling in the calm serenity of the holy place, she felt calmer. Margaret had been responsible for the little chapel, actually a small stone room within a tower of the king's house. It was a simple place with its carved oak altar upon which two golden candlesticks with pure wax tapers now burnt. As she completed her rosary, she became aware of another within the little chapel, and looked to see the queen's confessor, Father Turgot, standing before her.

"Would you like me to pray with you, my lady Mairin?" he asked her. He was a stern, but kindly man.

"Please," she answered him, and he knelt with her.

When they had finished their prayers he asked her, "Shall I hear your confession, my lady?"

"Oh, yes!" she told him, honored that he should ask her, for he usually heard no confession but the queen's. She was suddenly very aware that she had not been to confession since her arrival in Edinburgh. What would Father Turgot think of her? Placing her hands in his she began the words of contrition, and if the priest was shocked by what she told him, he gave no sign of it.

When Mairin had finished, the cleric said wisely, "Your sins are small, my lady, and you have suffered deeply. The fears you now suffer for your husband who must tomorrow defend his honor and yours are a much greater penance than I could ever impose upon you." Putting his hand upon her bowed head, he blessed her and said, "Go in peace, my daughter." Then he helped her to her feet, for she was so clumsy with the child.

Returning to her apartments, Mairin found that she could doze a little, but she awoke the moment Josselin moved from the bed. "Where are you going?" she asked. "It is too early for the combat." Why did her own voice sound so strange in her own ears? she wondered.

He did not seem to notice. "I would go to lauds, and be blessed."

"I will go with you," she said, nervously flinging back the coverlet of the bed.

"No! I want you to stay here, Mairin. I must be alone with my thoughts this morning. I cannot worry about you now!"

He left her, but Mairin could not sleep. Arising, she dressed and went to the Great Hall to find Dagda. "He would not let me go to the Mass with him," she fretted. "He said he needed to be alone. What is the matter with him, Dagda?"

"You should not go to the combat today, my lady," came the blunt reply.

"He is my husband! He goes to avenge our honor! Of course I should be there!"

"No, you should not," came the equally positive reply. "Under normal circumstances, Lord Josselin would be proud to fight this battle before you, but you are shortly to bear a child, and he fears that having never seen a combat to the death before that you may become fearful and miscarry of the child. He worries for you when he should be concentrating upon the battle to come."

"What you are saying is that my presence could possibly be responsible for endangering my husband, and alter the outcome of this battle." Mairin looked thoughtful.

"He will win whether you are there or not, for God is on his side, but it would be easier for him if he did not have to bear the burden of your presence."

"What will people say if I do not go, Dagda?"

"When did you ever care for what people said, my lady Mairin? Escort him to the field of honor, publicly declare your love for him, and then depart back to the queen's bower to await your lord's return."

"Why did you not tell me this before, Dagda?"

"Because you would not have listened, my child, would you? From the purple shadows beneath your eyes, I know you have spent a sleepless night. I believe you are more amenable to reason now." The big man put his arm about her, and gave her a hug. "You are more amenable at this moment, are you not?"

"Aye," she admitted.

"Then you will do as I suggest?"

"Aye, Dagda. I will wish my lord Godspeed, and then I will await his return away from the field of battle."

When Josselin learned that Mairin had changed her mind, and would not stay to view the combat, his entire mood lightened, and she knew that Dagda had been right. Had the battle to come been part of a tournament, it would have begun in mid- to late afternoon. Combat as a spectacle was apt to get out of hand as the blood lust of the combatants rose, and only the darkness brought on by night could force an end to such a tournament. The combat today, however, would be between the two men only, and so it had been scheduled for two hours before the noon. Although the stands set up about the field of honor were filled, there was no gaiety involved. This was a serious matter.

Mairin had dressed carefully for the occasion in her royal-purple skirt, and a rich lavender brocade tunic top. Upon her bosom rested a beautiful gold, enamel, and pearl cross that had been given to her by the queen along with its heavy red-gold chain. Her hair was dressed simply in two thick plaits that hung down on either side of her head, and upon the top of her head was her gold veil and chaplet. She was visibly full with her child, and she carried her condition proudly as she escorted her husband before the king. There was a formality to what was about to happen, and looking at his wife, Josselin said in a loud voice:

"Lady, by your word and in your behalf do I put my life in jeopardy to do battle with Eric Longsword. Ye know the cause to be just and true."

"My lord," answered Mairin, "it is as I have said wherefore ye may fight surely for the cause is just and true."

Josselin de Combourg then kissed his wife, publicly touched her protruding belly in what appeared to be a blessing, and then without another word, Mairin turned and walked proudly back toward the queen's bower.

"*Mairin Aldwinesdotter!*" Eric Longsword shouted after her. "Will you not wish me good fortune? Will you not wish the father of your child good luck?"

For a moment Mairin had stopped, frozen in horror at the sound of his voice. She had not noticed him there, though of course he must have been. Her greatest concern had been for her husband. Now for the briefest moment she debated turning and raining curses upon his blond head, but she realized, with sudden clarity, that the greatest damage she could do Eric Longsword now was not to acknowledge him at all. Lifting her head high she continued on toward the queen's bower.

Just a few moments remained before the actual combat began. Pushing Loial aside, Dagda carefully checked over Josselin and his equipment. The knight was dressed in a full-length mail suit called a hauberk. His pointed helmet was fashioned with a nasal guard. He carried a kite-shaped shield of azure with a *bend or* dividing the halves of the shield. On the upper half of the shield was a *rose or*, for the *rose or* was a part of his father's crest, and Raoul de Rohan had given his son permission to use it. The device upon the lower half of the shield was a *star or* he had taken in honor of Mairin, for to him, the star was representative of an enchantress. Across the *bend or* was the lettering *Honoria Supra Alis*, Honor Above All, the motto that he had taken for his own. The most important part of his equipment was a double-edged sword with its simple crossguard, and its hilt with a large counterweight. Dagda plucked a hair from his head, and ran it along the sword edge. It split immediately.

With a smile he looked up at Loial. "Very good, lad," he approved. Then he swung his gaze to Josselin. "You are ready, my lord."

High up in the queen's bower, Mairin heard the shouts of encouragement from the spectators as the battle began. Instinctively she shivered, and felt the child within her womb almost leap as her heart accelerated. She could not see the field of combat from where she was, and she was all alone. Even the queen's lowest serving wenches had gone to watch what was, to them, an exciting spectacle.

I cannot be afraid, she told herself. God is on our side in this matter. Only Eric Longsword's death at Josselin's hands can cleanse my honor, and wipe away the doubt of my child's paternity. When Josselin overcomes Eric, everyone will finally know that I have not lied, for Mairin was not so stupid that she didn't realize that many of the Scots court believed Eric Longsword's story despite the queen's trust and faith in her friend's word.

Once again she wondered, as she had wondered so many times before, why Eric Longsword had not actually raped her. Why he had believed as he pushed his fingers into her resisting body that he was possessing her in a normal manner. He had always spoken to her as he committed his abuse upon her, and afterward, as if he were actually having her. Not once had his mask of self-confidence and certainty ever slipped. She had come to believe that he really did believe he was possessing her fully, completely, and in a normal manner. If that was so, then Eric Longsword was really as mad as she had so often accused him of being.

Below her and away from her line of vision, she could hear the roars of the crowd watching the battle. Dear God! Why had she agreed to cloister herself like this? She should be there in the king's pavilion watching and encouraging her husband on to victory! Then suddenly Mairin realized that a great silence had fallen over the field of combat. She listened hard, but she could hear nothing at all but the wind which blew softly about the tower.

Mairin could feel her whole body clenching with fear. What had happened? Why had they stopped shouting? I must go to Josselin, she thought, but her legs would not function. She could not move at all for a long moment, nor could she seem to even draw a breath. If he's dead, I want to be dead too, Mairin said within her heart. Then a mighty cheer arose from the battlefield, and in that instant, Mairin knew that her husband had been victorious.

Grasping at a high-backed chair to keep herself from falling, she sagged against it and the breath was expelled from her lungs in a single great whoosh. A small moan of relief echoed about the chamber. Her entire body relaxed with relief. She drew in several deep breaths, and felt strength pouring back into her legs. Now she could go to him and everything would be all right. She took a step forward, and to her total surprise, water gushed down her legs in a great flood. Stunned, she stopped in her tracks as the reality pierced her brain. The child was going to be born, and it was several weeks too soon. Paralyzed with new fear, she found that once again she could not move.

Margaret and her ladies rushed into the chamber to embrace her, but she waved them away. It was the queen's mother, the lady Agatha, who realized what had transpired. Gently she put reassuring arms about Mairin, and guided her to a chair.

"Have you any pains?" she questioned Mairin.

Mairin shook her head.

"You must not be frightened, my dear," said the lady Agatha. "This is your second child, is it not?"

"It is too soon," came the reply.

"How soon?" came the reply.

"Three weeks, perhaps four," Mairin gasped.

"It will be all right," soothed the queen's mother. "Many a child has been born a few weeks early and survived to be an old man."

"I want my husband. I want Josselin!"

"I will send one of the girls for him immediately," said the lady Agatha, "but we must get you to a comfortable place, my dear, and out of these wet garments."

"My lady Margaret! He is all right? He was the victor?"

"Aye, Mairin, your lord husband is fine, and Eric Longsword is dead. He will never trouble you again, my dearest friend."

"Thank God!" said Mairin, and then she fainted, slowly sliding from the chair onto the floor.

She awoke to find herself back in her own bedchamber. Her garments had been removed. There was a soft woolen shawl about her shoulders, but other than that, she was nude. She lay upon her bed. The lady Agatha was poking busily at the fire in the corner fireplace, and one of the two shutters was drawn upon the single window.

The older woman straightened up, and seeing Mairin conscious once more, said, "Will you let me stay with you, my dear? I know that you must miss your own mother at a time like this."

"Thank you, my lady," Mairin replied, striving to remember her manners even in this situation. "Where is my husband? Can I see Josselin?"

"Of course," replied the queen's mother. "He and that white-haired giant of yours are fretting in the antechamber. Let us cover you with the coverlet, and then I shall bring them both to you, for your giant will not rest until he sees for himself that you are all right. Who is he?"

"He raised my mother and me," said Mairin. "It is a long story, lady."

"You will tell me afterward." The lady Agatha smiled and then she went to fetch Josselin and Dagda.

"You are injured!" Mairin cried as her husband entered the tiny room and approached the bed. He was naked from the waist up, and there was a fresh bandage about his shoulder that was already seeping blood.

" 'Tis nothing serious," Josselin reassured her. "How do you feel?"

"My waters broke, which means the child will come early, but I have no pains yet. Come closer, my lord, and let me see your wound."

He sat down upon the edge of the bed, and Mairin, sitting up, undid the badly wrapped bandage. "I am all right," he protested.

"You will not be if that wound is not properly dressed," she fretted.

"He wouldn't let me do it," said Dagda, coming in behind his lord. "Nothing would do but that he rush to find you and tell you that he was all right."

"*He* is dead," said Josselin. "He will never again hurt you, or terrorize you, enchantress."

She nodded, and then said, "I must dress your wound, my lord. My lady Agatha, would you hand me a camise? Dagda, I will need moss to pack the wound. You know the land. Can you find it nearby?"

"I gathered some earlier in anticipation, my lady Mairin. I will fetch it."

The queen's mother did not argue with the younger woman. She found Mairin's behavior quite commendable. She was not yet in labor, and her husband needed her attention. She handed Mairin the requested garment, asking as she did so, "Will you need hot water, my dear?"

"Yes, my lady, and clean cloths for bandaging, and wine to clean the wound." Mairin struggled into her camise, and then rose gingerly from her bed. Her belly was quiet as if the child was resting in preparation for its labors to come.

Josselin put his arms about her for a long minute, and they stood together in sweet embrace. Gently he nuzzled her hair, and she gave a little murmur of happiness. "I was so afraid," she told him. "I could not see the field of battle from the queen's bower, but I could hear the shouts of the crowd. Then when it grew so still . . ."

"I had driven Eric Longsword to his knees, and it was then that I killed him," Josselin said quietly.

"But he wounded you."

"A lucky blow," Josselin said with a careless smile.

She stood back from him, and looked closely at the deep gash that was now crusted over with dried blood. "If he had been any luckier, you could have lost the use of that arm. There is a muscle there that, had Eric severed it, would have left you with a withered arm. Oh, Holy Mother! Look at those bruises!" Her hands ran anxiously over his torso, his other shoulder and arm.

Josselin winced several times, but his humor was well intact. "Lady," he teased, "stop, I pray you, before I forget you are about to bear a child this day."

The lady Agatha, reentering the room, heard this remark and chuckled. It brought back so many memories, for she and her late husband often teased each other thusly. It was the sign of a happy marriage. "Here is some of what you need to begin, my dear," she said to Mairin. "I will check the kettle on the hearth to see if the water is hot."

"Sit down upon the bed," Mairin commanded her spouse.

"I will assist you," said Dagda, who crowded into the small room bringing the requested moss with him.

Mairin nodded, and the queen's mother could tell immediately that they had worked in tandem before. She stood quietly to one side, knowing that if she was needed, Mairin would ask. Dagda handed a small basin to Josselin to hold. Mairin held her hands over the basin while Dagda poured wine over them. The big man whisked the first basin away to replace it with a second, this filled with boiling water. He handed his mistress a piece of clean cloth, and dipping the cloth in the boiling water, Mairin began to soak away the encrusted blood about the wound. She worked in silence for some minutes until finally the gash was clean. Dagda had three times replaced the hot water, which quickly became bloodied, with fresh water, and Mairin had used at least half a dozen cloths before she was satisfied. Although the heavy bleeding had ceased, the wound was fully open and oozing now. The water basin was replaced once again, and Dagda poured fresh, dark wine into the new receptacle. Handing Mairin a small clean sea sponge, he braced his lord's shoulder as she disinfected the wound with the strong wine. Josselin winced but slightly.

"I must cauterize the gash," Mairin told her husband. "If I do not, it could open again. You can't lose any more blood."

"Very well," he said. He had had wounds cauterized before. It was not a pleasant prospect.

Dagda had placed a dagger on the grate over the fire in the hearth. Now, its blade glowing red, he removed it and carefully handed it to his mistress. She never hesitated. Pressing the blade over his wound, she successfully closed it. For a moment the little bedchamber was filled with the stench of burning flesh. Josselin gave a loud groan, and he swayed where he sat for the briefest moment, his eyes closing with his pain.

Mairin was very pale, and from the peculiar look on her face, the queen's mother suspected that her labor had begun. She would say nothing, the lady Agatha suspected, until her husband's wound was fully tended. She watched as Mairin tenderly packed the cauterized gash with cool moss, and then fussily rebandaged it, standing back to examine her handiwork. Satisfied, the young woman poured her husband a small goblet of the strong wine and handed it to him, but not before the lady Agatha had seen her put in the liquid a small pinch of powder from a tiny pouch that Dagda offered her. "It's a painkiller," Mairin said by way of explanation. "There's juniper, wormwood, and tansy in it." Then an open spasm of pain crossed her face.

"My lord de Combourg," said the queen's mother, "I think I must ask you to arise and give the bed back to your wife. She has been so concerned with your condition that she seems to have forgotten her own."

"I am all right," Mairin protested weakly.

He gulped the medicined wine she had handed him in a single swallow, and then standing, helped her back to the bed. "You have done more than your duty, lady," he said quietly. "You are indeed your mother's daughter. Eada will be proud when I tell her of your conduct."

Mairin chuckled. "Aye, my lord, I am indeed my mother's daughter, and she taught me well my duties as a wife."

The lady Agatha could see this was some little joke between them, and so with Dagda, she busied herself cleaning up the evidence of Mairin's doctoring. Then with the big man's aid, she prepared the room for a birthing chamber. Although she had never had the help of a man in such a situation, Dagda did not seem out of place here. She could not help but be curious.

"Have you ever seen a child born?" she asked him.

"Aye, gracious lady, I have. I was present at my lady Mairin's birth, and that of her little daughter, the lady Maude."

How very curious, thought the lady Agatha, surprised to find his answer did not shock her. She nodded to no one in particular with approval as Dagda placed several plump pillows behind Mairin's back, elevating her to a half-seated position. He certainly seemed to know exactly what he was doing, and seeing her obvious curiosity, Mairin said, "We have some time before us, my lady Agatha, and so I will explain Dagda's position to you."

The queen's mother listened, fascinated, as Mairin unfolded the story of her background, and Dagda's. She saw no reason to disbelieve Mairin, and the younger woman obviously spoke the truth, for her husband did not deny her words. Still, it was a story worthy of the bardic tales she had heard sung in the Great Hall of many a castle during her long lifetime. She could readily believe that the huge Irishman had slain hundreds in his time, and yet brought to God by the gentle monks, Dagda had become the keeper of that most fragile of life forms, a female child. It was a beautiful story, and she found herself touched and brought close to tears several times during its telling.

Mairin had paused several times in her recitation to breathe with a pain. Her labor was light, and remained so for the next several hours. She had sent the men off at one point to eat the main meal of the day in the Great Hall. She knew there would be a celebration in her husband's honor, and she wanted him to be there. He would find it easier awaiting their son's birth among the men of the court, she knew.

"Stay with him," she ordered Dagda. "I will call you both when it is time."

They had gone off, and Mairin had dozed for a bit. The queen and Christina had come to see how she fared. They had spoken for some time, Margaret telling Mairin of the combat. Josselin had been the perfect knight, fighting with honor and skill. Eric Longsword had been vicious and dishonorable, spewing a constant and vituperative stream of foul lies about Mairin and himself in hopes of rattling his opponent. Josselin, however, had closed his ears to Eric's words, and slowly and steadily beaten the man back, leveling punishing blow after punishing blow upon the kidnapper of his wife until finally Eric had fallen to the ground and Josselin de Combourg, without a moment's hesitation, had plunged his sword through his enemy's hauberk, and straight into his heart.

"How was he wounded?" Mairin asked the queen.

"It was in the beginning," said Margaret. "At first Eric fought silently against your lord, but when he found he could not easily disarm and defeat him, he began to speak his foulness. His first words started Josselin, and for a moment, his guard was down. It was then Eric struck his blow, but immediately Josselin recovered, and never again did he allow his opponent the advantage.

"Mairin, I hope you will not misunderstand, but I have given orders for Eric Longsword to be buried in hallowed ground. He was an evil and arrogant man, but he was shriven before the combat, and I must therefore consider that his was a Christian soul, and eligible for honorable burial. My conscience would not allow me to do otherwise."

"Nay, Margaret, I hold no grudge against Eric Longsword. He was a tragic man, but he has paid for his crimes with his most precious possession, his life. Perhaps he will be happier in the next world than he was in this world. I shall pray for his poor soul."

The queen smiled, pleased. "I knew that your heart was a good and a forgiving one, Mairin. Remember, when you return home to your beloved Aelfleah, that you will always have a friend in Margaret of Scotland."

The queen departed with her sister, and Mairin dozed once more. When she awoke it was evening, and her labor began in earnest. For the next several hours she sweated and strained to bring forth the child from her pain-racked body. There was little the lady Agatha could do but offer Mairin encouragement, an occasional sip of wine, and wipe the beads of perspiration from her brow. Every now and then she would arise from her place at the laboring woman's head, and check the infant's progress. Finally, when she deemed the time right, she sent a serving maid for Josselin, who needed no encouragement to return to his wife's side. Dagda returned with him, and together the two men waited in the little antechamber to be called to Mairin's side. Finally, the lady Agatha stuck her head through the door between the rooms and said, "The child's head and shoulders are born, my lord. If you would see your child's first efforts at life, you must come now!"

The two men squeezed into the chamber, placing themselves one on either side of Mairin while the queen's mother bent from the bed's foot, and helped to ease the child from its mother's body. Not quite fully born, the baby howled loudly, and even Mairin, in her final labor, smiled at the sound. Then giving a push, she expelled the infant out into the world.

"It is a boy!" the lady Agatha cried, holding the screaming and bloodied baby up for them to see. Then she put the child upon his happy mother's belly. Mairin having quickly expelled the afterbirth, the older woman cut the cord that had bound mother and son, and swiftly cleaned her patient up while a smiling Dagda took the baby, and gently wiped the birthing blood from him with warm oil and a soft cloth.

Feeling useless, Josselin slipped from the room. He had barely looked at the baby, afraid of what he might see. Suddenly, all the old fears and doubts had returned to plague him. All the terrible and foul words that Eric Longsword had spat at him this afternoon before Josselin had finally killed him—words he had shut out of his conscious mind at the time for fear of losing his control and, ultimately, the battle with his enemy—now flooded back to torture him. He could almost hear Eric Longsword laughing at his plight from the fiery hell to which he had surely been consigned. Mocking him with the knowledge that it was his son, and not Josselin's who would be called the de Combourg heir.

Weeks ago he had sworn to Mairin that he had believed her story that Eric Longsword had not raped her. That the child Mairin carried in her womb was his child. That he had no doubts, but God have mercy upon him, he did have doubts. Mairin was the most beautiful woman he had ever seen. Surely the most beautiful woman in the world, and no normal man having her in his possession, desiring her as Eric Longsword had desired her, could not have taken her fully and completely.

"My lord?" Dagda was at his elbow. "The lady Mairin would see you now."

Slowly he went back into their bedchamber, and there was his beloved enchantress propped up against the pillows smiling proudly and radiantly, the swaddled baby settled within the crook of her arm. Pushing the damning thoughts into the dark reaches of his brain, he smiled back at her, and for the first time, gazed seriously upon the infant. Large round blue eyes stared back at him to his complete amazement. In a strange way, the child reminded him of little Maude, but for the blond fuzz that topped his head. Maude's hair had been dark.

"Here is your son, my lord," Mairin said quietly. "Here is William de Combourg. I swear upon the True Cross that he is your child. Will you recognize him as such?"

He knew he must answer in the affirmative, and yet he hesitated, and in that moment, the king entered the room with Margaret. Gratefully, he turned to greet the visitors, but not before he had seen the disbelief and hurt spring into Mairin's eyes.

"Josselin, my friend," said Malcolm Ceann Mor, "I have to tell you something that has been discovered while preparing the body of Eric Longsword for his burial. My wife has never doubted Mairin's assurances that her captor never forced himself upon her, and for my Meg's sake, I believed it also. Your wife did not lie, though I know there were those who did doubt her.

"When the body was stripped of its garments to be washed prior to preparing it for its burial, it was discovered that Eric Longsword had no genitals."

"*What?*" Josselin felt both relief and amazement pouring through him in equal amounts.

"The man had no genitals," the king repeated. "Once he did, but he was obviously injured severely in some battle of the past few years. He used a reed to aid him in peeing, but as for his cock and balls, they have been long gone. There are terrible scars, but nothing else remains to attest to his manhood. I thought you would want to know. Now let me see this fine son you have had a hand in producing."

Silently Mairin handed William to the king, and then she said, "I would consider it an honor if you and the queen would stand as godparents to *my* son. Will Father Turgot baptize William tonight?"

Margaret glanced at the new parents, and realizing that there was something very wrong, she quickly said, "Of course he will. Here, Malcolm, give me our godson. We will go immediately to the chapel, and see that young lord William is pronounced a good Christian before the hour is out."

The room quickly emptied but for Mairin and Josselin. After a long silence broken only by the snapping of the dry apple wood in the fireplace, Mairin said quietly, "I will never forgive you, Josselin."

"You must," he said. "I cannot go on without you, enchantress. I tried to believe you! I wanted to believe you! I thought I did, but as I stood in the anteroom just a few minutes ago, all the terrible things that Eric Longsword said to me this afternoon came thundering back, and for the briefest moment, I admit to my doubt."

"You would have continued to doubt me and to doubt William had the king not brought us the information that he did."

"*No!*" He denied it, feeling greater shame now than he had felt before, for he knew what she said was true.

"I will never forgive you, Josselin," she repeated, and seeing the cold anger in her dark violet eyes, he found himself more afraid now than he had ever been in his entire life.

"You must forgive me, enchantress. I love you, and I recognize William as my trueborn son!"

"*Too late,*" she hissed at him. "You are too late, my lord. William is *my* son, and *mine* alone! *I will never let you have him!*" Then she turned her back to him, and Josselin de Combourg knew that of all the battles he had faced in his life, the battle now facing him, the battle to win back his wife's love, would be the hardest battle all.

Chapter 17

❦

When William de Combourg was two weeks old, his parents began their journey home to Aelfleah. He had been a strong and healthy baby from birth, and he thrived further in the bright autumn air of his travels. He made his journey resting comfortably in a heavy cloth sling which enabled him to ride cuddled against his mother's warm breasts. When he was hungry, Mairin merely drew a breast through one of two slits she had made in her tunic top, and popped a nipple into William's eager little mouth. The infant's appetite was quite prodigious, and the motion of Mairin's horse seemed to have no ill effects upon him.

Mairin was overly protective of her son, clutching him to her bosom possessively whenever Josselin came near. Although she did not create any overt scandal, her attitude was enough to unnerve Josselin. He dared not remonstrate with her publicly, for before others she appeared to be the sweetest-natured woman and an obedient wife. She did not speak to him, however, unless he spoke to her first. Her demeanor was a modest and quiet one.

Dagda, watching her, knew better. The dark side of her Celtic nature was asserting itself strongly, and he knew that she plotted revenge against Josselin de Combourg who she felt had wounded her so deeply. In Mairin's entire adult life, Dagda had never seen her so coldly angry at anyone as she now was at her husband, and Dagda thought that his mistress was wrong. It was not fair, he thought, for her to have expected Josselin to disbelieve Eric Longsword's story. Mairin seemed to forget that, had her captor been fully endowed with all his parts, she would have indeed been raped, and the paternity of her son, quite definitely, in doubt. Dagda thought that the mere fact that Josselin had tried so hard to accept his wife's word should have exonerated his momentary lapse of blind faith.

He was probably the only person who might challenge her attitude, and Dagda did. "You are treating the man shamefully," he scolded Mairin several days after little William's birth.

"Has he not treated me shamefully?" she argued back.

"Nay," said Dagda bluntly, "he has not. He publicly accepted your word when others would not. He has been a loving and a kind husband to you. Sometimes I think he is better than you deserve."

"He would not have acknowledged *my* son as his heir had not the condition of Eric Longsword's manhood been brought to light. He doubted William's paternity, and for that, I will never forgive him. A woman knows the father of her own child! Especially when she has never known any man but him." Mairin glowered at the Irishman.

"Agreed!" replied Dagda. "But you cannot be certain he would have denied William, my lady Mairin. He but hesitated a moment. Perhaps it was to clear his throat. Perhaps not. Josselin de Combourg is but flesh and blood. He is no saint. Whatever private devils he may have had troubling him, he kept them to himself. You were not there upon the field of honor. You did not hear the words with which Eric Longsword taunted him. I did! That he did not go mad is a miracle, and a testament of his love for you. Why will you not forgive him?"

"Do you know the kind of life he would have condemned my son to by not acknowledging him? He would have made William a bastard, and not even a bastard like himself. At least Raoul de Rohan admitted to his paternity where Josselin was concerned. Josselin would have denied William on suspicion alone, condemning him to the life of a fatherless bastard, and shaming me in the process, for mine is a tale that could hardly be repeated over and over again each time an explanation was due. Josselin would have denied his eldest son his rightful place and his inheritance. I will not forgive him for it!"

"Then you are either a fool, or your wits have been disarranged by this experience," snapped Dagda. "Maire Tir Connell would have never behaved in such a fashion."

"Spare me the stories of my sainted mother," Mairin snapped back, sending him a withering look. "She died in her fifteenth year. I am practically twenty."

They took their leave of King Malcolm and Queen Margaret, and the many friends they had made at the Scots court.

"I am verra sorry to see ye go," Angus Leslie said. "I hope the next time we meet, 'twill not be in some damned battle."

"Let us make a pact then." Josselin grinned. "You stay away from the English border, and I'll stay away from the Scots."

The laird of Glenkirk chuckled. "I think yer right, Joss. 'Tis time I, like ye, took my wife and went home where the politics of our two countries canna reach us."

The two men gripped each other's hands in a grasp of friendship, and then parted. The king and the queen presented Mairin with a silver goblet for their godson. It was beautifully wrought, and had the de Combourg seal upon it done in silver, azure enamel, and gold. The new mother thanked them, knowing that this was the first heirloom to be received by the now English branch of the de Combourg family of which her son was the firstborn.

The queen embraced Mairin, and said softly, "Do not answer me now, for you would but answer me in haste, Mairin, but you must eventually purge your heart of this anger you now feel toward your lord husband. Forgive him, my friend. You will not be happy until you do."

Forcing a smile, Mairin thanked the queen for all her kindness, pointedly ignoring that good lady's plea, and feeling guilty at the saddened look she saw in Margaret's eyes as they met hers in final farewell. I am right, Mairin thought stubbornly. *I am right!*

Mairin's heart raced joyfully at her first sight of Aelfleah. They had traveled slowly and carefully for both her sake and the baby's. Now as she looked down upon her home for the first time in ten months, it was early October and from the vantage of the hillside upon which her horse stood, she could see the beeches, the oaks, and the birches splashing their russet, scarlet, and golden tones amid the deep green of the pines within *The Forest*. Then her eye was irresistibly drawn to something upon the heights of the western hills, and Mairin gasped.

"Aldford," she said, amazed. " 'Tis finished!"

"Not yet," Josselin answered his wife. "There is still a great deal of interior work to do, but it can be done during the autumn and the winter months. The castle is defensible now, however. When it is finished, the king has said he will come, and our old friend Eadric the Wild has agreed to pledge his fealty to William then. In the meantime, he has promised me he will keep the peace."

"I imagine he would keep the peace now. The lesson of Northumbria cannot have been lost on him."

"Would you like to inspect Aldford tomorrow?" he asked her.

"If it would please you, my lord, that I do so," came the deceptively meek reply.

"I would think you would want to since it is soon to be your home, and you its chatelaine. The family apartments are quite spacious, and I have arranged for fireplaces in all the major rooms."

"I will never leave Aelfleah to live in your castle," she said sweetly. "You built Aldford to keep the king's peace. Although I have not been happy to have your beacon of a castle drawing strangers to this manor, as a good servant of the king, I allowed it. I did not, however, promise you that I should live there."

"I am Baron Aldford," Josselin said through gritted teeth, "and William is my heir. Aldford will one day be his, and he should live there until he is fostered out."

"You will never take *my* son from me," she said in a low voice, "and as I do not intend living at Aldford, neither will William live there, my lord."

"He is my son too, Mairin."

"Are you certain of that, my lord?" she replied mockingly. "You were not so sure upon the day he was born. You would have denied him despite my assurances. It took the sight of poor Eric Longsword's mutilated body to convince you of William's paternity! In the moment that you doubted me, you gave up all claim to William, my lord!"

"We cannot go on like this, Mairin," he protested to her.

"Like what, my lord? I will be a good and faithful wife to you, as I have always been. I will tend your house, and bear your children, but you shall not have William." Then before he might argue further with her, she pointed with her finger as they were descending the heights and said, "Look! There is mother, and she has Maude with her! My God! Our daughter is walking! I left her an infant in arms and she is walking now! Oh, damn Eric Longsword! How much else have I missed?"

Eada wept with happiness to have her daughter back safely once again, and she was ecstatic at her first sight of baby William. "Look, Maude," she said to her granddaughter, holding the baby at the little girl's level, "here is your baby brother. His name is William."

Maude cast a jaundiced eye over the swaddled bundle. "Wi!" she said. "No! No!"

Mairin laughed, and dismounting, swept her daughter up into her embrace. "You must not be jealous of William, my poppet," she said, nuzzling kisses on Maude's soft little neck. "Mama loves you as much as she always has."

Maude turned her head and looked into Mairin's face. "Mama?" she said.

Mairin's eyes filled with tears that threatened to spill over down her cheeks. "Yes, Maude," she told her daughter. "I am your mama, and I will never leave you again."

Maude gave her mother a sunny smile, and then she said, "Down!"

"She wants you to put her down," said Josselin. "She walked at thirteen months and hasn't stopped since."

"I am capable of interpreting my child's needs, my lord," Mairin said icily as she set Maude upon her feet, and took William from her mother. Then she turned and walked into the house.

Eada looked at Josselin. "What on earth is wrong with Mairin?" she said.

"Your daughter is a stubborn, unforgiving, and impossible creature," he snapped at her, and turning, stamped after his wife.

"I will explain," said Dagda wearily to Eada, "but first you must give me a cup of cider, for my throat is parched from the dusty travel."

Together Eada and Dagda entered the house, and she settled him by the fire in the hall, a wooden cup of freshly pressed foaming cider in his big hand. "Now," she said, seating herself opposite him, "what has happened between them?"

Dagda took a long sip of the sweet apple liquid, and then set about to explain what had caused the problem between Mairin and Josselin. As he finished the main body of his tale, he observed, "You know how she is when she feels she has been betrayed. Suddenly, everything is all black or all white. There is no in between for her. Remember when Basil was murdered? She convinced herself that he had not loved her at all. It was several years before she could face the situation honestly, and admit to the real tragedy of her first marriage."

"But she was still a child then, despite the status of her marriage. She is a woman now, and she must behave as such."

"You are her mother," he answered. "You tell her. I have done my best. She will not listen."

Eada did not wait. She went immediately to her daughter, who was ensconced in the solar feeding William. "What is this that Dagda tells me?" she demanded.

"What *is* it he tells you?" Mairin replied innocently.

"Do not dare to play cat and mouse with me," Eada said sharply. "There is a breach between you and Josselin which Dagda tells me you will not allow to heal. Why?"

"If there is a breach between us, mother, it is of *his* making, not mine."

"Tell me," Eada begged her daughter, her tone softening. "I might be able to help."

"I am certain Dagda has already told you, mother, and there is nothing more than that. Josselin refused to recognize William as his son when he was first born, and for that, I will never forgive him. William is my son now, and mine alone."

"I did not refuse to recognize him!" Josselin said, entering the solar. "That is something your own mind has invented."

"I pronounced him your trueborn son, and asked you if you recognized him as such. When Maude was born you practically tumbled over yourself to answer that query, but with William, you said naught until King Malcolm came to inform you of Eric Longsword's deformity. Only then did you accept my word that William was your son!"

The subject of the discussion heard loud and frightening voices. Beneath his cheek his mother's heartbeat accelerated alarmingly. Worse, her nipple slipped out of his mouth, and he found himself denied his sustenance. William de Combourg howled with fright and outrage at this sudden turn of events.

"Look what you've done!" Mairin raged at her husband. "You are terrorizing *my* son! Leave us at once! I hate you!" She pressed the baby close to her chest, slipping her nipple back between his lips which effectively silenced him. The silvery baby tears upon his fat, rosy little cheeks touched her to the quick, and she sent Josselin a black look.

Eada took her son-in-law from the solar, and together they descended the stairs back into the hall. "Let her be for now, my son. She has worked herself into an evil Celtic temper, and I am afraid that no one can reason with her right now. If we refuse to pander to her mood, I am certain that her anger will eventually cool."

"In all the time we have been married, I have never seen her like that," he said.

Eada chuckled. "Women," she said, "change more often than the weather. You have had an unusual spell of dry sunny weather, Josselin, but everyone knows that after the sun comes the storm. In this case, it is a particularly violent storm, but it too will pass, and the sun will shine once more. Until then, we can do no more than seek shelter and hope for the best."

"Did you ever get as angry at your husband as Mairin is at me, mother?"

Eada chuckled again. "Once," she said, "Aldwine made me so angry that I went out in the hills and hid in a cave for three days. I almost frightened him to death, I fear. When I arrived back at Aelfleah, he swore on his knees never to intentionally anger me again." A sad little smile touched her lips. "He never did either," she finished.

Despite Mairin's apparent reticence, she had gone up the hill the following day to see Aldford. She was totally amazed by what she found, for the castle was practically completed. Riding through the gatehouse, she entered the outer ward. Her guide was one of Dagda's younger sons, a ten-year-old named Scandy.

"The lord was wise to build on rock," said Scandy. "When it rains, the courtyard don't become a bog of mud."

They passed through the inner curtain walls into the inner ward. Here Mairin found that half-timbered buildings had been only recently constructed about the edge of the entire inner ward. They would add to the castle's living space for the family, their retainers, and their servants. With Scandy dogging at her heels, she inspected it all.

There was a Great Hall with its soaring arches of oak that were, even now, being carved decoratively by local artisans. The Great Hall had three fireplaces, and one large window space that did not yet have its glass. It would have to and would be a great expense. There were several smaller windows with stone windowseats built in on either side of them that would also have to have glass. Like all the windows in the Great Hall and the living quarters, they would be fitted with wooden shutters.

The kitchens were marvelous, and whoever was chosen to cook for the castle would find no fault with the design of his workspace. Water could be brought directly to the stone sinks by means of a pipe that led to a cistern set within a corner tower. There were ovens for baking, cooking, and smoking both meats and fish. Separate areas were set aside for the storage of wine, beer, and cider, as well as a creamery where the milk might be set for skimming. The creamery was a large enough room so that cheese could be made there and butter churned.

One small additional room intrigued her, for she had no idea of its possible use. "What is this place for?" she asked Scandy.

"For you, lady. The lord said there was to be a place for you to store your herbs and medicines."

Delighted, Mairin inspected the room. There was a small stone sink in it, and Scandy further informed her it had its own private cistern to supply it with water. Stone counters with slate tops had been built into the walls which had been already carved with niches for storage. There is even room for my oak table, Mairin thought, already deciding with what to fill the wall niches. Then she remembered that she was not going to live in Aldford, and the smile on her lips was replaced with an angry frown.

"Lead on, boy!" she instructed Scandy irritably.

Although the castle's towers were basically the same—each had two stories and an attic—two of them had differences. Beneath one, a dungeon had been hewn from the rock of the hill upon which Aldford stood. And the north tower of the castle was to house the chapel. The structure contained one soaring room rather than two levels of one room each. The altar area was fitted into the curve of the tower. Walking across the bare oak floors, Mairin thought it would be beautiful when it was finished.

The family apartments of the castle were spacious and light. Located upon the second floor of Aldford, they contained a family hall, a solar, a chamber for bathing, guestrooms, and six bedchambers. There was even, Scandy noted pridefully, a special apartment for the children. This area contained a large anteroom with a fireplace and several additional bedchambers. Another wing of the castle contained living quarters for Dagda, who was Aldford's bailiff, for the cleric who would be chosen castle chaplain, the barber/doctor, the cook, and their families. There were barracks for the soldiers to be garrisoned in the castle, and a separate set of rooms for their captain.

Below the barracks were the stables and the kennels. Scandy pointed out where the falconry and the dovecote were, even now, being built. Beneath the kitchens, he told her, were storage rooms for additional foods in case of siege. Under the blacksmith's shop was a small armory. There was no doubt that the plan for Aldford Castle had been a well-thought-out one. Set upon its rock base with only one means of access, it was virtually impregnable. Mairin felt a thrill of pride sweep through her. Someday it would all belong to William.

"Well," said Eada to her daughter, seeing her return from the castle, "what do you think of Aldford?"

"It is impressive," Mairin said honestly. "I believe the king will be pleased."

"When do you think it will be ready for habitation?" Eada asked.

"By the spring for certain," came the answer. "Are you planning to live there, mother?"

"Would you prefer I remain here, my child?"

"The choice is yours, mother, but I would like it if you stayed here with me and the children."

"*What?*" Eada looked puzzled.

"I do not intend living at Aldford," said Mairin calmly.

"Daughter," came the reply, "you go too far, I think. If you continue on like this, you will drive your husband into the arms of another woman."

"I am a good, faithful wife, mother," Mairin replied. "My husband has no cause for complaint."

"Except that your disposition these days is an evil one. If I did not know better, I would say you were possessed!"

"It is time for William to be fed," came the answer, and Mairin departed the hall where she had been speaking with her mother.

Looking after her, Eada sighed deeply. She understood very well that Josselin had hurt Mairin, but standing aside and looking at the situation, she could also understand both sides of the issue. According to Dagda, and she took his word, for he had been there, Josselin had publicly accepted his wife's version of her kidnapping which, in the end, had turned out to indeed be true despite the improbability of it being so. Still Josselin had had his doubts, even if he had kept them to himself until that fatal moment. Eada considered his behavior admirable under the circumstances. She could not think of a single man of her acquaintance over the years, except possibly her Aldwine, who would have believed Mairin's tale.

Mairin, however, expected complete loyalty from her husband. Her first marriage to Prince Basil, when she had been so total an innocent, obviously had left its mark. Her whole life, she had been cosseted and loved, but for the little time between Ciaran St. Ronan's death and her coming to Aelfleah. Even then, she had had Dagda loving and protecting her. The enormity of what appeared to be Prince Basil's betrayal of his bride had obviously left a stronger impression upon Mairin than any of them had realized. She wanted the impossible of Josselin, and it would have indeed been impossible for any man to meet Mairin's inflexible standards of loyalty in love.

Eada wanted to help Mairin and Josselin back to the happiness that they had shared before her daughter's kidnapping from York. She believed with all her heart that they truly loved one another, but she also knew the longer it took to heal the breach between them, the more difficult it would be to heal it, for with each passing day, the wound was allowed to fester, the gap between the lovers grew wider and deeper.

Then one afternoon when Mairin had been home but two weeks, a messenger came down the hill and across the river up the road to Aelfleah. The horseman was from the queen who was back in Normandy, and he bore a message for Mairin. Offering hospitality to the messenger, Mairin broke the seal upon the parchment he carried and unrolled it. Her violet eyes widened as she read the message within.

To Mairin of Aelfleah from Matilda, Queen of England, and Duchess of Normandy, Greetings.

Your half-sister, Blanchette of Landerneau, wishes me to ask you if she would be welcome at Aelfleah. She desires to meet you, and to personally convey her thanks to you for your kindness and generosity to her, despite the evil done you by her mother. It is my desire that you offer her your hospitality until early next summer when she will enter my own endowed convent in Caen with my little daughter, Cecily. Since I know the great kindness of heart you possess, and that you would not refuse your queen such a small request, I have taken the liberty of sending the lady Blanchette on to England. She travels but one day behind the rider who has brought you my message. As always, you have my prayers. I think of you often.

The letter was signed with the queen's signature, and Matilda's seal.

Mairin stared at the parchment for several long moments, and then she handed it to Josselin. He quickly scanned it, saying as he finished, "We have no choice."

"Is it not enough that I have provided handsomely for the daughter of *that* woman? Must I open my home to her as well?"

"What is it?" asked Eada, totally confused.

"The queen is sending my half-sister for a visit," said Mairin sarcastically. "Is that not wonderful? We must keep her until next summer when she enters her convent."

"The child is not responsible for what her mother did to you, my daughter," Eada said sharply. "When will she arrive?"

"Tomorrow," said Mairin shortly, and Eada laughed aloud.

"She does not give us much chance to refuse, this queen, does she?"

Suddenly, Mairin saw the humor in the whole situation, and she joined her mother in laughter. "If you could see her, mother. She is the prettiest woman, but she is no bigger than a minute. Yet she can terrorize the king if she is denied her way. I have heard it told she even blackened his eye once. Well, there is nothing that we can do to prevent Blanche de St. Brieuc's daughter from coming to visit with us, and so I suppose we must make the best of the situation and welcome her."

"Remember that she, like you, is Ciaran St. Ronan's daughter as well, Mairin," said Eada. "I think if you try to think of her more as your father's child as you were, and less *that* woman's offspring, you may find your half-sister easier to accept. If her heart is with the church, she cannot be an evil person as was her mother. It seems to me that Blanchette St. Ronan is reaching out to you, Mairin. Do not turn away from her because of her mother. Judge her on her own merits. How old is she?"

"She was to be born the winter after the autumn I was sent from Landerneau. It is autumn of the year 1070, and I will be twenty shortly. Therefore, my half-sister will be fourteen this winter." She looked at Josselin who had been silent all this while. "I remember you telling me you never met Blanchette. Is that truth, or another of your lies?"

"I have never lied to you, Mairin," he said quietly.

"You have also not been entirely truthful with me," she said.

"I never met Blanche's child," he said.

"We will put the children in with us," Mairin decided, "and then Blanchette can have Brand's old room."

"It is a pity," Eada remarked sweetly, "that Aldford is not habitable yet, for it has lovely guestrooms. I am going to enjoy living there. This old house seems quite primitive in comparison."

"I have never noticed," Mairin replied sharply, and Josselin hid a smile. "We will have to hurry if we are to have my half-sister's room ready, for the Blessed Mother only knows exactly when she will arrive tomorrow. It could be before noon."

It was not, however, until early the following afternoon that Blanchette St. Ronan and her escort arrived from the coast. Mairin's first glimpse of her half-sister reconfirmed once again her abilities to see what others did not. Months before, she had seen a sweet-faced girl, and Blanchette was indeed that same sweet-faced maiden having, Mairin realized as she looked closely at her half-sister, all of Blanche's features. In the mother, however, they had been sharp features. In the daughter, they were softened. It helped that Blanchette had Ciaran St. Ronan's deep blue eyes and rich russet hair.

Mairin had found herself dressing carefully that morning, for first impressions were important. She had chosen her black taffeta skirt with a gray brocatelle tunic top embroidered with gold. Upon her chest she wore Queen Margaret's cross, and in her ears were the fat pearls and garnets. Her hair she chose to wear loose, but for a simple gold band, and Eada smiled at this small vanity shown by her daughter.

Blanchette had traveled with an English nun, Sister Frideswide, a plump and jolly little woman with a deep laugh who was returning to her convent which was but two hours further on from Aelfleah. The good sister would not even stop to accept Aelfleah hospitality, for she feared she could not reach her home before dark if she did. The king's soldiers escorting her were obviously disgruntled at having to spend a night outside the convent walls eating smoked fish and sour wine when they might have been at Aelfleah. Josselin understood this, and invited them to return to his manor after they had delivered the good sister.

Their captain had thanked Josselin, and the lord of Aelfleah suspected that Sister Frideswide would reach her destination in record time, much to the regret of her bottom. The nun and her escort thundered off, and Josselin turned to observe the first meeting of the half-sisters. For a long moment the two women stood and looked at one another. Young Blanchette was modestly attired in indigo blue, her russet hair hanging in two braids. Her head was covered with a simple white veil.

"Welcome to Aelfleah, sister," Mairin said quietly.

"Do you look like our father?" Blanchette asked. "I always wondered what he looked like."

"Yes, I look a little like him, but I also have some of my mother's features too. Our father was a handsome man. You have his eyes, and your hair is his color." Mairin drew the girl into an embrace. Then she set her back gently. "Come, let us go into the house. There is a wind today in the valley and the air is chilly. I would not have you ill after such a journey."

"Did our father love you very much? Do you think he would have loved me also?" There was a poignancy to Blanchette's questions.

"Did your mother not tell you of our father?" Mairin asked.

Blanchette sighed and shook her head. "She would not speak of him except on rare occasions. She said it distressed her too much, but my nurse, Melaine, said that he was a good man."

"Melaine was your nurse? She was mine also! How is she? Does she still live? What of old Catell? Did you know her also?"

"The witch woman?" Blanchette seemed horrified. "She was condemned to be burned when I was four, but when they went into the Argoat to take her, she was not there, and to my knowledge, she was never seen again. They said that the devil came for her, and took her away."

"More than likely she escaped them to move to another part of the forest," said Mairin dryly. "She was an amazing old woman with a great knowledge of healing."

"You knew her?" Blanchette's deep blue eyes were round with fascination.

"Aye, I knew her. She taught me many things having to do with herbs and healing. She was an interesting old lady, but what of Melaine?"

"She still lives. It was through her I first learned of your existence, although mother never knew I knew. Melaine said that my mother sent you away before I was born because she claimed you were bastard-born. The queen says you are not, and that Landerneau belongs to you, not me. I am so glad! I never liked Landerneau. It always frightened me, surrounded by the forest as it is. Except that Hugo died of the measles, we were to be married this coming summer, and I would have had to live there. I have always felt so guilty that you were sent away."

Mairin led her young half-sister into the hall of the house and settled her by the fire, for the girl looked chilled. "Bring wine," she ordered Nara who was hovering nearby. Then settling herself into a chair facing Blanchette, she said gently, "Melaine should not have told you about me. None of what happened between your mother and me was of your making. Like me you are innocent."

"How old are you?" asked Blanchette.

"I will be twenty in six more days," Mairin said. "When were you born, Blanchette?"

"I will be fourteen on the twenty-third of February next," came the reply. Then Blanchette's eyes grew round and her hand flew to her mouth to stifle a cry. "Holy Mother! You were only five when mama sent you from Landerneau. Oh, I am so ashamed! I am so ashamed!" and she began to cry.

For a moment, Mairin was stunned by the girl's apparent depth of guilt over her mother's behavior. Then with a sigh of resignation, she stood up and drew her half-sister into an embrace. "Do not weep, Blanchette," she said quietly. "It was not your fault. Remember, you were not even born then."

"She did not like me," Blanchette sobbed. "She did not like me at all, and when Melaine had her second baby, mama called her back from the village so she could nurse me. Mama said no lady should allow her breasts to be spoilt by the constant tugging of a baby's mouth, but Melaine said 'twas unnatural for a woman not to want to nourish her own daughter." Blanchette wept harder.

Damn Melaine, thought Mairin. She always did chatter too freely and without heed for the feelings of others. To her great surprise, Mairin heard herself saying, "I am sure that your mother loved you, Blanchette. Did she not arrange a fine match for you with a powerful and important family? It appears to me that she surely had your best interests at heart when she did that."

Blanchette raised her tearstained face to her half-sister. "You are so good," she said worshipfully. "How can you be so good after what mama did to you?"

Mairin's arms dropped from about her sister, and she gently resettled the girl back in her chair before sitting down herself. It was plain that the girl had a desperate need for love, for she, poor child, had obviously never had any. Still, she did not want Blanchette idolizing her to the point of sainthood, for Mairin knew better than most her faults. "I am not good in the sense you imply, little one," she began. "My mother was an Irish princess, a Celt in every sense. The Bretons are also a Celtic race, but their proximity to the rest of Europe has taken them further from their origins than the Irish. Do you see that large man with my husband? His name is Dagda, and he had the responsibility of raising my mother, and when she died, she put me into his care with our father's approval. I will tell you his story one day, Blanchette, but for now, all you need know is that Dagda was once one of the most feared warriors in Ireland. He has raised me as a Celt, and we forgive nothing.

"I never forgave your mother her treatment of me. I longed to revenge myself upon her, and when the opportunity arose, I grasped at it like a drowning man grasps at a straw. At no time, however, was it my intention to hurt you. You are of my blood. As for your mother, that was a different case, but she might have escaped me except that in her own personal desperation, she made a fatal mistake.

"Your mother had met my husband several years prior to his coming to England with the king. When she learned of his good fortune, she managed to gain a place for herself amongst the queen's ladies when the queen came to England to be crowned. She implied to the queen that Josselin would welcome her as his wife now that he had found his good fortune. My husband has known the queen since late boyhood, and she is fond of him. She believed she was doing Josselin a favor by transporting Blanche de St. Brieuc to England. You can imagine her deep embarrassment and her indignation when she learned otherwise.

"Josselin had never told me of this acquaintance with your mother, particularly having learned of her part in defrauding me of Landerneau. He thought that, as we would never meet, it was unnecessary to reveal the association, but finding her with the queen he confessed all to me, and it was then I decided to wreak my revenge upon *that* woman. I am no saint, Blanchette, as you can see."

"You heard me, didn't you?" Blanchette said softly. "You heard me calling to you for help! I know you did!"

"*What?*" Mairin looked somewhat startled by the intensity in the girl's voice.

"Melaine said you had the gift," was Blanchette's reply. "She said you could hear the voices on the wind, and that if I called to you, you would hear me because we are sisters."

"And why did you want my help, Blanchette?" Mairin was quite fascinated, for she remembered how quite unbidden her sudden knowledge of her half-sister had come into her conscious mind. Could the girl reach out to her?

"Hugo died of measles, and when he did I realized that, although I would have wed with him, I really did not want to marry," said Blanchette. "All of my life I have found myself drawn to the church. I have always been happiest in prayer, but when I spoke on it to mother once she told me that I was being foolish. She pointed out to me how lucky I was to be joining the Montgomerie family who are important and rich.

"Actually, they have always frightened me, for they are big, loud people, and they never speak softly when they can argue and shout. I was sent to them when I was just four, and the betrothal agreement was settled. Hugo was five then. He had three elder brothers, and a sister, Isabelle, who was my age at the time. His mother was always with child. There was a new little one every year until Hugo's mother died in childbirth with a stillborn son. I was nine that year. My lord de Montgomerie rewed almost immediately, and the new wife took up where the old had left off, but she was a poor frail creature who died within two year's time, having not been able to successfully produce a living child, though she lost three. Again Hugo's father remarried, but this time, he chose a big healthy woman much like his first wife. She was a widow with six children of her own, and she brought them all to live at the castle which made it even more crowded and noisy. The lady Yvonne gave my lord Montgomerie a ten-pound infant son in less than a year of marriage." Blanchette shuddered nervously with her memories, and sipped for a moment on her wine before continuing her tale. "Then a measles epidemic swept the castle. Hugo, Isabelle, and three of the lady Yvonne's children all died of it. I, and several of the others who had been ill, survived.

"When finally everything was back to normal, the lord de Montgomerie realized that with Hugo dead, I was no longer bound to his family. He was ready to send me back to Landerneau, for he had no more sons not already betrothed, and I was just another mouth to feed. Then the lady Yvonne suggested that I be matched with her second son, Gilles, who had not yet been betrothed. It was no wonder. He was a horrible boy whose head was too big for his body. He was always trying to catch girls alone. I told the lady Yvonne that, although I would have honored the marriage agreement that my mother had made for me with Hugo de Montgomerie when we were children, since I was free of that entanglement I preferred to dedicate my life to God and enter a convent. She beat me, and locked me in a tower room with only bread and water for weeks. She said I would stay there until I changed my mind. Each day she would come to demand my consent to a match between her son and me. Each day I refused, and was beaten for that refusal. Finally after several weeks I was released, but everyone in the castle treated me like a pariah.

"It was then, Mairin, that I remembered what Melaine had told me about you before I left Landerneau. That you had a gift, and were a magical creature, perhaps even an enchantress like the great sorcerer Merlin's lover, Viviane. I tried to reach out to you, to tell you of my plight, and of how very much I wanted to give myself to God. I thought surely God could not punish me for seeking the only aid I knew available to me. I felt that if I was wrong, God would show me the error of my ways, but, instead, there came word from the head of the de Montgomerie family, and from Queen Matilda herself, that I was to be sent to the queen at Caen. That I was to be allowed to dedicate my life to the church.

"I knew then that you had heard me. That you understood, and that you had helped me. The queen told me that my mother was dead. She gave me the first official word I had ever had of you, and she told me that you knew of my desire to give myself to God. She said that you had offered, out of pure generosity, to dower me into the convent of my choice. Then she asked me if I should like to be received into her very own Abbey of the Holy Trinity with her own little daughter, Cecily. Oh, Mairin! I could not remember ever having been so happy! The little princess and I were to have gone into the convent this past summer, but she has been ill, and so the queen decided to wait until next summer to send us.

"When I learned that, I asked the queen if I might be allowed to come to England to meet you. I have no other close relatives, for our father's family is gone, and I never knew my mother's family except for one funny old bishop who died years ago. I hope you are not angry with me for coming."

"Nay," said Mairin quietly. "I do not think there is anything you might do, Blanchette, that would anger me." She reached out and patted her half-sister's hand, thinking all the while how strange it was that this poor little waif had reached out to someone she had not known at all, could not have been certain was still alive. "When you called out to me," she said to the girl, "did you not consider the possibility that I might be dead?"

"Oh, no! I knew that you were alive!"

"How?" demanded Mairin.

Blanchette shrugged. "I just knew," she said.

Mairin smiled. "It is possible," she said, "that you also have a gift of sorts, little sister."

"Nay!" came the quick denial. "It would not be proper and godly for me to have such ability."

Mairin could not help but chuckle at her sister's reply. The child considered it perfectly proper to reach out with her mind to Mairin, but rejected the idea that in being able to do so she might have that same gift that allowed her elder sister to hear her. This, however, was not the time to argue such fine points with Blanchette, whom Mairin suspected as being woefully ill-educated. Growing up as one of a litter of many children in a large Norman castle, she knew, did not guarantee formal knowledge. There was time to learn all she needed to know though, and so for now she would simply make the girl feel welcome.

"I am glad you are here at Aelfleah, Blanchette, my sister," she said. "This is where I grew up after I left Landerneau, and this lady is the mother who raised me." Mairin reached out and took Eada's hand as she approached her daughter's chair. She had heard most of Blanchette's story. "This is the lady Eada. Mother, how would you have Blanchette address you?"

"I would have her call me mother as do you and Josselin," came the reply. "Poor child! Your life has not been an easy one, has it? Well, you are safe in the bosom of your real family now, and we shall try to make you happy while you are with us." She looked down at Mairin and said pointedly, "Have I not been tellng you how fortunate you are to be so surrounded with love, my daughter? And here is poor Blanchette who has been so alone all of her young life."

A small smile played at the corners of Mairin's mouth. Eada was hardly being subtle, but suddenly Mairin began to wonder if perhaps her mother were not right. Perhaps she should forgive Josselin. Then she pushed the thought from her head, saying to her sister, "Would it please you to call the lady Eada mother?"

"Ohh, yes!" Blanchette said happily, and once more tears threatened to overflow her lovely soft blue eyes.

"What of me?" said Josselin, joining them. "Will you not introduce me to your sister, enchantress, or are you still too angry at me to do so?"

"My lord husband, Josselin de Combourg," said Mairin without formality.

Josselin's green-gold eyes twinkled with mischief. "My lady Blanchette," he said warmly, taking the girl's dainty hand and raising it to his lips to kiss. "I bid you welcome to Aelfleah."

"My lord," said Blanchette in return, removing her hand from his grasp with an expertise that caused Mairin to stifle a giggle.

Regaining control of her emotions, Mairin called to Dagda to come and meet Blanchette. The big man joined the family grouping, and looked down into the girl's eyes. She returned his gaze shyly, but she did not flinch from his piercing gaze. Finally, Dagda smiled.

"I see much of your father in you, my lady Blanchette," he said approvingly in his deep booming voice.

Blanchette smiled for the first time, and Mairin thought how very, very pretty she was. "Oh," she said, "you could not have said a nicer thing to me, Dagda! You knew my father, did you not? Please tell me about him."

"I will be happy to tell you all I know of Ciaran St. Ronan, child," said Dagda, "but I find I am growing powerfully hungry. The supper hour is at hand, and I am not a good storyteller on an empty belly." He looked at Blanchette with seemingly critical eyes. "You look as if you could use some good meals," he said. "Our good Aelfleah food will soon fatten you up."

"Come, child, I will show you where to wash away the dust of your travels," said Eada. "We have prepared my son's old room for you. Brand would have liked you. He liked all the pretty girls," and Eada led Blanchette away.

"Well, enchantress, are you sorry that she is come now that she is here?" Josselin demanded of her when they suddenly found themselves alone.

"Nay," Mairin answered him. "Poor child! She has not had an easy time, has she? Blanche, it appears, could hardly wait to foster her out to the de Montgomeries. How different it would have been for us both had our father only lived. I do not think anyone has ever told that girl she was loved.

"I remember we once discussed Blanche's intelligence, and decided she had little. Now I know we were right! Imagine giving her baby to my old nurse for safekeeping. Melaine adored me, and although she would never have been so cruel to anyone deliberately, she could not resist whispering to Blanchette of me. Now I wonder if my poor little sister's desire for the convent is to escape her mother's sins or atone for them? Or does she have a genuine calling?"

"You will have time over the next six months to find out, Mairin," he answered her.

"Aye, I will," she said thoughtfully; and then, "Josselin?"

"Yes, enchantress?" He had taken Blanchette's place in the chair opposite his wife.

"Josselin, I am sorry for the anger between us," she said in a rush of words. "My mother has told me over and over again how fortunate I have been in my life, always surrounded by love, and though I heard the words and knew in my heart that she was right, I could not put the anger I felt in my soul from me. I am still not certain I can, and yet seeing little Blanchette today, hearing how lonely her life has been . . . It makes me realize that I do not want to continue fighting with you, my lord."

"Mairin, I never meant to hurt you," he said, "and I would never harm William."

"I know that," she answered him, and then she sighed deeply. "I do not know why I get so angry. It felt like such a betrayal of me when, in that single instant, you seemed to doubt me. I remembered what had happened before . . . in Byzantium with Basil . . . when he betrayed me."

"Basil betrayed you?" He had not heard this before. "How? With another woman?"

"With a man," she answered softly.

"With a man?" Josselin looked stunned.

"The people of Byzantium are different from us in some of their manners and ways," Mairin said quietly. "They are apt to take lovers of the same sex, and no one thinks it strange. Before my first husband wed with me he had a male lover. His name was Bellisarius, and he was the most famous actor of his time in Constantinople. He murdered Basil, or so they told me. Then there were others who claimed that the two men had committed suicide so they might always be together.

"I was very young when I married Basil. He was a very wonderful man. He was as handsome as I am beautiful. He was educated and kind, and had a marvelous sense of humor. I had a blissful, if brief, life with him, but I came to him a complete innocent. He made certain that I stayed that way, sheltering me tenderly, even as my parents had sheltered me from the world. Imagine my shock at his death, and then the gossip surrounding that death! For some weeks I lost all memory of him and our life together. It was a terrible time. When I did regain my memory, I decided that Basil had never loved me, that he had deliberately and wantonly betrayed me. Later, I came to realize that that was not so. He had loved me, and I was fortunate to have had so tender and thoughtful a first lover. I will never, however, be certain of how Basil died, and that will haunt me all my days.

"I trusted Basil completely, and so I trusted you, Josselin, for is it not a wife's duty to cleave unto her husband? Your doubts seemed, at the time, an even worse betrayal than Basil's, for that apparent betrayal threatened my baby more than it threatened me." She laughed somewhat ruefully. "I have behaved very childishly, and I am not a child any longer as I was when Basil died."

He understood so much now! Things he had never before comprehended that had seemed mysterious about her. Leaning forward, he reached out and took her two hands in his. "I am not a wildly handsome and clever prince, Mairin. Neither am I a saint. I am but a rough knight, a servant of the king, a simple man. But I am a man who loves you, enchantress, and I will always love you. I may not always understand, and there may be times as we grow older together that I lose patience with you, but I will never stop loving you." He raised her hands to his lips, and tenderly kissed them, the backs, the palms, the soft skin of her inner wrists. His green-gold eyes met her violet ones in silent pledge.

"Pax, my lord?" she said softly.

"Pax," he answered her.

Eada, returning to the hall with Blanchette, saw their two heads together, and observed Josselin kissing her daughter's hands. Mairin sat quietly and unprotesting. There was a smile upon her lips now, a smile that Eada had not seen in the weeks since she had been home. She turned to Blanchette, saying, "I think your coming, child, has worked a miracle, and I thank God for it."

"There is nothing I would not do for Mairin," said the young girl fervently. "Oh, Mother Eada, do you think she will love me despite my mother's behavior?"

"I know my elder daughter," said Eada, giving Blanchette a small hug about her slender shoulders. "She loves you already, child. Mairin's temper is pure Celt, but her large heart is also Celt. What she gives she does not give lightly, nor does she take away a gift once given. You have come home at last, Blanchette St. Ronan, and we welcome you to Aelfleah with all our hearts."

Blanchette could feel her own heart swell with happiness at Eada's words. She suddenly realized that all of her life she had been seeking a family. Now she had found one in the most unlikely manner. She settled comfortably and happily into life at Aelfleah. Very much in awe of her elder sister, she nonetheless adored Mairin openly. As for her niece and nephew, Maude and William delighted her as the population of children at the de Montgomerie castle had not. Perhaps it was because these two children were her family. Her blood relations. Blanchette found that for the first time in her life she was genuinely content.

"I wonder what her mother would say to see her here with us?" Mairin chuckled to Josselin as they bundled together in bed the night before her birthday.

"Blanche would be envious, I think. She was a mean-spirited woman," he answered, "but let us not speak on her, enchantress."

"What shall we speak on then, my lord?" Her voice was teasing as was her manner. Her eyes danced mischievously in the golden light of the single candle by their bed which cast dark shadows upon their fair bodies.

"I should rather not speak at all," he said with meaning.

"Then what shall we do, my lord?" They both lay on their sides facing one another, propped upon an elbow. "I am at my lord husband's command."

Reaching out, he cupped her head in his big hand, and then leaning forward, he kissed her soft lips. "Does this give you ideas, lady?" he said low.

"You must promise me not to bellow lest you wake William," she replied demurely.

"I do not bellow," he protested.

"You always say that," Mairin laughed, "but you do!"

"William won't know what we're doing even if he does awaken," Josselin reasoned.

"And how fortunate that Maude has expressed a desire to be with her aunt Blanchette," chuckled Mairin.

The hand that had held her head in embrace moved about to caress her face. Gently he rubbed his knuckles against her cheek, down around her chin, and up the other cheek. With a barely audible sigh she pressed against his hand. His fingers played over her lips, and opening her mouth she nibbled at them playfully with sharp little teeth. Their eyes met, and they smiled at each other. Trailing his fingers between her breasts, he pushed her long red-gold hair aside so he might feast his eyes upon those magnificent twin glories. Her nipples hardened beneath his very ardent gaze.

Lying back, Mairin drew her husband's head down to the valley between her breasts, and breathing deep, he inhaled the faint lilac fragrance she seemed to favor that clung to her skin. He rubbed his cheek against her breasts grumbling as he did, "Will you please get a wet-nurse for William, enchantress? It is extremely unfair that these beauties," and now he fondled her breasts lovingly, "be the sole possession of a toothless babe unable to appreciate their finer points." He licked teasingly at a nipple, and almost immediately a pearl of her milk appeared which he appreciatively lapped up.

"My lord," she half-protested, "would you deny your heir his only sustenance?"

"Let some fresh-cheeked farmer's wife with big tits like cow's udders give him sustenance," Josselin said. "These beauties should belong to me alone!"

"Oh wicked and lustful man," she scolded him laughingly, "perhaps this will help ease your ardor!" With a playful push she rolled him from her and onto his back. Then before he might protest this treatment, Mairin mounted her husband, clasping him between her milky thighs and looking down at him archly. Her lovely breasts thrust boldly forward, their moss-rose nipples easy temptation. "Well, my lord," she said, "must I tell you what to do next? You are usually quite full of wicked ideas."

Reaching up, he began to play with her breasts, teasing at the nipples with delicious expertise, causing her stomach to flutter with pleasure, and her secret place to throb with eager longing. Unable to control herself, Mairin's slender hips wiggled with growing excitement, grinding themselves down quite provocatively into his groin. Just when she thought she could bear no more of these delights, his two hands clamped about her neat waist, and he slowly impaled her upon his aching shaft. Mairin's back arched, and with a little moan she threw her head back, her eyes closed.

"Ride me," he growled fiercely. "Ride me, enchantress mine!"

With almost mindless obedience, she heeded his order, leaning her breasts forward to brush against his chest, her hands bracing themselves on either side of his head. Reaching up he held her hips which worked themselves up and down, up and down in sensuous rhythm, her still-tight sheath encasing and releasing his hot manhood as his mouth hungrily fastened itself upon hers, kissing her with wild abandon.

When he saw her visibly beginning to tire, he swiftly and gently rolled her back over so that now it was he who was mounted upon her. Mairin's arms tightened about Josselin's neck. She was vaguely aware of their change of position, but she was far too lost in pleasure to be fully cognizant of anything. It had been like this since their blissful reunion of five days prior. *Why*, the thought drifted through her mind, why did I ever deny myself this joy? She could feel him, hard and hungry, within her tingling body, thrusting, withdrawing, thrusting, withdrawing until she thought she would explode with happiness, but instead she seemed to crave even more, and she could not understand it, for their coupling was the best it had ever been.

"More," he groaned against her ear. "Ahh, enchantress, I want more of you!"

She heard his plea, yet she did not fully comprehend his words. Still, she wrapped her legs about him allowing him deeper penetration of her body, and Mairin felt him shudder against her. She soared within the endless sky of their mutual passion, her hands smoothing down his long back, tangling within his tawny hair as she rode the wave of her love for him. Within her own body she could feel the tumultuous tremors of her own passion beginning to come to a soaring crest. Her nails dug into the flesh of his back, scoring him cruelly, and she heard her own voice moaning with sweet fulfillment as together they were swept over the peak.

"Ahhhh, enchantress! Ahhhhhh!"

As the pleasure filled her body, leaving it weak and sated, Mairin giggled softly. "You see . . . you bellow, Josselin," she teased him lovingly.

Lying atop her still, he took her face within his two hands and tenderly kissed first her nose, and then her lips. "I suppose," he said with a lazy grin, "that I do, but you wouldn't have me any other way, I hope."

"Nay, my love, I wouldn't," she admitted.

Then suddenly from the cradle in the corner, the baby began to cry.

"Damnation," grumbled Josselin.

"What, my lord?" she said. "Would you deny William his turn?" Arising from their very tumbled bed, she hurried across the floor to gather up their son. Returning to the bed, Mairin settled herself cross-legged, and pushing her hair aside, put the baby to her breast. With almost smug contentment, William suckled noisily, his round baby-blue eyes gravely viewing his father who enviously watched. His chubby baby hands kneaded busily on his mother's flesh as he went about the serious business of eating.

"Is he not the most beautiful boy in the whole world?" Mairin cooed at her son.

William took a moment to belch noisily, and then continued nursing.

"Enjoy it while you may, you little glutton," Josselin warned his heir. "Those glorious tits will soon belong to me again, and me alone. I have no intention of sharing them with you any longer."

William ceased his nursing momentarily at the sound of his father's voice, and his little head swung about in Josselin's direction.

"He understands you!" Mairin was amazed. "I truly believe he understands you," she said, carefully putting her nipple back into the baby's mouth.

William nursed more thoughtfully now, his previously loud smacking noises somewhat subdued.

Josselin chuckled. "He had better understand me," he said. "This is but the first of our confrontations as father and son. One day he will be big enough to beat me, but not now! Do you hear that, you little piglet? I am master here!"

"Bully," Mairin said.

"Kiss me, wife!" he commanded her, and leaned forward.

With a little smile, Mairin pressed her lips to his in a kiss she meant to be brief, but somehow she could not seem to draw away from him. The kiss deepened. Her lips softened and parted. Their tongues eagerly entwined in passionate embrace. It was heaven, Mairin thought fuzzily, and then without warning Josselin pulled away from her.

"*Tomorrow,*" he said through gritted teeth, and with an emphasis she could not mistake.

Looking down at her sucking son, and then back at her husband, with his smoldering gaze, Mairin was forced to laugh in rueful understanding. "Tomorrow," she agreed.

They sat together watching as William greedily finished his meal, one suspicious eye upon his sire all the while. Gradually his small fuzzy round head drooped against his mother's warm breast in sleep. Their eyes met and they smiled at one another.

"I am so happy," Mairin said quietly as she arose and tucked baby William into his cradle.

"It is what I have wanted," he replied. "It is all that I have ever wanted for you—that you be happy with me." He stood and took her into his arms, his lips brushing tenderly against hers. "Ahhh, enchantress mine," he said. "I am surely the richest of all men, for I have you, I have our children, and I have our home. What more could any man or woman want?"

"There is nothing more, Josselin, my love," she answered him softly. "This is everything! Together we possess the world, you and I!"

Through the narrow bedchamber window the evening star shone in all its blue-white splendor; but Mairin and Josselin were so caught within the magical web of their own love that they did not notice the clear still night acoming because for them a new and more hopeful era was even now dawning.

ABOUT THE AUTHOR

Bertrice Small is a *New York Times* bestselling author and the recipient of numerous writing awards. In keeping with her profession, she lives in the oldest English-speaking town in the state of New York, founded in 1640, and works in a light-filled studio surrounded by the paintings of her favorite cover artist, Elaine Duillo. Because she believes in happy endings, Bertrice Small has been married to the same man, her hero, George, for forty years. They have a son, a daughter-in-law, and three adorable grandchildren. Longtime readers will be happy to know that Nicki the Cockatiel flourishes along with his fellow housemates, Pookie, the long-haired greige and white feline, Honeybun, the petite orange lady cat with the cream-colored paws, and Finnegan, the naughty black kitty.